Dodger

Dodger

James Benmore

Based on a character created
by Charles Dickens

Quercus

First published in Great Britain in 2013 by

Quercus
55 Baker Street
7th Floor, South Block
London W1U 8EW

HB ISBN 978 1 78087 465 4
TPB ISBN 978 1 78206 194 6
EBOOK ISBN 978 1 78087 466 1

10 9 8 7 6 5 4 3 2 1

Printed and bound in Great Britain by Clays Ltd, St Ives plc

Typeset by Ellipsis Digital Limited, Glasgow

For my parents, Henry and Eithne.

'It's all up, Fagin,' said Charley . . . 'the Artful's booked for a passage out . . . To think of Jack Dawkins . . . the Artful Dodger – going abroad for a common twopenny-halfpenny sneeze-box . . . without no honour nor glory!' . . .

'Never mind, Charley,' said Fagin soothingly; 'it'll come out, it'll be sure to come out. They'll all know what a clever fellow he was; he'll show it himself, and not disgrace his old pals and teachers . . . What a distinction, Charley, to be lagged at his time of life!'

From *Oliver Twist,* Chapter XLIII

Part One

Part One

Chapter 1

The Silver Sneeze Box

*Wherein the reader learns of how my carefree childhood
was cruelly snatched away by a cold-hearted magistrate with
no regard for my youthful promise*

We was a gang of six and we was swooping through the London
crowds like low-flying jackdaws, fast, thieving and beautiful to behold.
It was the first day of May and the people of the city was all dressed
in their Sunday finery, not least us, the happy students of the Saffron
Hill School of Finders Keepers. We was scudding through the dusty
lanes towards Covent Garden, where we hoped to find the choicest
trinkets that London could offer, and we was all very much feeling
that spring buzz. I was leading the thing, as was natural, and close
behind me was my best pal, Charley Bates. After him came Jem
White, Georgie Bluchers and Mouse Flynn and that, I now reflect,
should have been all. Five has always been more than enough to
work a spring crowd; in truth the ideal number of boys to go finding
with was three. One to distract, the other to dip and pass, and the
last to make the dash. But what with the day being so merry and
fresh we was all feeling companionable and so was stuck together
like toffees in sun. All of these boys was gifted in the art and had it
just been us then it would have remained a very pleasant and productive morning. But we also had Horrie Belltower dragging along behind
us and this stupid oaf proved to be my undoing.

Horrie was not one of us. I had never taken him to Saffron Hill because I knew the Jew would not be interested. He was too old and too lumbering. He looked and smelt as if he'd been dredging through the riverbank all night, so shabby was his clothes. We was all dressed up flashy and colourful in proper gentleman's attire, with studs, rings, gold chains and such, so we didn't much care for the look of him in his dirty coat and faded neckerchief. On top of this he was too feeble-minded and fat-fingered to make a living in our chosen profession. As a thief, all he was good for was the kinchin lay – jumping out in front of young children what are running errands for their mothers in the genteel districts and taking their sixpences by force. No one respected the kinchin lay, an idiot could do it. What Horrie couldn't do was turn himself invisible like we could, he couldn't put himself just outside a cove's sight and stay there no matter which way their heads may turn. But worse than all this, he was slow. And we all hated slow.

We slid by the corner of Jarrett Street, where a big crowd was distracted by the puppet show. Mr Punch was busy battering his wife with a stick and he squawked a friendly *That's the way to do it!* as we brushed past tailcoats and gowns, finding ourselves all the richer for it. We was well pleased with our earnings and was itching for more when Mouse asked me where the Belltower boy was. We looked back towards the puppet booth and saw Horrie still stood among the crowd and watching the story.

'Good riddance,' said Jem. He had been vexed with me all day for letting Horrie tag along but until now had not shown the steel to say it. 'I thought we'd never shake him.'

Charley was most amused at the thought that, any minute now, the gentlemen either side of Horrie would feel that their pockets was lighter and grab him as the culprit. The younger boys laughed too and only Jem was sharp enough to see there was nothing droll about that. He turned to me.

'We ain't going back for him, Dodger. Least I ain't.'

The other boys stopped laughing and looked at me in wonder at the very idea.

'He's got nothing on him,' said one.

'He won't say nothing,' said another.

'And even if he does, so what?' asked a third, 'he ain't even met the Jew.'

'I know Horrie ain't much,' I said. 'But friends is friends. And if any of you lads was in a tight spot, then I would just as soon come to your aid.' This remark made an impression upon Charley and the two younger boys and they nodded at me with due admiration. Jem, though, was having none of it.

'Tell that to the workhouse boy,' he said, referring to a recent incident what had led to all sorts of trouble for the Jew. 'If this Horrie wasn't a relation of yourn, then you would just as happily stroll off.'

I ignored this slur against my good character and spoke to the others. 'You lot go to the courtyard off Crick Lane to compare findings. I'm going back for Horrie and, while I'm there, I may feel like collecting some more valuables for my trouble. We'll meet at the broken pump in ten minutes.' I emptied my pockets of my morning's work and handed them to Charley for safekeeping. These was some handkerchiefs of the finest silk, two ladies' purses containing eighteen sovereigns between them and, what was most impressive, a gold watch and chain what I had liberated from an old gentleman's vest pocket. The boys *oohed* and *aahed*, as well they might, as these findings was worth more than all theirs put together. I dangled the ticker from its chain so they could see its value and I tossed it to Charley. I was the only one among us what dared to do vest pockets.

With that I shot Jem a hard look to remind him who was top-sawyer around here. Then I put my hands in my pockets, so as to strike an idle pose, and went sauntering back to the scene of my freshest crime whistling a carefree tune. Those boys may well have wondered, as they watched me stroll away, as to why a clever thief of distinction, such as myself, would be risking the grab for one such as Horrie, a boy that we had long since nicknamed the Fartful Podger. The answer to this lay in my regrettable dealings with a woman I was once unfortunate enough to live with. A wicked, conniving old hag called Kat, who I often had cause to wish that I had never even met. But it is a sorry truth that you cannot pick your own mother.

The last time I had seen this Kat Dawkins was two nights prior in the taproom of the Three Cripples public house. This was a safe establishment in Saffron Hill where I could often be found after a hard day's work drinking and conversing with like-minded individuals. On this particular evening I was in the back room playing cards and enjoying a nice pot of beer with Len Pugg, Precious Tom and some Chinamen. Normally these gentlemen would not have gambled with someone of my tender years, considering as they did that such behaviour was an unnatural corruption of childhood innocence. However, earlier that day I had pinched some high-quality cigars from a Mayfair tobacconist and so they agreed to overlook my youth. The little room grew smoky, the conversation ribald and I soon won a tidy sum using skill, bluff and nerve, as well as a second pack of cards I had hidden just below the table. Just as I was about to clean them all out with my royal flush of diamonds, the door of the taproom blew open and in burst my mother like an unfortunate queen of spades. I had not laid eyes on the woman in eighteen months but here she was, just as I remembered her, wild-haired, starey-eyed and shrieking like a banshee.

'Here you is!' she screeched, making Precious Tom, who is of a nervous disposition at the best of times, spit up his whisky and drop his playing cards on to the table where we could all see them. 'Here, among thieves and low characters, just as your father ever was! Shame on you, gennelmen, for corrupting him so!' I was sat at the furthest end of the round table, facing the door, but my fellow players had their backs to her so they was good and startled. She circled the table, slapping them all on the back of the head and laying curses upon them, and the poor confused Chinamen reacted as though she was an officer of the law and made for the exit. As they left they pushed past Barney, the landlord of the Cripples, who was following her in from the front bar. He was swearing that he had tried to stop her from coming back here but that she was slippery as an eel and had dodged him. His meek apologies though was no match for her violent wailings.

'You have given me nothing but agonies since you was first placed inside me, you ungrateful wretch!' She grabbed my ear and began her striking of me. 'I have borne countless miseries for you, young wastrel, I've sacrificed my own comfort for yourn, and never once have you heard me repine!'

If these charges had been made against me in a more delicate manner, then I could have answered back. I would have refuted the image that she had painted of herself as a selfless mother, as well as her claim that I had never once heard her repine. But at the time I was unable to make these arguments, bent over as I was and covering my face against her sharp whackings. Then Len Pugg decided that he had stood this interruption for long enough and he rose from his seat to knock some sense into her. Len was a hero in that vicinity due to his prowess in the boxing line, and behind the bar of the Three Cripples there was displayed many pencil sketches of him in the ring knocking men out. But here he faced a challenger of a different sort, and no sooner had he risen to his feet than Kat reached inside her petticoat and produced a flash of metal that caused him to stop cold.

'Sit, Pugg!' she spat, pointing the knife towards him in a way that created a strong impression that she had used it before, and not just for skinning rabbits. Precious Tom cried out like a woman, Barney begged her to take it outside and Len sank back down. 'I's come here to talk to my Jacky,' she said. 'And my Jacky alone. If you gennelmen would be so kind as to piss off out of my face, then we shall both bid you goodnight.' She hoisted me from my seat and tugged me out of the room. 'It's long past his bedtime, the poor lamb.' Then she pulled me through the front bar, which was full of drunken associates of mine. They was all singing along to a bawdy tune being played out on the piano and none of them saw fit to come to the aid of a young boy being led out into the night by a woman with a knife pressed to his ear. But then the Cripples was a smoky inn, so let's be generous and say that they must not have seen me. Outside she near pulled my arm clean off as she dragged me through a maze of back alleys and crooked lanes until reaching one, all dark and dripping, where only the rats could hear us talk. She pushed me against the slimy wall and grinned at me. 'Well,' she said, 'ain't you going to give your dear old mum a kiss?'

'What you after?' I demanded.

'That's pleasant,' she replied, all innocence. 'I travel all the way from Seven Dials just to visit my angel child and this is the greeting he gives me. I'm after nothing, Jacky, nothing other than what is due me.' My belly turned with the beer and cigars. I felt like I was going to empty my dinner right out into the dirty lane if she wouldn't stand back and let me breathe. She started brushing down my coat of all the sawdust from the Cripples and spoke gentle. 'All I wants from you is returns,' she said, 'and not for me, you understand. But for your older brother Horrie, bless his simple heart.'

'Half-brother,' I said. 'We ain't got the same dad.'

'Half is still half,' she winked, wiping the dust away, 'even if it ain't the good half.'

She began telling me that she felt that I had done her a wrong turn as a son. I had benefitted, she felt, from all that she had taught me at an early age, such as how to pinch my own supper from the markets, and by what means a lady's clothing may be penetrated by small, searching hands. And all she had ever prayed for, she said, was that one day I would be able to use these skills to provide for my mother in her dotage and for my slow-witted brother who was not born as gifted as I. But, she lowered her voice to stress the depth of my treachery, instead I had applied my talents for the good of some Jew to whom I owed nothing, whilst my family was starving to death. As she said this last thing I thought I spied a tear glisten in her blue eye and thought, not for the first time, that she could have made a success of herself on the stage if life had turned out differently.

'I saw Horrie two days gone,' I answered back. 'He's good and fat for someone starving to death.' Her hand was like a claw around my neck.

'Clever lad, ain't you?' she hissed. 'But you won't feel so clever when someone starts whispering about your Hebrew friend and his little school up there.' She banged my head against the wall. 'Horrie needs to learn the ways and means with which to make his living. He eats too much, he drinks too much and he's about as much use around the house as a hole in a pisspot. You come by with your little friends on Sunday and take him out to work the crowds.' She released me from her grip and stepped away. 'And mind he don't get pinched,' she added before taking her leave, 'else it'll turn ugly for all.' I dropped on to the muddy ground and, sure enough, my guts started emptying. By the time I raised my head to wipe away the spew, my mother had gone.

So that is why, two days later, I was having to edge my way back into the puppet-show crowd to fetch Horrie, squeezing past ladies and gentlemen whose pockets I had picked just moments before. The former owner of the gold watch was so engrossed in the entertainment that he had yet to perceive his loss and every eye was still on Mr Punch, who was now hitting a police constable good and hard with his stick. Everyone was laughing at this while my half-brained half-brother just stared, mouth open, as if the whole scene was giving him ideas. I worked my way through, stepping over stray dogs and trying not to disturb the baby carriages, and sidled up close. He had helpfully managed to position himself between two large gentlemen, both of whom, to my trained eye, looked to be the taking-the-law-into-their-own-hands type. I tapped him on the shoulder and addressed him most genteel.

'Horace, good fellow,' I said, 'do come along. We have an appointment with some right distinguished personages elsewhere for whom we must not be late. Let us leave this vulgar entertainment and proceed forthwith.' Horrie turned his fat head and looked at me as if I had took to speaking Russian, so I stamped on his foot and whispered, *'Move your fat arse!'* This woke the dreamy lump up and he remembered where we was and what sort of trouble we was in. He nodded and I led him out of the crowd, both of us trying hard to avoid notice. We was not helped in this by Horrie stepping on the tail of a young lady's pet dog. The dog yelped, a baby cried, eyes turned upon us and I had to make a grand show of petting the noisy creature until Mr Punch won back his audience's attention.

Once out of the crowd we quickened our feet until we was clear of Jarrett Street. The two of us then hid ourselves deep within a fresher crowd, what was watching a procession of musicians and acrobats pass along Great Knaves. There was stilt-walkers, people on tambourines, jugglers, drummer boys, all creating a fine distraction. People was stopping on both sides to enjoy the sight and I nudged Horrie to say that here was good pickings. He was busy gawping though, just as before, at the fellow on the tallest stilts, as if the whole thing had been laid on for his entertainment alone.

'Let's get stones,' he said suddenly. 'Let's get some stones and chuck 'em at the wooden legs. See if they tumble.' He snorted like a pig and I looked at the boy amazed that we could ever be of the same blood. I used to remind myself, in such moments, that Kat Dawkins was a wicked liar and that in all likelihood she had found one of us as a baby, abandoned in an alley. If this was true I also hoped that I should be the one that would prove to be the foundling.

'It's May Day,' I reminded him. 'We ain't out to have fun.' I was vexed with Horrie for getting so distracted and I had a mind to do a Len Pugg and wallop him hard. I stopped myself because violence is lowering and also because he was much bigger than me and would most likely wallop me back. So instead I just asked him if he felt ready to try his hand. 'Just do what you saw me and the others do. And keep your wits sharp. You ain't robbing kinchins now.'

We walked along with the crowd. Horrie was moving close by, all stiff and with a fierce look on his face, and I fretted that he would give us both away. I told him to saunter like I was doing, trying to capture the air of a gentleman at leisure but he didn't understand. 'Do you want me to look at 'em or don't you?' he asked. What could be done with him? Some boys just don't have the aptitude for this line of work.

There was lots of rich people strolling about and I fanned them as I brushed past. When you've been practising the art for as long as I have you become good at fanning the outsides of pockets and with only the lightest touch I could tell you to the nearest shilling the value of what was within a person's tailcoat. This crowd's pockets was bulging with fogles, tickers and other trinkets and I was itching to take them for mine. I felt as though they was mine and that these people was the thieves and my stealing of them was a stealing back. It stung when I realised that I would have to let them stay where they was just because I had no faith in Horrie as an accomplice. If this outing was going to be an education for him, then we would need to start off with something simple.

Further along, at the corner of Knaves and Goswell, I saw a cove who was ripe for this purpose. Sitting at a table outside an inn was a portly, bald-headed gentleman in a blue velveteen coat that spoke of money. He was alone, scribbling into a notebook, and he raised his head every few moments in order to see the coming procession before returning to the book as if describing what he saw. A writer, I thought, pleased. Picking the pocket of a writer is akin to stealing from a baby carriage; they is a dreamy-headed lot. This one seemed oblivious to the world about him so lost was he in his words and I signalled to Horrie that here was sport. As we approached him he reached inside his coat and produced a silver snuffbox that glinted in the sun. He took a delicate pinch of snuff and put the box back into his coat, the street-side pocket no less, from which it stuck out for anyone to see. He was ever so accommodating and couldn't have made this easier if he'd tried. I was feeling the tingle as we drew near and, with the drumming and the whoops and the cheers covering my words, I instructed Horrie as to what was expected of him.

'You dip, I dash. As practised.'

'I dip?' he said.

'Yeah, you dip.'

'I want to dash.'

'No. You walk ahead, dip, I come fast behind, you pass, and I dash. Right?'

'Why should you get to do the dashing?'

'All right. I'll walk ahead and dip. You dash. But Horrie, dash don't mean really dash. It means sauntering off quick. Inconspicuous. Don't just run for it.'

'In-con-spic-a-what?' he said. I told him what it meant. Stone me, he was stupid.

The procession of stilt-walkers and acrobats was nearing the inn where our silver snuffbox was waiting for us and the crowds was at their thickest. The spectators was mixing in with those that sat outside enjoying the acrobats, and this writer cove was surrounded by people, any of whom could snatch his snuffbox if they'd only had the steel. I walked a few paces in front of Horrie and veered towards the cove whilst pretending to watch four lady acrobats stand on each other's shoulders, one on top of the other. This produced a roar of amazement from the people, and various gentlemen that sat outside the inn, including this writer, got to their feet to clap and cheer. I brought my body close to him, laughing loud at the lady acrobats, crossed my arms and pressed myself against the blue velveteen coat. As a fifth lady began climbing the others and the crowds held their breath, I inserted my left hand, covered from view by my right arm, into the pocket. My

JAMES BENMORE • 14

fingers removed the snuffbox and I coiled it up into my hand so as not to be seen. Then I unfolded my arms, just as the crowds began their mad clapping, and moved my hand behind my back, so that Horrie could just take the box and just glide away with it.

Horrie did not glide away with it.

Instead there my hand remained, the snuffbox waiting to be passed to another hand that just would not come. I left it there, open to the street, for five or six seconds, which in pickpocketing is too long for anything to happen. So I curled it back into my own pocket and carried on down the street, careful not to look behind to see what had happened to the boy. And then all this shouting was heard.

Stop that boy! Stop him!

This is when dash meant really dash and my feet took to running before the cries was even out. I darted headlong into the crowd, away from the cove, and weaved my way through the spectators at great speed. I was heading towards the direction of Goswell Street, where I knew I could lose myself down an alley, but the people about was now agitated and the voices of *Stop that!* and *No, boy!* grew louder and panicky and I wondered if I would make it past the people who was turning and gasping in shock. And then there was this scream, a woman's scream, followed by more screams and some crashing noises and the people became hysterical and the crowd began to lurch and I was squashed between other bodies what had begun dashing about in all manner of directions. There was more shouting of *Seize that boy!* and *What boy?* and then *The boy with the stones!* and I knew then that all these cries was not in reference to my activities.

I turned back towards the procession to see what the fuss could be about but I saw nothing more than the backs of gentlemen gathered around where the acrobats had stood. I approached with caution, still ready to dart if need be, and as the backs parted I saw the five lady acrobats all lying across each other on the stone street, crying in pain. Near them was a stilt-walker who had also come down hard into the crowd. His stilts was snapped and he was face down on the cobbles with blood trickling out underneath. The drumming had stopped and some selfless gentlemen was attending to the fallen women by running over with offers to rub their bruised bodies. I cast my eyes about for my partner-in-crime, Horrie Belltower, knowing that he would be close by, and saw him just outside the inn, being grappled to the ground by four large men, two of whom appeared to be policemen. He was red-faced and crying out for his mother.

I surveyed this ugly scene and decided that it was not for me. Nothing could be done to help Horrie now. I had tried to be a good influence on him and teach him our ways but there are some youths that will always be trouble and I'm sad to say that he was one of them. If my mother should feel a grievance against me for allowing him to get pinched, then I would tell her the honest story and say she should take it up with Horrie when he was finally released from jail. The men was dragging him away so I shook my head at the shame of it and turned on my heels. I was planning on meeting Charley and the others, if they was still at the pump, where I would enjoy telling them the whole sorry tale, when, just as I was leaving, my coat was grabbed from above and I was hoisted up.

'You, my young shaver,' said an angry voice, 'is going nowhere!'

It was a rough man what had got hold of me, who had been creeping up behind in an unsporting way while I had been watching the chaos. I tried to escape, but his grip was tight and he pulled me towards himself with one hand and knocked me hard on the head with the other. 'Stop your wriggling!' he said, with breath that stank of the gin-house, and he began going through my pockets. I cried out at this injustice and demanded to know for what reason was I being abused in this here fashion. Some of the crowd, what was still gawping at the injured acrobats, turned to look, but they seemed to consider my struggles to be an even fresher entertainment and did nothing to help. I called for the police, knowing that they was all busy with Horrie, in the hope that this would startle the man into loosening his hold, but he just laughed.

'I *am* a policeman,' he said, 'and I've been watching you from that there window.' He nodded his head towards the building opposite and to the second-floor, which overlooked the street. 'I saw you and the other boy work the street together. You were stealing from coat pockets while he threw stones by way of distraction. Very clever! But not so clever as could get by me. Oh no!' I was vexed with this person, first for the grab and second for thinking I would ever work a plan as stupid as that. I had no love for policemen – they was ordinary men what work against their own class – and I bit this one's hand good and hard. He just struck me harder than before. And then a voice spoke on my behalf.

'Good sir,' it said in a gentle tone, 'I pray, do not treat the lad with such viciousness. He is just a child after all. Do you not have children yourself?'

'Certainly I do,' replied the man. 'To speak truth, I have a son the same age as this one.' And then he boxed me on the ears once more. 'And I don't care for him much neither.'

'Please,' continued the voice, 'do not debase yourself with brutality. What on earth has the child done to deserve such ill treatment?' I wriggled towards my champion so as to display my innocent, helpless face and to encourage him in his heroism, when I made the ironical discovery that he was none other than the writer cove in the blue velveteen coat.

'Check your pockets, sir,' said the rough policeman. 'You will find them lighter for this item.' And then he produced from my pocket the silver snuffbox.

'That's mine,' I cried. 'I takes snuff myself. You've no proof it belongs to him! Let me go!'

But the man remained cold.

'Yours, hey?' he said. 'So is this your name engraved upon it then?' He showed me the lid of the box and then passed it to the cove. 'Or is it perhaps this gentleman's?' The writer peered at his own property through his little, round spectacles and gasped in surprise.

The engraving read:

MR SAMUEL PICKWICK, Esq., G.C.M.P.C.

'Bless me,' he said, and he began searching through his coat-pockets as if expecting the box to be in two places at once. He seemed a decent sort of cove but he had something of the simpleton about him. 'I didn't notice the loss,' he said eventually, half smiling, like someone who has been the victim of a most rare magic trick. 'He must have the touch of a feather, this boy.'

The magistrate who presided over my trial days later was less enchanted by my mastery of the magical art of pickpocketing, however. I was shoved into the hot and heaving police office, full of watching women and crying babies, and I had to speak loudly to make myself heard. I was one of countless unfortunates what was put forward for sentencing that morning and Constable Hodge was telling the court that I was a troublemaker. I had just enjoyed two nights' hospitality in an Old Bailey cell under his protection and I still had the bruising to show for it. Not that Jailer Hodge was responsible for these; in truth he had tried to stop me from getting bruised-up the night before. The good fellow had chanced upon me getting a kicking from Constable Hummerstone in the outer yard, which I had broken into during my third try at escape. Hummerstone was applying his boot to me with enthusiasm when Hodge had ordered him to stop.

'Hummerstone!' he cried. 'Have you run mad? The whole prison can hear you.'

'I caught the rascal again, sir,' said Hummerstone sweating. 'You should see the damage he's done to his cell door. Lord knows where he keeps getting the chisels from.'

'But can't you see he'll be red raw? He'll use those marks against us in court. I'll take him back to the lower cells while you get him a nice soft cushion. Then we'll take turns punching him while the other holds it between.' He was a kind old soul, Constable Hodge.

I promised Hodge and Hummerstone not to peach about their violent ways, if they swore not to bring up my escape bids, but I still found plenty to say to the magistrate. I addressed the court in a most familiar manner and accused the police of entering into a conspiracy against me. When my arresting officer gave his statement I threw some nice insults across at him and I then asked the magistrate to hurry things along as I had an appointment in town after lunch. I then declared that I had several good character witnesses sitting just outside the doors and when they couldn't be found I said they must have gone to lunch. None of this amused the officers of the court but it went over very well with the watching crowds, who liked to see some cheek in the face of authority. I saw few people I recognised in the crowd, which was as expected, as my sort of people tend to steer clear of the police office.

The magistrate was having none of me. He had a head on him what seemed to be made out of red brick, like it was weighing down into the rest of him, and this discomfort may account for the harshness of his judgment. Seven years transportation he gave me, just because I was a notorious criminal well known to the law in many a locality. He couldn't have cared less about my promise and talent. I was booked for a passage aboard a ship what was to sail me down the Thames, away from my home city, and take me around the world to Australia, where it's nothing but heat, flies and hard labour, and no one has invented anything worth pinching except for some queerly shaped sticks. A place where the sun makes a mockery of Christmas, and if St Nicholas shows up he wonders if he hasn't read his calendar wrongly. Australia, where a lesser lad would have remained, withered and died.

But the Crown was soon to discover that, like the boomerang, I was not to be chucked so easy.

Chapter 2

The Booted Cat

Wherein I relate my happy return to British shores after six years away. I am much changed

Sometimes, in the more fashionable novels, there comes a part in the story what is so very unpleasant that the cove narrating it will spare his reader the horrible details and write something such as *No words can describe the horrors that I endured*. This is never true — there are always words to describe anything.

Take my voyage out to New South Wales by way of argument. Some of the words I could use to describe what it was like to travel on a six-month voyage down in a hold with fifty other convicts include: *starving, sweating, spewing, shitting, fleas, rats, cockroaches, shackled, flooded, underfed, airless, freezing, boiling, rotting, punching, kicking, unwanted, sexual* and *advances*. Stick some of them together in the same sentence and you get a fair idea of the transportation experience. But where is the use in dwelling upon such an ordeal when my return journey at the age of nineteen was so much more agreeable? I sailed aboard a magnificent vessel called the *Son and Heir* what was transporting wool back from the colonies, and myself and a man named Warrigal stayed in a large cabin what rivalled the captain's for comfort. This luxury had been paid for by my new benefactor, a Lord Franklin Evershed, and his generosity did not end there. Warrigal and myself would parade around the top deck, as our ship sailed across the equator, dressed in our fine tailorings and bearing other signifiers of wealth, and these did much to make up for my rough accent and unvarnished ways. Although I had spent my youth picking the pockets of people of their class, the other travellers did not seem to suspect me of criminality and I was pleased that they was ready to believe that I could have made my fortune at such a young age. Warrigal, they all agreed, was an unusual choice of valet, but he seemed an attentive servant and they was sure he would be happy in London society. Perhaps, suggested Captain McGowan as we shared a pipe one evening as we watched the Canary Islands fade into the distance, I should consider giving him a nice English name when we arrived home so that he should fit in better. I gave this idea some thought and, when the ship docked in to Dover on a miserable November day, I had almost started to believe our story myself and was sorry to have to wave goodbye to the crew.

Warrigal and myself walked down the unsteady gangplank of the *Son and Heir*, harassed by the wind and rain, with carpet bags over our shoulders and each carrying an end of my trunk. We made straight for the local booking office to see what could be done about a coach to London and when we got into the mouldy little room we found other wet people making the same enquiry. The clerk behind the counter was an oily-skinned, belligerent lad what I took to be about my own age and he was telling everyone that he was sorry but the last coach to London for the day had just been taken and there was an end to it. He didn't look very sorry and, as I pushed my way through the dispersing crowd to the front of the counter, he took a long lazy look at me, then at Warrigal, and then turned his eyes back down to a newspaper he was pretending to read. I impressed upon him the importance of me and my valet securing a passage to the capital forthwith and

I hinted that there could be something in it for him if he could arrange events to my satisfaction, wink wink. But either the lumpen youth misunderstood my subtle insinuations or he lacked the spirit and capability that you would have found in a boy from the rookeries. He thumbed to a posting bill pasted on to the wall behind him that told how the next carriage out wouldn't leave until six o'clock the next morning.

'You won't find another coachman what'll take you to town in this weather,' he yawned, his eyes still not leaving the paper, 'so you can either book yourself into an 'otel or you and your black are welcome to bed down in the stables with the 'orses. Either way, you ain't getting out of Dover tonight less you plan to foot it.' I was somehow getting the impression that this waste of blood and bones doubted my credentials as a gentleman. I held a silver-tipped cane in my hands which I raised to my lips and made a *hmm*ing noise as if pondering upon these suggestions and, as he turned the page of the paper, I hit him over the head with it. He cried out in pain. 'What's that for?'

'Apologies,' I said, all concerned. 'Just thought you wanted rousing, that's all. You was so very taken by these tales of crooks and lowlives −' I tapped his copy of *Bentley's* − 'that you must have imagined you was talking to one of them. You ain't. You is talking to a respectable gent what appreciates a bit of manners.' The room was now almost empty save for some gentlemen drying themselves off and Warrigal who was standing by my trunk and staring out of the doorway towards the rain. He was dressed in a brown greatcoat and wore a top hat as splendid as any Englishman's but his thoughts must still have been on the other side of the world. 'This here is my servant,' I said, pointing my cane at him, 'and as such is not accustomed to sleeping in stables. The last carriage to town has been booked, eh? Well, unbook it then, because

I don't plan to spend one more hour in this here town.' I smiled at the boy to show that I was a reasonable gent but I still held my cane in a way that made him flinch every time I moved it.

'Bravo, sir,' said a voice from behind me. 'A swift but gentle knock to the head is the surest way to combat insolence. You were right to strike him.' I turned to see a man in a clergyman's collar who had been watching me close throughout the whole perform- ance. At a quick glance I could see that he had no valuables about him worth pinching. His clothes was not special and nor was the cheap timepiece he had pinned to his waistcoat. He was the sort of cove you would hardly be aware of if he lived in your same street, and had he not spoken then I would have never have noticed him.

'If it is a carriage towards London that you want, then perhaps I can assist,' he continued in his pleasant way, 'for I was the man that booked the last coach. My name is Reverend Albert Cherry and my family and I are headed towards the suburbs. If you would care to travel with us we will happily take you, and perhaps you can book into the Booted Cat, the same inn where we are to lodge. I fear that is all the progress you are likely to make today.' I told this Cherry that I feared he could be right. Then accepting his kind offer I said that I would like to pay for my share of the journey, but that if he had his heart set on letting us ride with him for free then I wouldn't insult him by refusal. He had not actually mentioned that the ride was gratis but now he was stuck with it.

'Dawkins is the name,' I told him, offering him my hand, 'and it's a pleasure to make your acquaintance. You can help my valet carry this luggage if you care to.'

'Good gracious, Mr Dawkins,' said the game fellow as he grabbed the end of my trunk and lifted it with Warrigal. 'This is a mighty weight.'

'You're not wrong, Reverend,' I said as I buttoned up my coat and readied myself to head back out into the wet. 'You'll find it easier if you lift with your knees,' I advised him. 'We don't want you to be doing yourself a mischief now, do we?' Before picking up my other bags I reached into my pocket for a coin. I tossed it towards the clerk and thanked him for his trouble but he was a clumsy catcher and was busy searching on the ground for it as I walked out. He needn't have bothered; it was Australian money.

Outside the rain was letting off but I had to step around a great many puddles on my way to the coach so as not to muddy my expensive shoes. The reverend was chattering away as he carried the trunk and I admired how much puff he had in him for his age. He was all questions. From where had I travelled? How long had I been away? What on earth was Warrigal? I kept my answers good and short like Evershed had warned me to.

'There will be just enough room for you to join us inside the carriage, Mr Dawkins, but your valet may have to sit out beside the coachman.' He didn't look to Warrigal as he said this, despite being nearer to him. 'He will be rather exposed to the elements, I'm afraid.'

'Oh, you needn't worry about Peter Cole, reverend,' I replied. 'It'll be a treat for him to feel the drip of English rain on himself after all those years of living in heat and dust. I imagine he'd be disappointed if we didn't let him ride outside.' I also took great care not to look at Warrigal as I spoke, especially since it was the first time he would have heard his new name. We reached the coach that the reverend had booked and I saw that it was a larger, grander vehicle than I had expected and seemed a bit plush for a simple clergyman. The rest of his family was already inside and the horses waiting to go as Reverend Cherry explained to the coachman about the new arrangements. The coachman eyed

Warrigal with suspicion as he helped him stow my luggage, and I saw the reverend give him a shilling to let Warrigal sit beside him. Once they was sat atop, Reverend Cherry said that all that was now left for him to do was to introduce me to his family and we could set off. With that, he pulled open the carriage door and revealed something well worth travelling back from the other side of the globe for. They was four women in all, a wife and three daughters, and these girls was as sweet and as delicious a set of English Cherries as I could have hoped to have met upon arrival home. I smiled and doffed my hat to them as their father explained that I would be joining them on the journey.

'My family, this is Mr Dawkins, a businessman, and he, like us, has just returned home after many years abroad. Mr Dawkins, allow me to introduce to you my wife, Mrs Cherry . . .' Mrs Cherry was a plump, pink-faced woman who, as I took her hand to kiss it as a gentleman should, let out a little gasp as though it was the most exciting thing that had ever happened to her. From this I reasoned that it was not difficult giving thrills to a clergyman's wife. '. . . And our three daughters, Constance, Amelia and Lucille.' Their three pretty, bonneted heads was smiling out at me and I guessed their ages to be between sixteen and nineteen. *So*, I thought as I removed my hat and climbed into the carriage, squeezing myself good and tight between Amy and Lucy, *the good reverend does have something worth pinching after all*. Once the reverend was settled inside I tapped the roof of the carriage with my cane and we was on our way towards London.

I was, you must remember, still a young fellow who had spent most of those difficult years wherein a boy becomes a man stuck in a penal colony surrounded by convicts, soldiers and aborigines. So for me to be now pressed in a small space among three lovely roses, all sweet smelling and in the fullest of bloom, was having a strong effect upon my senses. The coach was rattling gently as it trundled along the stony ground and this created a nice jiggling sensation inside the carriage, which made looking at the Cherry girls in their white cotton dresses even more appealing. We had travelled less than half a mile when I had to find an excuse to place my hat over my lap in order that it should hide the dirty great dart that had begun to grow beneath. Also, it must be noted that during my time away I had grown into an attractive fellow myself, not handsome in a traditional way but there was some young wives of the ship's crew what had fallen for my rakish charms while their husbands was busying themselves on the top deck and away from their unlocked cabins. I knew I had good looks enough for those smiling ladies to welcome me in whenever I paid them a visit, so I was now hoping now to press a similar advantage upon these three fair maidens.

All this time Reverend Cherry had been talking about how he and his family had just returned from Bombay where he was doing missionary work and I was making a good show of pretending as though I cared. He was saying how the girls had been well educated there, and had been raised as paragons of Christian virtue, but he was worried about how they was to fare now that they was back in England. They was so innocent, he said, and London had a reputation for wickedness. He hoped they would not prove corruptible. The dearest prayer of him and his wife was to see all three girls wedded off to successful men of distinction so that they would not have to worry about their financial futures. But they met so few eligible bachelors abroad, he sighed.

'There was one young man though,' he beamed, touching the hand of the girl sat next to him, 'an officer in the navy, no less, whom we had the pleasure of meeting while he was stationed in India, and who developed a strong admiration for our little

Constance.' This did not surprise me as I was sat opposite the buxom Constance and as we bounced along the hilly path I found I was developing a strong admiration for her myself. 'Before he returned to England,' continued her father, 'this man came to me and asked for her hand. I can honestly say that it was the proudest, happiest day in the lives of myself and Mrs Cherry.'

'And you were delighted too, weren't you, Constance dear?' twittered the mother like an idiot bird. Constance looked as though this was the first time anybody had asked her opinion on the matter and she returned a weak smile. I wondered why Mrs Cherry thought that she would be in any way excited about marrying a man too miserly to give her an engagement ring as I had noticed that, buxom though she was, she had no decent jewellery about her for me to steal.

'And so you find us, sir,' Reverend Cherry continued, 'on our way to reunite these two lovebirds. William has requested that Constance be brought to the town of Welling in Kent where the wedding preparations are already under way. His family, as I understand it,' he lowered his voice to a whisper, although who he thought was listening in I don't know, 'are rather affluent, I believe. They even arranged for this carriage.' He winked.

'If only we could find such suitable husbands for our younger daughters,' commented Mrs Cherry. She paused and looked to her husband as if waiting for him to say something. He said nothing so she asked me herself. 'You seem rather young to be a businessman, Mr Dawkins. What line do you say you are in?'

'Sheep shearing,' I told her.

'Sheep shearing?'

'That's it. The shearing of sheep. Down in Australia I've got some farms with my name on the outside and plenty of sheep to put in them. The world will always need wool.' Reverend Cherry agreed that this was so and said that I must be quite prosperous indeed if my clothes was any indication. 'I keep the wolf at bay,' I said. 'If you lie down under a blanket tonight,' I assured him, 'there is a strong chance it'll be made of Dawkins wool. We export shiploads of the stuff.' The reverend and his wife seemed most impressed with this boast and, to the left of me, I could feel young Lucille sitting up a little straighter. To my right, however, Amelia was still looking out at the green fields in a sulk, showing herself to be the harder to impress of the two.

'Do you hear that, girls?' cooed her mother. 'Dawkins wool! I can't say that I've ever heard of it, but I am certain that I shall. To think that I will be able to tell people that we once shared a carriage with the famous Jack Dawkins of Dawkins Wool.' Sat opposite me, Constance was tilting her head to one side.

'Will you stay in England very long, Mr Dawkins,' she asked, 'or must you soon return to Australia?' Her eyes were full of curiosity and I had a feeling that her fiancé was not too close to her thoughts at that moment, which served him right for not giving her an engagement ring.

'I imagine that Mr Dawkins must have a sweetheart back in Australia waiting for him, Constance,' said Lucille, with all the subtlety of her mother. 'Do you have a sweetheart, Mr Dawkins, back in Australia, waiting for you?'

'No, Miss Lucy I do not.' I made the sad face. 'It seems that I have been so very industrious that I have just not had the time to find anyone worth sharing my fortune with. Perhaps I never will.' This made Constance, Lucille and Mrs Cherry all of a cluck and they was quick to say that I was mistaken in thinking it. Reverend Cherry promised me that the Lord had made matches for every beating heart and that mine was sure to make herself manifest before long.

'Sometimes, Mr Dawkins, He hides these things beneath our very noses. Isn't that so, Amy?' All of the other Cherrys looked towards this middle child as if this was her cue to deliver her one line in a play that they often acted out. But she just shrugged and raised her hand to her mouth to yawn. Reverend Cherry was a smooth performer though and he changed the subject quick to what a delightful creature his youngest daughter was, while his wife looked at Amy with a burning eye. The rest of the journey was taken up with Lucy this and Lucy that, as both her parents was keen for me to know of her every skill and accomplishment. Several times I was told that she could speak French, German and Dutch, could play the harpsichord, dance a quadrille and sing like an angel, as if could I care a tinker's tit for any of that. The reverend was boasting of how she had always been an obedient daughter and that she was sure to prove a pliable wife for some lucky fellow. Lucy blushed to hear herself spoken of like this and she gasped and giggled to hear any nice compliment that I chose to sprinkle on her. I told Mrs Cherry that her three daughters had better watch out when being introduced into London society as the Indian sun had turned their complexions to such a pleasing brown that this, on top of their blonde loveliness, was sure to send the lesser beauties of the city into violent fits of jealousy. Lucy and Constance was as delighted with my flattery as I had expected them to be, and their mother clapped her hands in joy, but, much to my surprise, I heard a small scoffing sound from the girl to my right. That Amy Cherry seemed not to be susceptible to my gentlemanly charms was a source of annoyance to me, as she was more interested in gazing at passing hedges than in anything I had to say. I was starting to wonder as to what her problem might be. Here was I, Jack Dawkins of Dawkins Wool, a successful capitalist and silver-tongued charmer, and here was she, a penniless clergyman's daughter without a jewel on her, and yet still she was treating me like I was some common boy from the rookeries. I hoped that her father or mother was fixing to give her a good talking-to later that night for being so ill-mannered.

On the coach trundled and the day began to darken. It was easy to see that the accomplished and pliable Lucy was a ripe Cherry just waiting to be squeezed, and just a few more lies and worthless promises was all it would take for me to pop her. But, as we neared the end of the journey, I had started to lose my appetite for her, so unsettled was I by her sister's indifference. Amy was a pretty girl, this was a truth not to be denied, and the more time I spent in that carriage with these sisters the more I began to think her the most appealing of the three, although it seemed as though this Cherry had the hardest stone within. I decided to not waste another moment more thinking on her.

Finally we came to a large coaching inn where Constance Cherry was to be reunited with this William cove about who I had heard such big talk. The painted signboard flapping in the wind and the drizzling rain showed a cat wearing leather boots what was strutting his way past a sign what pointed towards London. It was a large place and most inviting, with an ostler waiting to take care of the horses, and through the window a crackling fireplace could be seen. Our coach came to a stop and out stepped three men holding umbrellas. The first of these strode right up to the door and opened it for us before the coachman had even got down from his seat, declaring, 'Constance, my love, I feared you were not coming!' The reverend beamed and told me that this was William Faith, the fiancé of little Connie, and I raised my eyebrows as if I never would have guessed. This fancy cove greeted all the Cherrys as if he was marrying the lot of them, and to see the way the reverend and his wife acted he may as well have been. He helped the women down from the carriage as his two friends held the umbrellas above their heads and we all moved to the sheltered part of the inn-yard to shake hands as the coach was unloaded. Once Faith had finished fussing over the wellbeing of the Cherry family he turned to introduce the two coves flanking him. The first was a lad called Martin, about my age, and shaking his hand was like being handed a dying fish. He was a junior officer in the navy we was told, and Reverend Cherry responded to this information as if it made him the new Lord Nelson. But whether Martin was his first or last name I cannot now recall as he made little impression upon me. The other man though was harder to ignore. He was tall and beardless with grey side-whiskers that was as stiff and as bristly as a used brush and he was old enough to be William Faith's father. He was introduced as Wilfred Bracken, a great and faithful friend of the family, and I found myself wary of him right away. His face was the colour of pot ashes, his skin all pitted with smallpox scars and his hands was big and grabbing, out of all proportion with the rest of his bony self. He put me in mind of something from one of those gothic novels that I had been given to read back in the colony, a creature what had been stitched together from the dead parts of others, and I did not care to look at him.

'Gentleman,' said the reverend, 'allow me to introduce to you Mr Jack Dawkins, a new and valued acquaintance of our family.' I gave them all a little bow and said how did they do.

'Dawkins, you say?' asked the miserable Bracken, and I half expected a thunderclap to accompany him, so doom-laden was his voice.

'Yes,' Mrs Cherry answered for me, 'of Dawkins Wool. Perhaps you have heard of them? They are quite famous, I am told.'

'Are they?' said the creature, and he looked me up and down like he was measuring out my coffin.

The reverend was explaining to William Faith about how we had met, and I said that I needed lodgings for the night as I was leaving for London the very next day. Faith was sure that the landlady of the Cat could find me a room and said we should all get inside out of the rain.

'And perhaps later, Mr Dawkins, you might care to join us all for a private dinner? That is, if you and your family don't object, Reverend?'

'Not at all, young William. It would be a joy for us to have Mr Dawkins attend. And for Lucy especially, I imagine.' He winked at his youngest, who was a picture of shrinking bashfulness. Amy didn't look like she thought my attendance would be a joy though. The snooty mare was barely listening.

'Very good then,' said Faith. 'I shall tell the landlady to set another place and we will meet again at . . . Who in fiery blazes is that?' I turned to see what they was gawping at. It was only Warrigal, who had come up behind me with the luggage. He had been helping the coachman unload not just my trunk and bags but also those of the Cherrys, and now he was standing as still as a statue waiting to be told what next. He was drenched with rain and his crunched black face was glaring out at us from under his soggy hat as though he was busy putting curses on us all.

'Oh yes,' I said. 'It's just my valet, Warri— Peter Cole. He's a docile one, I promise you. He's what they call an aboriginal – there are whole tribes of them down in Australia – and he's proven himself to be as faithful and as hard-working a servant as I have ever had.' William Faith apologised and said that he had not realised that this was my servant and that he would ask the landlady if another room could be arranged for him. At this, a sharp hacking cough came out of Warrigal what made every head turn on him again.

'Don't put yourself to all that trouble,' I told Faith. 'Peter Cole will be happy sleeping on the floor of my room, if we get him a blanket. It may sound rough, but he's used to sleeping outside at home so he won't mind. We've an early start tomorrow after all.' The whole party glanced at each other as if this was most unusual and also cruel. But William Faith was an agreeable fellow and he took Constance by the arm and led us all through the low door of the inn and into the main bar where a rosy-cheeked landlady was waiting to greet us. She told me she had the perfect room for myself and Warrigal and would send a chambermaid along with an extra bedding shortly.

'Perhaps they will be made of your own wool, Mr Dawkins,' Mrs Cherry said with a smile, and I smiled back saying that perhaps they just might. And so we was all directed to our separate chambers in the rambling old place, down passages and up staircases, and I made a special note of where the Cherry girls was staying just in case I should need to know. Warrigal and myself was struggling with the heavy trunk and Faith told us that dinner would be served in just over an hour. Once we was inside our room we dropped down the trunk, locked the door behind us and Warrigal flopped on to the large mahogany bed.

'That ain't for you, Warrigal,' I said, hanging my hat off a peg on the wall. 'You could have had your own chamber, you know you could. I can't be expected to lie on the floor. Not with my back.' Warrigal stared at the ceiling. He hadn't said one word to me since he'd got to England and it didn't look like he was going to start now. 'That's where you're sleeping,' I told him, pointing at a rug on the floor in front of a small fireplace, 'and very cosy you shall be. But the bed is mine.' Still he said nothing. He just lay there like a sooty corpse and ignored me. I busied myself around the room, taking off my coat and unpacking some of the clothes and toiletries that Lord Evershed had supplied us with and preparing myself for dinner. 'Come on now, enough of this,' I said after a time. 'Ain't we friends?' He gave no response. I took some boot polish out and started work on my own shoes.

'Is it because you was made to sit out in the rain?' I asked. Still nothing.

'Is it because I keep calling you by another name?' I finished on my shoes and asked him if he wanted me to do his. He nodded, unlaced them and passed them to me. I did a good job and they came up lovely. I showed him how shiny they was and placed them by the door.

'Something is troubling you, Warrigal, and I think I know what. You think I shouldn't be sniffing around these Cherrys when we have more important things to do, that's what you think. You think I was wrong to tell them my name when we was told not to draw attention to ourselves. Well, Warrigal, maybe you is right, but where, I ask you, is the harm in it? We've done nothing but travel for months, so why not enjoy ourselves on our first night in England?'

Just then the chambermaid knocked on the door and I half opened it so she couldn't see Warrigal lying in my place. 'A pillow and a blanket,' she said, handing them to me, 'for your valet.' I thanked her, she curtsied and I shut the door and went over to the fireplace to lay them out. Warrigal was now propped up on the bed with two large feather pillows behind him. He looked at me like I was just one of those flies that was forever buzzing around his head back in Australia.

'You is a malingering wretch, Warrigal, that's what you is,' I told him as I buttoned up my evening shirt. 'Stay there then, if you feel so strong about it. I don't care if you lie there till morning. It's you that has to watch over me, remember, and I'm not sitting up here with you all night.'

I turned my back on him and picked up a small looking glass in which I inspected my collar and brushed my hair. In the reflection I could see Warrigal still lying on the bed and looking at a clock upon the mantel. He reached for his fob-watch that was chained to his waistcoat and began setting it to English time in a lazy way. I wished I knew what was going on inside that head of his. I wondered, as I watched him, if he was thinking about the pact we had both made with that red-coated devil, and how he was going to kill me, if and when the time came.

Chapter 3

Shiny Things

*Containing further particulars of that evening
and of the dinner I took with my new acquaintances.
Romance was in the air*

'It is very good of you to insist that your valet serve us at dinner, Mr Dawkins,' William Faith was saying, 'but quite unnecessary. I believe the Booted Cat is fully staffed.' Warrigal had been helping to pour the drinks and serve from the soup tureen throughout the starter. I said that it was good practice for him and that he was enjoying himself greatly. Mrs Cherry commented that he was the very model of a valet.

'My father had an attendant once,' she said, 'and he was forever vanishing when needed. But your Peter Cole seems rather devoted to you. He's very much your shadow.'

'Isn't he just,' I replied, and I knew that Warrigal was now sat behind me on a chair against the wall watching me eat, his eyes fixed on the back of my head. He knew he had to busy himself if he was going to be able to stay in the dining room with me, and the dirty imp wouldn't let me out of his sight. He would play out his part in public though. He knew what Evershed would do if he didn't.

The dinner had started badly, this was true, as I had shown myself to be a man who lacked proper breeding. I had entered the private room and sat myself straight down while the other four men was stood behind their chairs waiting for the Misses Cherry and their mother to seat themselves first. These ladies made matters worse by taking forever about it, and I could see Amelia Cherry smirking at my rough manners. I had no clue as to which of the many knives and forks I was to be using and when, but I was sure I was the only one there who knew how much they would fetch in a Whitechapel pawnbroker's. I was contemplating numerous strategies to smuggle these items away later on when something happened that pushed these idle wonderings away. William Faith had got down on one knee and was talking to Constance.

'My darling,' he began, 'what a brute you must think me. To have asked for your fair hand and to have requested that you travel across continents to live here as my wife without ever having once presented you with that which any tender bride could reasonably lay claim. Here, my turtledove.' He reached into his waistcoat pocket and produced a tiny felt-covered jewellery case which I knew from the insignia to be of the highest market value. Constance gasped, her sisters and mother squealed with excitement and the reverend and myself leaned over, knowing this was to be something special. Faith opened the case slow, as if he had bought it from God's own jeweller, and as soon as the lid parted and the light could catch it we saw the diamond glint from within. 'It is the finest cut,' he told us, 'for the sweetest heart.'

It certainly was a beauty. He took the ring from its case and placed it on her finger and the light bounced it in all directions. Mrs Cherry did not know what to do with herself to see such a vision and she looked fit to faint. All three Cherry girls was now in tears of happiness and as Constance leaned forward to receive Faith's courtly kisses I could see in the eyes of Lucy Cherry that she had forgotten all about Jack Dawkins of Dawkins Wool. This was a small concern for me, however, as by this time I had lost all interest in anything either of the two younger Cherry girls had to offer me. It was Constance now who had my full attention, Constance, who was holding out her finger to display her prize for everyone to see, who passed it underneath my very nose to be admired. Sweet, innocent Constance who could not have possibly known what a deep stir her teasing actions was causing within me. I have always had a weakness for shiny things – it's something I cannot help – and I knew then that there was no chance I was leaving that there diamond on that there finger. I wanted it for mine and there was an end to it.

'Bravo, William,' said Junior Officer Martin once we had all settled ourselves. 'It is a quite brilliant stone.' Around the table everyone agreed and then Bracken, whose big hands was dabbing away at the pea soup around his lips, spoke for the first time that evening.

'It is an exquisite stone to be sure. Rose-cut, I think. I suspect it comes from the new diamond mines in South Africa, and is three carat. It's quite rare and must have cost you a small fortune, William, although it would be indelicate of me to try to guess how much. The ring itself is less expensive and you purchased it from a jeweller's called Lillertons in Hatton Garden. It has been designed in the style of ancient Rome and the image of the snake coiling about itself is a Roman symbol of eternal love. This design has become particularly popular ever since Prince Albert bought one like it for our young Queen as an engagement ring. Correct me if I am wrong.'

'As ever, old friend,' Faith said smiling, 'nothing escapes you.' The spooky old cove nodded and returned to his soup. Faith went on: 'But however could you tell all that from just a quick glance?'

'A lucky coincidence, nothing more,' said Bracken. 'Retrieved a stone just like it for Lillertons some time last year. Could even be the same one, its kind is so rare. A most extraordinary case.'

'I beg your pardon, Mr Bracken,' Reverend Cherry asked, blinking, 'did you say you *retrieved* one last year? What on earth can you mean?' William Faith laughed and apologised for not explaining.

'Our Mr Bracken is a somewhat celebrated professional in the capital. He is one of Sir Robert's men.'

'Sir Robert's?' someone asked.

'Yes. A bobby. A peeler. One of Sir Robert Peel's original Metropolitan police officers. We have the honour, ladies and gentleman, of sitting with Detective-Inspector Bracken of the Yard.'

All of a sudden I had lost my taste for the soup. I preferred it when I thought Bracken just a thing from the grave.

'I dare say you have been away from London for so long, Reverend Cherry,' Faith continued, 'that you won't be aware of the wonderful progress that has been made by men like Bracken here. Gone are the days of the Bow Street Runner and his ineffectual attempts to maintain law and order. In recent years an organised force of men has emerged who are more persistent in their pursuit of the criminal class. And Wilfred Bracken is universally recognised as the best of them.'

Wilfred Bracken did nothing to deny this compliment; instead he just bowed his head as the Cherry family all made noises to show they thought he sounded right heroic. Faith went on to say that Bracken was the scourge of the rookeries and that thieves trembled to hear his very name. He then insisted that Bracken tell us about his exploits as if this would be a great treat for us all. Bracken was agreeable and cleared his throat.

'The case to which I refer,' he said in a low, serious voice which

I felt was at odds with the merry occasion, 'was the Case of the Pimlico Pincher. You may have read about it in the *Police Gazette*.' The ladies all shook their heads. Of course they hadn't read about it, or anything else, in the *Police Gazette*, as well he knew. But they all leaned closer into the table to listen to him, his lifeless old face looking even more ghoulish in the candlelight. 'Lillertons jewellers had been contacted by a lady calling herself Countess Mariana Velez. She had written to them explaining that she was an ambassador's wife currently staying in the fashionable area of Pimlico and that she wished to purchase some jewellery to wear at the Spanish Embassy Ball. She arranged for a brougham carriage to collect an assistant from Lillertons and bring him round with a selection of diamond rings and ruby necklaces for her consideration. The assistant arrived at the address where a housemaid led him into the front room of a fully furnished house and told him, in her thick foreign accent, that Countess Velez was sick upstairs in bed. Would he mind handing over the rings and necklaces for her to take up for inspection? The assistant, like a fool, agreed and it was almost ten minutes before he tried the door and realised that he was locked in. The so-called maid had fled with the jewels and it wasn't until the real owners of the house returned home that it became apparent that there never was a Countess Velez and that somehow this woman had gained access to the place through craft and villainy.'

Everyone looked good and shocked at this and I also acted as if I could never believe such deviousness. But inside I was amused as it was an old ruse and I was pleased to hear it still worked.

'Upon arrival at the scene I interviewed the jeweller's assistant and he estimated that the housemaid had been around two-and-forty. Her accent was Spanish, he said, although when pressed he admitted that in hindsight there may have been traces of Italian in it. Despite this, he told me, he had simply not found anything suspicious about her, she had seemed so comfortable in the place. The only remarkable thing he remembered was her eyes. They were odd-coloured, one green, one blue.'

Inside me, as he said this, something went cold.

'Then I spoke to the lady of the house. She was in a state of some distress as it had now emerged that some priceless family heirlooms had also gone missing from her bedroom. I took an inventory of what was lost and asked her if she had noticed anything irregular in recent days. She told me that that two days prior to this she had been accosted, while travelling on an omnibus, by a strange woman who had tried to sell her soap. This woman, whose age she estimated at two-and-forty and whose accent was Irish with traces of Scottish, had travelled next to the lady for long enough to pick a key from her pocket and press it between two bars of soap thus giving her all she needed to make a perfect replica. When asked if she remembered anything about her appearance the lady mentioned her eyes. One green, one blue.'

'How extraordinary!' said Mrs Cherry. 'Odd-coloured eyes. I've never heard of such a thing. Have you, Mr Dawkins?' I shook my head and lied.

'Our next task was to locate the driver of the brougham carriage. This was made simple as the man himself had already complained to the police that he had received counterfeit notes for a job that involved collecting a jeweller from Hatton Gardens and taking him to an address in Pimlico. He told officers that he had been paid in advance and until now he had not closely inspected the money. The woman who paid him was . . .'

'About two-and-forty, with odd-coloured eyes and a dubious accent.' Faith laughed.

'Precisely, William. This time Welsh with traces of Indian.' His listeners was now good and hanging from his every word and he moved his gaze from face to face as he spoke. He never looked towards me though. Warrigal had got to his feet to fill up my wine glass but I put my hand over the top of it to stop him. 'I recognised the notes instantly,' continued Bracken as though he was giving evidence in court. 'They were the handiwork of a notorious forger named Inker Finch, whom I had arrested years earlier and who had been recently released from prison and was now residing with his wife in Camberwell. My constables and I sped round to his home directly and we interrogated him with some urgency.' I could tell by Bracken's big hands and heavy manner that his idea of an urgent interrogation was more about actions than words. I felt sorry for this Inker Finch. 'The interrogation was effective and we soon established the whole story. Finch claimed that he had not wanted to return to his criminal occupation but had been forced to by a woman whom he knew to be highly dangerous. She had visited him one night, armed with a knife, and told him that she felt he owed her a debt and that she would cut him from gut to gizzard if it wasn't repaid. Finch was frightened and felt that he had no alternative but to produce the money himself through his old art. He gave us her address in Seven Dials and we proceeded there directly. As we kicked down the door of her lodgings we discovered that she was in the process of packing her things to leave the city but had not counted upon us catching up with her so soon. Her bags were half full, a chambermaid's outfit was burning in the grate and, as we entered the room, she exited by the second-floor window. She jumped down on to some hay in the alley below whilst clutching a case that could only contain the stolen jewellery. My officers and I jumped out after her. We pursued her through a series of winding, twisting alleys and were closing in when she reached a courtyard filled with

vagrants and other undesirables. Here she opened the case and
tossed the contents into the air, her plan clearly being to create
such chaos and delay that she herself could escape. The jewels
were scattered around the courtyard and the denizens of the slum
reacted like ants around sugar. I ordered my officers to remain in
the courtyard and see that every last jewel was safely retrieved and
accounted for while I alone continued the chase. She had gained
some distance by now and had crossed over on to the other side
of Drury Lane but I was the quicker runner and I bounded over
the street, narrowly avoiding phaetons and cabriolets, and saw her
vanish down a side lane between two theatres. This was an error
on her part as the lane had been closed off, and I grabbed hold of
her leg as she attempted to climb the wooden fence at the end of
it. She kicked and swore at me and, as I forced her to face me so
I could see for myself those odd-coloured eyes, she scratched at
me like a cat. She was more animal than woman and I had never
come across her like before.'

'She sounds positively ghastly,' said William Faith as he motioned
to Warrigal to top up his glass. 'Foreigner, was she?'

'Not at all,' said Bracken, continuing to look at everyone except
me. 'She was the product of our own monster city. Her name . . .'
he paused, the bastard, and I remember thinking, *Don't drag it out*,
'. . . was Katherine Dawkins.'

There was three or four dead seconds before anyone said anything
when they all must have been trying to think as to where they
had all heard that name before. Then Mrs Cherry's witless laugh
broke the silence.

'My, Mr Dawkins, would you credit it?' she said. 'To think you
share a surname with such a curious person!'

'This Mrs Dawkins,' continued Bracken, as if he himself had
not yet noticed the coincidence, 'was a notorious figure in the

London underworld. She had been arrested for various offences over the years and was well known to the local authorities. Whether there ever was a Mr Dawkins is a matter of speculation, as it seemed this dissolute woman was forever attaching herself to various crooks and ruffians and often took their surnames regardless of whether or not she married them. She was the mother of two boys by different fathers. The first was a slow-witted simpleton who fell into bad company and was soon taken by the law, but the younger lad, well, he was an altogether different case.'

Our soup bowls was being removed and so he paused in his telling until all the servants, save Warrigal, had left the room. Then he went on. 'This child, when still a child, gained himself a reputation as being one of the most brazen thieves in the metropolis. Taught at his mother's knee to steal and cheat, he became a talented pickpocket and then fell under the control of two criminals, an elderly Jewish fence with an Irish name and a violent housebreaker with a terrible temper. A more villainous pair of mentors he could not have hoped to have found than these men, Fagin and Sikes, and they soon had him schooled and working the streets of London, where he became known by a well-earned nickname, the Artful Dodger.'

'The Artful Dodger!' laughed William Faith, shaking his head. 'What a colourful soubriquet!'

'Do you know,' piped up Junior Officer Martin, 'I seem to recall that name. I think I once read about his arrest in the *Newgate Calendar*.'

'You may well have done,' said Bracken, 'for arrested he was and made an example of. The magistrate, who recognised an unrepentant sinner when he saw one, sentenced him to transportation for life. He was sent to an Australian penal colony where he would be put to work for five years and then given the chance to become

a law-abiding Australian. But he was never, under any circumstances, allowed to return to our shores.' He looked around the
table from face to face but he still never looked to me. His listeners
was all staring straight back at him, not sure of what he was getting
at.

'Do you know what they get the prisoners doing during their
incarceration out in New South Wales, Mrs Cherry?' he asked.
Neither she nor any other Cherry answered. 'Sheep shearing,' he
told her, and took a swig from his glass, draining it dry. One by
one the other dinner guests was turning their heads towards me,
all save for Mrs Cherry, who was still confused by the question.
William Faith spoke next, his voice a lot less jovial than before.

'What was his Christian name, Wilfred? How old would he be
now?'

Bracken was looking into the bottom of his empty glass. 'He
was called Jack,' he said, and he lifted his big old pointing finger
and directed it right at me. 'And he would be exactly the same
age as our young friend over there.'

The room went quiet and Bracken turned his head to look at
me for the first time. 'The family resemblance is uncanny, Mr
Dawkins. Your green eyes match but, that apart, you are just like
her.'

William Faith was vexed. He threw down his napkin, pulled
back his chair and stood up. 'Is what Mr Bracken says true,
Dawkins?' he said, trying to look tough in front of his fiancé.
'Are you this Artful Dodger character he tells us of?' A gasp came
out of Mrs Cherry. She'd only just caught up, God love her.

I reviewed the situation and decided not to worry about it. I
just undid my collar button, leaned back in my chair and spoke
to the man sitting behind me. 'Peter Cole,' I said, 'why don't you
do us both a good turn and run upstairs to our chamber? Fetch

me that letter from the Governor that I keep in my trunk and bring it down here for Inspector Bracken's perusal. I think he may find it makes right interesting reading.' I couldn't hear any noise behind me so I turned to lock eyes with him. '*Warrigal!*' I said, as if to a disobedient dog. 'It'll take you less than one minute. And clearly' – I nodded towards Faith and Martin, who looked like they was fixing themselves for a fight – 'I ain't going nowhere.' He rolled his eyes to show how bored he was and slowly got to his feet, but his path to the door was blocked. I had not seen Bracken move from his seat but move he had and now he was stood in the doorway, a meaty hand stuck out at Warrigal making the sign for stop.

'If you think this fellow is to make his escape, Dawkins, you are mistaken. I am just as curious about what he is doing in our country as I am about you.'

'Inspector Bracken,' I said, 'everything you have said tonight is true, or at least most of it is. I am that same Jack Dawkins what once was known as the Artful Dodger and that crooked woman you arrested is my mother. I do not deny it.' I turned to Reverend Cherry, who had a look of horror on his face that was quite a picture. 'But I am also Jack Dawkins of Dawkins Wool, Reverend. I've earned my money the honest way and have made a success of myself. Everything I said to you and your family was pure and honest and if you will let me I shall prove it to you. I was sent to Australia for pickpocketing, this is a shameful truth. I was told never to return, this is also true enough. What you have said that is not true' – I turned back to Bracken – 'is that I am an unrepentant sinner, and that the letter will show. Among my papers upstairs is a document written by the Governor of New South Wales what pardons me of all previous wrongdoing and will attest to the goodness of my newly reformed character.' Bracken narrowed his eyes. 'Send someone with Peter Cole if you're worried he'll bolt. And while we're waiting for him to get back' – I reached for the wine and started giving my glass a refill – 'you won't mind if I finish off this bottle.'

It was decided that Junior Officer Martin should go with Warrigal to fetch the letter, which was funny to me as, if Warrigal should have wanted to run for it, I couldn't see how that useless drip was going to stop him. The rest of the party stayed in the dining room and watched me drink. Lucy Cherry seemed to be most upset with me now and it was a fair chance that she had gone off the idea of being Mrs Dawkins. Constance Cherry was also looking at me with disgust, covering her ring hand as if she now realised what peril it was in.

'Perhaps,' said Faith to Bracken, 'the ladies should be excused from witnessing this ugly scene. You and I can accompany Mr Dawkins to another room, and if this letter acquits him, as he assures us it will, then we shall all be back before the main course.'

'No!' This was from Amelia Cherry. 'I want to see what happens!' She looked at her parents with a fierce eye that said that they had better not dare to take me away. Then she got control of herself and spoke more genteel. 'Mr Dawkins has had his character publicly denounced. It is only fair that he should be given the chance to defend himself just as openly.'

I smiled at her. 'That's very kind of you, Amy, I do say. I look forward to winning back your good opinion and we will all put this messy business behind us.' She smiled back, her cheeks flushed and her eyes shining at me like two well-cut stones from a new South African diamond mine. I could tell what she was about.

Warrigal returned carrying the letter and Junior Officer Martin reported that he had not let him out of his sight and that their trip upstairs had passed without incident. I expect he thought he should be given a medal for his trouble. I told Bracken to open the letter and to feast his eyes. 'If this letter is a forgery,' he said, snatching it from Warrigal, 'then I shall recognise it as surely as I would an Inker Finch pound note.' He opened the envelope and read.

> *28th June 1844*
> *Government House*
> *New South Wales*

To Whomsoever it may concern,

Let it be hereby shown that the convicted felon Jack Dawkins, having satisfactorily served his five-year sentence, has been granted a full release and pardon by the British Crown under my authority as the Governor of New South Wales.

His liberty has been given under the advisement of Lord Evershed. It is the opinion of this inestimable man that Mr Dawkins has undergone a complete moral transformation and is now a fully reformed individual. He has worked hard to better himself during his incarceration and has had his soul renewed by the teachings of Christ. He was a model convict and stands as a testament to the success of the transportation and penal colony system.

Having established himself as a prosperous farmer and exporter of wool, he has expressed a wish to return to the country of his birth in order to attend to his business affairs there.

There can be no better character witness than Lord Evershed, whose reputation ranks among the highest in the

*Empire. And so we have agreed to grant this wish and have
overturned the previous ruling.*
   Signed,
   Sir George Gipps,
   Governor of New South Wales

*Postscript. His manservant, the aborigine, is also free to tread
on British soil.*

'Well, Wilfred,' asked Faith, after Bracken had gone over the letter
a couple of times, sniffing at the broken wax seal of the Crown,
holding the paper up to the light and peering close at the signature at the bottom, 'what's the verdict?'

Bracken handed the letter to him. 'It seems that Mr Dawkins
here,' he said, all doom, 'has powerful friends. The letter is genuine.'
Faith read it aloud for all to hear and all five Cherrys applauded
with delight at the words.

'"A complete moral transformation",' said the reverend, shaking
his head in wonder. 'What a miracle.' Faith strode up to me with
his hand out and I stood to shake it. He said he was sorry for
doubting me and Martin said the same thing to Warrigal. Bracken
of the Yard, though, still stood there with a face like a dinnerless
dog.

'I think,' said Amy Cherry to Faith, with a wicked grin on her,
'that your policeman friend also owes our Mr Dawkins an apology,
William.' And then she looked to Bracken to see what he was
going to do about it. He made a grunting noise and returned to
his seat.

'I believe we have two more courses to be served.' He unfolded
his napkin and placed it on his lap. 'And it would be a pleasure

to listen to Mr Dawkins tell us more about his remarkable change of fortunes.' He had all the charm of a gravedigger, that one.

For the rest of the dinner I was an entertainment to everyone, save for Inspector Misery. The reverend and Mrs Cherry was most moved to be told of my terrible upbringing under the wicked influences of the city and of the cruel and villainous characters there encountered. William Faith and his friend Martin enjoyed hearing of my Australian adventures; of how, when still a godless criminal, I had tried to escape from the settlement and got myself so lost in the outback I had very near died of thirst, only to be tracked down by Warrigal and returned to the camp where forgiving doctors nursed me back to health. I told them about how brave, noble Warrigal had saved my life on two other occasions and how, now that I was reformed, I was in turn saving him by turning him from Warrigal the savage into Peter Cole, a Christian valet. This was greatly approved of and their heads turned to smile on him but he just stared into nothing and ignored them. I told them that it wasn't the way of the abo to get emotional in public.

How I went from bad apple to good egg was a story I told with much carefulness. I knew it was important to show how, on one hot night in the colony, Jesus had appeared in a dream and finally talked some sense into me. But I also wanted to hint to the middle daughter that I wasn't changed all that much. It is a truth universally acknowledged that some girls love a rotter, and Amy Cherry seemed to be one of them. While she may not have cared a tuppence for wealthy Jack Dawkins of Dawkins Wool, the story of the Artful Dodger had been more successful in touching her girlish heart. She was sat opposite me at the crowded table and announced to everyone present that she felt most ardently that Mr Dawkins was not to blame for his bad behaviour. This was indeed the case as, under the table, she had removed her dainty shoe and we had been enjoying the occasional unseen leg stroke ever since the pudding was served and it was very much her that started it.

'This tart is divine,' said reverend Cherry, and I agreed with him. He was unaware of the goings-on down under and had been asking me many questions about my moral education in the colony. I told him that I had been taught to read and write by the teachers there who had used Matthew, Mark, Luke and John. But in truth I had been taught to read much earlier than that in the London rookeries by Mr Fagin, who had used the *Newgate Calendar* and *Dick Turpin*.

Chapter 4

The Strike of the Midnight Hour

Showing how the Devil makes mischief for restless sleepers

'It is simply wonderful to me,' said the reverend as dinner came to its end and our plates was cleared, 'that a fine young man such as Mr Dawkins here, whose crimes could only be the fault of our modern society, should be cast away so casually, only to return home again a Whittingtonian success. I find his story to be quite . . . oh, what is the word?'

'Unbelievable,' said Bracken, his voice cold.

'Yes, unbelievable,' agreed the reverend. 'And inspirational,' he added, and everyone, except Bracken, agreed that it was. Bracken's hard face suggested he still considered our modern society to be an innocent bystander in the story of my life.

We all stood up to bid each other goodnight and Junior Officer Martin said that my story was of such a heart-warming kind that I should consider telling it to some novelist cove to put down in a book. I told him that I might do better than that and write the thing myself. He laughed, as if the notion of me writing my own book was very droll, and told me that he looked forward to reading such a curious work of literature one day. I wished him good luck with the naval career and said that I hoped he wouldn't drown.

Mrs Cherry, who had developed a taste for elderflower wine as the evening had gone on, was unsteady on her feet as she passed me out of the dining room and, holding on to her husband for balance, said that it was a pleasure to meet me, and insisted that I call her Annabel from now on. Amy Cherry was next. We locked eyes and I kissed her hand in a slow, saucy way to let her know that what had passed between us that night was special and full of meaning for me and that we was two hearts that was beating as one.

Then I did exactly the same thing to Lucy, just to make Amy jealous.

But the hardest goodnight I had to make was the one to Constance as she and her fiancé passed by. She held out her hand with the diamond ring on it and, as I took it in mine and pressed my lips close to the precious jewel, I felt as though my heart was breaking. That I would have to abandon any attempt that I may have made to take it for my own, just because of the watchful, distrusting nature of Inspector Bracken, was a source of great sadness and vexation. But the hateful man seemed to know every-thing about me, from my family history to my every secret thought, and so I would have to kiss this treasure goodbye and not risk its liberation.

Bracken himself had slipped off without saying goodnight to me. On top of everything else, he was an ill-mannered sod.

By half past eleven we was back in our bedchamber and Warrigal was being just as bloody-minded as before. He had put on his white nightshirt and matching cap and had climbed in under the great covers of the big bed without saying a word to me. But I was not sleepy and had lit a large candle so we could sit up and talk about the day's events as I had done with the other convicts on Abel's Farm.

'Well done on fetching Evershed's letter, Warrigal. That got us out of a tight squeeze, eh, my old covey?' He was busy plumping the feather pillows as I spoke. 'What a thing to have had the very policeman who arrested my mother there at the table readying himself to do the same for me, eh? What a thing!' I shook my head and chuckled as he placed pillows behind his head. 'And do you know what that Amy girl was doing underneath the table as we ate our pudding? She had taken off her dainty shoe and was . . .' I stopped talking as the room had suddenly turned black. Warrigal had leaned over and blown out the candle.

I did not care to sleep on the rug by the grate just yet so I went over to the window to see what was outside. Our room overlooked the inn-yard where the stables was and, though dark, there was just enough moonlight to see what was where. The cobbles was clean from dirt, washed by the day's rain, and the yard was so peaceful you could hear the horses snore. As I looked on it I found myself thinking about that beautiful diamond that was in the room three doors down. I wondered whether it was still on Connie's finger or whether she had given it to Faith or to her father for safekeeping. I imagined not. A girl like her, what had just been given a ring like that, would not part with it so soon. She would not be sleeping with it still on though, that was certain. She would have taken it off and placed it in that little jewellery case and hidden it somewhere in the bedchamber, the same one she was sharing with her sisters. The sisters would know where it was, though. One of them might even creep over in the night and open the case themselves perhaps, once they was sure that Connie was asleep, just to take a quick peek, a piece of harmless fun.

Somewhere my in head, a plan was forming.

But what use was there in forming plans of any sort with this man Bracken ever alert to my thieving ways? If he wasn't here, I thought, sleeping in a chamber between mine and theirs, if he didn't know my name and that of my closest criminal connections, then perhaps I would be bolder. I would somehow, perhaps through Warrigal or by some cleverer means, get a secret message to Lucy Cherry, the youngest daughter and the biggest pigeon, who, if not for Bracken, would still think me just a rough yet respectable businessman. The message would tell her that I was much taken with her beauty, her grace and her many accomplishments and that I was requesting to see her alone in the stables at the strike of the midnight hour, so I could unburden my heart to her. She would come scurrying, as would be natural (perhaps wearing a thin silk nightdress or whatever these girls wear in bed) and I would drop to one knee before her and tell her of my love. I would ask her where was the use in my being a wealthy capitalist if I was alone with no one to share my fortune and would she please be my wife. She would accept my proposal – this was also natural – and I would reach into my pocket and get out a ring. This ring would be one from my own collection, a cheap one from among the many treasures that I carried in my trunk. It could be the stoneless one that I had stolen from the market in Rio, where the *Son and Heir* had docked for a day, and for which the street trader had not even bothered to chase me. Or, better still, the one with the roughly cut stone that I had taken from the cabin of the ship's prostitute, Elena, the one that Captain McGowan had never in public accused me of taking for fear that I would tell Mrs McGowan who it was what had given it to Elena in the first place. And, once this ring was produced, I knew that there was one thing I could count upon for certain and that was the look of deep disappointment upon the face of sweet Lucy when faced with it.

She would try to hide her feelings, a well-mannered young girl like her, she would tell me that she thought the ring lovely. But

I would tell her that I could see how shabby an offering it was to give her after Constance had been presented with so superior a jewel earlier that night. She must think me an unworthy vagabond, I would say, to expect her to wear such an ugly trinket. After listening to her protest I would then promise to make amends as soon as I got to London next day, where I would march straight into the grandest jewellers and buy her a diamond ring bigger and brighter than her sister's. She would squeal with joy and we would embrace and I would kiss her with some force. Then I would confess to her that I was ignorant about diamonds and jewellery and that I had no clue about what sort to get her. If only, I would say, I could get another look at her sister's ring, then I would know what qualities was desirable in such a diamond. She would then scurry back upstairs and then scurry straight back down with the ring in its case and we would gaze at it together, and she would educate me in the difference between it and the one that I had presented her with, telling me exactly what she would like to wear on her own hand. Then I would take her in my arms, rendering her insensible with my kisses, and I would make the unseen switch. Once both deeds was done I would prop her back up and, after helping her to pick hay out of her hair and back into her night-dress, I would say that it was wrong of us to take her sister's ring, even if it was just for innocent, romantic reasons, and that she must return the ring case to where she found it and not even open it again for a peek. She would agree – by now guilt would be gnawing at her from all sides – and when the lovely Constance opened it on the following morning she would shriek in horror to see Elena's ring winking back at her. By which time myself, Warrigal and her real engagement ring would be hidden deep within the crooked streets of London.

It was a fine scheme but even I, a boy of optimism, could see it would have been full of danger and possible mishap even without this obstacle of Bracken. But there was no harm in going over such imaginings on a sleepless night; this was something Fagin had taught me during the days that I had spent living above his kitchen in Saffron Hill. He had said that a buzzing mind is a brilliant mind and that it was only natural that I was kept awake at night by devious thoughts and hatching plots as so was he and we was two articles what was cut from the same fine cloth. From my first days under his care he had let me sit up with him through the night and had kept me entertained with his tales of swindles, dodges and other trickeries. He let me watch as he counted out his stolen trinkets, something he would never let the others do. He would tell me that I was the best of them, his top-sawyer he would say, and that he could see in me a younger version of himself what would grow to be just as dazzling a thief, something I took to be a very great compliment. The day he coined my nickname, which he did with typical generosity in front of all the other boys, was the proudest day of my young life. He was a jewel of a man.

And what was troubling my young mind on that lonely winter's night, was that tomorrow I would return to him, after six cruel years of separation, with nothing to show for it. Him, what had welcomed me into his warm home after I had run away from my lunatic mother and given me, and countless other children like me, kindnesses, shelter, friendship and encouragements, and had only ever asked that in return we should prove ourselves industrious for him. This man was like a father to me, and all I had to present him with was two worthless rings that I could have found lying in a Chelsea gutter. What would he make of me then?

If only, I found myself wishing again, I could somehow take that diamond ring that lay so close by and offer it as a gift to my Fagin. I would surprise him in his kitchen, having got past the watch-boys and the locks that I was so familiar with, and he would be startled to see a well-attired young gentleman standing before him in his sacred den, smiling. Then he would blink and recognise me and ask if this was young Jack Dawkins he saw before him what was snatched away at such a young age. I would answer by coolly slipping my hand into my coat pocket and pulling out the ring.

'Maybe you can find a home for this, you dirty old fence,' I'd say, and then toss it to him across the room. Upon catching it his eyes would light up as he saw the quality he held in his fist. Then he'd dance his merry jig and tell me that he always knew I would come back to him.

I was interrupted in this pleasant dreaming by the sound of hurried footsteps coming up the hall, like those of little mice. They reached up to my room and ran straight off again. It was a second before I saw that something had been slipped underneath the door. I tiptoed over, careful not wake the bad-tempered abo, and I picked up a little card that smelled of ladies' perfume. On it something was written in ink, and in a feminine hand, but I could not read what, as the room was too dark. I crept over to the candle and took it to the table at the far end of the room. I lit it, with one hand covering it from disturbing Warrigal, and read.

'My Darling Jack,' it began, 'I cannot sleep for thinking of you. If you should leave tomorrow and never see me again I think I should die.' I smiled in the dark as I realised that the fish was on the hook, and kept reading. 'Meet me in the stables at the strike of the midnight hour if you feel as hotly for me as I am sure that you must. There we can plan our escape as I cannot spend another hour living with my stultifyingly stupid family. We can live off the money we will get from pawning Constance's engagement ring, which I have already taken for mine. Make haste, my rough diamond.' The note was signed with the initials *A.C.*

It was five minutes to twelve. I went over to the window to look at the stables and saw a shadow dart across the inn-yard. Someone wearing a black cloak had entered through a side door and had left it ajar. What a puzzlement, I thought, that Amy Cherry, who had been so cold at first, was now so very warm that she was willing to ruin herself for me and give me her sister's ring without me having to do a thing for it. I put on my greatcoat and thought about how this would work. At the very least I should get the pleasure of deflowering a young virgin and that alone should be worth the trip outside. I opened the door, slow and silent, and took one last look at the sleeping Warrigal before entering the corridor. As I tiptoed my way down the passage I passed the room where Inspector Bracken slept and thought about what he would do if I was to run off with Amy. He would know to track me down to Fagin's, that was certain, but if I got there in time, and the Jew could move the jewel quick enough, it would be impossible to trace. I could tell the law that Amy and I was planning to wed and that we had run off to get a marriage licence and neither of us knew anything about no missing diamond. If pressed, I could say that Warrigal could have took it. I trod on. As I passed the room where the Reverend Cherry and his wife slept, a thought struck. *Call me Annabel*, she had said. I stopped, looked at the card and the initials and I sniffed it to see on who could I place the perfume. It was hard to tell. Could it be that the feet I was feeling under the table did not belong to Amy but those of an older, plumper Cherry? She had drunk too much wine and had a playful look about her all evening. I considered this and decided that, in either case, it would turn out to be an adventure. I trod on.

Downstairs in the inn I saw that the door leading out to the yard had been left ajar by this A.C. and I stepped through. I crossed the courtyard, reached the door of the stables and went through.

It was dark in there, and stunk of horses and leather. The door swung shut and someone stepped out from behind it. The tread was heavy, a pair of man's hands was around me and I was pushed against the saddle bench. I thought I would be sick as a horrible fear took grip of me. *My name is Reverend Albert Cherry*, he had said.

I cried out in terror and the horses was startled and woke. I could feel him pressing his weight down into the back of me and he reached for both my hands and forced them behind my back. Then he pulled me, with surprising strength, and threw me against the wooden wall where I was at his mercy.

'No girl. No diamond. Sorry to disappoint.' He forced me to face him. It was Bracken. I was right relieved.

'"A fully reformed individual", eh?' he said, banging my body against the wall with every question mark. '"A complete moral transformation"?' *Bang*. 'To me, sir, that letter was as transparent as glass.' His big fists was grabbing my collar and I was sure of only one thing. Amy Cherry was not coming.

'Would a man truly changed by the teachings of Christ fall for such easy bait?' *Bang*. 'I think not. You're a thief, sir, even worse than your rotten mother.' I kicked him then but he just laughed. 'Gnat bites. That's all your kicks are to me, sir. Less than gnat bites.' He picked me up and walked me past the watching horses to the other end of the stable. There he banged me against the far wall. He must have done this just to show me and the nags that he could.

'I'm a respectable businessman!' I told him. 'You can't treat me in this here disgraceful fashion! Get your hands off!' I struggled some more but he seemed to enjoy brutalising me and so I tried to reason with him. 'I come down here for the sole purpose of telling the author of that card that they should behave themselves. And now I know the author to be you I still say it. Behave yourself!' Bracken released me from his clutches and I dropped to the ground. My back hurt terrible. 'My letter is real.' I drew the perfumed card and flicked it at his shoes. 'Yours ain't. Tell that to the magistrate.'

'You are not under arrest, Dawkins,' he said. 'At least not yet. I just wanted to see if I was right about you. And I was.' He picked up his card. 'I know some things about this Lord Evershed whom the Governor mentions in his letter. Your character witness. The Bow Street Runners used to speak of him. Many years ago, when they still policed the capital, his wife turned up dead. The Runners didn't like the stink of it but, being only Runners, they did little to investigate.' He knelt down and looked me in the eye. 'Your letter may be real, but it stinks even so. It stinks because he does and so do you. I am the new police and I will make it my business to find out what it stinks of.' He prodded me in the chest with his big finger of justice. 'And I shall solve the mystery of you.'

He got to his feet and walked to the stable door. Just as he opened it he turned to me, still on the ground. 'A warning: stay out of my city. When we catch you again, as I am sure that we shall, it won't be transportation like it was before. This time we shall hang the very breath out of you.' He paused and looked into the night, speaking slow and cold. 'Just as we hanged your rotten mother. Goodnight.'

I was in that stable for another hour after he had gone, alone with my thoughts. Just as I was readying myself to leave I realised that someone was standing in the darkest corner watching me.

'Warrigal!' I said with a start as he made himself known. He was still wearing his white nightshirt and cap and looked like a ghost. 'You frightened the eyelids off me. How long was you there?'

'Long time,' he said. There was a silence and I thought that he must have followed me out of the room and been shadowing me all along. It was the sort of thing he would do.

'Crying,' he said.

'No, I'm not.'

'For mother. Sorry business.' So he had been there, the crafty spy, and heard all.

'Yeah,' I said. 'Sorry business.'

We walked back across the yard and found the door to the inn still open. Then we crept up the stairs and through the creaky passages towards our chamber. As we passed Bracken's room I imagined him to be still awake, listening out for us and writing the time of our return down in a little notebook. When we was inside our room I whispered to Warrigal that we would hire a carriage before breakfast and leave for London before anyone else woke up. We was drawing too much attention to ourselves, I told him. He nodded.

'Take the good bed,' he said, and went over to the grate to settle himself on the floor, 'for the bad back.' I thanked him and he said nothing. I blew out the candle.

Chapter 5

Monster City

In which I return to the haunts of my youth.
A painful chapter in this here history

All of my boyhood Christmases, if my recollections serve, was happy and white. It was as if a giant chambermaid had stood above old London Town and spread a great silken sheet of white across the city, beautifying all parts, even the rookeries. The snow fell just as heavy on the broken old slums as it did upon the Queen's new palace and it did a perfect job of hiding the muddy filth of Jacob's Island so you would never guess at the squalor beneath if you did not know the place. At Christmas, what was dirty and derelict was made pure and new and this was true not just of the outsides of buildings but also of the insides of the souls living in them. Mean men, men what would step on the likes of me at any other time, would turn soft in the head on Christmas morning and start giving away their money as if it was their last day on earth. They would recover their wits by Boxing Day of course, and return with force to their spiteful and miserly ways, but by then the damage would be done and they was ruined.

In Fagin's den spirits was as high and as festive as in any great home and the merry old gentleman, Jew though he was, knew how to celebrate. Every year, at the crack of dawn, he would dress up in the same green gown with white cotton lining, hide his features under a fluffy false beard and climb up into the attic room where the smallest infants slept to wake them all as old St Nick. He'd have a bag flung over his shoulder full of toys and they would squeal their heads off as he'd open it and hold them out as prizes to whichever small hand could snatch them away fastest. These toys was the newest made, painted wooden soldiers, toy trumpets, small bears, all of them found the night before under pine trees what stood inside the richest homes in London, where they had been waiting for Bill Sikes to break in and grab them. The snatcher with the most amount of toys would be declared the winner and also be given a special paper crown to wear in victory, while the boy what failed to snatch any toy at all would be told by Mr Fagin that there was a lesson for him and that he would not be given any pudding in punishment for his slowness.

During my early years there, as was natural, I was always top snatcher, but soon I grew too old to play for toys and Fagin gave me and the other older lads cigars and whisky for gifts instead. He would ask us to be good and responsible though and not to blow smoke in the faces of the below-tens as we all sat at the table eating our steaming goose. The place would be decorated with holly stolen from off the back of a country cart and after dinner, while the Jew played blind man's buff and Snap-dragon with the children, Bill would kiss Nancy under the mistletoe, his dog Bull's Eye would lick away the last of the plum pudding and we'd all sing carols until dawn.

These memories was flooding upon me as we entered London on the first morning of my return. It was four weeks until next Christmas, and we had much to do in that time, but the dark early morning reminded me of its approach. Christmas day, what I had always very much looked forward to, was now a coming terror to me, thanks to Lord Evershed. If I did not complete the task that the red-coated devil had set for me by then, I would be the steaming goose and Warrigal would be the one to do the carving.

As decided, we had left the Booted Cat before the cock crowed and found an apple-man in the neighbouring village what had agreed to let us ride in the back of his cart to the winter-fruits market in Covent Garden. We was grateful for we had not wanted to book a carriage from the inn as Bracken would be sure to discover where we went. The day had advanced and the sky had turned the colour of tombstones by the time we crawled over Waterloo Bridge. We jumped off at the Strand without the driver seeing, leaving no gratuity save for two dozen apple cores. Then we footed it to Golden Cross to book a carriage to Saffron Hill.

I had woken in a black mood due to the words of Bracken the night before and my already sore back was still stinging from his manhandling. But now I was moving again through the rush of the city and, although much encumbered with our luggage, I could feel myself getting lighter. It seemed that in the six years that I had been away London had grown rich. I could see it in the people who brushed past us moving in the other direction; they was finer, handsomer, even more bejewelled than I remembered them. The carriages what raced past us was sleeker and more beautiful, the streets was cleaner and even the pigeons was looking plumper. By the time we had loaded our bags into a shiny two-wheeled cabriolet I was feeling that London buzz again.

'To Saffron Hill!' I told the cabman once Warrigal and myself was seated 'the Field Lane end'. The cabman stopped readying the horses and turned his pockmarked head to me.

'A cab like this, to a place like that?' he said as though I was mad. 'It'll be another shilling.'

'What for?'

'Well, I'll never get a fare back for one thing,' he replied, 'and for another, robbers.'

'You're the robber,' I said, but agreed to the shilling. Then he drove the horses out into the fast stream of carriages and I was on my way home.

'This here is Fleet Street,' I said to Warrigal as we sped along, 'where our many great writers live and work. And that great building up there –' I pointed proudly towards the blackened dome ahead – 'is St Paul's. A man named Wren built it. And up that alley there is where a prostitute named Cracked Alice almost bit the pipe off some magistrate.' I thought it was important to give Warrigal as much information about the city as I could, if he was going to find his way around. Whether he was taking any of it in was hard to tell. 'We'll be nearing Newgate soon,' I added darkly, 'where they hang people.'

The closer we got to Saffron Hill the narrower and dirtier the lanes became and we saw fewer horse-drawn carriages and more donkeys and dog carts. There was many street urchins darting about, in gangs of three or four, and they was all dressed in clothing two sizes too big for them. Halfway up Shoe Lane I saw a boy leaning against a wall eating an apple and wearing a hat that he had twitch back into place more than once. He was a dirty, snub-nosed boy and he was eyeing our cab, eyeing me, with a smirk like he knew something I didn't. We locked eyes as the carriage passed and then I turned my gaze to the other side of the road. And there I saw someone that I knew, someone I recognised, walking ahead of us in the same direction. A woman, red-haired and full-figured, wearing that green cotton dress that she always wore and moving with that same pleasing wiggle. I leaned out of the cab and whistled to her.

'Nancy!' I called out. 'Nance! It's me, girl. The Artful. I'm back at long last!' I told the driver to pull alongside her as she hadn't heard me and I adjusted my clothing to its full advantage. I was excited for Nancy to see me returned and looking prosperous as I was always her favourite. The cab drew close enough for me to tap her shoulder with my cane. She turned and looked at me unsmiling. She had a harelip.

'Sorry,' I said. 'I thought you was someone else.' She stared at me with stony eyes that was nothing like Nancy's and I wondered how I ever mistook her. I got back in the cab and the driver pulled away. Behind us, down the street, I heard the snub-nosed boy laughing about something.

The old vicinity seemed smaller than I recalled. The driver, white-livered beggar that he was, refused to take us further than Holborn now that it was growing dark and so Warrigal and I walked our heavy luggage down the stone steps into Saffron Hill. The crooked lane ran ahead of us like a rabbit warren and out of the many dirt-smeared windows I could see faces peering from the darkness. They may have been looking at me, they may have been looking at Warrigal. Most likely they was looking at our luggage and guessing at its value.

'This is Fagin's,' I told Warrigal as we came to a numberless, knockerless door. 'It don't look like much, true, because he likes to keep things low. But inside it's full of treasures.' I held my cane against the grey-painted door and knocked the secret knock. No one answered. 'They must have changed the secret knock,' I said to Warrigal. 'I'll try another.' I tapped out another secret knock, which was meant to signify that the knocker had urgent news, but was surprised when nobody answered this one either. 'Plummy and slam!' I then shouted. This was one of the watchwords we had back in the old days and I hoped it would alert him to who was calling. Still no answer. 'I know a way in through the upstairs back window,' I said to Warrigal. 'But it involves climbing up the guttering and I don't want to get my new clothes all slimy. Maybe you could have a go.' Warrigal said nothing but pointed up to the top windows. One of them was boarded up with wood, as was many of the windows along the lane, but through the other a light could be seen burning. 'So they are in,' I said, most aggrieved. 'They deaf or something?' I stepped back, put my fingers to my lips and whistled loud enough to set dogs barking.

The light in the top window began to glow all the brighter as someone came towards it with a candle. Then a face appeared, just as it got close, but the light was snuffed out as though the person was on purpose trying to hide their features. It was too dark to tell who was looking down on us.

'I'm looking for Fagin,' I shouted up. 'Mr Fagin, the old Jew. He used to live here, about six year ago. Him and a gang of kinchins. Open the door so I can talk.' The face drew away from the window and the glass went black.

As I waited in hope that this person would answer the door I looked at the old house more close. The door was a different door, heavier than the one I remembered. Someone had been drawing pictures low down on the walls in black chalk. 'See, Warrigal,' I said, pointing at them, 'children will have done that. I used to draw etchings on the walls too when I first came to live here. Birds and snakes and the like. Fagin used to blow up something terrible when he saw them.' I looked again at the chalkings. 'Never drew teardrops though.'

Then came a woman's voice from behind the door, high and strangulated, like that of a parrot. 'Who is it?' she shrieked. 'What d'ye want?'

'A gentleman by name of Jack Dawkins,' I replied. 'And I want to talk about Mr Fagin.' At the very mention of his name the woman groaned aloud.

'Leave us be, why don't you? We're Christians in this house. Honest Christians. Leave us be.' She began this hysterical sobbing and I looked to Warrigal in wonder at it. He was now sat on the trunk, his coat buttoned all the way up to his chin on account of the wind, and his hands was rubbing together. I had forgotten how this lane channelled wicked gales on these dark winter days.

'Look here, my lovely,' I said with firmness. 'If you was a houseful of prizewinning nuns it wouldn't impress me. Just open the door so we can converse like respectable types. We're at the mercy of the elements out here.'

'Can I help you fellas?'

I turned to see a large, burly man walking towards us down the steps from where we had just come. He was carrying a tin tray with other metal items in it, knives, forks, tools and such. He had a serious head on him and his expression was that of a man who had no clue who we was but was going to do something about us anyway. He marched up to Fagin's door and demanded to know what was our business.

'I'm glad you've asked,' I said. 'I am here making enquiries about a man named Fagin what once lived at this here address. He's an elderly gent of the Hebrew persuasion. You'd know him if you'd met him – he's a merry old boy.'

'I never met him,' said the man, his voice a solid boom, 'and nor did Mother. If you've come here to cause trouble I won't stand for it. It's honest Christians who live here now. You go away and tell the others that. You go and tell how John Froggat said *no more*.'

I was taken aback by this outburst. 'No more what?'

'No more bricks,' he said, pointing to the wooden window. 'No more taunts. No more persecution. No more of this!' He pointed to the chalk tears. 'Your man Fagin has been gone nigh on six years. Leave us be, why can't you!'

'Six years?' I said. I was feeling sick again. The wind was blowing through my open collar and felt sharp against my neck. 'But . . .' I was stumbling my words, thinking of Bracken, 'where did he go?'

'You mean you don't know? You haven't heard?' I had not, I told him. But I was starting to get an awful feeling inside of me. 'To Newgate he went. To the gallows. They hung the man in punishment for his evil. Hordes of people came by here soon after the murder of the woman Nancy. A great mob they were, and they smashed in the door and dragged the devil out by his beard. They pulled him into this here street and crowded round him, men and women, spitting and tearing at him and throwing stones at his head. He begged like an animal, so they tell me, and when the police arrived he was so bleeding and desperate that – in the name of Almighty, son, steady yourself!'

John Froggat was interrupted in his narration by the sight of me staggering over and collapsing against the wall of the house with my hands over my face. I seem to remember Warrigal jumping up from the trunk and stopping me from falling further. There was a terrible wailing noise that shot through the lane which may have been the wind or may have been made by me, and a clatter of metal as John Froggat dropped his tray in order to help revive me. I sank down the wall to the level of the black chalkings, which I now saw was not meant to be of tears at all. They was of nooses.

We was all silent for a bit and then the timid voice spoke from behind the door. 'They cleared off yet, John?' it asked.

'No, Mother,' replied Froggat. 'Perhaps you should open the door now. This young feller could use the warmth of a fire.'

'I thought you said you was a Jew?'
'I did, my dear.'

'Then how come you're allowed to eat pork?'

'How come you're allowed to pick pockets?' He winked and turned the sausages over with his toasting fork. We both laughed and I took a swig from my coffee pot while waiting for my breakfast. I liked these mornings when the other boys was out and it was just us.

'I'm very glad we've got this chance to have a little talk, Dodger,' he said, placing a sizzling plate of bacon, eggs and sausages on the table in front of me. 'Very. We seldom get the chance these days, what with all the comings and goings. How many Christmases have you spent under my roof now?'

'Dunno.' It was four.

'Do you, by any chance, remember that present I gave you two Christmases ago? Not the snatching presents, my dear – ha ha, you took plenty of them for yourself. No, I mean the special present that I told you to keep safe.'

'The prince,' I said.

'That's him. The prince. Tell me you've still got him, Dodger. Tell me you ain't given him away to one of the younger boys.'

'I've still got him somewhere. Why? He ain't valuable, is he?'

'Dear me, no. There's nothing valuable about a rattly old wooden doll, no matter how handsomely it's painted. No, its only value is of the sentimental kind. But I would hate to think you'd lost him, Dodger. I told you to keep him safe now. He had a spell put on him that wards off evil spirits.' I scoffed to show him that I was too old for that sort of talk. Fagin chuckled. 'You think me a silly old fool, don't you, my dear, with my old superstitions? Well, maybe you're right. But you just keep him handy, Dodger. He'll bring you good luck if you do, and bad if you don't.' I'd finished my plate and he took it away to be washed while I drained my cup. 'You're a good lad, Dodge, the sharpest there is. Why, if all my students were as sharp as you we could all retire young and do the genteel.' He put the plate in a bucket of soapy water and went over to the clothes horse to count the handkerchiefs. 'Talking of which, we could always use more pupils around here. There are plenty of poor unfortunates lying in the streets just starving to death. It breaks my heart, really it does. If you see any hungry lads out and about who you feel might benefit from the education that we provide, don't hesitate to make an introduction.' I told him I'd keep an eye out. 'Good boy, Dodger. After all, what harm can it do?'

That was the last time we ever spoke, myself and Fagin, just the two of us.

'I thought he said he was a gentleman?' Mother Froggat said to her son.

'He did.'

'Then how come he grew up in this crap-house?'

Mother Froggat was boiling cabbage and a pig's head in pots over her fireplace, the same fireplace Fagin was forever cooking his sausages over. She said she didn't like the look of either Warrigal or myself but had agreed to let us into her home after John Froggat had said something to her about Christian duty. She was now doing us our supper as we warmed ourselves near her fire but still could not bring herself to speak straight to us. She was a short teapot of a woman in cheap cotton and was snappish and unfriendly in the way that frightened people often are.

'I would guess that he was one of this Fagin character's boy thieves, Mother,' said her son, who sat at the wooden table watching us close. 'Is that right, Mr Dawkins?' I nodded and just looked into the flames. I had not said much for most of the hour that I had been back in that house, just answered some of their questions and asked some of my own. We was all drinking this tasteless tea out of pewter pots and I was feeling ashiver. John Froggat had told me I looked unwell and I could feel the sweats coming on. Once he had learnt that we had travelled all the way from Australia and had no other lodgings he had said that we could stay the night if we promised to behave ourselves.

'I knew he was a thief,' said Mother Froggat. 'I could tell it in his eyes as soon as I saw him out of the window. He has the look.'

'Then it's just as well we've nothing worth stealing, isn't it, Mother?' the son said. 'And that I'm here to put a stop to it if we did.' He had a young face, this John Froggat, but his hair was as grey as iron filings. His eyes was watery, as if from lack of blinking, and his arms looked like they was made of oak. He had been telling me about what had become of my old criminal associates and said that he was sorry that it was causing me such distress. I told him not to worry and asked him to carry on.

According to what he told me, Bill Sikes had killed Nancy. It was a famous murder about which all of London had heard tell. He had heard from someone that she was planning on peaching upon him so he smashed her skull open with a pistol in the bedroom they shared together and then finished the job off with a club. Housebreaker Bill, who had been a hero of mine for his daring at burglaries, someone that I had often wished I should grow up to be, had worked upon the face of pretty Miss Nancy until it was unrecognisable as a human head. So mutilated was she that the girl who found her, a girl who I took to be her friend Bet, was sent mad by the sight and was removed to an asylum where, as far as John Froggat knew, she was still. When word got out about the murder the city was sent into a frenzy and the killer was hunted down to Jacob's Island, where he hanged himself from a roof in full view of a vengeful mob and from where his dog also fell to its death. Soon after that, in a show of force by the new Metropolitan Police, the old Jew was taken and hung and then all their known associates was rounded up. Crackit, Chitling, Kags, Pugg – men whose names was as familiar to me as those of uncles – was executed in what Froggat called 'a great culling of the criminal class'. All of this, I thought, must have happened within the weeks after I had got lagged. Perhaps within days.

'Well, this is pleasant talk for the table,' said Mother Froggat. 'Change the subject, John, it's putting me off my cabbage.'

'What was the charge?' I asked, ignoring her. 'Against the Jew?'

Froggat blinked at last. 'I'm not sure, son,' he said. 'I don't know if anyone ever said. I think,' he spoke as if unsure of what he meant, 'that the city had just had enough of him.'

I have always hated to be thought of as a poor guest but on hearing this I just couldn't help myself.

'He was a *fence*, was all!' I shouted, banging the table and unsettling the plates. 'You don't hang fences!'

'Steady, son. I know you're upset, but just steady now.' Outside the weather was all melodrama, wailing winds and sobbing rains and the windowpanes made to rattle. This did nothing to improve my mood.

'It wasn't just that he was a fence, son,' he said, after we had all lit from the candle. 'It's that he was a kidsman, a corrupter of children.' He said this in such a way that suggested that I, of all people, should know this. Mother Froggat had taken down the linen that was hanging from ropes and, at John's asking, had gone upstairs to find bedding for us. 'There was one boy here, an orphan so I was told –' John flicked his ash into an empty pot – 'who somehow or other got in with some rich folk who, by a rum coincidence, it turned out he was related to.' He leaned back on his chair and breathed out. 'And this boy peached upon the whole lot of them. When people – rich people, I mean – got wind of what your Fagin was running here, a school of thieves as it was, well, that was the end of it.'

'What was his name?' I asked. 'This orphan.'

'Couldn't tell you, son,' he said, putting out his half-finished cigar, 'and what does it matter anyhow? It's history now.' He yawned and rose from his seat. 'Well, it's late and we rise early tomorrow. You will leave with us. Mother will have readied some bedding for the two of you in the attic room.' He began snuffing out the candles and shooed the cat off the lap of a blind man what was asleep in a rocking chair before draping an old blanket over him. The cat dashed up the stairs to the dark rooms above. 'I told you, there's a room behind mine which was took by my brother before he grew consumptive and died. You should bed down there – it's more comfortable.' I thanked him but said that I very much wanted to sleep in the attic. 'For sentimental reasons,' I said by way of explanation. 'It's where the younger kinchins used to sleep when first I came here. I've happy memories of it.'

'As you like,' he said. 'But hark this: there is nothing worth stealing in the bedrooms of either me or my mother. They will be locked throughout the night anyhow. This kitchen, where Uncle Huffam sleeps, is unlocked yet also has nothing of value in it. In spite of that, should I catch either you or your friend creeping about in the night, or if Uncle Huffam is disturbed, then there will be a reckoning.'

'Mr Froggat, you and your family have nothing to fret about,' I told him. 'I never steals from people who are poorer than myself.' These words was true although I did not know this until after I had said them. Warrigal and myself then lugged our bags over our shoulders. 'Don't bother to show me the way up,' I said. 'I remember it well.' Froggat handed us two cleft sticks with lit candles in them and then, leaving the trunk in the kitchen with Uncle Huffam, we climbed the stairs to the landing above. The floors was so creaky and loud with our footsteps it was hard to see how we could have crept about the place even if we had wanted to. We said goodnight to John and found the small, rickety ladder that led into a tiny trap in the ceiling and we climbed up.

There was a reason why only the youngest boys ever slept in the attic and, as I squeezed my grown self up into it, I imagined that the place had shrunk. I stood and dipped my head under the low roof and turned to help Warrigal up after me. Once we was both through I looked about for the two lanterns what hung from the beams. It was hard to see in the long dark room but, as I lit them with my candle, the bright rays shone around the space and I was hit by the suddenness of my memories. There was the same four beds that we used to fight over, with the scratchings on, by which we had marked them as our own. And there was still toys scattered about the place, dusty and unused, a moth-eaten, cobwebbed bear that had once belonged to Mouse Flynn and the toy soldiers with which we had played war what was now broken and left underfoot like they had died in battle and not been buried. The walls was marked with chalkings of animals and lines where we had measured ourselves growing tall. On the beams above was our names, or what we could spell of them, carved in with knives. There was 'Jem WITE', 'CHarly', 'Blukers', 'mowse' and, at the top, 'Jack DAW'. I pointed at 'Jack DAW' and told Warrigal that this was me and then I showed him a chalking next to it of a bird flying upwards with his beak pointing down. 'I did that,' I whispered.

Warrigal was sat on the bed by which Mother Froggat had left the blankets and looked to me as though he had no time for my reminiscing.

'So –' I smiled – 'see where the beak points to.' With my finger

I followed the line from the beak down to a thick floorboard near the wall. Warrigal understood and rose from the bed.

'There?' he said.

'There,' I said back and with my hand told him to open his bag. He pulled out a claw hammer and chisel and walked over to where I was crouched. The floor creaked and I told him not to move around so much as I took them from him. I went to work prising up the board as quiet as I could, knowing that John Froggat lay in the room below, most likely staring up at this very spot on the ceiling. But after some minutes' labour I had the board out and passed it to Warrigal who, quiet and soft, put it on a bed. Then I reached my hands down under the floor and felt something cold and rusty just where I had expected it to be. I grinned at Warrigal, pulled up my old metal box by the twine that I'd tied around it and took it over to the bed nearest to the lights. The lid was not easy to remove after all these years and it made an unfortunate, loud squeak as I got it off. Then I placed the box on my lap and started searching through. At the top, acting like a cover for the rest, was a folded copy of the *Newgate Calendar* which my mother had given to me when I was seven. It had turned a deep yellow and the weak, brittle pages was crumbling at the edges as I handled it. On the cover was a story I had read many times of how a treacherous servant had violently beaten his employer, a great lord, to death with a heavy candlestick when caught in the act of stealing the family silver. He was caught by a Bow Street Runner who had pursued him all the way to France and dragged him back to Newgate where he had been hung by the neck until dead. The man's name was Michael Dawkins and I was once told he was my father.

Underneath that was some breast-pins, fogles and a now colourless fob-watch what I had kept as souvenirs of my first ever outings.

But below all these was the real treasure and I was relieved to see it was still there. I pulled out the wooden toy and showed it to Warrigal. It was a mahogany-coloured doll of an Indian prince, with turned-up toes and bright-painted clothes, a blue coat with yellow lining and red trousers, and its white-teethed face was smiling up at me. It was an exotic thing and I remember being well pleased when given it. I shook it and heard it rattle. Warrigal leaned in to get a closer look.

'That it?' he said.

'That's it,' I replied.

'Go on,' he whispered.

'No. We've made too much noise. We'll put the room back to how it was and then we'll leave good and early. We'll take a glim tomorrow.' Warrigal looked vexed but nodded and together we laid the floorboard back down, after having put the box back in its place. The only thing we wanted to take from this room was the prince.

'Give,' said Warrigal, holding out his hand once we was readying ourselves for bed.

'Piss off,' I said, climbing into the bed still holding on to it and pulling the blanket over myself. 'It ain't his yet.' He cursed under his breath but went over to the lanterns and blew out the lights. I knew he wouldn't fight me for it tonight, not when the Froggats could hear. Once I was sure he was in his own bed I rolled over and pulled my knees up, so as to sleep in this bedstead that was made for children, and I placed the prince on the pillow next to me. I looked at it and thought about the man who had given it to me for a Christmas present. The man who was both my father and mother. It was hours later when at last I got to sleep.

Chapter 6

Red Meat

Containing a good deal of blood.
The more sensitive reader may wish to skip it

It was hot, Australia hot, and close by I could hear the horrible screaming of wild beasts.

'Meat for the lions, Dawkins!' jeered Lord Evershed as the whip cracked just by my ear, causing me to flinch. 'That's all a thief is fit for. Meat. For. The. Li. Ons.' There was a whip crack for every full stop and my head turned this way and that as I begged him to knock it off. But he looked to be enjoying himself, the nasty old brute.

I was in these rusty convict shackles and my back stung from the whipping. I had this tight iron collar around my neck with which I was being pulled through the colony like some dangerous dog. Ahead of me, through the blinding sun rays, I could see it was Warrigal what was doing the pulling. He was as naked as Adam but covered in that white body paint his people slap over themselves whenever they is feeling celebratory. It was so thick on his face it made him look more like a pantomime clown than a proud aborigine. I shouted over to him to stop. Was we not friends? I asked him. But Evershed just cracked his whip again and repeated his comments about my use as lion meat.

The big tent was not dirty and ripped like all the other convict tents but clean white with red stripes. It was just like those of the travelling circuses in America I had seen in pictures of and, as I was dragged through its opening, I could see there was a full house for this here show. Inside the seats was lined with spectators, many of them people I recognised from picking their pockets in the London streets, and they was all grinning at me and pointing.

'Picture if you will, ladies and gentlemen, a great big juicy steak!'

In the dead centre of the ring stood Ringmaster Evershed, now wearing a red coat and clutching a cat-o'-nine-tails. He was stood next to a giant cage with a red sheet covering it and from inside animal roars was getting louder and more terrifying. The cage shook with great violence and the crowd gasped.

'Because that,' Evershed went on, 'is what we have before us. For your delectation tonight . . . Mr Jack Dawkins!' As the crowds clapped and cheered Warrigal began prodding me with a stick to move forward. When I was a nose-length from the cage, Evershed pulled back the covering with one strong stroke, the bars of the cage fell away and I was screaming good and hard. Warrigal then poked me in the side of the head with his finger and I jerked my head to look at him. He was fully dressed and sat over my old bed in Saffron Hill. It was morning.

'Shut up, you,' he said. 'Too much noise.'

The tiny bed was soaked in sweat and the very second I recalled where I was I began feeling for the wooden toy I had gone to sleep with. It was gone. I looked to Warrigal and saw the blue hat of the prince's head poking out of his pocket.

'You thieving imp,' I said, most vexed. 'Fancy pinching a cove's property while he is fast asleep like that. I would never stoop to such unsporting behaviour.' I got out of the bed and took off my nightgown. '*I* only steal from those what is awake,' I said. 'Because an Englishman must have his standards.'

I began to dress as Warrigal looked out of the small window through which the light was shining in. It overlooked the crooked lanes of the vicinity and I could hear the church bells chiming eight times. I could tell that Warrigal was troubled about something even before he turned to me as I was belting up my trousers. 'Animal screams,' he said.

It took me some seconds to catch on to his meaning. The wild screams I had heard in my dream was still carrying on now and they was dreadful upon the ears. 'Smithfield meat market,' I told him as I buttoned my shirt. 'Must be slaughtering day. Those poor beasts are having an 'orrible time.' I searched around for my shoes and then looked to him. 'Can you remember where I left my hat?' I asked him.

I had put it downstairs with our trunk in Fagin's old kitchen with these Froggat people. When we got down there we found the man and his mother at breakfast. There was two pots bubbling over the fireplace, one what smelt of oats and another what they was using to boil up some more watery tea. Mother Froggat was spreading mouldy butter over a hard bread roll for blind Uncle Huffam, who was still in his rocking chair and lost in his own little world. He seemed put out when she offered him a plate of almost nothing, and the cat was nowhere to be seen. He must have been off getting his own breakfast if he had any wits.

It had been weighing upon my mind that the night before I had given this family the wrong impression of myself. They could have been forgiven for thinking, on account of all the fuss I had been making, that I was some sad creature deserving of their pity. I wished to correct this impression as I strutted into their kitchen.

'What a dreary old dump you poor beggars are living in,' I said.

'These are dismal surroundings, I do say!' I ran my finger along the dresser and pulled a face like I had never before been in such a filthy hovel. My hat was hanging from a chair and I picked it up and started blowing upon it as though it was covered in dust. John Froggat looked up from his bowl of stodge and asked if I could ever find it in my heart to forgive his humble family.

'Because if we'd 'a known Your Lordship was going to grace us with your presence, we'd 'a tidied up a bit.' He looked to his mother, who laughed her hacking laugh, although I found the joke to be weaker than her tea. Uncle Huffam joined in too, though it was doubtful he knew what he was supposed to be chuckling about. Then John turned his head round to Warrigal all slow and serious. 'Mr Whatever-your-name-is,' he said, 'if you have a tongue in your head perhaps you can remind this young prig that we know he grew up in this very house and by what class of people he was raised.'

'Thieves!' cried Mother Froggat, making poor old Huffam jump and ask where. 'And murderers! The criminal class!' She held up her head as if posing as a figurehead for some ship called the *Grumpy Trout* and went on. 'We may not have much,' she told me, 'but we're not to be looked down upon by the likes of you.'

John took another swig from his pot and looked at me steady. 'Make another flash remark,' he said, 'and my next answer will not be so jolly.' I saw that his hands was covered in these little cut marks and that on the table next to him was his tray of metal objects. I decided not to enter into a quarrel with him as this would have been lowering behaviour for a quality gent such as myself, especially considering he was within reaching distance of several sharp knives.

'Don't go misunderstanding me.' I smiled at Mother Froggat while avoiding her son's steely looks. 'I wouldn't look down my nose on a nice old bird such as yourself, honest I wouldn't.' I cast my eyes about the barren room, with its empty shelves and cupboards what I knew was empty without even opening them. 'But I remember this kitchen when it was stocked full of tasty eatables: penny pies, sweetmeats, crumpets, Chelsea buns . . .' I wandered over to the grate and pointed to a wire what overhung it that she was using to hang socks off. 'My friend Fagin, dear old soul that he was –' I ignored her scoffs – 'used to hang rashers of streaky bacon from that before sunrise and let the smell of them cooking fill up the whole house. Us boys would all tumble out of bed and be down here ready for the day.' I picked up a skillet and spun it by the handle. 'These was always cooking eggs or herrings or juicy great sausages. The food we had in those days was . . .' I searched for the right word, '. . . glorious.'

'What's that?' said Uncle Huffam, and he sniffed the air. He had only pecked at his bread and was now letting the plate just rest on his lap. 'We having sausages, are we?' In his excitement he was causing his plate to slide down to his knees. It was about to fall off but I grabbed it before it could shatter on the floor. Mother Froggat did not thank me for rescuing her crockery though.

'Now look what you gone and done!' she said instead. 'You've gotten him all excited. And for what? Nothing!' She took the bread roll which had fallen on to the floorboards, brushed it with a napkin and put it back in his unsteady hands. I snatched it straight out again.

'Yes, we are having sausages, Uncle Huffam!' I announced. 'Big juicy saveloys. And bacon if you fancy it. And the tastiest rumps in Smithfield!' On hearing this old Huffam clapped with delight as if he was being paid a visit by the breakfast fairies and I gave the last grey hairs on his head a good rustle. I turned to Froggat and went on. 'I for one am starving and so I'm sure is my valet over there.' I tossed the roll over to Warrigal who caught it in one hand. 'I promised him a decent British breakfast for our first morning in London and that is what we're getting. You fine people have been so generous that I shall be happy to get victuals for the lot of us.' I stretched out my arms, hat in hand, like a politician making big promises at the hustings. I cannot say I expected John to jump up and dance a jig of glee at my words but I was hoping for a bit of a thank-you. But he just carried on eating his porridge.

'Last night, Mr Dawkins, you said you only had foreign money about you,' he said after a time. 'It was why you couldn't pay for your lodgings. I should be interested to know how you mean to go about paying for this breakfast.' He leaned back in his chair and sipped at his tea. 'They don't take Australian coin at Smithfield, you know.'

I waved it off and put my hat on. 'Don't you go worrying your handsome head on that score, Johnny my new-found friend. You leave those messy particulars to me. And please,' I added as I made towards the coat pegs, 'call me Jack.' I took down the coats and weighed the difference. Mine was lighter and was this very dark blue what would hide any bloodstains but it was also of a tight cut. It could take bacon or leaner steaks but would not be much use for hiding thick slices of meat. Warrigal's coat was more suited to our purpose though. It was heavy, brown and loose on the insides with wide and deep pockets. You could hide a whole pig in that, I thought. I was feeling most pleased at the prospect of this spree and the thought that I would be sharing my findings with these Froggats made me feel a proper Robin Hood. I then made to pass by where John Froggat was sitting, when I found my path was blocked by the rude obstruction of his leg. He had put his foot up on the wall and spoke in a way that I found most menacing.

'But I do worry, Mr Dawkins,' he said, removing his tree trunk of a leg from out of my way and standing tall in front of me. My eyes came up to his chest. 'In this house we earn our breakfast the honest way. By working and spending. We don't take what ain't ours.'

'We're Christians!' his mother squawked, in case I'd forgotten.

'Just so,' John said. 'Mother takes in laundry. I sell metalware. Uncle Huffam, when he's feeling up to it, plays his fiddle on street corners for pennies. We may not have much but what we have is ours, fair and square, let no man deny it. This meat you're telling us of,' he said in a heavy voice, 'we won't be wanting it.' Uncle Huffam leaned over from where he sat and patted his nephew on the arm.

'Well said, boy,' he nodded. Then he looked back to where he thought I was still standing. 'Nick us some kippers instead, son.'

'No, Uncle!' said John with much firmness. 'We won't be accepting nothing stolen from this young man.' There was a wail of despair out of Huffam. 'I'm sorry,' John said to him, 'but it won't be honestly bought and so would turn rotten in our stomachs.' He stepped out of my way so I could get to the door. 'I will ask you not to come back here once you have left, Mr Dawkins,' he said. 'This is no longer a house of thieves.'

It was wet, London wet, and close by I could hear the horrible screaming of wild beasts.

'You're starting to stink, Warrigal,' I said as we lugged the trunk through Cow Cross Street towards the sound of a thousand bellowing butchers. We was up to our shins in mud, had still not breakfasted and I was finding the noise of tortured cattle coming out of the ring-droves to be most upsetting. Warrigal was in as dirty a mood as I and gave me a look to answer that I was no rose in bloom either. Neither of us had taken a bath since our last night on the *Son and Heir* two days ago and our rain-drenched clothes was now in need of a good wash. The marketeers was pushing past us with dead carcasses over their shoulders and, even though the rain had stopped, the puddles on the uncobbled streets was dark pink from the dripping blood.

I had never liked Smithfield; it was a place what held unpleasant memories for me. Many years ago, when still doorknob high, I had spent a night in the pens there. I had run away from my mother's home in the Dials after another one of her screaming fits and had hid under some tarpaulin with the urchins. We had awoke to find ourselves surrounded by bullocks, sheep and other livestock all crushed and tethered together and suffering many cruelties. It was a nasty scene of drovers goading their cattle, cracking their hocks, twisting their tails, breaking off their horns and stabbing their eyes to get them to move. The following morning I walked the streets of Clerkenwell hoping to pick enough pockets to afford lodgings for myself and the other lads when, and this was the only time it had ever happened in my distinguished career, I was grabbed by the arm as my hand was deep inside a coat pocket. The hand and coat belonged to a man who introduced himself as Mr Fagin and I never had to sleep in that market again.

'It was rotten ingratitude, is what it was!' I moaned to Warrigal as we passed the market stalls selling sirloins, ribs, rumps and veiny parts. I was still on about the ignorant Froggats – I had been ever since we had been pushed out of Fagin's front door – and about the grievous mistake they had made by refusing my offer of free meat. 'It's Uncle Huffam I pity,' I went on as our noses followed the smell of fried sausages. 'To go on starving a hungry old man like him when there is all this for the taking –' we approached

the sausage man, who was shouting loud, boasting of the quality
– 'is a cruelty I could never inflict.'

But it was not Uncle Huffam I pitied but my poor orphaned
self. I had not wanted to be cast out of my once happy home and
in truth I had hoped that the Froggats would let us lodge in the
dead brother's old room until we had made other arrangements.
I had said this to John Froggat as he had pushed us down the staircase and out into the street but he answered that he would never
trust that our money was clean. Just as he was about to slam the
door on us I asked if this was Christian of him. Should he not be
prepared, in the name of all things Jesus, to give me a second
chance? While he was ruminating on this I pressed on. Would he
at least let me buy one of his metal saws which I had spied in his
tin tray and for which I had enough English coins to pay? I swore
within the sight of God that there was nothing dirty about these
coins, they was honestly come by and that he could accept them
in good conscience. He asked me what I wanted to do with a
metal saw. I tapped my nose and said that I needed it for secret
business. The door slammed shut.

It was not true that we had no English money about our persons,
Evershed had given us pursefuls to make our task easier once we
was over here, but I did not want to hand them over to a simple
sausage man. Here was I, so young and artful, blessed with the
talents to pinch from any stall I cared to, but now, because of this
burdensome trunk, I was reduced to paying for my breakfast like
some law-abiding commoner. I bristled at the indignity of it.

We fed ourselves under some shelter by an alley, with Warrigal
sat upon the trunk, and watched the bustling market. Bloody
cleavers was everywhere, cutting up swine, and I considered the
chances of stealing such an implement. The market still stank of
dead animal but it grew quieter as the slaughtering neared its end

and I was gratified by this. The sounds of squealing pigs being all of a sudden silenced was ruining my meal and my thoughts turned to poor doomed Nancy. I was finding the vision of Bill, and what they say he did to her, to be most disturbing. She was beautiful, at least in my memory she was, and I had dreamt of her often while away. I was wishing that Bill had not been so clumsy as to have fallen from that rooftop so that I could have had the satisfaction of pushing him off myself.

'My goodness!' I then heard someone say. 'It's the Artful Dodger!'

It was a girl's voice, sweet and happy, and for a second I thought it was Nancy herself calling out to me. I looked across the road to where the streaky bacon was hung and saw instead a beautiful young woman dressed in red and twirling a matching parasol to shake off the raindrops. 'Jack Dawkins,' she said. 'It is you!'

'It's me all right,' I called back to her, my gloomy mood vanishing the very instant I saw her. 'I've come back to you at last. Come over here and kiss me.' On hearing this she laughed in delight and came running straight over, dancing her way around the puddles. I opened my arms wide to catch her and she threw herself into them and kissed me on the cheek. Some watching washerwomen scowled to see her behaving with such brazenness but we was both too happy to care.

'But they sent you to Australia!' she said.

'Didn't care for it,' I told her. 'Missed you too much.'

'Missed you too, Jack,' she said, squeezing me tight. 'I so hoped I would see you again. Are you back for good now?'

'Oh yeah,' I answered, and held her close to me, breathing in her perfume and stroking her hair all gentle with my fingertips. 'I'll never leave you again.' And from his place sat on the trunk, and in spite of the hard expression still stuck on his face, I got a sense that even Warrigal was a little touched to see so tender a reunion.

I still had no idea who she was though.

'Let's get a good look at you then,' I said, holding her out in my arms and trying to recall how I knew her. 'You've grown up lovely, you have. Just lovely.' She was younger than me, about seventeen, and she had a figure what was most fetching. Her scarlet dress struck me as a bit pricey for one of her class and this told me that she was either on the thieve or earned her living on her back. Either way she was good at her job, as I had only ever sniffed that perfume before on rich ladies. The only rum thing about her looks was the hat. It was tall and stiff and, in spite of the dainty flower tied upon the rim, it seemed like that of a man.

'You're dressed up like a real gen'leman,' she said as her fingers stroked my superfine coat, passing over the bump made by my pocket watch. She had the touch of my profession, I could tell that. 'Fagin would be ever so proud. He always said you were the best of them.' And it was then that I made a very sudden and pleasing realisation. This was Ruby Solomon, this was.

'You're Ruby Solomon, you are,' I told her, as if she herself was in the dark about her own identity. 'Fagin's little girl.' She stepped back from me and placed her hands on her hips.

'Have you only just remembered me?' she asked, annoyed.

'I haven't thought about you for years.' I laughed in wonderment at how much she had altered. 'You've transformed into a right beauty.'

'Well, that is as maybe,' she huffed, and turned her cheek towards me in mock indignation. 'But I cannot believe you haven't thought on me once while I've been here pining for your return every day for three long years.'

'I've been gone six years.'

'Have you now?' She shrugged. 'Well, it felt more like three.'

During the years that I lived at Saffron Hill there was only ever one girl what was allowed into our gang and she was this here Ruby. As a matter of principle Fagin was always very strict about letting girls into his den – he didn't even like us having sweethearts come to visit let alone would he teach any of them the tricks of his trade. He said that the female sex was a talkative sex, too talkative for safety's sake, and considering his own downfall was due to Nancy's indiscretions it seemed he had a point. He also said that girls was too often the source of fisticuffs between boys and he preferred to keep things harmonious between us. But with Ruby it was different. He treated her as though she was his own daughter which, considering how close he was to her mother, was thought to be true. The Widow Solomon had died when Ruby was very young, but Fagin spoke of her as if she was the greatest love of his life and he used to take Ruby to visit her graveside often. There was an old uncle what would come to visit her on occasion but he was too poor and feeble to take care of her and so, as was typical, Fagin took responsibility himself and gave her a home. Ruby was a great favourite with us boys, so happy and mischievous a child was she, and her fast little fingers made her a wonder at the snatching game. The old Jew was never more fierce than when acting as her protector and if he ever caught any of us treating her bad, such as the time Crisper got caught trying to set light to her hair, they would be cast out into the night no matter how cruel the hour. But Ruby still had to earn her lodgings, same as the rest of us, and she soon proved to be a good distracter. I remember when she was still small I took her promenading around the many pleasure gardens in the spring where the well-to-do would stop and comment on the delightful child in her fine pink dress and beaded necklace what had been stolen just for her. As they bent in, to coo and kiss and tell her how adorable she was, their dress pockets was a dipper's delight and such excursions proved most profitable.

As was natural, Ruby was besotted with me. I was two years older than her, as handsome as a hero and as silver-tongued as a villain. And, let's not forget, I was top-sawyer after all. She followed me everywhere, or she tried to, and she made a proper pest of herself, considering she was only little. But six years later, seeing her all grown up and looking and smelling of stolen money, I realised what she meant to me. She made me feel glad to be home.

'You make me glad to be home,' I told her, and went in for another squeeze. She laughed and let me hold her but the magical moment was ruined by the sound of Warrigal clearing his throat. He had finished eating and was looking at his pocket watch with a face that was reminding me we still had business to attend to.

'And what might your friend's name be, I wonder?' she asked.

'Warrigal,' said Warrigal before I could say Peter Cole.

'Charmed to meet you, Warrigal,' she said, curtsying as if he had said Prince Albert.

Warrigal just stared back at her.

'Warrigal's my valet. I have a valet now.'

'Blood,' said Warrigal, and he pointed at her.

'The reason I'm back, see,' I continued, ignoring him, 'is that I got this pardon from the Governor of New South Wales. You ain't going to believe this, Ruby, but I'm in the sheep-farming business now and business has been most—'

'Blood,' said Warrigal again.

Ruby looked to Warrigal and then quick back to me. She raised her white-gloved hand to her forehead. 'Oh no,' she said. 'Oh dear no!' And then I saw three red lines dripping down from under her hat and on to her brow. 'Oh, Jack,' she said, her voice sick as she saw my expression change. 'I wish I'd never seen you.'

She hitched up her skirt and with one hand placed the other on top of her hat and took to running in the direction of Cloth Lane. I chased straight after her, and Warrigal in turn chased after me. Her parasol and our trunk was both left on the pavement untended.

'Ruby!' I shouted as she scudded into an alley. 'Come back! I want to help!' She ran halfway up the narrow path until she reached a water pump which could not be seen from the street and there she stopped dead. She was facing the stone wall, as if ashamed to be seen, and I caught up with her and touched her on the shoulder. 'You're hurt,' I said. 'Let's have a glim.'

Still with her back to me, she raised her hands to her temples and lifted that queer hat up so I could see what it hid. There, resting on top of her crown, was a thick slab of steak what was leaking blood all down her head.

'This never happens,' she cried as she turned to face me. She looked as vexed as I had ever seen a person, although this may have been on account of the redness which had spread down to her tearful eyes, making a right old smeary mess of her. 'I gets it home in time most days. You were a distraction to me, Jack Dawkins!' She took the steak, flung it into the hat and handed it to me as she bent over to shake her dripping hair out into the lane, grumbling about how hard it was to rinse out cow's blood. I looked inside the hat, as Warrigal caught up behind, and saw that it was lined with newspaper what had soaked up some of the blood but had not stopped it seeping through the rim. Warrigal looked cross with me for running off but I handed him the steak and turned back to Ruby. She was trying to wash the blood from her hair and so I yanked at the pump while she held her head under it.

'How did you get that in there without being seen?' was the first question. 'And what for?' was the second. 'It's only a steak, not worth messing up your pretty hair over.' Once she had washed her hair and face she straightened herself up, shook her head dry and snatched her hat back.

'It's for Jem,' she answered, tying her wet hair into a bunch. 'He eats steak and not much else. And where else can a lady hide such a thing?' She was starting to calm herself and then went on. 'I peruse the meat counters while twirling my parasol and then, when a gust of wind blows by, I make like I'm all feeble and I drop it on to the counter between me and the butcher. By the time I've raised it back up there's a steak under my hat.' She took the steak back from Warrigal and put it back in the hat. 'It's easy when you practise.' She put it back on her head and asked me how she looked.

'Jem who?' I asked back. 'Jem *White*?' Ruby nodded and then held her chin up as if to ask what of it. 'What are you doing going around pinching steaks for Jem White of all people? He's big and ugly enough to steal his own dinner by now surely.'

'Jem is my fancy man,' she said in an *I'll have you know* voice. 'We live together in Bill and Nancy's old place. He's the flashest crook in the rookeries. Top-sawyer. And if he says he wants a steak, then a steak he must have.'

This information could not have surprised me more than if she had said that during my time away Queen Victoria had given birth to an elephant prince. Jem White was not cut out to be top-sawyer – he didn't have the fingers for it. Charley Bates was the only boy that could touch me on that scent and even he knew his place. But now I was having to listen to Ruby witter on about what high fashion Jem had been keeping her in ever since she became his kept woman.

'My parasol!' she cried out all of a sudden. 'I've dropped it.' And then she hitched up her skirt again, hand on her hat, and ran back to where she had left it. Warrigal and myself followed close behind and when we ran back out on to the street we found a gang of four boys about to lift our locked trunk off in the other direction.

'Get out of it!' I shouted at them. They dropped the trunk and scattered and, as they disappeared in every direction, Warrigal bent down to check that the locks had not been opened.

'It's gone,' complained Ruby about the parasol. 'It was a present from my Jem. He'll be furious that I lost it.' The market was now emptying of people and it reeked of rotten offal. She wrinkled her nose in disgust. 'If I catch the little urchin what took my gamp,' she said, 'I'll wring his neck like a chicken.'

'I should like to reacquaint myself with your Jem,' I told her. 'And all the others. Where do they lurk?' She looked back to me and at last her face began to brighten.

'They'd all love to see you again, Dodge', she said and touched me on the arm. 'Jem, Mouse, Georgie, Herbie Sharp . . . They all still talk about you like you never left. I'm sure Jem'll let you back in the gang.'

Let me back in the gang? The cheek of her. I *was* the bloody gang.

'Go to the Cripples the night after next. They'll be there betting on the rats.'

'I will,' I said, pleased to hear it. 'It'll be nice to be reintroduced into London society.'

Finally, after many large hints from Warrigal, our conversation came to its end. Ruby held out her hand to feel for raindrops and made to leave. As she said goodbye and scurried away I called out after her. She was crossing the busy street away from the market but I was loud enough to be heard over the noisy hoofs of the traffic.

'It was good seeing you again, Rube,' I said, raising my hat to her as carriages passed between us. 'Sight for sore eyes.'

She smiled back at me. 'Go to the rat pit,' she repeated. 'You'll have fun. But be warned, they might not let your ugly friend in.'

'Warrigal will be fine,' I told her.

She blew me a kiss. 'I was talking to Warrigal!' she said. Then I heard her mischievous laugh as two large shires pulled an omnibus between us, obscuring her from me in much the same way that a parasol at a meat counter would. By the time the packed carriage had passed she was gone. I could still smell the perfume on me though.

The church bells was now counting to ten and, as I wound my gold timepiece to match it, I remarked to Warrigal that Ruby had a fine nerve saying that I was the distraction. We lifted up the trunk and made towards a coach stand, both agreeing that we should head straight towards the address I had written down on a small card inside my wallet. It was an address of a man in Greenwich and had been given to me by Lord Evershed when he bid us farewell at Botany Bay. This was the man we was supposed to take the doll to as soon as we had it in our possession and I wanted to waste no time in delivering it. Warrigal, who was treading in ankle-deep puddles all the way along the road, offered no objection to this plan but said nothing, as was his way. So I just let him dwell upon whatever he cared to while my own thoughts turned back to our simple errand.

It was a rum business, this finding and delivering of my old toy, but the reward for a job well done was my freedom. However, the penalties of failure was terrible, and I did not like to dwell on what would have happened had the doll not been where I had hoped. I had experienced many bad dreams on the voyage back to London, imagining that I would get all the way back to the old attic and be disappointed in my search. The thought had been a torment to me ever since Lord Evershed had reminded me of the brown-faced doll six months before. But now that the grinning prince was safe inside Warrigal's pocket I could at last begin to breathe easy, knowing that I would soon be out of Evershed's clutches. He was a wicked fellow, of this there was no doubt, but then so was most of the people I had grown up with so I had decided not to hold it against him. I had met the man while serving time in Australia and it was there, on a penal colony on the opposite side of this here world, where I had first learned about the curse of the Jakkapoor stone.

Chapter 7

Abel's Farm

*Treats of the place I was sent to for incarceration
and of the people there encountered*

There are coves in this world, those who are flatter of mind and straighter of purpose, who do not see things in the way what I do. These sorts of coves, and perhaps you are one of them, might think that my getting packed off to Australia at a tender age was not the outright disgrace that I saw it to be. They might feel that I should have been grateful for the magistrate's decision and try to tell me that the London from where I had been banished was a very wicked place for one of my class. It was all filth and rats, disease and danger. Most of my associates, they might remind me, had met with bloody ends soon after my transportation but I had survived by being sent away. I was the lucky one. I was spared.

Convicts on Abel's Farm was forever being told how lucky we was. In London we was looked down upon by the gentry just for being born poor and living in slums where there was only one privy hole for every hundred arses. But over in Australia we was being given a chance to better ourselves. If we was to put aside our thieving ways and behave like respectable gents, if we worked hard and played the game, we could rise high in that new world. We could serve our sentences and then become proper Australians if we cared to. We could buy cheap land what was bigger than all

Poplar and farm animals or plant crops. We could marry another convict, make an honest woman of her, give her some babies, be our own masters. Now, they would say, would that not be a fair life?

No, I would answer, it would not. Because what these coves have never understood is that London was my home and there was an end to it.

Old Abel Magwitch, the sheep farmer whose name hung over the place where I was sent to sweat, he must have felt the same way as me. He had been transported for thievery many years before and had done wonderful well as an emancipist, making himself a tidy fortune breeding stock. He, who had lived little more than a beggar back in England, had made himself a king down there, an example to us all. Why then, many asked, had he just vanished from sight one day never to be seen or heard from again? Some among us said that he had heard London calling him back like a mother. This I believed as I could hear her calling too.

'"It was the night after the storming of Seringapatam,"' I said to my fellow convicts one boiling afternoon in captivity, '"and the brave soldiers of the British East India Company had breached the walls of the citadel, shot the troublesome sultan in the head and stripped his body of all its jewels. They had laid waste to the enemy and, as dusk fell over the cannon-blown palace, their business had moved from slaughtering to plunder."'

I was sat sweltering on a rickety fence and I fanned myself with an old copy of *Bentley's* what I had stolen from Mr Pebble, the English teacher. Inside that was the first chapter of *The Curse of the Jakkapoor Stone* by George Shatillion and I was now relating what I had read there to my less educated companions. I used to describe scenes I had read in the *Newgate Calendar* to the other pickpockets in London and I was happy now to provide the same service for these illiterates as long as it got me out of the sheep shearing.

'"The redcoats swarmed through the palace which, as they had hoped, was a treasure trove of diamonds, sapphires and other jewels, hidden in every room and hanging off enemy corpses. Fine silks was pulled from doorways and windows, statues was smashed for their encrusted gems, and the doors of the treasury was blown open with gunpowder to get at the gold bars within."' I smiled as I watched my listeners shear their sheep, knowing I was making their labour more pleasurable. 'It makes you proud to be British,' I said to them.

'Will you ever shut that bloody mouth of yours, Dinkins?' snapped Sergeant Allhare, who was watching over us with his gun. He knew full well what my surname was; he was just being a turd about it. 'Get back to work before I shoot you dead and we can all get some peace.'

We was in one of the sheep-pens on the farm and the others was knee-deep in wool. I was in the company of this soldier, three aborigines, two convicted prostitutes, four convicted thieves and two dozen sheep. All we needed was a partridge in a pear tree and it would have felt like Christmas. The abos and convicts was working so hard that I had decided to entertain them with this story what begins in the middle of a true historical battle but soon takes a turn fantastical. A corrupt English officer steals the ancient stone of Jakkapoor and spends the rest of his life being hounded by a vengeful *vetala*, which is what your Indians would call a genie. The story has the vetala showing up in London and threatening to lay a curse upon the officer's innocent daughter if he doesn't hand over the stone. What happens after that I couldn't tell you, as Mr Pebble only had the first three chapters. But during my time in Australia the novels of George Shatillion had been great favourites of mine and I had become fanatical about him. He was the greatest living Englishman, I would tell anyone who'd listen, and I was forever visiting the small library in the penal colony and pinching whatever they had of his back catalogue. My very favourite was his first novel, the now classic *Thimble and Pea*, peopled as it was with fences, pickpockets and other irrepressible Londoners what reminded me of home. There was an old Jewish villain in it called Ikey Slizzard who was, for me, the best thing in the book.

I carried on reading out the story for them in spite of Allhare's empty threats. There was no danger of him shooting me – he would get in too much trouble. The only way he would have been allowed to was if I had made a run for it and this would not happen as I had long since given up trying to liberate myself. I had made three separate escape attempts during my first year in the colony and each time some aborigines had been sent to track me and drag me back. This was just as well as I would have starved to death if they hadn't and, seeing how I had to suffer through harsh whippings upon every return, I soon lost my taste for taking flight.

'The rest of you can start taking your wool in,' said Allhare, spitting upon the ground. He was sat upon his horse and looked as bored with the sheep as I was. 'Dinkins and the blacks will finish the rest.' The others took their metal buckets into the barn and he rode off to talk to some other soldiers what was approaching on horseback. There was only a few more sheep to shear but I got off the fence to help the aborigines finish the job as I had become familiar with some of them over the last few years. Convicts and natives was not known to get along well on the farms – the aborigines looked down on the convicts because we was criminals, and the convicts looked down on the abos because they was enslaved. But we was both serving under the whip hand of the British Empire so I was prepared to be congenial about it and engage them in friendship. I soon learnt a lot from them about this land, about what you could and could not eat in the outback and about the customs of their tribe. In return they seemed happy to listen to me tell them all about my own country and how much better it was than theirs.

There was not much more shearing to be done on this particular day but the sweat was dripping heavy from my brow as I toiled. I took off my brown convict shirt and wiped my face with it and it was then that I saw something what I knew could only mean trouble. Sergeant Allhare, sat atop his horse over by the farmhouse, was still talking to these two well-dressed coves what had ridden in and who looked most out of place on a sheep farm. They was dressed in neat black suits like they was a pair of account- ants and as they spoke to Sergeant Allhare I saw him look over to where we was and point straight at me. I turned away fast, unsure of what this could mean. My instinct was to crouch down by the livestock in the hope that I would be obscured from their view. But as I tried to busy myself and not draw more attention I could hear three sets of hoofs ride over to the pen and Allhare call my name out.

'Dawkins,' he said but not to me. 'Jack Dawkins. This is him.'

From my low position I squinted up at the three riders. The sun was behind them and I held up my hand so I could see them better.

'Are you Dawkins?' said one of the little men in a nasally Australian accent. 'Jack Dawkins?'

'From Saffron Hill?' said the next. I said nothing and looked from one to the other as though I did not understand this strange language they was speaking.

'It's him all right,' confirmed Allhare. 'The boy you were asking after. He never shuts up about himself.' The two men seemed to be ignoring him and just kept their eyes on me.

'He's about the right age,' said the first to the second after I said nothing in response. 'And the records say the lad is on this colony. I think His Lordship will be satisfied.'

The second man still stared at me and I found myself holding his gaze for a few moments. 'Known any Jews?' he said after a time and then laughed. And then without waiting for my answer the two men turned their horses around, thanked Allhare for his trouble and galloped away leaving me with the distinct impression that I had not heard the last of whatever this was all about.

Most mornings in Australia I would be woken either by these great shafts of sunlight beaming in through the gashes in our ripped tent or by some insect trying to fly its way up my earhole. But on this morning, just two days after I had been paid that mysterious visit, I was awoken before sunrise by a man's gloved hand being placed over my mouth and a whisper what was most menacing.

'Up,' said the voice, and I blinked my eyes open and started to see the strange and unfamiliar face of an aborigine man glaring down at me. This man was not like the ragged natives what I knew from the farm; he was dressed in a gentleman's brown coat and hat, wore a gold ring in his ear like a pirate and the hatred what all the others tried to keep hid from the English was here undisguised. 'Up with me,' he commanded. 'Come.'

'Get up, you little bugger,' said the voice of Sergeant Allhare who was stood behind him. He was holding a candle what reflected a great distorted shadow of both of them upon the walls of the tent. Then the aborigine leaned down and yanked me up from my grassy mattress, forcing me to my feet. I will not lie to you and say I went without fuss.

'Murder!' I shouted, waking up all the other sleepers in the tent. 'They're dragging me to me death, boys! Do something!' The aborigine's hand was around my mouth once more but my fellow convicts was now all woken and watching as I was bundled away. I heard Allhare tell them that everything was all right, that I was just being taken away for a nice chat.

'Go back to sleep,' he said as I was dragged away screaming, 'and don't worry yourselves about it.'

Outside, in the centre of the colony, was some soldiers and a much older man in a long scarlet coat smoking a cigar. He was stood beside a covered vehicle what transported us prisoners to and from the colony. I could not see his face too clear as the morning was still dark but he was dressed not in uniform but more in the manner of a rich man. He wore a high stovepipe hat and his whiskers was well-barbered but, as I was pulled towards him by the soldiers, I did not find him genteel. This man, for all his seeming wealth, was one whose pockets I would never dare to pick.

'This is him, is it, Sergeant Allhare?' he said, his English voice deep and regimental.

'Yes, Your Lordship,' replied my keeper. 'As promised.' The man reached into his coat and I flinched, expecting a weapon. Instead he pulled out a thick wallet full of notes and began counting them out.

'This is more than we agreed upon,' said the man as he handed them to Sergeant Allhare. 'I expect complete discretion in return.' Allhare took the money and said that his lips was sealed upon the matter. 'Keep them that way. Now have your men lock him in the back of the van. My associate can keep an eye on him.' I put up a good struggle as the soldiers forced me into the back of the dark carriage and the aborigine took the lantern and climbed in with me. Once we was bolted in I struggled to see his face in the dark as his lantern was held low. I heard the cigar man say something to the soldiers; it sounded like a warning, a *not a word of this to anyone*, and then they was heard getting into the front and the horses drove away.

The hold of the prisoners' van was strong and wooden and the windows was covered with tarred sheets what was loose enough to let air in but not so I could see well. But the man opposite lifted his light up to hang in the centre of the hold and this gave me my best look at him so far. I remember thinking I had never before seen a face so evil.

'What's this about?' I demanded of him. 'Where you taking me?'

'Shut up, you,' he said. 'Too much noise.'

We trundled on in silence for what felt like an hour. Through the cracks in the wooden planks I could tell that the sun had come up and the hold's juddering grew more violent as we travelled up and down rocky paths. We splashed through brooks and other shallow waters and every so often I could hear the driver of the vehicle yelling at the nags to go faster still. I was feeling sick with terror at what these men meant to do with me and the speed of the carriage soon became so strong that I had to hold on to the seat to keep from sliding off it. Just as it seemed that we would never stop racing, the horses reared up, the carriage came to a sudden halt and I was sent hurtling from one end of the van to the other. The aborigine hadn't moved. He just looked at me and said nothing.

Next I heard some heavy boots jump down from the front and tread around to behind the carriage. Locks was turned, bolts slid away and, as the door was pulled open, sharp sunrays flooded the van, causing me to flinch. 'Pleasure to meet you, Mr Dawkins,' said the red-coated man in a manner that sounded lighter than that in which he had spoken to Allhare, 'you have had a rare stroke of luck.' I looked over and saw his grey wrinkly face clear in the daylight. He was most handsome for an old boy and he was talking to me as though I had just won a raffle. 'I hope we can do business together, you and I.' Then he addressed the aborigine. 'Bring him out of there, Warrigal,' he said. 'And escort him into the house.'

Within half an hour I sat upon the wooden veranda of this big stone house which overlooked the River Hawkesbury, breakfasting with an aristocrat. Lord Evershed was sprinkling sugar on to his half of a grapefruit as we sat on opposite sides of this round table and then he passed the sugar bowl over to me so I could do the same to mine. I took the tiny silver spoon and sweetened both the fruit on my plate and my coffee as he finally brought the conversation around to business.

'Tell me, Mr Dawkins,' he said, watching my face with great intentness before asking me a question I would never have expected, 'does the name Fagin mean anything to you?'

It was a beautiful place he had brought me to – the clear green water was nothing like the brown murk of the Thames and the sound of it flowing was most pleasing. There was no one else here except for Evershed and myself and a small number of aboriginals what he seemed to employ as servants, including this Warrigal cove. After I had finished with the sugar bowl I picked up the cup by its saucer, said cheers to his health and drank the coffee down.

Evershed did not say cheers back. Instead his smile thinned and I could sense his body stiffen. When he next spoke his voice was a little quieter, his tone a little more threatening.

'I asked you a question, Mr Dawkins,' he said as I placed the cup and saucer back on to the white-sheeted table. 'The polite thing to do is to answer it.' I picked up the larger spoon, scooped out the fruit segments and slipped grapefruit into my mouth. I let him wait while I swallowed it. In truth I was most surprised to hear the name of my old teacher and friend spoken out here in Australia and I could not imagine what business this high-born toff could have had with him. But the old Jew had taught me many valuable lessons over the years and the highest among these was how, should anyone important ever ask, he did not really exist.

'Fagin, you say?' I mused, and made a great show of giving it some thought. 'Can't say I've heard the name before. Is it a mister or a missus?'

Evershed's eyes left me for the first time since I had sat down and he glanced over to the man standing by the door, who was eyeing me like a sheepdog watches a ewe. Warrigal then crossed over to stand just behind my chair so I could not see him but could hear his breath. If this was done to intimidate me then it worked, although I took good care not to show it. Evershed then pushed his own chair back and stood up. 'Come now,' he said, and circled the table towards me. 'Mr Fagin from Saffron Hill. He's said to be a notorious fence and corrupter of children. A kidsman, I believe they call it. I have been informed by some private investigators here in Australia that you and he were close once.' He stood over me now, crossed his arms and rested his buttocks on the table. 'Tell us what you know of him,' he said.

'Can't help you.' I shrugged. 'He sounds a proper shady one, this Fagin. I try not move in such circles if I can help it.' I tapped the crockery with the spoon and listened to the sound. 'Bone china?' I asked.

Lord Evershed chuckled then. 'Honour among thieves, eh? Well, I call that admirable, Mr Dawkins. Very admirable indeed.' He then looked to Warrigal and I heard knuckles crack. I dropped my head down into my knees and waited for it.

The strike came, much to my surprise, from in front rather than behind. It was Evershed's own fist that smashed into the side of my face. My chair toppled and crashed to the floor, my dropped cup shattering against the desk. My head stung like he had opened it and I felt my temple for blood. There was hot liquid on my face and all over the wooden floor but I soon saw that this was just splashed coffee. 'What was that for, you vicious sod?' I demanded. 'I've done nothing to deserve it.' Evershed kicked me in the side hard and through my pain I could still marvel at how much strength he had in him for someone of his advanced years. I was on all fours and trying to stand as his polished gaiter shoes came close and the left foot stepped down hard upon my fingers. I cried out in pain but he just pressed down the harder. Then he removed his foot, reached into his waistcoat and handed me his silk handkerchief. I took it and wiped away the coffee.

Warrigal then helped me back into the chair, as innocent as if he had just watched it fall out from under me. Then he touched my face and turned it towards him. 'Bad,' he said, and tutted. 'Red tomorrow.' He fetched a little dustpan from just inside the house and wiped away the smashed crockery before taking a cloth to the spillage. Then he went back to his place just behind my chair.

'I shall ask again, Mr Dawkins,' said Evershed, taking his seat once more, 'and perhaps we will have more luck with you this time. Does the name Fagin mean anything to you?' I held the handkerchief up to where his fist had struck and said nothing. 'Don't be unreasonable,' Evershed sighed. 'He is in no danger, if that is what bothers you. Neither are you.' I dabbed the bruise all sceptical. 'This is a job interview of sorts and you're being very stubborn. The job is in London and, if I think you and I can do business, then you will be sent back there a free man. I have the ear of the Governor of New South Wales.' He pointed through to the house where there a hung a large picture of a man what I now assumed to be the Governor himself. 'We are very old friends, he and I, and I assist him in his duties here in Australia in an unofficial capacity. It would not be difficult for me to obtain his signature on your pardon. Not with all I know about him.'

I considered these words and wondered if they was true. To return home to London with a full pardon and to be reunited with Fagin and the others was all I wanted at that time. I could not have asked for a greater wish if an Indian vetala had granted me three of them. But, as the poets tell us, 'A Fool Trusts He Who Has Just Punched Him In The Face' so instead I kept my council.

'Mr Dawkins,' said Evershed as Warrigal's knuckles could be heard cracking again, 'I'm waiting for your answer.'

'Fagin . . .' I said after a long pause. 'Yeah, I recall the name.' Evershed's smile returned as he sat up straight. 'He was a horse I lost three guineas on.' A second punch, this time from Warrigal, landed in my left cheek and I was back on the floor. Now I bled hard.

'A pity.' Evershed sniffed as he began eating his breakfast. 'A great pity. I had hoped you were going to be more sensible than this.' Then he spoke to Warrigal. 'The fellow is an impossibility.'

'Take away?' asked the aborigine.

'Back to the colony?' said Evershed between mouthfuls. 'It's more than he deserves. I've a mind to just feed him to some hungry pigs.' I raised my hurt head and looked to him. He looked back as if wondering what I even was, let alone what was to be done with me. Then after he had finished his half of the grapefruit and had begun eating the rest of mine he spoke again. 'Let's try something different. Back in his chair.' Warrigal forced me back up as Evershed cleared his throat.

'An easier question this time, Mr Dawkins. If you have never heard of this man Fagin then let's try someone a little more famous. Does the name George Shatillion mean anything to you?'

Warrigal stood behind me with his hands on my shoulders forcing me not to go anywhere. I did not think I could take another punch. 'Course,' I said with sullenness, 'everyone has.'

'Everyone has,' Evershed agreed. He laughed then but the laughter was hard and mirthless as if daring either me or Warrigal to laugh with him. 'Who is he then?'

'He's a novelist.' I answered. 'The greatest living Englishman.'

Evershed's fist bashed down upon the table, making the china wobble. '*He's a thief and a bastard!*' he shouted, his face reddening. 'A faithless jackanape! And he's very far from being the greatest living anything now. They buried the unconscionable shit in Highgate Cemetery some months ago. And when I return to London I intend to visit his resting spot and piss all over it. What do you say to that, sir?'

'Well, his stories weren't for everyone,' I answered. 'I found them to be most entertaining myself.'

Evershed laughed as though he had been presented with a stupid person. He began to calm himself and crossed over to the writing desk. 'You and his legions of other admirers will be disappointed to learn that his final serialisation, *The Mystery of Mary Sweet* it was called, will forever go unsolved.' He then pulled out a sheet of paper from the desk and turned back to me. 'But as one mystery closes –' he rolled the paper up into his fist and motioned for me to stand – 'a clue to another is revealed. I assume you are familiar with his story *The Curse of the Jakkapoor Stone*?' I nodded that I was. I told him that I had been telling other convicts about it only a few days before. 'Then you'll be delighted to learn that you are in the company of the lead character,' said Evershed.

I thought about what he might mean and remembered that the name of the corrupt English officer in the story was called Nevershood.

'I have never encountered anything as fantastical as a vetala,' he said as he went over to the door and opened it. 'But it was I that took the real Jakkapoor stone.' He motioned for me to follow him. 'Let us take a walk along the river, you and I. And I will tell you the truth behind the fiction.'

Chapter 8

A Thief and a Bastard

Wherein Lord Evershed tells me of how
he was robbed of something priceless

A breeze cooled my face as we strolled along the Hawkesbury together and every so often Evershed would use his silver cane to point out the more unusual birds what twittered in the oaks above. It was as if we was two idle gentlemen on a Sunday jaunt and it was only my brown convict clothing and my cut face that said otherwise. Warrigal followed at such a distance that he was not part of our conversation but could still catch me should I try to run for it.

'If there is one thing I cannot abide, Mr Dawkins,' Evershed said, 'it is a thief.'

'Me neither,' I said, dabbing the cut with his handkerchief. 'Rotten little buggers.'

'And yet throughout my life,' he went on, 'there have been many foolish men who have dared to accuse me of being one.' He stopped at a brook and looked off into the distance. He was a queer sort and seemed to be drawing into himself as he spoke. Then he carried on walking.

'George Shatillion never accused me, but he *insinuated*, the coward. What is worse, he made his insinuations in print by modelling the villainous lead character in that wretched book of his upon me and therefore bastardising my own heroic actions.'

He shook his head and tutted at this but I found myself most impressed. If anyone ever put me in a book I should be proud.

'Many years ago, during the time of the mad king, I served with distinction in India during the Mysore Wars as captain of the 19th Light Dragoons. Like this fellow in the book I was there at the storming of Seringapatam and I did more than any other to bring about victory for the Empire. My speeches had enflamed the soldiers before battle, I had led the charge over the citadel walls and my claymore was the first to clash with the enemy sabre. Yes, as Shatillion depicts, it is true that the conquering heroes of John Company indulged themselves most shockingly in looting and rapine once the fighting was over but British blood does not cool quickly. The citadel, and everything in it, was now the rightful property of the Wodeyar dynasty but we had fought savagely on their behalf and the men were now as wild animals. I remember sweeping through the many rooms of the palace yelling my commands and punishing any looters whom I caught in the act. I shot one man, a colonel's nephew no less, straight through the eyes for daring to make free with one of the dead sultan's concubines. But despite this I could not have brought order to chaos if I was a thousand Captain Eversheds, and it was not long before I elected to leave them to their indulgences and pursue my own prize.'

He lowered his voice now as we passed along the riverbank as if he was concerned that hidden ears lurked behind trees.

'I had heard of the fabled jewel of Jakkapoor and about the powers it was said to grant to those who possessed it. I had been told two nights before by the uncle of Prince Mummudi that the Wodeyar people believed that jewel's loss had been responsible for all their previous defeats. Legend tells that those who hold the small black jewel are blessed with great fortune, but should one

lose the stone then they would be beset by bad luck until the day
that bad luck destroys them. Of course, as an Englishman I have
little time for foreign mysticism, and yet. . .'

Evershed let the sentence hang there for a bit before continuing.

'I found the jewel at last in an ancient temple, encrusted upon
a statue of a God, and I knew it instantly. Something about its
blackness called to me and I prised it out with my sword and took
it for my own. This is not stealing,' he said, and looked at me
steady, 'because the enemy had fallen. To the victor the spoils.'

He waited to see if I was simple enough to disagree with him
before continuing.

'And yet years later when George Shatillion learnt that the jewel
was in my possession he tried to paint me as some sort of mercenary thug rather than what I truly was, an imperial servant merely
helping himself to a small and just reward. I have always despised
fat and comfortable men like Shatillion; they are hopeless in battle.
They write about murder as if it were the worst thing in the world
and yet they know nothing of killing. They just sit like cowards
behind their desks using only the poison of their inkwells as a
weapon.'

There was much hatred in his voice as he spoke about my
favourite novelist and, gentleman though he was, I thought he
was going to spit. His hand moved up to his waistcoat and he
pulled out something small and gold what glinted in the sun. It
was a locket on a chain.

'It was Shatillion who stole,' he said. 'He did not face me in
battle like a real man and take what was mine by force. No, he
crept in the night as thieves do and took what was precious.' He
held up the locket for me to see and opened it. 'What do you
think?' he asked.

'It's beautiful,' I told him, wanting it for mine. 'Is it solid gold?'

'I'm not speaking of the locket, fool,' he said. It was only then I noticed there was a picture inside. It was a small but very life-like pencil sketch of a fair young girl with flowing hair and a lovely long neck. She was about eighteen and I liked her almost as much as I did the locket.

'Very nice,' I said. 'She your daughter?'

'This is Louisa,' he answered. 'My first wife. And I draw your attention to what the former Lady Evershed is wearing around her neck.' I peered closer and saw that the woman had a tiny black jewel hanging off a necklace.

'The Jakkapoor stone?' I asked.

'Yes,' said Evershed in a flatter voice than before. 'I gave it to her as a love gift. She wore it always.' We came to some daffodils what was in our way. He just trod across them. 'She even wore it when she was with him,' he muttered.

He was several steps ahead of me now and it was as though he wanted to get away from what he was telling me. I looked behind me to see if Warrigal was still following. His eyes had not left us. I quickened my pace and caught up with Lord Evershed, who seemed to be ranting to himself under his breath.

'George Shatillion had her for his whore,' he seethed. 'That is the crux of the thing. The how and the why of it do not concern you, Mr Dawkins, and I have no intention of telling you any more about the shameful business than I have to. But the fact is that you need to know the bare bones of the affair if you are to be of any use to me at all, so here they are. While I was abroad, attending to matters of Empire, the only woman I have ever loved, my young bride Louisa, found herself seduced by this ridiculous dandy. Their affair soon became common knowledge in gossiping London society and they ran off together, taking the jewel of Jakkapoor with them. I suspect that the priceless jewel was the real reason that Shatillion had made her his prey in the first place but I will never be certain. Whatever his purpose, he took my wife and my treasure and both were lost to me forever.'

We was facing the river now and stopped to sit upon a rock. In the trees above, the noise of the kookaburra was like cruel laughter. Evershed's fingers stroked his moustache and he looked lost in his thoughts. I could not imagine what any of that had to do with my Fagin or with me.

'Shatillion was a famous man,' Evershed continued. 'Loved and cherished by the people of England, they would forgive him any scandal. But once fallen, a woman stays fallen forever. The respectable world closes itself to her. As soon as his passion cooled then George Shatillion simply returned to his wealthy wife and was welcomed back into polite society. Louisa, however, found herself an outcast. She disappeared from public sight, taking only one thing of any value with her: the jewel around her neck.' Evershed gripped his cane and looked as though he wanted to thrash something. I felt the need to inch away from him. It was as though he had forgotten about me and was talking to himself, throwing up all these old memories like a sickness.

'So you want to find her,' I asked, filling the silence, 'and get the jewel back off her. Is that the thing?'

Evershed shot me a look that said I was understanding nothing. 'She's been dead for seventeen years, Dawkins.' He sighed. 'The police fished her body out of the Thames about a year after she had gone missing.'

He waited as a mob of kangaroos bounced past us in the distance, as if worried that they would overhear him.

'I was in England then, trying to locate both her and the jewel, and they came to tell me that a young woman had destroyed herself by jumping from Southwark Bridge. When they found her she was wearing a necklace that identified her as my wife. The stone had been removed but the inscription on the back read: "To my darling Louisa – I shall treasure you always, Franklin." A gift from me to her in happier times. I was in agony.'

'I'm not surprised,' I said, recalling the beauty of the woman in the locket and wanting to sound all sympathy. 'It must have been heartbreaking.'

'Heartbreaking?' Evershed snorted and rose to his feet again. 'Because the bitch had died? Nothing of the sort. She had betrayed me, Dawkins, or have you not been listening. I was glad to hear that she had suffered.'

His stare dared me to challenge him for his callousness but I did nothing of the sort. 'Why was you in agony then?' I asked instead, although I already knew the answer.

'Because the Jakkapoor stone was missing of course! It was my imperial prize and I had been beset by bad luck ever since I had given it away. Just as the legend had said I would be. I simply must retrieve it before bad luck destroys me.'

Oh dear, I thought as we walked towards a high iron bridge what crossed the Hawkesbury, and I started to make sense of who I was dealing with. This Lord Evershed, for all his aristocratic airs and military talk, was a lunatic who believed in foreign nonsense about magic jewels and cursed fortunes. Had he been born into my class then they would have thrown him into Bedlam and forgotten all about him but instead here he was, strutting about the Empire and getting himself into a hot state about lost trinkets.

'George Shatillion musta had it,' I suggested. 'Couldn't you have just bought the jewel back off him?'

'Buy it off him?' Evershed's reply was loud enough to be violent and we was far along the high iron bridge for him to throw me to my death. In spite of his age he was a bigger man than me, and Warrigal was close enough by to aid him. 'Offer money to the man who cuckolded me? I would rather turn on my own sword.' Then he stopped walking and turned to look over the river, forcing me to do the same. 'I set my lawyers on him instead and demanded that he return my property at once. He sent back one terse reply, the only communication he ever deigned to send me while alive, saying that the jewel was no longer in his possession. Soon after that he became reclusive. He spent his time writing his novels in hiding as if in fear for his life. He seemed impossible to get to.'

It was then that Lord Evershed pulled from his pocket the piece of paper he had taken from the writing desk on the veranda. 'Until six months ago. When the clumsy fellow finally slipped and fell from a great height. An even greater height than this one.' I looked at the water below what sparkled in the sun's rays. It was a long way down. 'He was walking alone along a cliff edge in Kent and a gust of wind must have taken him. At least that is what the coroner's report said.' Warrigal was not far from us now, leaning against the rail of the bridge, alert for any order.

'Shatillion left a will,' sniffed Evershed. 'And in this will were some written documents that he had left for his biographer, some autobiographical fragments. These fragments, which a faithful servant of mine managed to acquire from the biographer, were not meant for publication until after *my* death, would you believe? I have a copy of their contents here, sent to me by my man in London, and they reveal a great many secrets. Including who it was that gained possession of the Jakkapoor stone. Do you think you can guess who that person might be, Mr Dawkins? I'll give you a clue. The document describes him as a fence and a kidsman.'

'*Fagin?*' I asked in proper disbelief.

'Indeed he,' replied Evershed with some relish. My surprise must have been plain to see but I could no longer hide my interest. I was at a loss to imagine what the Jew's involvement could be in all this.

I could feel Warrigal drawing near, his fists clenching. Evershed's voice became a threat.

'Mr Fagin,' he said through stained teeth. 'The same Mr Fagin that you claim never to have heard of, Jack Dawkins, despite my private investigators identifying you as his only known associate currently imprisoned here in Australia.'

Warrigal now stood beside Evershed and the two of them had me pressed tight against the iron rail of the bridge. My terror was building fast as Evershed grabbed my shoulders with his hands and kept on talking.

'There is much more to this story than you can imagine, Mr Dawkins,' he said. 'It is even more fanciful than one of Shatillion's own fictions. There is a small wooden toy at the heart of things and an orphan child to whom it was given. But you shall never hear the rest of this tale if you continue to insist in this wrong-headed refusal to cooperate. Now, I shall ask you one more time . . .' He spoke slow and with menace. 'Have you . . . ever heard . . . of a man named Fagin?'

The sudden recollection came upon me of a time when the old Jew had presented me with a rattly old doll and told me to keep it safe. I looked at the two of them and considered how high we was up from the river below.

'Come to think of it, Your Lordship,' I said to him, 'that name is starting to sound a bit familiar.'

Chapter 9

Deals and Devils

In which my services are engaged

As we walked away from the bridge and back to the path there was so many conflicting emotions at work within me that it was hard even to concentrate on where I was stepping. My nerves was much shaken on account of having just been spared a long plummet to my death, but even this powerful sensation was nothing compared to the thrill at what I had just been told. The Jakkapoor stone, the priceless treasure what had inspired so much bloodshed and literature, had been placed inside a little wooden doll. A wooden doll what I was now certain had been given to me when I was only a kinchin.

'He must have stolen it,' I said, lit up with excitement. 'Fagin, I mean. He must have pinched it from Shatillion or somehow swindled him out of it.' I chuckled at the thought and did nothing to disguise my love for the man. 'My eyes, he's good. The best thief in all London.'

Lord Evershed, bastard that he was, must have known that Fagin was dead at this time. I now have no doubt that this information would have been found out by those private detectives what had tracked me down, as well as being mentioned in Shatillion's document. But I had shown Evershed my loyalty towards the Jew and, maybe because he knew that thoughts of reunion would spur me on or perhaps out of sheer cruelty, he chose not to share this fact with me. Instead, as we followed the path back to the stone house, he told me what Shatillion had written about Fagin and the story of how they had first met.

'George Shatillion was a young writer when he first encountered your Mr Fagin. He was writing his debut novel and was on the hunt for inspiration.'

'Like Ikey Slizzard!' I exclaimed. 'The villain from *Thimble and Pea*. You know, he always reminded me of Fagin. So that's why.'

'The Jew had tried to swindle Shatillion with a game of chance when they had met on a street corner and Shatillion, who was no fool either, had caught him out. But rather than report him, like an honest Englishman would have done, Shatillion instead insisted that Fagin take him on a tour of London's lowest haunts so he could get a taste of the underworld for his book. He would disguise himself on these outings to blend in among the criminal class, adopting the persona of an old Jew much like Fagin himself. This went on for many years, long after the book was published, and it seems as though Shatillion had become a little too accustomed to the delights of the gutter, often losing himself in gin-houses, brothels and gambling dens. He had a special weakness for playing cards and before long he found himself owing a substantial amount to some nefarious villains who Fagin had introduced him to. Shatillion was told that Fagin would cover the debt for him but that now there would be a terrible and very public reckoning if it was not paid. In the document Shatillion asserts the idea that Fagin had orchestrated this turn of events in order to place the novelist under his power. He refers to the Jew in very unflattering terms, calling him a "wicked trickster" and a "vile devil".'

As Evershed told me all this my heart swelled with affection. Of course Fagin had arranged all that. It was so like him.

'To worm his way out of this predicament,' Evershed went on, 'Shatillion hatched a scheme. He offered to pay Fagin off with the Jakkapoor stone.' At this part of the telling he began to growl again. 'This was soon after his abandonment of Louisa. He had left her with only that very jewel, the last thing she had to trade with. Louisa had hidden the Jakkapoor stone, what she often referred to as the black heart of India, inside a blue-coated wooden doll that resembled an Indian prince. But it was Shatillion whose heart was black and he stole the doll away from her and took it for his own.'

The stone house came into view and Evershed kept talking as we followed the path up to it. 'Oh yes,' he said, 'Shatillion's document is full of expressions of regret about the theft and he tries to justify his actions on superstitious grounds. It seems he hoped that the curse of the jewel would soon bring destruction down upon Mr Fagin. He had just finished writing *The Curse of the Jakkapoor Stone*, the book that so callously mocks my military triumph, and his head was full of how dangerous the jewel was and he claims he was protecting Louisa from its curse by taking it from her.'

A fat lot of good it did her, I wanted to say as we stepped back up towards the door of the house and Warrigal unlocked it. Evershed seemed to sense this thought and waited until we had entered a dark mahogany study what let in little sunshine before continuing.

'Shatillion did not understand the curse,' he remarked as we both took our seats in red leather chairs and Warrigal lit us some fat cigars from a wooden case. 'Its power is not over those who possess the jewel but over those who subsequently lose it. The curse is a punishment for letting the jewel go.'

I nodded as he came out with this, fixing my face to look as interested in it as possible. But inside I just wished he would get back to the business at hand as I cared nothing for silly curses. I only wanted to know about this doll.

'So Fagin accepted the jewel as payment,' I said, knowing that with his magpie's eye for real treasure he would have known at a glance that the stone was of a rare kind. 'And then what?'

'I was hoping that this part of the story you could explain to me, Mr Dawkins,' Evershed replied after his cigar had been lit. It seemed he did not want to smoke these on the veranda, although this would have been more natural. 'The Jew's behaviour becomes most unaccountable at this point, even to Shatillion. He writes that the jewel was left inside the wooden doll and given to a child – a child he described as his favourite. Now why on earth would a greedy old villain like him do a thing like that?'

Because he cared about me, I wanted to reply. Because I was his favourite and like a son to him. But this was something a love-less old fool like Evershed would never understand and so once Warrigal had lit my own cigar I just leaned back in the chair and winked at him.

'You've come to the right man, Your Lordship,' I said. 'I'll get that jewel back for you, don't fret yourself on that score.' Evershed leaned over to me, his eyebrows raised.

'Do you mean to tell me,' he asked, 'that you know where it is? That you were the child it was given to?' I puffed out the smoke and had a little cough before answering. I wished Warrigal would open a window.

'I don't like to say,' I replied at last, as I was concerned that if I told him where the jewel was he would just telegraph this servant of his back in London to fetch it and I would be cheated out of my liberty, 'but if you can see to that full pardon you spoke of earlier –' I shrugged – 'then I can guarantee satisfaction.'

Evershed nodded and stiffened in his chair. The room was becoming most smoky now and I knew that we was not outside because this was the most secret part so far. A bargain was being done what not even the birds could listen to.

'Very well,' he said without smiling. 'Then you will be freed from your penal servitude and engaged on an errand, Mr Dawkins.'

I took another puff on my own cigar and smiled. Things was going my way at last.

'You will return to London cast as a gentleman. I will provide you with everything required to make this seem plausible. Warrigal will accompany you, posing as a servant so that his appearance is not questioned either, and once the stone is retrieved you shall hand it to him to bring back to me. You will then be allowed to go back to your old life in London.'

With the cigar in my teeth I clapped my hands and let loose a cry of joy.

'That's very well, that is, Your Lordship!' I laughed. 'I like that very well indeed!' But Lord Evershed did not join me in celebration.

'But mark these words,' he said instead, and pointed the cigar what was held in his left hand at me. 'Do not think about failing me. If you have the jewel, as I suspect you do, then you will take it to be verified by my servant in Greenwich. If you should be so foolish as to try to run off with it, then Warrigal here will play sheepdog and return you to the pen.'

I looked to Warrigal, whose expression said nothing.

'If you are lying to me,' he continued, 'and there is no jewel, or you cannot find it, then there will be severe consequences. Warrigal knows this as much as anyone. You are very much his responsibility.' I could not tell from looking at him whether or not this was the first Warrigal was hearing of this.

'Warrigal has killed men at my command on previous occasions,' Evershed continued looking to Warrigal as he spoke. 'And furthermore, he knows that while he may be out of reach from me in London –' he took one last strong draw from the cigar – 'his people will not be.'

He then snuffed the rest of the cigar out into an ashtray.

'It is in both your interests that the jewel is found and returned. I'm a vengeful man, Mr Dawkins,' he said as he breathed out the last of the smoke. 'And nobody who has ever crossed me is currently living.'

An hour later Warrigal was sent over to Government House to get a signature and an official seal for my pardon. I had made the deal and was going home.

Part Two

Chapter 10

What the Prince was Smiling About

*In which the charms of London fail to impress
one foreign visitor*

Warrigal sneezed.

'Bless you,' I said, and handed him one of the many handker-chiefs I had pinched during my short time back in London. 'Only next time, be a good fellow and do that into this. We don't want your snot all over this fine upholstery, thank you very much.' We was racing through the London streets in as sleek and as sporty a cabriolet as I could whistle down from Smithfield Market, and I was enjoying the ride much more than he was. As we galloped through the city streets, past St Paul's and down to Monument, I remarked to Warrigal that this was exactly the sort of carriage I was going to buy once I'd stolen enough to pay for it. 'Either this or one of those tall phaetons,' I said, pointing at one coming the other direction over London Bridge. 'But custard-coloured with red stripes and a horse as lean as this one.' Warrigal just carried on emptying the contents of his nose into my fogle and said nothing. 'Get used to that,' I told him. 'It happens all the time here.'

Warrigal had begun complaining of the cold just after we had said goodbye to Ruby Solomon at Smithfield Market and was now turning as pale as someone of his complexion ever could. This did not surprise me, considering the chill of the city. Even I, a boy what had suffered through many a London winter growing up, was finding the weather a shock after six years in sunnier climes so what effect it was having on Warrigal I shuddered to think. 'Don't you worry,' I assured him. 'The moment we get to Greenwich we shall book ourselves a room in some cosy tavern and have ourselves a nice hot meal. And then we'll smash open our friend there,' I pointed to the doll still sticking his head out of Warrigal's coat pocket. 'He won't be smiling so much then.'

My failure to procure a metal saw off John Froggat or to pinch a cleaver from the market meant that the wooden prince was still in one piece. If the late Lady Evershed had somehow hidden the jewel inside then there must be a way of opening it but I could not fathom as to how. We had tried cracking him open with our hands, but the Indian wood was too just strong. We had also considered placing him in the street for a shire horse to step on but, fearful that this would damage the jewel within, we had decided to wait until we was safe inside.

We was under instructions to take the jewel to an address in Greenwich where this servant lived for him to inspect. The servant was called Timothy Pin, and once he was satisfied it was the real Jakkapoor stone he would message Evershed, let me go and send the jewel back to Australia with Warrigal. So both of us to was keen to make our way straight there. I was looking forward to this journey as I have always loved a good train terminal and London Bridge is one of the finest. It's loud, dirty and bustling with sleepy travellers from Kent who would not notice if their spectacles was removed from their noses, so distracted are they by the shock of the city. I could not wait to get among them and begin practising my old art again. However, as our driver reared up outside the station doors I saw something what challenged the romance of train travel. There, among all the many comings and goings of the station, I spied several of these blue-uniformed fellows in their hats striding about as if they owned the place, all eyes and suspicion. These new bobbies had become the scourge of London while I had been away and I was vexed with my fellow Londoners for allowing this to happen. I was old enough to recall the old Bow Street Runners, and although they was a joyless bunch of bleeders at least you knew where you was with them. They was just the fat, wheezy dogs to our nimble, clever cats and they would usually give up the chase if we made it hard work for them. But these peelers, like that bastard Bracken we had run into, they was taking it all far too serious. I watched two of them force some luckless prig through the doors of the station and then march him off in the direction of a police office. I would have to tread lightly, I told myself, if I was to get on in this faster, crueller London.

'We should avoid the train,' I said to Warrigal after we had inspected the inside of the station for a short time. 'It'll be crawling with more of these peelers looking for pickpockets and we don't want the attention. We'll get a riverboat to take us to Greenwich instead. You'll enjoy that,' I promised him. 'It's a lovely way to see London.'

But Warrigal did not enjoy the boat ride much. An evil wind whipped up the river and lashed our cheeks as we rowed and, while they helped to speed our journey along, these blasts did nothing to improve Warrigal's humour or his health. He coughed and spluttered and violent shivers began to run through him and, as we passed the Tower of London, he could not have been less interested as I told him about the ravens. Instead he just held on to the rudder lines and watched myself and the waterman do the rowing.

'Sorry about my valet, Gaffer,' I said to the strong-armed

waterman who was sat behind me and whose boat it was. 'Colonial servants are never much use on English soil, I tend to find.' He just huffed and carried on rowing these long strokes in time with mine. It was a long journey, considering the boat was carrying not just the three of us but also our heavy trunk, and it took us most of the afternoon. By the time we got to Greenwich darkness had begun to settle and Warrigal looked paler than I had ever seen him. As the waterman and I helped him out of the boat, I told Warrigal that I was sorry that I had made him take the riverboat now. If I had known, I said, just how sick the river would make him, then I would have suggested some other form of transport. But in truth I had guessed full well what a torment the river ride would be for him and I was glad to see that he had gone through five handkerchiefs on the way down. He looked ready to pass out, while my aching arms had grown good and strong with all the rowing. For the first time since I had met him I had the feeling I would be the favourite should the two of us come to blows.

I paid the waterman with more of Evershed's coins and we made our way to the nearby Trafalgar tavern and booked ourselves a room with supper and a warm bath included. The plan was to open the doll here, release the Jakkapoor stone within and knock on Timothy Pin's front door bright and early the next day. I asked the landlady if she could send up a hot meal as soon as possible and she said there was a table in our chamber already set for the guests. 'It's roast pigeon tonight,' she said as if she had just described some rare English delicacy rather than a bird common enough to be found on any rooftop in the rookeries.

'This pigeon,' I asked her, 'is it tough?'

'We serve the tenderest pigeons in London, sir,' she answered.

'Pity,' I said. 'Cos I like my meat good and chewy.'

This landlady, who was not much older than myself but carried herself like she was someone's mother, was nothing if not hospitable. 'Well, for a few shillings more I could get some of our beef sent up instead, sir.'

'Is that tough?'

'As old boots,' she replied. 'You won't be disappointed.'

'I like the sound of that,' I said, and reached for my purse. 'We'll need a proper carving knife as well then –' I counted out a generous amount for her – 'with teeth like a crocodile's.'

'We have such a knife in our kitchen,' she said as she took the coins and jingled them in her hand. 'We'll be up with your supper shortly, gentlemen.'

The chamber we had booked into would have been very pleasant had Warrigal and I been a pair of fresh honeymooners rather than two rough coves who hated one another. It was decorated in the French style, like one of those rooms in the molly-house what Precious Tom used to run and where some of the softer lads would go to work. It was all crimson drapes and gilded walls, with a copper-leafed bathtub and silver candelabra laid out on the small round dining table with all this fine crockery. There was a large double bed with a pink blanket and pillows and a queer uphol-stered red chair what was curved at the top and long enough to lie on.

'That there is a *chaise longue*,' said the maidservant, pleased with her own mastery of language. 'Or fainting chair if you prefer. Your servant should find it most comfortable. There are blankets for him in the cupboard.' She curtsied and left us, and the very second the door shut behind her Warrigal and I went to business. He pulled the prince out of his coat pocket and we rushed over to the foot of the bed where we had placed the trunk and flung it open. I found the hammer and chisel what we prised up the floorboard with the night before resting on top of everything else. I told him that we could use these to smash open the doll if the carving knife I had ordered should turn out to be of no use. Warrigal, whose brow was dripping with sweat, pushed me aside and began throwing our clothes and other possessions all over the floor.

'If you're expecting me to clean all this up, Warrigal,' I said as he emptied the trunk of everything in it, 'you is much mistaken.' But he just reached into the bottom of the trunk and started pressing down at the sides. Then, much to my surprise, I watched as he pulled up the wooden base and revealed a false bottom to the trunk. There, lying flat at the base, was a long sharp knife, a coil of metal wire and, of all things, a boomerang.

The sudden appearance of this secret blade, what gleamed as though it had never been used, was most unsettling. It was no Australian bush knife, what would have been good for cutting through wood, and nor could I imagine any butcher using it to carve through fleshy meat. So thin and sharp was it that the only job I could imagine it to be fit for was the kill stroke. It had been packed for me, not the prince, and I froze as Warrigal pulled it out and pointed it at me. 'You hold,' Warrigal said as he got to his feet and walked over to the small table, 'and I cut.' He placed the doll half over the edge with its face looking downwards like it was a French aristocrat waiting for the chop. Then he sneezed again.

'You want to cut the doll open with *that*?' I asked.

Warrigal wiped his face with his sleeve and nodded. 'Come hold,' he said.

'I'll hold the knife,' I told him. 'You hold the doll.'

Warrigal swore at me and coughed. Then he just started cutting into it himself, one hand on the doll, the other slicing back and forth with the knife. He made it look like a right struggle and the wood kept slipping from his hand and he almost cut himself on the blade. Then another attack of sneezes took him and he staggered back from the table and almost dropped the knife, so violent was these explosions.

'Warrigal, you're acting like a mad person,' I said. 'She'll be up in a minute with a proper carving knife and then I'll do it. You ain't well.' He ignored me and walked the doll over to the window what overlooked the Thames, the knife still clutched in his other hand. He unlocked the catch and lifted it half up and a wicked chill blew in causing him more misery. He's about to throw himself out into the river, I thought for one horrible moment. But then he placed the doll on the windowsill and tried dropping the window down on to it. The window was too stiff however and again he nearly dropped it. 'You've got a fever,' I said. 'The best thing for you to do is get under them covers until supper comes up.'

He turned to me, his eyes watery from the sneezing, and looked as though he wanted to argue. But instead he just sucked in his teeth, walked over to where he'd hung his coat, pulled another hankie from out of the pocket and blew his nose loud. 'Stupid country,' he said when finished.

Soon after he was lying underneath the pink goose-feathered blanket and I was sat on the fainting chair watching him sleep. The doll was propped up on the bedside chest next to him and beside that was that deadly knife. The more I contemplated the nasty thing the more fearful I became. I had always feared that Warrigal would carry out Evershed's orders to kill me if he had to, but it was most disturbing to see the implement what he was most likely to use. He and I had been travelling companions for many months now and I had been stupid enough to hope that perhaps he had grown fond of me in that time. That perhaps, when our business with Evershed was done, he may even look upon me as a pal.

But he was an assassin, nothing more, and I was a fool to think he would even pause to run me through should he need to. I knew that in his weakened state it would be well within my interest to snatch that knife from him as well as to reclaim the doll. I reached down to my bluchers, unlaced them and slipped my feet out, as soundless and as slow as I could. There was some sort of celebration going on in the room below ours; a fiddle was playing and there was clapping, laughter and stamping about, and I hoped that this would cover any creaking floorboards I might step on as I began to move towards the foot of the bed, cautious as a cat. Once there I whispered his name to be certain he was asleep.

He did not stir.

I moved to the chest, quicker now in case he was just feigning sleep to trap me, and I laid my two hands on both knife and doll. Then, in less than an eye-blink, I was back on the other side of the room.

Just then there was a knock and someone called to say that supper was ready. I looked to Warrigal, but he did not seem to wake even for this. I walked over and let in two servants what was carrying hot plates of beef on a chafing dish, a bottle of red wine and, on a little silver tray with some other cutlery, a knife so perfect for cutting through a wooden doll I could have imagined a blacksmith fashioning it especially for that purpose. They began setting it all down upon the table and I asked them to be as quiet as they could on account of my ailing valet. If they thought there was anything peculiar about a servant asleep in the master's bed they did not show it and instead began apologising about the noise from downstairs.

'A wedding party, sir,' said one of the servants before he left. 'They could carry on for hours like that, I'm sorry to say. I'm amazed your valet can sleep through it.'

'Well, he comes from a very noisy place,' I said, and shut the door behind them. Once alone I tiptoed back over to Warrigal, saw that he was still snoring all gentle and then crept back to the table. The plates of beef, boiled potatoes and greens looked delicious, as did the little jug of gravy what sat between them, but I had business to attend to before I could tuck in. I cleared some room on the table, placed the doll back over the edge and began sawing through it, slow and steady. Behind me I could hear Warrigal give a little cough and I turned to see him roll over on to his side facing the window. Once I was sure he was still not awake I turned back to the doll and continued to work upon it. The prince's face was smiling up at me as I cut just above his chest, and I made sure that the stone what rattled inside was safe down by his belly. It took some effort to saw even halfway through and I thought that this was why Fagin had chosen it to contain something so valuable. I could feel my blood getting warmer with excitement as the knife continued its journey through my childhood toy. Even though I could have had no clue as to how priceless it was when I had been given it that Christmas I still valued it enough to hide it under that floorboard and keep it safe. My eyes began to prick as I sawed on and thought about kind old Mr Fagin and how much he loved me. If only he was alive today, I thought as I was almost far enough through to just crack the rest with my hands, so that he could see what freedom his gift had bought me. *He had left it to me*, I thought as I put the knife down, *his favourite*, I took the helpless prince's head in my hands, *in the hope that it would one day make me a gentleman*, I cracked the head back in one strong movement, *but could he ever have guessed that one day it would buy me my liberty?* The head came clean away and I lifted the bottom part of the doll up over the table as if raising a toast to the wonderful gent. 'Here's to you, Fagin,' I said aloud. 'I don't care what others may say, you was always a diamond to me.' And with that I tipped the contents of the doll on to the white-sheeted table below.

Something fell out and then bounced into the gravy boat. I stuck my hand straight in after it and felt around. It was smaller than I had imagined. I pulled it out and wiped it clean with a serviette and looked at it resting in the palm of my hand.

It was not black. It was not a jewel. It was just a common pebble what you might find in any street in the world.

'That dirty old Jew!' I cursed aloud. 'That rotten, double-crossing, stinking old bastard!' I hurled the pebble across the room and it bounced off the walls and landed inside the bathtub. 'I'm glad they killed him!'

I sunk on to the chair and dropped my head into my hands. I was angry, betrayed, heartbroken to discover that the gift was worthless after all. I had been so sure when I had heard that Fagin had left the jewel to a young child that this could mean nobody other than myself. Who else could it be? And where had he hidden the jewel if not inside this doll? I had no one to ask, now that he was no longer alive.

But the thing what troubled me most of all was my terror at the thought of what I was going to do now. Evershed would want me dead. I could hardly go to this Timothy Pin and tell him that I was very sorry but I had been mistaken. There would be consequences. I should run for it now while I still could.

I started to slow my breathing and wondered if this was wise. There was a chance, I reasoned, that Evershed would be more understanding than I was giving him credit for. Perhaps all his talk of severe consequences was just bluff. He might even thank me for my efforts and tell Warrigal to just bring me back to Australia where we would hear no more about it. Perhaps I was worrying over nothing.

I was interrupted in my wonderings by the sudden awareness of something being placed over my head from behind me. Some hands passed my ears and it was as though a bag had covered me although no bag was there.

'Warrigal?' I said, and went to turn around to the bed. But my throat suddenly caught on fire and I was yanked out of my seat and pulled back in a strong, violent motion. I could feel him behind me, pulling me close, and the pain in my throat got tighter than ever and I grasped up to it and tried to call out but no sound came. Then I realised that I could not breathe. My fingers reached my neck and there I felt the metal wire being pulled tighter and tighter. I kicked out but my legs gave way under me as he forced me to the ground, his knee hard in my back, pushing in as the wire pulled out.

So it's a garrotting, is it? I thought as the wire cut into my skin and my whole body began to shake from lack of air. *God help me. I think I would have preferred the knife after all.*

Chapter 11

Greenwich Mean Time

*Warrigal and I enjoy a frank and forthright
exchange of views*

I think, on reflection, that it was not being able to talk what made being garrotted seem such a horror. My typical response in any situation where a cove tries to attack me was always to try to reason with the mad fool, to make them see sense. Leave it out, Warrigal, I wanted to say, as I felt his two arms behind my neck tighten into a vice and pull the wire tight. This is all a bit unnecessary, don't you think? But, as I tried to give it voice, my mouth just made a low wheeze.

So terror took grip and my whole body shuddered throughout. My heart began hammering, I could feel my eyes ready to pop and my limbs started this wild thrashing. I tried to kick the small dining table over, in the hope that the clatter would distract him enough for me to throw him off, but it was just out of reach. My hands had been pulling at the wire to try to get some air but, as I tugged it away from my neck, I felt the crushing worsen. He had double-looped it, the vicious sod, and I was making one wire the tighter by trying to free the other.

My arms made a grab for his ears. But his knee was pushing into my back so hard I could not reach. One thing was clear: he had done this many times before. I was overcome with fear and could see no way of besting him. I was done for.

And then he sneezed again. His face was so close behind my head that it felt, to my trembling self, as though there had been an explosion in my earhole. But for a second his grip was loosened, his knee removed, and that second was all what was needed. I had the fingers of one hand under both loops and I tugged them from my neck as with the other arm I reached behind and grabbed him by the ear. Then, with arms strong from the afternoon's rowing, I hauled his sickly body over my shoulders and he landed, with an almighty bang, on the floorboards in front of me.

I staggered away from him, freed my neck from the looping wire, and in I breathed. My throat was in agony and I cried out for water. All the sound what came out however was a long, terrible rasp. But there was no time to recover as, cat-like, Warrigal was back on his feet and glaring at me in rage. Then his eyes darted to the fainting couch, my eyes followed and all four rested upon what lay there. That evil knife of his, what stretched out along the upholstery like an idle duchess just waiting to be taken.

We both sprang for it and clashed into each other as we did so, landing on the curved end of the chaise longue. Warrigal had hold of the knife handle but I had my arms over his and we struggled there on the raised side of the furniture until the lower end left the ground and the whole thing toppled back, sending both of us tumbling down hard on to the floor. The thump of the wooden boards was good and loud but, on account of the revelry going on in the room beneath, it went unheard as Warrigal and I rolled around on the big rug, locked in battle. Finally he managed to free himself and kick me away but I was on my knees faster and over to the dining table, where I grabbed the carving knife what had cut open the doll. Then, with him one side of the round table and me on the other, we stood there eyeing each other, both armed with blades and ready to move quick if the other did. His knife was longer and more deadly but mine could be vicious if he let me close enough. It was, as your chess players might say, stalemate, and at last I could try to talk to him.

'Behave yerself, Warrigal,' I said in a thin voice what was drowned out by the din below. 'I can find . . .' *cough* '. . . find stone. Kill me . . .' *cough, cough, cough.* On the table in front of me was a small glass of water. I raised my finger in the air. ''Ang on a bit.' With one hand still pointing my knife at him, I used the other to pick up the glass. Warrigal just watched me drink it back as if waiting to hear what I had to say. I hoped his blood was starting to cool, but his face was still hate-filled. Once I had drained the water I put the glass back on the table and felt a good deal better.

'Right,' I said, my breaths coming in and out much stronger. 'Where was I? Yeah. I told Evershed I would find the stone before Christmas. That still gives me four weeks. What we'll do now, you and me, is—'

'What we do now,' he hissed, his nostrils flaring, 'is I kill you.'

He moved around the table to get at me and I moved the other way. Then I changed direction as he did and we danced like this for a few seconds.

'Whoa, yourself,' I shouted, brandishing my own weapon at him. 'If you catch me we'll go down together. Mine ain't as sharp as yours but it'll do some proper damage. Think like an Englishman, Warrigal, and just let me go. You can tell Pin I gave you the slip.'

'You die,' he spat, 'or my people die. Like that.'

'Your people?' I asked, unsure of what he meant. 'What have they got to do wi—'

'My people on Honey Ant Hill!' he shouted then as though I had not been paying attention. 'Evershed says, if no jewel then *consequences!*' This last word sounded unnatural in his mouth. I then recalled what Evershed had said about Warrigal's people being within his reach and I knew that Warrigal thought that Evershed would carry out his threat against them should the jewel not be delivered. He must have felt that murdering me was his only way of stopping this and so it was either my life or that of his family. In his heated state I could see his eyes getting watery and I started to understand that this was not anger I was looking at. It was fear.

'Warrigal.' I spoke as if he was making a fool of himself. 'They'll be all right. I know coves like Evershed of old. They're all talk. He ain't gonna—'

'Massacres!' he shouted at me. 'Done it before.'

I knew from the natives on Abel's Farm that massacres against the aboriginals was not unheard of, but I could not believe that Lord Evershed would organise such an attack. However it was clear that Warrigal did and I could think of nothing else to calm him with than an apology. I held out one hand in a gesture of peace but kept the other one gripped fast around the knife.

'I'm sorry, Warrigal,' I said. 'I really thought the jewel was in that doll and that is the truth with no lie. But if it ain't there, then, you got to believe me, I can find it.' I was thinking aloud as I spoke, going over the possibilities. 'Shatillion wrote that Fagin gave the jewel to a child, his favourite. There weren't that many of us. If it ain't me, there are only two other possible boys that he could have meant. We'll find them together and get the jewel. It's the clever thing to do. Much cleverer than killing me.'

Warrigal was listening now and I could feel the violence lifting away from him. I began lowering my knife-hand in a show of trust. There was a silent moment while he thought about this and so I decided to press my luck.

'Why should the likes of Evershed set you and me against each other like we was two rats in a pit to be bet on? Convicts and natives have more in common with each other than we do with him. If we're going to survive his wicked game then we need to work together.'

I could see I was starting to get through to him. He became stiller, his breathing softened but he still held that knife as though ready for business.

'If you kill me,' I went on, 'and come home empty-handed then what is to say he won't carry out his threat anyway. A high-born man like him expects satisfaction and my head on a plate won't be enough.' I placed my own weapon down on the table now, but with my hand still on it in case he pounced. 'Better to help me find the real stone instead. It's the best chance we got of saving your people from getting slaughtered and, be sensible, you ain't gonna find it without me.'

He looked to my hand and, still slow, I removed it from the handle of the knife. Then he looked to the long blade he held in his own. If he made a move now I would be helpless against him, but I had a feeling the storm what raged inside him was passing. He looked back to me as I stroked my stinging neck.

'Put the knife down and let's work this out. We've come too far, you and me, to have it end like this. And, you know, killing me won't help matters.'

There was a pause and he eyed me hard. At last he nodded. A small but clear nod and he twisted his hand so the knife pointed away from me before he too placed it on his side of the table.

'Before Christmas,' he said at last.

I nodded back. 'That's it. Yeah. We'll have it by then. No need for—'

Then, with one swift kick, I sent the entire dining table crashing towards him. The food, crockery and stabbing implements was all scattered across the floor and Warrigal stood surprised. My hands was on the back of the small wooden chair and I charged with it towards him, meaning to smash it into the side of his face, but he, with sudden quickness, darted away in time. The chair leg swung past him, missing his head by a hair, and I tried to swing it back again to catch him the other way. Only this time the weight of the chair was against me and Warrigal caught it with his hand. We wrestled over it in the centre of the room, with the rug getting bunched underneath us, before one of us must have hurled it away to the other side of the room. I saw it land straight into the fireplace and by the time my head turned back to Warrigal his clenched fist connected with my right cheek. I staggered back as his other fist hit into my left and I almost tripped on the rug. I do not know if Warrigal had ever been inside a boxing ring in his life but this two-punch assault suggested that he would have been good at it.

However, I had always fancied myself as an amateur pugilist myself and so the sharp, strong uppercut what struck into Warrigal's chin probably came as a shock to him. My knuckles stung as they connected, telling me that they must have done him some harm, and as the rug shifted beneath his feet I seized my advantage, grabbed him by his nightshirt and charged with him over to the corner of the room where the bath screen was. The screen, one of them thin zigzag pieces of work what is meant to hide a lady's modesty, was made out of this light wood and it offered no resistance as I pushed Warrigal into it. It collapsed around him as he fell to the floor and I lost no time in finding something to hit him with while he was down.

Beside the fireplace was these three tin buckets of water what we was meant to heat over the grate before bath time. I decided that one of these would be ideal for striking a cove with until he could not get up but first they needed emptying. So I got hold of the biggest one, stood over my fallen opponent and tipped the contents all over him. He wriggled on to his back as the water splashed upon him and he looked so sad and soggy that I decided that I did not have the stomach to beat him with the bucket after all. I decided instead to just leave him, wet and hopeless, as I made my sharp exit. There had been enough violence for one night, I told myself. I would be merciful in victory.

Then he kicked me between the legs. The pain was like no other and I doubled over, the bucket dropped and I fell on to my side. 'You rat!' I said to him, my voice an unmanly squeak. 'That weren't sporting.' I could hear him getting to his feet and so in an instant began struggling to mine in spite of the agony. But Warrigal was up before me and I steeled myself for a hefty killing blow. It did not come and instead I watched as he walked, dripping water all across the floor, over to the door at the other end of the chamber. The key was in the hole, and he turned it and took the key out. There was no escape for me that way.

He walked over to the overturned fainting chair and lifted it back on to its feet. 'Sit,' he said, and stepped away from it. 'We talk.'

I stood to my full height, not easy considering the bruise to my bollocks, and told him it was about blooming time.

'That's what I been telling you!' I said to him, as though the part where I had tried to smash his head open with a chair had never happened. 'A good chat solves everything. Not fisticuffs.'

'Sit,' he said again.

I did not want to as I was certain it was a trick and he would run me through with his knife as soon as I was comfy. That blade was still on the floor, the same distance from each of us, but Warrigal no longer seemed aware of it.

From the room underneath ours there was still the tremendous noise of the wedding revelry. A piano was playing, as was competing fiddles, dancers stamped about, drunks was singing as loud as they could. The racket Warrigal and myself had made would have gone unheard by everyone around and the sound from below set a queer background noise for our tense scene above.

I rubbed my neck and felt the deep raw cut left by his wire. I saw the garrotte curled on the rug amid the smashed crockery and next to it the severed top of the wooden prince.

'You near took my head off with that thing,' I complained. Warrigal said nothing. He had moved over to the far wall and his arms was crossed. 'I dare say I've got a nasty mark now thanks to you.' Warrigal nodded. There was a looking glass above the fireplace and I stepped towards it, careful not to turn my back upon him. I lifted up my chin and saw a long streak of red circling my neck. It looked even worse than it hurt. 'Ouch. That'll never heal. I shall have to start wearing a thick neckerchief now, you rotten abo.'

Warrigal mumbled something I did not catch. I asked him to say it again. Then he ran a finger across his neck.

'Red tomorrow,' he said. 'Sorry.'

This was a surprise. He had never said anything of that sort before. His eyes was still watery from all the sneezing but I looked into them to see if he was lying. I had known him long enough to know that he was no kind of actor. He could not even play my valet without giving off an air that I worked for him. In truth, I thought as I searched his face and saw some regret looking back at me, I had never seen him lie before. He was artless in that way.

'So you should be,' I answered, my voice still wheezy from the attack. 'Disgraceful behaviour, coming up from behind me like that.'

His chin raised and the hardness was back. 'Two boys?' he demanded. 'Who?'

To have sat in that long, low chair would have placed me at his mercy and so, to show him that I was ready to talk but also to keep my distance, I instead crossed over to the bed and sat at the end of it. He then moved round to the chair and we began to discuss our problem like two sensible fellows.

'There was a lad called Eddie Inderwick,' I told him. 'Steady Eddie, we called him. He was older than me and had moved out before I went to live with the old man, but he would come and visit often. Fagin used to hold him up as an example to the rest of us; it would make me good and jealous listening to these praises. We'll track down this Eddie and see if he has what we need.'

'And?'

'The other boy is my best pal, Charley Bates. He was the only other what I could recall Fagin liked as much as me, on account of how jolly he always was. He was a delight of a boy was Charley and I could see him being Fagin's favourite because he was my favourite too.'

'If not?'

'If it's not with either of them then he could have hidden it anywhere, but I know his old haunts and I've more chance of finding it than anyone. I know how Fagin thought.'

Warrigal pointed his chin towards the pebble on the floor and tutted.

'All right, I admit that was a bit of a poor surprise,' I said, and shook my head. 'It seems my confidence in being Fagin's favourite was ill-judged. Never mind.' I got to my feet and paced around the bed. I might have allowed myself to get good and gloomy thinking on this disappointment. I was his favourite, his top-sawyer, he had told me often enough. So how could he have given the jewel to another?

But I did not dwell on this for long. I have never seen where the profit is in self pity and I had no use for it now. Instead I started telling Warrigal what our next move would be.

'First thing tomorrow,' I said as I began to pull back the big quilt what he had been lying under earlier, 'we head back into town.' Warrigal shivered. He was still ill from this afternoon's river trip and looked unwilling to repeat the experience. 'Only this time we shall take the train.' I began fluffing the pillows, making it clear to him that it was my turn to crawl into the big bed. It was only fair, I felt, considering he had just near choked the life out of me. 'And we shall go straight to see Jem.'

'Jem?'

'Ruby's fella, my oldest pal. Or leastways he was once. One of them. Ruby said him and her now live in Bill and Nancy's old crib and I know the very place.'

'Where?'

'I'll take you there tomorrow. We shall head off after we have given this place a good clean.' The table was still overturned, our dinner on the floor. 'We can't leave it looking like this. We're not animals.'

I went over to the small wardrobe and pulled out the bedding and walked it over to him. As I drew near I felt him stiffen as though readying himself for another sly strike but I placed the bedding at the end of that long settee and told him that he should find it comfortable. My boots was under the chair. I longed to reach for them but dared not to.

'You can have that beef if you don't mind eating off the floor.' I yawned and began reaching for my nightclothes. 'But I for one am getting an early night. Much to do tomorrow. Much to do.'

★　★　★

But of course I did not sleep. The noise from the wedding celebrations below still thumped up through the floorboards with no signs of abating and I just lay there and thought. Soon after I had rested my head, Warrigal walked about the chamber pinching out the candles and I peeped through my covers and watched his dark shape bed down upon the chair. His sneezing and coughing had been replaced by a quiet sniffle but his breathing was still heavy. I watched the blankets what covered him rise and sink, rise and sink, and after a time I thought I heard snoring. It was hard to make out anything above the downstairs din but the more I listened the more confident I became. I then rolled over away from him and looked to the large window what overlooked the Thames. It was now, I reasoned, while the sounds of carousing would still cover any noise made, that I would have to make my escape.

I may have convinced Warrigal that he needed my assistance to track down the Jakkapoor stone but I could not think of any good reason as to why I should keep him – a fellow who was under orders to kill me and had just proven that he was ready to do so at the drop of a stone – around me. I knew where Jem and Ruby dwelt and he did not and that was to my advantage. They was the only people whose address in London I did know, so it made sense for me to head there without him. I would just leave him here in Greenwich and he would have to explain things to Timothy Pin without me as I hunted for the jewel alone. Because there was a strong chance that neither Eddie nor Charley had the Jakkapoor stone either and if that proved to be so then I needed to do a disappearing act before Warrigal or anyone else working for Evershed could get to me. Perhaps the lives of the people at Honey Ant Hill was in jeopardy but that was not my problem. I had my own neck to consider.

Warrigal lay next to my hat, boots and coat and I did not have the courage to try to snatch them back before leaving. He still had the key of the door about him so I could not have exited that way either. However, I had noticed that the window was still unlatched from where he had opened it earlier and it was close enough to my bed for me to slip out without him noticing. I moved under the bed covers, like a snake under sand, and poked my head out of the lower part of the bed. I was an arm's reach from the window and I lowered myself to the floor as soundless as I could. I turned my head back to Warrigal to make sure he was still sleeping. I could see, from under the far side of the four-poster bed, that there was no movement, so I dared to lift the window enough to make a large enough opening for me to squeeze out through. There was a squeak as I did so and I snapped my head back to Warrigal. He did not stir. I lifted the window up a few more inches and my knuckles, raw from the punching, felt the sharp air of the late November night sting them in a warning not to proceed. I chose to ignore it. It was a choice between facing the outside chill hatless, shoeless and wearing nightclothes, or staying here with a murderer. I wasted no time and pulled my body through the thin gap and out into the night. Once I was out on the veranda I shut the window behind me and every bone within me rattled with the cold. I looked about me and wondered what to do now.

The night was moist and foggy and I could not see below me to where the Thames ended and the bank began. From this height I could not even make out if a boat was moored below or if I would jump into the black river. Before I had crawled outside I had been thinking how easy it would be to plunge in and then swim to one of the nearby boats, row it to a causeway and climb the stone steps back up to the bank. I now saw the foolishness of this scheme as I was sure to freeze and be swept under by the current. However, to the left of the veranda was a long flagpole what waved the Union Jack above the roof and I looked down to see to where it led. Underneath our veranda was another wider one what led out from where the dancing and music was coming from and I would be able to climb down this flagpole and on to that. I leaned over and saw the many flickering lights shining out from the three tall windows underneath that lit up most of the veranda. But the outside areas in between the windows and at the far sides was cast in deep shade and would be easy to hide in. The pole led straight down into one dark corner and so I grabbed hold of it, threw my legs over the side of the balcony and began shimmying my way down.

It was a fair distance down to the lower floor but I have always been a nimble boy, and with vicious winds whipping me downwards, I soon lowered myself on to the platform below. But, just as my feet touched the floor, I noticed something I had not seen from the balcony above. There was two people already on this veranda before me, both hidden in the dark far corner and trying to be as quiet as I. It was a young man and woman and they was having at each other with much vigour. Neither of them noticed me drop down on to the other side, so consumed was they by each other's passions, and I could tell by the silent murmurs and secret gropes that these was not our innocent newlyweds. The man, a gentleman it seemed, had his hands already under the lady's dress and his own breeches was down by his ankles which, considering how cold it was, made me want to salute the determined cove. It was clear that they had sneaked outside so that he could be the ruin of her and they had been most helpful and left the glass door nice and ajar. I peered inside to where the merriment was carrying on and saw that this was some sort of large dance hall where many happy couples was bouncing around, clapping and spilling glasses of wine about as they did so. Drunken ladies was slipping over on to their backs and gentleman was roaring with laughter as they locked arms with one dancing partner, spun her around, released her and grabbed another. They was all dizzy and distracted and so I slipped straight in, stepped past a fiddler and made my way over to the door.

'Not so fast, young gentleman,' called a female voice most severe and I turned to see a plump woman in an orange dress approach and grab me by the arm. Then she pulled me on to the dance-floor, cried, 'Here's another one trying to go abed!' and spun me about as all the other revellers clapped and cheered. Then she let me go, to lock arms with another man, and I found myself dancing with a second even plumper lady. Nobody seemed to question who I was or where I had sprung from but almost every lady in the place seemed most insistent that I take my turn on the floor with her. I made matters worse by being as good at dancing as I am at everything else and so was unable to get away as fast as I wanted to. But after having hopped and spun with every girl, and some of the gents, I reached the door and bid them all goodnight.

Out in the darkened corridor I saw two staircases, one leading up to where Warrigal lay and one leading downwards to the bar. I raced down this and stepped through the empty tavern where a few drunken wedding guests was chatting and drinking. There was a coat-rack close to the door and as I passed it I picked off the thickest one I could find and a matching green hat from off a peg. I dashed outside on to the cobbled streets, not even looking behind me to see if the owner of the coat or an angry aborigine was about to come charging after. I just began hopping off fast down the lane barefoot, away from my sleeping assassin. I was not even out of the tavern's tall shadow before my bare feet was aching and I cursed myself for not daring to take those boots before I left.

Chapter 12

Cuts and Bruises

In which I find myself poorer than a beggar

It took me over an hour but I at last found the vagrant I had been looking for. He was lain out in an alley stinking of vermin somewhere near Deptford, asleep in a doorway, his boots the only things of him what could be spied from the road. As my own sore feet tiptoed towards him I peered into the dark for any other unseen coves what might alert him to my approach but saw only a black cat peering at me from the shadows. I had passed this particular beggar a couple of times and had tried to look as inconspicuous as a man with no shoes ever can when hopping his way down an unpaved alley. Beside him lay an empty bottle of gin what seemed to have sent him into a deep slumber. He did not stir, even in spite of the heavy dripping from the ledge above, and I felt very certain that he would not waken as I began to untie his laces. Once the first boot was unlaced enough I pulled it off as gentle his mother may have many years before, careful not to disturb his sleeping.

I had boasted to John Froggat just the night before this that I never stole from those what was poorer than myself. I still prided myself that this was a truth, even though here I was removing the boots off a beggar and with no thought of paying him even a brass farthing in exchange. But it could be argued that this here beggar was indeed a richer man than I, with his thick-soled boots and his bellyful of liquor, so I chose not to question myself on it. In making the hard decision to slip out of a window and distance myself from a murderer I had also given up all the trappings of wealth what Evershed had supplied me with and now had no home, no money and nothing in the way of practical footwear. So the sight of this mendicant poking his old dirty farmer's boots out into my path struck me as a vulgar display of his own affluence and one which I could not let pass.

The second boot came off as quiet as the first and I dashed off quick before the cold night air informed the holes in his socks about the loss. Once I had run to the end of a flagstone path, and was certain that I could not be grabbed for the crime, I crouched down and put them on. They was made for a man with feet twice the size of mine and, with the large pea-green coat swiped from the tavern and the matching hat too big for my own head, I felt quite the clown. But the undersides of my feet had begun bleeding from small cuts caused by all the jagged, bottle-smashed lanes I had been walking down and the night was so cold that I did not find myself fretting too much about these concerns of fashion. Instead I carried on travelling further into London because, as has often been the way with me, I could not imagine in what other direction I should be headed.

Even with these much-needed boots on it was still a long and sorry night. I found myself drawn towards a great fire down by the riverside where many other homeless, miserable wretches was warming themselves while people from the City Mission served out soup and read from scriptures. One such missionary handed me a hot bowl and talked to me about Christ the Saviour as I slurped from it. Then, after I had licked the bowl clean, he asked if I could read and, on hearing that I could, he offered me a way of making some money. He wanted me to go among the large crowd of men and women reading aloud from a religious tract he gave me what was full of all the Bible's best bits. This I did, and spent the next two hours spreading the good word of the Lord among the lowliest creatures in the capital. I found that I was a natural preacher and was soon beginning to wonder if I could make a go of it as a clergyman if only such a comfortable position would present itself. For certain these vagrants seemed to be most captivated by my talk of the Lord's forgiveness and of redemption, salvation and the like. I soon amassed a tidy group of followers what was just as keen to hear my readings as those convicts was in Australia when I had read them extracts from Shatillion's books.

There was a young girl present at this dreary scene with whom I fell into a long conversation. She was younger than me but it was clear that her flower had already faded and it saddened me to think how poverty and vice had got hold of her like a disease. She had grown up among the fishermen of Great Yarmouth but had found herself seduced by some handsome rake who had then discarded her like a rag doll. Too ashamed to return home to the honest fisherman she had abandoned for a life of sin, she now haunted the streets and brothels of London cursing the very name of the man who had ruined her. If only she had given her heart more wisely, she said, to someone good such as myself, then she never would have ended up in this dreadful place. I told her that Christ forgave her and headed back to the missionary to claim the shillings I was owed.

These earnings was enough to pay for a ride to Whitechapel, and as the missionary counted out the coins I asked if he knew of a cab office what would be open at this early hour. He pointed me in the direction of a nearby dockyard and wished me luck in my journey. Before I left he asked if I myself had been moved by any of the scriptures I had been reading from. 'Oh yeah,' I said to keep him happy. 'I'm a changed man.' He smiled then and I went to leave him but, before I had taken even three steps, I felt a sudden need to turn back and tell him something.

'Look here,' I said as I checked both ways to make sure no one could overhear me. 'I've been hearing about some old soul lying drunk in an alley off the Creek Road. He's got no shoes on, the poor sod, because some little horror stole them from him while he slept.'

The missionary looked good and shocked by this. 'Are there no depths,' he asked me, 'to which the wicked will not sink?'

'Well, that's what I thought,' I said, 'so if any of you City Mission lot are heading in that direction then perhaps you can keep an eye out for him.'

The missionary promised that he would and so I shook his hand and walked off towards the cab office. The few hours that I had spent resting in that place had been good for my cut feet, which was already starting to hurt less.

It was the small hours of the morning by the time I got to the tangle of streets in Bethnal Green what I remembered Bill occupying like a dirty great spider. Ruby lived here now with Jem White and I came here tonight because Warrigal would have no clue to the address. The sleet was battering down as I worked my way into the centre of this run-down vicinity, trying to remember the quickest cut to his old crib. The first time I had ever met Bill Sikes was when Fagin had led me down this very maze back when I was small. He had presented me to the burglar as 'the perfect boy for an outing', meaning that I was small enough to crawl through any hole he had cut into the side of a house and also smart enough to know what to do once through it. Bill took me on many night-time expeditions and he often had me climbing up guttering to squeeze into an attic window or would force me through a removed door panel before knowing if there was any dogs on patrol inside. Even after I had grown too big for such tasks I would still be sent to this address to deliver secret messages or to fetch the booty whenever the Jew wanted to keep his own head down.

I found the dark, single-lamped street down which the two ill-fated lovers once dwelt and I hurt at the memory of how Nancy was no more. She had been a kind woman and I could not help but link Nancy and Ruby together in my mind now as I walked down the old lane to their dwelling. As much as I was keen to be reunited with my old pal Jem again, it was with little thought of him that I had travelled all the way here from Greenwich.

However, once I had arrived at Ruby's front door I became shy about knocking upon it with my fight-grazed fist. Just yesterday she had seen me in all my proud affluent glory, tailored and spangled like a gentleman with my very own servant and a hat what was firm and upright. She was sure to have told Jem all about how prosperous I had become and it was a sweet cream to imagine how this must have sickened my dear old pal. But, less than a day later, here I was appearing on their doorstep, drooping, beaten and weather-battered, with a sharp red cut-mark circling my neck. I now had all the grace and gentility of something a cat would deliver. Shame fell upon me with the raindrops but I banged hard upon the door nonetheless. I wanted to see her.

The wooden door was thicker than any of the others in that street but in its centre was a tiny peephole what someone had bored through. I pressed my eye against it to see if anyone in there was approaching but it was covered on the other side and all was blackness. I knocked again, my eye still against the peephole, and at last I heard footsteps from inside hurrying down wooden steps. A woman's voice called out that she was coming, the cover over the peephole slid back and an eyelash blinked back at me.

'That you, my sugar-mouse?' said a voice of soft concern. 'Lost your key again?' I pulled back from the peephole so she could see better who was calling. Jem, I imagined, was her sugar-mouse and it seemed he was out. Good.

'It's me, Rube.' I brushed my hair over with my fingers. 'Jack Dawkins. I've had a horrible night. Let us in, will you?'

The eye vanished, I heard the turning of keys and the unchaining of locks. Then the door opened and there she was. Ruby, looking lovely in her nightdress, the pale skin of her uncovered neck lit up by the candle she held low in a cleft stick, the features of her face still obscured by the shadows. 'You're soaking!' she said. 'Come inside quick.'

I stepped into the warmth and moved to hold her. 'Thanks, girl,' I said as I kissed her on the forehead. 'You've done me a bloody good turn.' I gave her a quick embrace and her body felt all warm against mine but she stiffened as I held her for too long. She pulled away and said, 'Shut the door after yourself, Jack. Or we'll both catch our deaths.' I did so and once I had finished chaining and barring it behind myself I turned back to face her. She was holding the tallow candle higher now and so I got a better look at her face. And there I saw something what shook me.

'Where did that come from?' I asked as I saw the bright purple bruise on her right cheek. 'You didn't have it yesterday.' My hand reached out to touch it but she flinched and the candle was lowered again.

'That's nothing,' she said. 'Let's get you upstairs and in front of a fire.' She turned and I followed her candlelight up the rickety staircase what I had walked up so many times before. Ruby came to the room where Nancy had lodged with Bill. And as she touched the door handle I was overcome with a dreadful realisation. I almost wanted to stop her hand from turning but it was too late. She swung open the door and I glimpsed the dark outline of that heavy oak bed what Bill and Nancy had once shared together, unmoved and facing out at me from the opposite wall.

This was the place he had killed her in, perhaps even in that very bed. It was an evil room and I wanted nothing to do with it.

'In you come,' Ruby said. 'You can help with the logs.' She entered her bedchamber, as if unaware that it was once the scene of murder, and began lighting some candles around the place. She then looked back to me and asked why I had not crossed the threshold myself. So, with much unease, I stepped inside and looked about me as the room became illuminated. They had changed the wallpaper – it was green with gold flowers now and not that bright crimson it once was – and the rug looked newer, but much of the furniture was the same: that cupboard where Bill kept all his spirits, the mantelpiece on which rested a large lead-weighted stick for defending the property with. I walked towards this life-preserver, to see if it could be the one that Bill had used, but Ruby called me over to help her light the fire. Once this was done I sat on a chair and placed my feet on the fender while Ruby went to the cupboard to fetch some drink. I noticed three heavy bludgeons in the corner and that underneath the bed the end of a pistol could be seen. I warmed my hands at the flames. This room just crackled with badness.

'What happened to your face?' I asked her as she took the chair opposite mine and we had chinked glasses.

'What happened to your neck?' she replied, and sipped at her drink.

'My valet,' I told her, rubbing it. 'We had a dispute and he tried to throttle me with a piece of wire. You can't trust these colonial servants.' I tutted in disappointment. 'You give them some work and this is how they repay you. I tell you, next time I need a man I'm going English.'

'Mr Warrigal done that?' She seemed surprised. 'He looked to be as gentle as a lamb.'

'Well, you aren't much of a judge of character then, are you? He's a vicious bugger and I'm glad to be rid of him.' I nodded at her face again. 'Your turn.'

Ruby had tried to cover the bruise with her hair but now her own hand went up to it and she pulled the tendrils away and tucked them behind her ear.

'Tripped,' she said all casual. 'Last night on the way home from the Cripples. Too many glasses inside me and I've only gone and walked into a gas lamp, clumsy bitch. It's as Jem always says – I'm a danger to myself when drunk.' She smiled at her own stupidity, but on seeing that I would not do likewise she changed the subject. 'I've got a pot of bathwater bubbling on the stove in the other room. You take your clothes off and I'll fetch it. Go on, I won't look.'

At the far end of the bedchamber was a smaller room with a basin and a tin bathtub. There was no door on this room, just a thin white sheet what hung from a wire above. When she came up with the first pot I went through and poured the water in and she went back to the kitchen to heat up another. Once undressed and inside the shallow water I began scrubbing away at my grubby feet using a bar of quality soap. Ruby returned and through a thin tear in the sheet I could see her tidying the place up. In spite of the dark history of this lodging house it was clear that Jem was doing well for himself. The strewn clothes and different dresses what Ruby was picking up and placing in the wardrobe was too fine for the woman of a common thief, and the room was an Aladdin's cave of jewels and other treasures, a big difference to the stark Froggat residence. I could see Ruby picking up various bits of jewellery and hiding them away in drawers and about her person too. She must not trust me, I thought, and felt affronted by it.

'So who's "Ruby in Red"?' I called through to her. 'You?'

This was a reference to the various posters I had seen pinned up on the bedroom walls what advertised these different music-hall performances. The most prominent, what was displayed above the dressing-table mirror, boasted of a star performer.

'My stage name!' she called back. 'Or used to be, more like.'

'What was you doing in music halls?' She answered by bursting into a bright rendition of the 'The Hardest-Working Milkmaid in the Country'. It was a lively tune and I made a good show of sounding impressed but I was not sorry when she stopped after one verse.

'I didn't think of the name Ruby in Red; Douglas did. Douglas Boyd was the man what produced the shows.'

'How did all this come about?'

Ruby went on to explain that after Fagin had been hanged, before she had taken up with Jem, she had been at a loss as to what to do. All the kinchins of Saffron Hill had found themselves homeless and the only relative she had was some filthy old uncle what used to visit every month or so. But it seemed that even he had vanished when the peelers started turning over their rocks in the wake of Nancy's killing and so Ruby was left all alone. She, what had not yet reached womanhood, had no other choice but to make her living on the streets as so many others girls was doing. Not wanting to become a prostitute she tried to earn her pennies by standing on street corners and singing bawdy ballads like the one I had just heard. Many men approached her, wanting more than just songs, but she told them she only wanted paying for music and if they was not interested in another chorus of 'Don't Act Coy Around the Butcher's Boy' then they should seek their pleasures elsewhere. She could not carry on like this for long without starving though.

However, just a short time after this, she was approached by a portly Scotsman by name of Douglas. This cove thought she had a very pleasing voice and asked would she be interested in a career in music halls. He told her he was a stage producer, bowing all gallant as he did so, and that she should come to Rafferty's Music Halls the very next day where he was auditioning for new performers. This she did and there he promised to take her under his care, put her up in a nice little apartment and make her his own pet songstress.

'Oh, I see,' I said, scrubbing between my toes. 'Like that, was it?'

'That's what I thought,' Ruby admitted, still talking to me from beyond the sheet. 'But he never did nothing.'

'Was he a molly?'

'No,' Ruby said, 'he was at one of the other girls, a dancer called Fanny, who was sweet on the eye but whose voice was as fresh as the guttering. Douglas favoured me as a performer though and after some years of working my way up to a star performer, he made me top of the bill at last.'

'I saw that from the poster,' I said. 'Must have been a good buzz.'

'I suppose,' she sighed. 'I never went.'

'Never went?' I leaned my head over so I could see better what she was doing. She was just sat on the side of the bed, staring at the poster. 'Why?'

'Jem didn't like it,' she answered. 'He had begun paying me

visits around that time, dressed up all gallant, a hothouse flower in his buttonhole, a bouquet for me every time. I had become quite taken with him. He's grown up most handsome since you last saw him, Jack – you'll be surprised when he walks in. I had never thought much of Jem back when we were all kinchins,' she then confided. 'He always seemed less comfortable in himself than either you or Charley ever was. But now here he was, tall, foxy-whiskered and spending his money as though it came from a pump. We reminisced about those wonderful days before the Jew got caught, and before long I was living here with him.' She left the room for a few moments to fetch up the second pot.

'But why should that stop you from performing at the music hall?' I shouted through to her. 'I'd be proud to have such a famous fancy woman.'

She shouted something back about Jem being the jealous sort and them having an almighty row about her parading herself around in front of strangers. 'We had a big blow-up about it,' she said as she came back in carrying the pot, 'and he talked me into not going.' I saw her twitch as she said this and I thought about her bruise again. 'I'm lucky to have him, you know,' she said, more to herself than to me. 'He's top-sawyer around here.'

'So you keep saying,' I remarked as I reached for the big hat what I'd taken from the tavern. I held it over the water so Ruby could not see my bits bobbing about below as she came through the sheet. 'Pour it straight in, Rube,' I said to her. 'This water's already gone cold.'

Ruby poured the boiled water around but not over me and I asked her what this Douglas had said after she cancelled the show. 'Don't know.' She shrugged. 'I haven't seen him in months. After passing up such a great chance I could hardly go back there. Theatrical types are not the easiest of – *what's all this?*'

'What's all what?' I said, turning around as she dropped the pot straight into the bath. She was staring at my back with her hand over her mouth and she had sounded so startled that I thought there had to be some large insect crawling up it.

'Who on earth done that to you, Jack?' she asked. I turned and realised that she meant the five lash marks streaked across my back. 'Was that Warrigal too?'

Over the years I had near forgotten about those marks, as it was rare to find the two looking glasses what would reveal them to me and I had never felt the need to try. They was courtesy of Sergeant Allhare at the penal colony five years ago in punishment for my misjudged attempts at escape and, although the pain had lasted for a long time afterwards, it was now a dim memory. The scars they left however was not meant to fade and I had been branded as a convict for life.

'Her Majesty done those,' I told her as she gasped in surprise. 'Or rather some dirty sod what works for her did. Never get transported, Ruby. It's a rough deal.' Ruby dropped to her knees and asked me if they still hurt. 'Not any more,' I said. 'Only if I don't get a good night's sleep or if someone hits me on the back. Run your fingers along them and I'll tell you if I feel anything.' This she did and, instead of making the lash marks sting, her smooth fingers was like ointment upon my skin.

'Poor Jack,' she said, and she brought her face round close to mine. Her hand moved from my back and up to my shoulder. 'You've been in some scrapes, haven't you, my love?'

With one hand still on the hat I reached the other one, still wet from the water, up to her face and tucked the hair behind her ear again. Then I stroked her bruise with the back of my fingers. 'Same could be said of you,' I told her. Then my hand travelled to behind her neck and I pulled her in closer for a kiss. I had a strong hope that she would not resist.

Before she even had the chance to kiss back we heard the squeak of the bedroom door handle as it turned and opened. 'Jem,' said Ruby, and she was up in a second and then through the sheet away from me. I could see, through the fine white material, that a man had entered with footsteps so light he could only be a burglar. 'Sugar-mouse!' Ruby said, and I saw her figure move towards him, only to be shoved away with force. From his dark outline I could see that the boy had grown tall, and his stillness unnerved me as I felt his head turn towards the bathroom where I sat, as unrigged as a babe, with only a hat to protect my wet self.

'Who,' he said in a deep yet familiar man's voice, 'is that through there?' I could hear a scuffle as he manhandled Ruby. 'And whose –' his manner was all violence – 'is that coat hanging from that knob?'

'It's Jack's,' answered Ruby, her voice so pinched that his hands must have been like a carpenter's vice around her cheeks. 'Jus' Jack's. 'Ass all.'

'Jack?' He shoved her away again so hard I could hear the thump as she landed on the bed. 'And who in hot hell –' he stomped over to the sheet separating that room from this and grabbed it – 'is Jack?' He pulled the sheet aside and revealed himself to me and me to him. He looked ready to strike.

'Jack Dawkins by name.' I smiled at him, the hat still covering myself. He stopped, fist in the air, and glared at me, confused. 'And you've grown up good and handsome I see, Jemmy.'

'Dodger?' he then said, blinking twice, as if scratching the inside of his head to make sense of the sight of me. I nodded and decided to hell with modesty. I placed the hat upon my head and leaned back in his tub.

'That's my name, Sugar-mouse,' I said. 'Sorry I never met you and the others at the broken pump, by the by. Got a bit waylaid.'

Chapter 13

Brother Starling

A thief worth stealing from

'"My letter is real, Bracken, you filthy coward," I said to him after I finished dishing out his punishment. Bracken just lies there at my feet, his nose broken, and begs me to stop punching and kicking him. "Yours ain't. Tell that to the bastard magistrate."'

Jem whooped in appreciation of my heroism and began banging the table with his mug of coffee. I had spent two hours regaling him with many colourful tales of my time in Australia and my long journey back, and this story, the story of my night spent beating up a policeman in the Booted Cat, had proved a particular favourite with him. 'You never done!' He grinned at me, leaning over his breakfast table and patting me on the shoulder. 'You never done that to a peeler!'

'I do what I please, Jemmo.' I sniffed and glanced at his lady. 'Always have done.'

Jem shook his head in admiration at this poetic retelling of my encounter with the law. As Ruby walked back to the table with two hot plates of breakfast, he grabbed her by the rump and pulled her to him. 'You and me both,' he said, and gave her a hard kiss on the unbruised side of her face, almost causing her to drop the meat and eggs all over the table. She did not complain; in truth she seemed to delight in his rough attentions.

The moment when he had burst into the bathroom, to discover a man wet and unrigged in the company of his kept woman, was indeed a delicate one. Even after he had recognised me as his old pal the Artful Dodger he still looked fit to give me a bloody good hiding. He was bellowing curses at me and calling Ruby all sorts of horrible names and it took some persuasion to convince him that events was not how they appeared.

'Don't give me that gammon!' he shouted loud enough for all of Bethnal Green to enjoy. 'If it ain't what you reckon it looks like, then how can you know what it looks like unless it's the thing what you reckon it looks like and not the other. Cos if it weren't what it looks like, it would not look like what it does!'

He had me there. 'I'm not sure I follow you, Jem,' I said.

He moved towards me and started prodding me in the chest. It was then that I noticed his hands was all covered in dried mud. 'It looks like you've landed in the wrong nest again, Jacko,' he said through his teeth. 'Looks like you're eating off the wrong plate!'

'Jemmy,' I reasoned, 'look at the state of me. I'm cut to bits.' I showed him the bruises on my arms, legs and the scar around my neck from my fight with Warrigal, lifted up my feet so he could see the cuts and leant forward to show him my lash marks. Then I got out of the bath and reached for a robe what hung from a hook. 'I'm not fit to be making love to anyone,' I said, putting it on me. 'I'm in too much agony. Ruby here was just nursing me, bless her kind soul, taking pity on a poor unfortunate what was dropped on her doorstep in disgrace. I knock on this door, the home of two of my oldest and much-missed friends, in the hope of finding some charity and she gives it to me. Then you come thundering in here looking to thump me as I wallow and making dirty insinuations about her good character. And she's just spent the last ten minutes going on about how much she loves you. What way is that to repay her, I ask you?'

This plea to his senses had a calming effect upon the boy and before long he was saying how good it was to see me again, even if I had been as bare as a newborn. He amused himself with a few flash remarks about how he did not mind Ruby seeing me unclothed after all as it reminded her of how spoilt she now was. We laughed about that, leastways I pretended to, and he went off to rummage through his clothes closet for something to loan me.

So, soon as the sun began to peek through the cracks in their thick black curtain, I was sat at his breakfast table, in a thinner man's shirt and corduroy trousers what I had to roll up at the bottom. We was then puffing on a clay pipe and laughing as though six years and a suspect bath incident had never passed.

'But enough of my tales of high adventure,' I said as I turned my half of the steak over with my fork. I half expected to see Ruby's black hair still stuck to it. 'What's the news round this way? I see you've moved up to the house-cracking line, Jem?' I nodded towards the big open bag what he had carried in with him. It glittered with silverware, necklaces and other choice jewels. 'You always was the ambitious sort.'

Jem nodded, leaning back after licking his plate clean. 'Yeah. Pickpocketing is for kinchins. Burglary's the game,' he said, and relit the cigar. 'Myself and Georgie Bluchers was at this cottage out in Kent last night. Took us forever to get there but between us we've stripped the crib clean. It's a fine business,' he declared, 'and tonight was a good haul.' He leaned over to a tin pot and flicked some ash into it. Then, once Ruby had left the room, he lowered his voice as if about to disclose something dead secret. 'If I do say so myself, I'm a natural at it. Quiet as mouse breath I am, when I wants to be. The flats of a house can be asleep in their beds and they won't hear me emptying the cabinets of diamond necklaces right beside them.' Then he shrugged and looked to be ashamed about what he was about to say next. 'But burglary is a two-man job if you mean to do it right and, well . . . I don't mean to speak ill of a friend . . .'

'Georgie?'

'Yeah.' He nodded. 'Georgie ain't so suited to the trade. Stomps around in those big boots of his, alerting the whole house to our activities. More than once we've had to knock out some butler or other servant what has been sent down by his master to bother us.' Jem pulled a cosh out of his coat pocket to show me. 'He's a liability, I tell you. It'll be the rope if we're caught.'

He sighed and drew on his pipe. He seemed to be eyeing me in that moment to see how he and I compared. He moved his belt buckle from left to right as though this was meant to signify something and then blew tobacco smoke out of his nose.

He had grown handsome over time, I thought, as I waited for him to resume the conversation. Or leastways he was what some women might consider handsome to be if they was simple or easy to please. He was taller than me – this was a vexing truth – and he had a beard what was blond and wispy. My own hair was black and thick and I wondered if Ruby would prefer that or favour instead his lightness. I swept my own hair to one side, to make a raven's wing out of it in the hope that Ruby might notice and mark the difference. But I could tell, as he stretched a yawn revealing how strong and long his arms now was, that it was going to be hard sport stealing his woman away from him. And this was a thing I had very much made up my mind to do.

'Take last night in Kent,' he said, glancing over to the doorway to make sure that Ruby was not about to come back. 'We're all masked up, a barker and a cosh each, and we've got the maid-of-all-work tied up in the parlour. The dogs are locked away safe in the cellar, the master of the place, this rich old landowner, is spending the night in London with his wife and daughter so we have all evening to strip his crib of anything that shines. Only we get surprised during the job by another fellow, a gardener what lives in a little barn at the bottom of the garden, just beyond the marrow patch. He hears the dogs, as well as Georgie's ruckus, comes to see what is what. Confrontation. Georgie gets agitated, hits him over the head with his persuader. Then the maid turns hysterical. "Georgie! You'll kill him!" The gardener turns to her, hands still on his thumped head. "Georgie?" the fellow asks. See, this maid, Fanny Cooper, is the sister of Cheap Jane from Crackity Lane and she and Georgie is sweethearts. It was she who told us the landowner and his family would be out and where the best jewels was hidden. She even took care of the dogs before we got there and we was only tying her up so things would look neat. But now, cos of Georgie's noise and her own stupidity, this nosey gardener knows that Fanny is in on it with us. We can't have that, and so it all went downhill from there.'

'You had to pay him off?' I shook my head in sympathy. 'Pity.'

Jem blinked. 'We didn't think of that, to speak true,' He shook his head as if I had just said something very clever. 'I wish we hadda done,' he sighed. 'That would have been tidier. No, we dealt with him by taking him back to the bottom of the garden where he should have stayed. Only now he's five feet under it.'

I laughed, thinking this a joke. Then I remembered the reddish mud on his hands and my laughter stopped.

'Georgie weren't happy about it,' he went on. 'Left me to do the job. But I said to him, if your Fanny coulda just kept that big mouth of hers shut, I wouldn't be having to club anyone, would I?' He began rubbing the cosh between his thumb and forefinger as if wiping it of something. 'Couldn't use a barker. Too much noise. That's why I got home so late.'

I had this sudden memory of him at eight years of age crying because one of the bigger lads had told him a story about how some skeletons had come to life. I could scarce credit this was the same boy.

At that moment Ruby came back in the room and Jem placed a finger to his lips. He did not seem to mind sharing his burglary tales with her, but the part about burying nosey gardeners under the marrow patch was for my ears alone.

'You must be exhausted after that walking, Jack,' Ruby interrupted. 'You can kip in our bed if you care to.' She went through the door into their bedroom and began straightening the blankets on that big four-poster. 'Jem never sleeps until the afternoon and I have to take his findings to the local fence.'

The big mahogany bed seemed to have taken root in that room and it looked back at me, uncaring and shameless. It struck an attitude, or so my sleep-starved mind supposed, of a dark beast what had feasted once and was now looking for its next victim. 'Not likely,' I said, and decided to raise the point. 'How can you,' I asked them, 'stand to keep the same bed what a murdered woman once slept in?'

'Why should we not?' asked Jem, wiping coffee away from his mouth. 'It's a bloody good bit of wood, that.'

'It's morbid,' I said, and appealed to Ruby. 'If you had any decency you'd saw it up for firewood and be done with it. It's a despicable travesty to have it still sitting there.' Jem laughed as though I was the one what was being a fool, but Ruby had gone very quiet. 'So no, in answer to your question, I do not wish to sleep in poor Nancy's bed, thank you very much.'

'Please yourself,' Jem said. 'Then you should bed down in Greta's room, below ours. Ruby has a key and the fat cow ain't been seen for days. Failing that, you can piss off to the nearest doss-house if you'd rather.' His laugh was boisterous and he walked up behind Ruby, who was clearing away the plates, and gave her a light grope on the behind. She jumped and told him to behave himself. 'We could do with a bit of private time up here anyway. Show him to Greta's room, Rube,' he said, unbuttoning his shirt and sitting on the edge of the bed. 'Then get yourself back up here.' He grinned as he patted the sheets.

This Greta, so I was told, was a young girl of industrious character what rented a downstairs room. She lived in a different part of London, where she supported her malingering father and four lazy brothers, but she came over this way for work whenever she could. Ruby told me that I could rest in Greta's bed for a few hours and then, at midday, she would be happy to go finding with me so I could start paying my way again.

'Are you boys all still going to the rat pit tomorrow night?' I asked Jem before taking my leave.

'Yeah,' he replied. 'My whole gang'll be there.'

'I mean Fagin's boys,' I said, unsure as to who he was on about.

'So do I,' he said, and shot me a challenging eye. 'Mouse, Herbie, Georgie, all the others. My gang.'

'Good then,' I said, and went to shake his hand. 'I shall look forward to reacquainting myself with your gang tomorrow.'

We both of us squeezed a bit harder than we might have done and Jem held my eye as he did so. He seemed unsure as to whether my return was a good thing or not. Then Ruby walked me down to where I could sleep for a while.

The bed in this room was black iron and big enough for two, although Ruby said it was not likely that I would be disturbed. Before she took her leave I took her by the hand and thanked her for her kindnesses. Ruby smiled and I thought her prettier than ever. She said she was happy I was back and I drew her close to me, close enough to kiss. 'I'm happy you're happy,' I said. 'Your smiles are a tonic to me.' She looked unsure of herself but pulled away and made to leave. Just before she shut the door I said her name again and she turned about. 'Now I'm back things are going to get better,' I promised. 'There'll be no more bruises from falling over. Not if I'm about.' Ruby gave me a look to say she did not know what I meant. 'I'll steady you,' I told her.

'Sleep well, Jack,' she said. 'See you in a few hours.'

Once in bed I lay facing upwards, and I could feel the whip-mark lines on my back and where her fingers had run along them. The plaster on the ceiling had crumbled from rot and I could see through to the thin wood rafters what ran under their room above. I could hear the door of that room shut after her and I heard Jem ask a question but could not make out what it was. She mumbled an answer and I could hear him ask her the question again, with more force. Their footsteps began shuffling and it sounded like a struggle. I sat up as I heard Ruby give a small cry like he was hurting her and I felt an urge to get back up there and pull her off him. Then a thump, as though something had been thrown on to that bed, and I was back on my feet and heading towards the door. I had a vision of Bill striking Nancy, and then another of that hapless gardener, and I was determined to prevent another violent crime from taking place. Another thump. I stopped with my hands on the door and listened. Then a rhythm of many quiet creaks began to be heard and I realised he was not hurting her at all. I took my hand off the handle and went back to the bed where I had to lie back down and watch those rafters above me pulse under the weight of the bed and listen to the girl I now wanted making love-noises for another.

It was a miserable moment. For all I knew the filthy sod would be banging away at her for hours.

Five minutes later he had finished. And, according to the clock on the mantelpiece, he was snoring noisily in less than ten. This made me feel much more confident about trying things with Ruby although, in all truth, if I had been out all night burgling houses and digging graves I'm not sure I would have dazzled her with my prowess either. But tiredness was now covering me like morning dew and I soon found myself sinking into slumber also. In my mind an image of Ruby in the arms of that there Jem persisted in my head even after my eyes was shut, and this caused me greater pain than the lash marks ever had. There was many things what was troubling me at that time. I was still grieving over the death of Fagin and, if I am to be honest, also that of my mother, madwoman though she was. Lord Evershed was no doubt going to want me dead as a result of failing to deliver the Jakkapoor stone and there was an aborigine somewhere in this city what would be happy to oblige him. Above where I lay sweet Nancy had been killed by her lover whose heroism I had once admired. And now, on top of this growing list of unhappinesses, I had fallen for a girl the music halls had once billed as Ruby in Red. I had only seen her twice since my return to London but she had, in that short time, stolen my heart like it was a steak in a market and made off with it under her hat. I was good and bewitched by my crimson sweetheart and I wanted to possess her more than the fattest wallet. That she was already spoken for, and that it was my old friend Jem doing the speaking, was an unfortunate obstacle but not one that made her any less appealing. Nor would it dissuade me from taking her regardless because, in truth, it just made me want her more. I am a thief in all things, even matters of love.

I cannot recall how long I slept in that bed but I do know that my dreams was strong, vivid and featured many shifting scenes in which Ruby was the star turn. In them she and I was busying ourselves making all manner of daring love and I was swearing to her my everlasting fidelity like I was a gallant knight of old. The kisses and caresses what she received from me was of a much more superior kind to those brief and half-hearted attentions she had received upstairs. This dream Ruby was a noisier and more appreciative lover then she had sounded above but, as is often the faithless way of dreams, she did not remain Ruby for good. Although I had been smitten with the girl for less than one day and my pure heart had already promised to be true to her alone, my tomcat of an imagination had already begun sniffing about for someone to betray her with. Ruby soon transformed into Constance Cherry, she what had worn that diamond ring I had wanted so much, and I did nothing to prevent the change. A person cannot feel guilty for what happens in a dream and I applied myself to this new bed-partner with as much vigour as I had to the girl I loved. But even Constance did not hold my dream's attention for long and she soon shifted into someone else, someone who had been visiting my dreams for many years.

Nancy. She was as glorious and as naked as the others and as we embraced I whispered about how lovely she was, even if she was much heavier than I had expected. She was on top of me then, her hair hanging down so I could not see her face, her legs astride and grinding down with force and the panting sounds she was making was rough and urgent. My dream self grew weary of her and, as wakefulness crept upon me, I wanted to look upon Ruby, to gaze on her face. So I reached up and pushed her hair away, and just before I did so I recall wondering who she would turn into now. I told myself that it was time to wake up but the woman above pushed my hand away as I reached for her hair and

I heard her murmur something in a voice I did not recognise. It was something about me showing her what I had and, as she continued to jump her now considerable weight up and down she was squealing in pleasure. I wanted the dream to go back to where it was, I had preferred it when it was just me and Ruby, but I could feel the heat in my loins bubbling up for release and I was powerless to stop it. The dream-girl's breasts was up and down like a pair of church bells on the Sabbath and, as my hips carried on thrusting away, I grabbed both as if to silence them. As I did so she threw her hair back, hair what was now orange and curly and did not seem to belong to anyone I had seen before, and she showed me a round unfamiliar face what was overheating with excitement. It was then that I made the startling discovery that I was no longer asleep.

'Sorry to wake you, handsome,' said the merry-faced girl as she continued bouncing away on top of me. My pipe was still solid iron from the dream and she was enjoying every stiff inch of it. 'My name's Greta,' she panted without stopping, 'and don't fret, I'll be finished up here in no time.'

Chapter 14

Favours

*A reminder that, in these hard times,
we must all make a living somehow*

This Greta was much larger than me and she pressed me down and held me captive beneath while she carried on taking her pleasure without ever having asked permission. I tried to put up a struggle, to push her off me and say that I was in love with another, but she was so very determined to have her wicked way that I could not resist. The squeaky iron bedstead made such an almighty racket as she pounded up and down that I feared we would snap the slatting and fall through it. As I rose up to stop her she pushed me back down, ignoring my attempts to tell her that I was not a willing participant in this here sweaty coupling.

'Tell that to the rest of you,' she giggled, continuing to ride the full length of my masculinity which, to be fair to her, was telling a very different story. And although I was much shocked to find a stranger astride me that morning I cannot claim that the experience was an unhappy one and before long I had given up fighting for my virtue and was very much getting into the spirit of the thing. ''At's a good boy,' she cheered me on. 'Girrit to me.' She was, as has been acknowledged, a lady of some carriage but, as my arms reached around her and my hands explored her large, magnificent body, I raced towards that magical moment with blissful abandon. Greta seemed to know this and, after reaching her face down to mine and covering it with kisses, she told me to give her fair warning. 'Say when you're ready to fetch mettle, lover,' she demanded. 'Say, and I'll climb off.' By this point my hips would not have stopped their happy thrusting had she pointed a pistol at my face and demanded me to desist. 'Don't let Greta down now,' she said. 'Let me know when it's time.' My arms squeezed her tighter than before, my jerks became all the more urgent and she was wise enough to take this as the best warning she would get. In a second she was off and lay beside me, her hand was around my stiff manhood and, with two clean strokes, she had helped me reach satisfaction all over the sheets. I sighed in relief and Greta gave her encouragement as I did so. 'That's a good lad,' she said as if proud of me. 'Better out than in.' We lay beside one another then, both breathing hard from our exertions, and I told her that this was the nicest thing that had happened to me since I had returned to England. 'So I see,' she said, as she wiped her hand on the sheets. Then she kissed me once more, a long, tender kiss what spoke of true love between innocents, and she stroked the hairs on my chest as I got my breath back.

'Now then,' she said, after lighting a small tobacco cigar what she had produced from a tin by the bedside for us to share, 'that'll be five shillings by my reckoning.'

'You what?' I asked, after drawing on the cigar.

'You heard,' she said, taking it back.

'What will?'

'*What will?*' she laughed, mimicking me. She tapped me on the nose with her finger, all playful. 'You're a funny one.' She took a puff and smiled. I sat up in the bed to see if she was jesting.

'What am I paying you five shillings for?'

Her sweet face then turned a nasty sour. She looked upon me

with fierce eyes, a look that was made even stronger by the two long puffs of smoke what blew out of her nostrils. 'You know why, handsome.' Her voice was a low threat. 'For my favours.' She tapped out the ash back into the tray and crossed her arms, ready for trouble. 'Don't be a bother now. We don't want to fall out over this, do we, me and you?'

This sudden demand for my hard-stolen money left me most flummoxed. I looked about for my nightshirt and saw that it had been thrown down onto the unvarnished floorboards and was covering the tramp's boots what I had stolen the night before. I had not draped it there and so I knew that this woman, while I was sleeping most happily, must have removed the shirt from me and tossed it there herself. It was possible, considering the hot and heavy dreams I had been having, that I had helped her off with it and put up no struggle as she positioned herself on top of me. But the fact remained that I was asleep and she had taken full advantage of my stimulated self for her own personal gratification. So the idea that I owed her even one bent farthing, let alone five blessed shillings, for the privilege of jumping up and down on me was not one I was ready to subscribe to.

'I'll be straight with you, my gentle dumpling,' I said to her after considering the matter for less than one second, 'the way I see it, you should be paying me.'

'*Paying you?*' she howled, as though she had never heard anything so outrageous. 'I like your cheek! Why ever for?'

'For my favours,' I countered as I reached down to the night-shirt before declaring, 'There's many a woman who would.' Her response was somewhere between a laugh and a screech but either way the effect was deafening.

'I ain't the one what dirtied the bedding, am I, sweet prince? The proof,' she grabbed at the sheet, 'is in this here pudding.'

I shrugged at her and pulled the nightshirt over my head. 'That is neither here nor there,' I reasoned. 'I did not agree to take you as a bed-partner and I never would have if asked. My heart belongs to another. And this other I would never stoop to betray.' I pulled the shirt down so it covered my parts once more. 'At least not for five shillings.'

On hearing this Greta released a great bellow what would have disturbed every man, woman, animal or child in the surrounding area. 'This is my room, you cheeky wretch!' she cried, getting all hysterical. 'My room where I works and brings men, young and old, back for my favours. They all pays me what they owes and so must you, handsome or no.' She was thumping me hard in the chest now, seething anger and I grew most frightened. 'If you creep into my room, and I don't recall inviting you in, then you're here for business. And you must obey my one simple rule. You fetch, you owe!' She pulled back and held her head up in pride. 'I have a malingering father and four lazy brothers to support. I don't expect to work for nothing.'

'Greta!' Ruby's voice came from behind the closed door. 'What's all this fuss? Who you shouting at? Is that Jack?' Her key rattled in the door and she entered to find Greta, naked and furious while I cowered next to her in the bed. Ruby was fully clothed in another red dress and she seemed most vexed at the scene she was witnessing.

'This ain't what it looks like, Rube,' I promised her. 'She forced herself upon me.' I pulled the strings of the nightshirt in tight. 'I begged her to stop.' Ruby looked to Greta.

'That ain't true,' Greta huffed. 'I never forced him to nothing he didn't want, the lying toad. It was all love and kisses until it came time to pay up.'

'I was fast asleep when she found me,' I cried in response. 'It was a disgraceful assault upon my innocent person.'

'Yeah, well, I ain't no bear in a fairy tale,' Greta continued. ignoring me. 'If I find someone lying in my bed I don't roar and chase them off, I get in with them and I set myself to work.' Ruby sighed as if this was something that was often happening.

'I let him in here, Greta,' Ruby explained. 'I thought you wasn't coming back until tonight.'

'Well, come back I did,' my attacker sniffed. 'And in my line of work you don't turn down easy trade when it presents itself.' She looked at me like I was a dog what had messed in her bed and shook her head in disappointment, 'And now he's trying to weasel out of paying me five well-earned shillings.'

Ruby listened to both our stories and then stood in judgement before us, like she had the wisdom of Solomon deciding whether or not to divide a baby in half.

'Jack,' she said at last, 'did you fetch or did you not?'

'Course he did,' said Greta, showing her the sheets.

'Then you owe Greta five shillings,' she decreed. 'Now be a good lad, pay the woman, put your trousers on and meet me upstairs. We've a morning's work to be getting on with.'

I did not have five shillings to pay Greta and this led to another almighty rumpus between us. I told her I was only kipping in her bed because I had no money and that if I had five shillings I wouldn't be nowhere near this crap-house in the first place. In the end she agreed to give me until this evening to pay her back and, now that she knew I was pals with Jem and Ruby, she said that she might even open an account for me with a view to future transactions. I had no intention of requiring her services ever again but I did assure her I was good for the money owed and that, in a gesture of goodwill, I would stand her a glass of gin in the Cripples some time soon. This softened her at last, and with the big white sheet wrapped round her she walked me to the door and curtsied all dainty as I left to go back upstairs to Ruby's. 'But don't be getting my shillings from no coiners,' she warned me before shutting the door, 'cos I always know a forgery.'

Upstairs in Ruby's bedroom Jem was lying in that menacing old bed of theirs, buried under three thick different coloured blankets and looking as likely to emerge as that gardener he had buried the night before was to rise up from the sod. 'Next time you sing one of your ballads,' I said to Ruby after hearing his arse carrying on like a battered trumpet, 'you should get Jem to accompany you. Audiences love a horn section.' She laughed but told me that I should not be making fun of her fancy man, not when he had agreed to lend me some of his finest togs to go finding in.

It was shameful to me that I had appeared at this address in the early hours of the morning with fewer possessions than a vagrant. I was most keen to get out among the people and practise my art so I could pay for my own things and not go on living off the charity of an inferior thief. Jem was top-sawyer now, this was clear from the flash clothes what Ruby was laying out for me to pick from, but I was itching to show her that this situation was only ever a fleeting one, an irregularity what had come about from my getting lagged at an unfortunate age and one what would soon be corrected. She might well have been impressed with his success as a cracksman up until now, I thought as I perused his many shirts, but today she would see a real thief in action.

The floor was strewn with many other male garments, shirts of flaring orange, trousers of garish green, and none of these much appealed. 'That superfine?' I then asked when she produced a black shirt and trouser set what looked to be of the highest quality. Ruby let me touch the cloth and it indeed felt like something worth having. 'I'll take it,' I said. 'I'm in a black mood.'

'I can't imagine why,' Ruby replied as she began opening more drawers and closets in the search for other genteel items what I might wear. 'You seemed to have had a fine old time with Greta just then.'

I could not tell whether she said these words in jealousy but I was hopeful that she had. As I tried on Jem's trousers and rolled up the legs on the inside, I reflected that it was hard to tell whether she cared about me or not and so I just grunted a reply and continued to peruse the many fine things that Jem had either purloined or purchased for himself with stolen money. I found myself feeling amazed and covetous at all the many possessions in that house. Ruby presented me with a thick scarf, what would hide the ringed scar Warrigal had left around my neck, and a coat in matching black. To adorn myself I had a choice of watches, chains, pins, rings and studs, all glittering gold or silver. If I was to move un-noticed among real quality today I would have to blend in with them.

'Tell me,' I asked once we had left the bedroom and I was sure that Jem could not hear. 'Does Jem wear a lot of these trinkets himself?'

'Course he does,' said Ruby, pulling out a pocketknife from a drawer to give me. 'He's as flash as anyone.'

'Does he have any favourites?' I asked, all casual, as I held the tiny silver knife up to the light of the window in mock inspection. 'You know, ones he keeps for sentimental reasons. From the old days.'

'Like what?'

'Like a small black stone or something,' I said, and peered at the quality of the blade, running my fingertip along it, and folding it into my fist to see how easy it would hide. I wanted my question to seem like idle chatter but I had to ask. 'Something what Fagin might have given him.'

'Search me,' she replied as she walked around the room putting things away and readying herself to leave. 'He ain't the sentimental type. But I'll ask him if you like.'

'No, don't do that,' I said a little too fast and I could tell she knew something was up. 'I'm just making conversation. You got them shoes?' She handed me a pair of Jem's shiniest black shoes and I had to tie the laces tight so they would fit. I doubted very much that Fagin would have given Jem the stone but I needed to start somewhere. Ruby began to put some coins into her little netted reticule bag and regarded herself in a small pier glass what was hung upon the wall. 'These fit perfect,' I said of the oversize shoes. I went over to Jem's hatstand and helped myself to the smallest. I was finding it most demeaning to have to wear a bigger person's clothes, as I had become accustomed to a tailored wardrobe in the last few months. 'Has he ever given you any little black jewels?' I asked her then, as she turned her pretty head this way and that in front of the mirror to see how her hair was pinned up. She seemed most preoccupied. 'As a gift?'

'Hmm?' she said, all slow and lazy.

'A jewel, Ruby,' I snapped. I had grown bored of trying not to sound suspicious; this was too important. 'A black jewel. Do you know of any?'

'No,' she said back, perplexed. 'Who has black jewels around here? And why do you want to know?' I told her it was just a curiosity and changed the subject. She pulled the drawstrings tight on her reticule and reached for her hat on the peg. 'Now let's get finding,' she said with firmness after checking the mirror one last time. 'I'm curious to see if your fingers are still as artful as they ever was.'

Chapter 15

The Touch

In which Ruby and myself spend a pleasant day together,
what takes an unpleasant turn when we encounter some
unsavoury characters

She was a tall specimen, this old plant what boarded the omnibus at Holborn Hill, and she brought with her into the carriage such a strong scent of violet water that Ruby and I knew she was coming long before she entered the carriage. The omnibus had paused to water the horses but it was already so bustling inside with travellers heading west that the young conductor should not have admitted any more persons no matter how perfumed they might be. From our positions seated inside the stagecoach we could hear the woman outside's rich aristocratic tones ask the conductor if he had room to take her to Kensington Gardens. And yet, in the way of people what are born with rich aristocratic tones, it was more of a command to make room than a request and one that the young cad would be a fool to disobey. She had the manner of the officer about her, this woman, regardless of her sex.

The inside was already packed with chattering ladies, grumbling gents, bawling children and one small dog. The dog was attached by a long string to someone, but that did not stop him from leaping from lap to lap. It felt like all of London life was in that packed coach headed to Oxford Street and it was to be a tight old squeeze for a lady of such formidable height. As the conductor opened the rear door and hollered through for us to make room for a little one we saw her long purple dress climb the steps of the carriage, her green velvet glove steady her on the rail and her grand flowery hat dip itself under the low door to gain entry. Ruby and myself was seated side by side but had not said a word to each other since we boarded at Shoreditch so as to appear as if we was not together. But we both knew that here, with these clothes, that perfume and those tones, was exactly what we had been waiting for. We shifted ourselves apart and made such a welcoming space that the high-stemmed lady had no choice but to bend her limbs down and share the bumpy journey snug between us. The conductor slammed the door behind him and banged on the roof to let the coachman know that the omnibus could rattle onwards.

'My, your fingers is like icicles,' Ruby said to the small girl sat on her right as she took her hands in hers and pressed them warm. 'We must write to this Father Christmas, if he's to be of any use to us at all, and get him to bring you a bright pair of woollens, mustn't we!' The little girl smiled and nodded but added that she still wanted all her toys what her mamma had promised. 'And you shall get every last one of them,' Ruby replied, tapping her on the nose all playful. 'A young lady like you deserves to.' Ruby had been working on this child for the past two stops and had built up such a familiarity with her that the new addition to the coach could be forgiven for thinking it was she who was the child's guardian and not the sullen nurse beyond, what just stared out of the window opposite ignoring her charge. The tall woman ignored their chatter and folded her long legs into as upright a position as possible until she was as close to comfort as she was ever going to get. On her right side I could feel her body stiffen into place, and near her hip, through the layers of material what made up her dress, I could sense a jingling bulge what could only be a full coin-purse nestling in an inside pocket. The gent opposite me had obscured himself behind a copy of *The Times* as if it was a shield keeping him separate from the chaos and noise of the coach. None of the other passengers looked to be taking much notice of me either. I dipped my hand into my own pocket and felt for the pocketknife.

'Brrrrrrrrr . . .' Ruby went on to the little girl. 'I don't care for these wintry days much. I'm all of a shiver. I'll tell you what –' she pulled her red-chequered shawl from around the back of her neck and began unfolding it – 'let's drape this over us for a bit. We need toasting up, we do.' The shawl was lain over her lap and that of the little girl, who appeared most grateful for it, and Ruby turned to her left and addressed our tall plant. 'There's plenty for you too, good lady, should you like some warmth?'

'I'm quite all right,' said the haughty woman, looking down upon her from her lofty position. She did not seem to notice as my closed hand left my pocket and crossed with the other so it rested near to her bulge. 'But thank you anyway.' This refusal of cover was a pity as there is nothing so helpful as to have a shawl placed over the lap of your neighbour when riding the omnibus. But it was a deft suggestion from Ruby nonetheless and I thought, as I turned the tip of the blade to touch the woman's dress, that she was proving to be a most able accomplice.

The lady then reached into the bag upon her lap and pulled out a bound book what looked to be one of the more fashionable novels. She opened it, removed the small ribbon of a bookmark and attempted to read despite the noise of the carriage.

'Ooh, how lovely to have a great big book like that,' beamed Ruby, her manner most friendly. 'I love a good novel, me, but can only ever get hold of the periodicals. You ever tried reading a novel in instalments like that, have you?'

'No,' sniffed the woman, her eyes not leaving the page.

'Well, it's a right confusion, I can tell you. You get hold of a second-hand copy of *Bentley's*, or some other magazine, and inside are these different chapters from different books. And you flick through it and it's all a bit long-winded and hard to read but, just as one story is getting going, it ends and you have to get hold of the next one. And I'm always missing out chapters and getting me episodes mixed up so half the time I don't know what's going on. And cos I'm the only one round in the family what's been schooled I have to read it out to all these others and they're all questions. What happened to the old gypsy woman what appeared out of nowhere? Why was the major all drugged and going on about ghosts? How did the blind soldier manage to escape his prison like that? I can never seem to find out so I just start making it up.' The woman turned a page and ignored Ruby. She did not seem to notice the blade of my small knife circle the part of her dress where the purse was. I grew confident.

'You don't have that problem with a thick old book like yours,' Ruby observed. 'You can just read the whole thing through from start to finish. What is it then?' she asked. 'One of them gothics?'

The lady sighed and raised her head away from the book. 'No,' she said. 'It is not one of *those* gothics. Nor is it one of those vulgar Newgate novels that are so popular in these periodicals of yours. It is a piece of realist literature by Mrs Sebastian Clement.'

The man opposite me was still engrossed in his paper, the omnibus cad was arguing with an elderly gent about the number of stoppages and the child was playing with the little dog. All the other travellers was lost in their own thoughts or conversations.

'Peculiar name for a woman' said Ruby. 'Most peculiar. She any good?'

'Sebastian is the name of her husband, dear girl. You've heard of the philosopher Sebastian Clement?' Ruby shook her head and the lady tutted in scorn at her ignorance. 'One of the world's foremost thinkers – of course you haven't heard of him. Well, this novel, *Teppingham*, is written by his wife, Lavinia, who uses her husband's name for reasons of decorum. And, in answer to your question, yes, she is very good. I consider her the finest novelist of the age. Indeed, of any age.'

As quiet as an insect bite my blade cut into her material.

'They said that about George Shatillion when he died,' said Ruby. The woman closed her book and turned her face down towards her.

'The fiction of George Shatillion,' she declared, 'bears very little relation to real life.' Slow but steady, my knife was slicing through the outer dress. 'Stolen wills, disappearing gypsies, ghosts. It would benefit someone of your class,' she informed Ruby, 'if you were to discard such sensationalism and instead pick up a book such as this.' She tapped the cover of *Teppingham*. 'This is a portrayal of provincial life which is mercifully free of endless incident and ludicrous coincidence. Rather, it explores the inner life of its characters, always a richer vein for the novelist.'

As she spoke I thought of my dead mother. It was she what had taught me how to cut open a woman's clothing like I was now doing and to slip in my hand unobserved. The thought of her meeting such a grisly end was enough to make me most melancholic. She and I had never enjoyed a loving relationship – I always knew she cared more for Horrie than she did for me, and her terrible temper did nothing to warm me to her. But I had never wanted for her to die a death so cruel and I now realised, what with all the endless incidents and ludicrous coincidences what had been happening in my own life, that I had been given no real time to mourn her loss.

'You see, Miss . . .'

'Flora,' said Ruby.

'You see, Miss Flora, the novel of character is vastly superior to the novel of plot. The former can inform the soul and comment upon our very humanity. The latter is prevented from achieving such grace as it is forever held down by the tiresome business of "What Happens Next?"'

My fingers gained purchase of the coin-purse but, as I tugged at it most gentle, I realised there was another piece of material between us, an inner pocket what I had not banked upon. Had the woman felt me pulling? Did I have enough time to cut some more?

'I don't believe I've ever read such a book,' commented Ruby. 'But I think I should like to.'

We was nearing the bottom of Tottenham Court Road, our next stop, and it was here I intended to get off the coach before my actions was discovered. My hand was still inside the lady's dress and I could feel her body alter as if preparing herself to do something. Should she now turn her head towards me I would be in as much trouble as some unwanted kittens in a sack. There was no way I could make it past this many gentlemen, least of all the conductor, before somebody grabbed me. I would be wrestled to the ground, arrested, tried and done for.

But instead this violet-smelling lady laid both hands upon her book, sighed again and handed it to Ruby.

'Here, child,' she said. 'A gift.'

'A gift?' asked Ruby. 'For me?'

'Yes. I want you to have it.'

'Really? Why?'

'Because, Flora, you strike me as a bright girl, if ill-educated, and I sense that your love of reading is as great as mine. I cannot bear to think of you rifling through those battered, haphazard periodicals, trying to make sense of the nonsensical, when within these pages true excellence awaits you. I can easily afford another copy. In fact, I shall buy myself one at the bookstalls this very day.' I had cut through the second pocket, my hand was on the purse. 'But it is my hope that with this gift I might inspire in you, someone who has been blessed with far fewer advantages than I, a truer education about what life is. And what matters most to we women of finer sensibilities.'

'Totnum! Court! Road!' yelled the cad.

The purse was out of her pocket and into mine just as the omnibus reared up at the stop and I was on my feet. 'This is me,' I told the cad, and he opened the door to let me out as I stepped over the little dog what was running around my feet. Its string though had tied itself around my feet and I had to laugh at the animal's mischievousness as I reached down to untangle it while wishing I could kick the thing for hindering the ease of my escape. Ruby, meanwhile, was still stopping the old girl from realising her loss by telling her how grateful she was for this surprise gift. She was an excellent actress, I thought, as she gathered her shawl up and made to leave also, so that I could have almost believed that the kindness of the woman was really affecting her soft heart if I did not know her better.

'That's very generous of you, Mrs . . .'

'Miss Trotwood.'

'. . . Miss Trotwood. I promise I shall read it all the way through from start to finish.'

'Do so,' said the old bat as she bowed her head. 'Learn from its lessons and then read it to others. But . . .' I heard the woman say to her as I paid the conductor his shilling, 'are you not taking your child?'

'Oh, she ain't with me,' Ruby explained as she too reached for her fare. 'I ain't sure who she's with.'

Once alighted I lost myself down Crown Street but not before peering around the corner to check that Ruby had got out of the carriage safely too. I saw her then waving at the departing green omnibus with much enthusiasm and it occurred to me that now she was taking the act too far. These theatrical types can be a liability on the job if you don't watch them.

Ten minutes later, as we had agreed, we met again in Soho Square to compare findings and there she was, sat on a bench reading this book. It was a shrewd way, so I thought, of making herself, an unaccompanied woman, look inconspicuous and I again marvelled at what a natural performer she was. Since we parted ways at the omnibus I myself had been strolling around the nearby Soho streets and there was many men what had bumped into me that morning in Old Compton, Frith or Greek streets who would have found themselves a lot lighter for valuables afterwards. I had about me three gold pocket watches and several fat wallets and I was keen to show this great bounty to her so she could see that I, and not her Jem, was the finest thief she knew.

'What a thing,' I said to her, all smiles as I approached the bench, 'that the old plant should just give you that book without you having to steal it or nothing. What a thing.' Ruby looked up from the book most surprised. She must not have seen me coming.

'Yeah,' she said at last. 'And look what's written in it.' She flicked to the cover page and showed me a signature with tiny little ink-blots splashed around it. Above this was written:

To my dear Elizabeth Trotwood, to whom I owe everything,
Lavinia

'Nice,' I approved. 'Signed by the author, eh? You should charge your Jew double for that.'

'It's about a young girl what is mistreated by those around her,' Ruby said as she placed the ribbon between the pages and shut the book. 'I ain't sure that I want to fence it.'

'Perhaps best,' I agreed as she stuffed it into her reticule. 'With that signature inside it could be tracked back to us. At least rip that page out first and burn it if you do. Anyway, look what I got!'

We stepped beneath an overhanging tree so we could not be seen from the street. I had spotted an unnerving amount of these new peelers on patrol and I was feeling cautious. From out of my pockets I produced the wallets, fogles and tickers what I had snatched in this vicinity as well as some choice items I had managed to pinch on the walk down to Shoreditch. I could tell Ruby was most impressed with my dexterity of touch and she made all the right noises as I displayed them in front of her. And then, as if this was top of the bill, I pulled out the bulging silk coin-purse I had removed from the lady's dress pocket.

'She must be very well off indeed, your Miss Trotwood,' I said, stroking the beaded decorations and fringing. 'This feels like all sovereigns.' I opened the purse and sure enough it was brimming with gold coins. 'What a find,' I laughed. 'Still top-sawyer!'

Ruby, however, did not appear to be as elated by this as I had expected.

'Do you think she'll be all right getting home, Jack?' she asked, biting her lower lip. 'Without no coins, how will she pay the omnibus cad?'

'Don't worry yourself,' I said as I counted out the sovereigns, getting more and more jubilant at their increasing value. I could not have wished for a choicer prize. 'She'll be all right.'

'Yeah.' Ruby nodded. 'A woman like that. All tall and sure of herself. She'll be all right.'

These coins was worth more than to enough to pay off Greta, buy myself some new tailorings and take Ruby out somewhere flash for luncheon. And I could now afford decent lodgings for tonight. 'Profitable,' I said as I dropped them back into the purse one after the other. 'Very profitable.'

'She was an interesting woman, weren't she, Jack?' Ruby said. 'Miss Trotwood. I should have enjoyed talking to her about books a while longer.'

'She was indeed, Rube,' I agreed as we set off back towards the crowds. 'That's what I missed the most about London during my time away. You meet such interesting people here.' I was keeping an eye out for peelers as we stepped across Carlisle Street. I took Ruby's arm in mine so that we would look like a respectable couple. She did not resist me, in fact it felt most comfortable. As we walked towards Dean Street we passed a short fat priest running towards the square. I doffed my hat as he passed and he smiled back.

'Seems a shame, don't it?' Ruby said.

'What does?'

'To thieve off a nice old bird like her.'

'Why's that then?'

These streets, I considered as we crossed through to Wardour, was not near populated enough. Nor did those populating them strike me as very affluent. We would need to head back to Oxford Street where the pickings was richer and then down to Regent Street.

'Cos she was kindly,' Ruby answered. 'And I always feel it ain't nice to steal off someone what's done you a good turn.'

We was getting closer to the big crowds now and I was keen for her to drop this line of conversation in case somebody over-heard us.

'She weren't kindly, Ruby, she was rich. It's no great thing to give a person a book if you have libraries of the things back at home.' I lowered my voice in the hope that this would encourage her to do the same. 'She most probably felt it was too heavy to go on carrying.'

Ruby lifted at her reticule, what was now busting at the seams with this big book inside it. 'Perhaps,' she said.

Just before we headed out into the thick stream of people I realised that Ruby's thoughts was not where they should be. I pulled her arm most gentle away from the thoroughfare and into a tiny alley where we could talk this through before proceeding.

'What's troubling you, Ruby?' I asked her. 'You seem out of sorts.'

'Nothing,' she said. And then, with a twitch of embarrassment, she asked, 'Jack, are we bad people?'

'Bad people?' I asked, most stupefied by the question. 'You and me? What makes you ask such a thing?'

'Because we're on the thieve,' she answered.

I did not know how to reply to such an enquiry. I had never before been asked anything like it.

'Course we ain't,' I said at last. 'The very idea!'

'But it's a sin, ain't it?' she went on. 'Thieving. Taking things what ain't ours from those what have done nothing to harm us.'

It was clear to me now that this crafty omnibus woman had worked upon Ruby's conscience in much the same manner that the sleeping beggar whose boots I had stolen the night before had almost worked upon mine. This was the danger of using conversation as a distraction for those you wished to touch. Sometimes they touch you back.

'Nothing to harm us?' I said. 'If it's Miss Trotwood you're speaking of, then no, she didn't do nothing to harm us.' Ruby raised her eyes to mine and I touched her gloved hand what held on to the reticule. 'But she never done nothing to help us neither, not she nor anyone of her class. And to me, that's as bad as harming us.'

I stepped out of Ruby's way so she could see the rush of people what was marching up and down Oxford Street. 'See them swells,' I said as we took in the sight of all these people in their splendid finery – the top hats, the tailcoats, the bejewelled necks, the fancy bonnets, the latest fashions. Popping in and out of different shops, arms full of brightly coloured gift boxes, Christmas presents for their loved ones no doubt. Backs straight, noses held aloft, like nothing in the world could harm them. All so handsome, all so polished. Respectable fathers, fashionable mothers, beloved children. 'Them swells, Ruby,' I told her, 'would not care a farthing if you or I was to drop down dead at their feet. They just would step right over us and hail themselves a hansom.'

Ruby did not seem shocked at my words. It was something she already knew and I was only reminding her. 'They know nothing of the streets we was born in,' I went on, 'though they glide by them every day on their way to somewhere cleaner. There is not one of them what ever gives a moment's thought to how we can live so poor and what can be done about us. They don't care if we're brutalised or kept ignorant. Their homes are grand and comfortable and if they see someone poor, outside in the cold night, gazing in through the window, then they draw the curtain and think no more about it. Perhaps they will call for a peeler who will come and shoo us away, for the peelers are their servants, not ours.' As I said this one such character plodded past and we both turned away to not draw attention to ourselves. Once he had passed we looked back. 'As long as we don't suffer inside their living rooms they don't care where we suffer. They are happy for us to starve,' I said, 'or to live as low as animals.'

I reached then into my pocket and pulled out the purse what I found on Miss Trotwood. 'And yet, when we behave like animals and hunt for what we cannot live without –' I made the coins jingle – 'they act as though we are the ones at fault and cry for us to be locked up or packed off to some dusty foreign place or, worse still, hung. There ain't one of them, Rube, not your Miss Trotwood, not the men in Parliament and not our new Queen sat fat and comfortable upon her throne, what would take our side if they did not need to.' I could tell from the way her eyes was beginning to lift that I was setting her right. She had no reason to be ashamed of her soft-heartedness but it was a quality people of our class could not afford. Our eyes did not meet then though; instead she looked over my shoulders at the tall houses behind. She seemed to start at something but I pressed on. 'They ain't our friends, Ruby,' I said, putting away the purse again, 'they're the opposite of that. They expect us to live off air and the nothing that they provide for us. Or they do not want us to live at all.'

Ruby and I was close together now, almost as close as we had been during my bath, and I felt the need to kiss her again. She looked back at me, our eyes locked and I saw a hardness in them.

'Jack,' she said then as if desperate to tell me something.

'Besides,' I whispered, stopping her from whatever she was about to say, 'it ain't like you'll ever see the woman again.' I moved closer and placed my hands on her waist. I tilted my head and went in for that kiss. I was desperate to know if she would respond.

'Flora!' a voice cried out. 'Get away from that boy. He's a thief!'

I turned my head and saw her, standing tall and furious on the other side of Oxford Street, her parasol, purple to match her outfit, pointing across at me, a thick slash along the pocket-side of her dress. She was flanked either side by two peelers, both of them taller even than her, but who both seemed to be having trouble seeing me through the roaring traffic between. 'That's the boy, officers,' she announced loud enough for all Oxford Street to hear. 'The boy from the bus! And look, he's about to molest that poor defenceless girl!'

Chapter 16

The Tiresome Business of
'What Happens Next?'

I am chased

The two peelers dashed across the street before she had finished
speaking, weaving in and out of the racing phaetons and hackney
carriages towards me. My hands was off Ruby in an instant and
my feet already charging back towards Soho. Ruby, I could hear,
was fast behind and not foolish enough to think that Miss
Trotwood would labour under her false impression for long. There
was enough distance between us and the peelers, what had still
not made it through the bustling shoppers, to exchange words as
we came to a crossroads.

'We're being followed,' she said.

'I can see that,' I panted. 'See you at the spot,' I said before she
scudded off in her direction. 'I'll hang back so they chase after
me.' I turned and saw the men, both tall, and leaner and fitter
than the old Bow Street Runners, make it across the street and
into the road where we were. I paused just long enough for them
to see which way I was going and then turned on my heel. My
first thought, as I ran, was that they would not chase after Ruby.
Her safety was the thing I prized above all others.

The second thing I prized above all others was my own safety
and, if I'm truthful, it was a very close second. I cut through into

the nearest turning in the hope that I would encounter a great crowd to lose myself in. But, as I had noted before, the back-streets was not well populated and I was unlikely to be able to hide behind this band of three small urchins what was frolicking in the street ahead of me. One boy what was trying to entertain the others by standing on his head with his heels in the air seemed to take a nasty tumble and fall flat on his back, an accident what could have been avoided had he not performed his feat straight in the middle of my path of escape. I could hear him making a right old fuss about it behind me but I did not stop to look back as I was already quickening my pace and dashing into another turning what led to a courtyard with a number of exits. This was always the best way for a cat to lose a dog and so the trick was bound to work on a pair of stupid peelers.

But once inside the courtyard I saw that it was occupied by a gathering of dustmen filling up their dirty great box-cart what they had left right in front of one pathway. The biggest of the men, what was ringing a great bell and calling for people to bring out their dust, was stood in front of another alley, but I pushed past him and headed down it in the hope that the peelers would think I'd taken the third, unobstructed, cut. However, before I had even made it to the end of that alley I heard something what surprised me almost as much as Ruby's earlier question. Back in the courtyard I heard the peelers ask the dustmen, in loud regimental voices, down what path I had vanished. And the dustman with the bell could be heard telling, as loud as if still calling out 'Dust Ho!', that I had just dashed past him and had gone in this direction. I was astounded by this betrayal. A working man, an honest labourer, taking sides against one of his own class. This would never have happened back in the time of the Runners. In those days most ordinary people knew better than to help a policeman; they kept quiet or even hindered those in authority to protect a poor man's hero like me. But now it was as though these new blue policemen, Sir Robert's Men, was respected by the people. Feared. Perhaps even approved of.

This was a most disturbing development for a thief, but this was no moment for dwelling on it and I was through to another narrow lane and then down an even tighter path before the peelers could blink. My heart was hammering even faster than my legs raced and, as I came to a low wooden fence and sprang over it, I found myself thinking of Kat Dawkins again. This was all very similar to the scene of her arrest that Inspector Bracken had described and I was scared that, if caught, I too would face the same grim fate. But the son was quicker than the mother and I crossed the yard I had landed in and was over the far brick wall before my pursuers had even reached the fence. Now obscured from their sight, I could make off in any direction I cared to, but as I headed off towards a maze of nearby streets I heard another woman's voice, rougher and shriller than Miss Trotwood's, informing the officers as to my movements. I looked up and saw an old woman leaning out of an overlooking window, her grey hair tumbling down and her arm pointed straight at me, screaming, 'That way, officers! After the wretch!'

It was starting to appear as though all the good people of London had turned police spy against me and that I could not feel safe until I was clear of them all. I should have lost these peelers by now but what with this, and the dawning realisation that this new breed of policeman was more persistent than any what had gone before, I saw that things was far more desperate than I first feared. If I was to dodge these villains for good then perhaps running fast was not enough. What I needed to do was to vanish. I needed an unlocked door or somewhere else to hide. It was then that I turned a corner and saw the open trap door outside of a public house, where the brewery drops the casks. This street looked to be deserted and so I dashed towards it in the hope of pulling the door shut after me and hiding in that cellar until the peelers had passed. The pub was old and dirty, the sort where you can tell just from looking at the outside that the landlord has yellow teeth and a cough. But as I approached it, I could not see anyone about and it was not until I got close enough to peer in that a massive head, what no doubt was attached to a massive body, popped out and shouted at me to clear off.

Back in my childhood I knew these streets well. I even felt as though I knew the people what dwelt in them. But now, a young man returned, I saw that all about me had altered and I grew afraid that I could not move about as free as once I had. The sounds of the peelers' boots was not far behind and I ran past the pub and into a lane what I remembered as being a clear route through to the nearest rookery, where I hoped folks would be more sympathetic. It was a narrow path of low houses with walls of sooted black and in it there was several poor persons ambling about. But, as I dashed down it, I saw that it had been fenced off at the end. I cursed aloud, knowing that at least one of my pursuers was close enough to see that I had taken this lane and I could hear him shouting those hateful words 'Stop thief!' as I did so. The fence was high and I knew that my only means of escape was to take a run at it, grab the top and haul myself over. I thought that if I could do this it was unlikely that the peelers would follow, no matter how dedicated to their profession they thought they was. I might even be able to haul myself up to the rooftops and escape that way. My feet sped up but, as I charged towards the fence, two men covered in soot tried to block my path and wrestle me.

'We got him, constable!' yelled the first as he made to grab at me. 'Come on, son,' he said to the younger chimney sweep behind, 'let's have him.' I shoved this older fellow in the chest and he fell back but I could not dodge the other, whose black hands was on my matching coat before I could pass. He was cursing at me for pushing the other with such force and told me that I was going nowhere until the peelers took me for theirs. I struggled to free myself but he was a bigger man than I and it seemed as though I was done for.

Then, and I am unsure as to where it flew in from, he was struck in the face by a thrown object and he released me in surprise. I bolted fast but I got a good glimpse at what had hit him before it clattered to the ground. It was a short wooden stick with a bend in it.

I was now free, but this encounter had slowed me so that I did not have enough of a run on to thrust myself over the fence. I tried anyway and jumped up as high as I could, but although my hands got purchase of the top I struggled to pull the rest of me over.

My legs was climbing upwards and my muscles strained to make it happen but the sweeps and a peeler was too close behind and, as I was about to pull my body over to the other side, the young sweep what had taken the hit came from behind and grabbed my left leg. I kicked out like an angry horse and he backed away but now the peeler was closing in and between them they would for certain take me no matter how savage my kicks was. I had managed to throw my other leg over the fence by now and had almost cleared it when the first peeler took hold and tugged at me hard. The fence what I clung to began this violent shaking as I fought to escape and I could see that on the other side was an empty courtyard. There was four pathways leading away from this one and if I could just get over there would be no witnesses to which route I would take. I could hear footsteps running down one of them though towards me and I knew that if this was the second peeler I would be trapped both ways. The peeler behind me pulled hard now and the sweeps tried to help him and I turned to spit at the cowards for aiding the police. But on the other side of the fence I could hear the footsteps run up to me and two strong hands grabbed right leg and I prepared myself to be taken.

Then a voice, familiar and deep, told me to give him my hand and let him pull me. I turned from the sweeps to the other side of the fence, where Warrigal hissed at me to keep fighting them. My arms reached out to him and Warrigal, with one foot on the fence, pulled me so hard that it almost seemed as though the rickety wood would come crashing down with me. I landed on top of him, he cursed and called me an elephant, but we was both already on our feet and off down one of the four pathways to freedom.

Whether that peeler was ever inclined to get one of his sooty admirers to hoist him over the fence and chase after us this history cannot record. For we ran so hard away from him, weaving through crooked alleys and hidden passages, that we had crossed three districts before stopping to catch our breaths. I made no attempt to run away from Warrigal now. I was so grateful for his assist-ance that it didn't even occur to me that he may still want to do me in and that I might have been better off with the police after all. Instead we moved quick through the streets, shoulder to shoulder and talking about what was the shortest and best cuts, as though we was old pals reunited. His sudden appearance had been such a pleasant surprise to me in so desperate an hour that I did not think to question where he had sprung from or how he could have known where I was. We was nearing a pie shop known as Mrs Cunningham's, by St Giles, the spot where I had agreed to meet Ruby should we come to be separated, and by now we had both slowed to a brisk and inconspicuous walk. Only then did I think to ask the man how in heaven he had managed to find me in time to swoop in and be my salvation.

'Never left you,' Warrigal replied darkly.

'I know you didn't,' I said back. 'I left you.'

Warrigal shook his head in weariness at my softness. 'You can't leave me,' he said as if imparting a secret. 'I'm your shadow.'

We came to a shop what bore the sign 'CUNNINGHAM'S' in faded green lettering and below that read 'HOT EELS, PIE, MASH AND MORE BESIDES'. I recalled having been here many years ago with my mother, who worked upstairs when I was a young kinchin. Kat never would have served pie and mash though – the upstairs floor of Cunningham's was where they sold the more besides. Kat used to leave me down in the steaming pantry with the big pots of eels swimming in circles while she took customers up the stairs for a half-hour at a time. It was not a place I had much fondness for and I wondered what made Ruby choose it.

Once inside I cast my eyes about and saw that Ruby was not there. In spite of this I led Warrigal over to a small table at the back, where we could order up some vittles and where I could keep an eye on the door for when she walked in. Mrs Cunningham, whose head had always looked to me as though it had been boiled in one of her own cooking pots, scuttled over to us as hot-faced as ever. She asked us what we cared for, winking as she did so, and down the side of her left cheek I noticed that she still had that scar. I wondered whether or not she recognised me from all those days when I had been left in the kitchen while my mother was upstairs but somehow doubted it. I would have been around ten years of age when I last saw her and, if the truth be told, the parting of ways between her and my mother was not amicable. I can recall seeing the two of them squaring off outside a pub at the corner of Seven Dials and Monmouth, Mrs Cunningham screaming accusations at my mother about some liberty she had taken with Mr Cunningham. Both of them was aflame with gin, and a large crowd poured out from the pub to watch as Mrs C called my mother a thieving odd-eyed whore and my mother replied by calling her a sweating pig-faced stink-hole who couldn't even keep her dog on the porch let alone a husband. Mrs C then tried to land a blow on my mother, encouraged by the spectators who was all taking her side. But Kat dodged and weaved before swinging her own arm, with a small blade out, and cutting straight into the side of the Cunningham cheek. Blood spilled and the crowd roared at the slyness of such an attack but I, still young and innocent, found myself feeling most proud of my mother as she took my hand and we fled before any violent recriminations could follow.

So it was unlikely that Cunningham's friendly wink was caused by some fond recognition of the adorable Dawkins child. Instead she wanted to insinuate that, if I was interested in more than refreshment, there was a number of ladies draping themselves about the tables and behind the counter what was available. These smiling sinners was an appealing sight, loose-haired, half-dressed, sitting themselves beside the many male patrons and making sweet talk. But I was devoted to Ruby and so I told Mrs Cunningham that we was only wanting victuals and ale.

'And for your Arab?'

'He ain't an Arab,' I told her. 'And he'll have the same as me and plenty of it.' I reached into the Trotwood's purse and produced one of her shining sovereigns. 'Keep the ale coming,' I said as I flipped it to her.

Warrigal's expression was as cross as ever, his arms folded, his coat buttoned up and I could see that the chill was still upon him. He was attracting a lot of attention as he sat there shivering as, although London was populated with many dark-skinned servants and beggars, few of these was as well-dressed and it was unusual to see a colonial sat with a gentleman such as I appeared to be. He would have looked more natural if he was to act like a servant around me but I did not have the nerve to tell him this, considering he had just saved me.

He sneezed then and I handed him a new handkerchief what I had found hiding in an old man's pocket when in Soho. 'If your whatever-he-is has the influenzy,' said Mrs Cunningham, who had returned with two pewter pots of beer, 'then it would be best for him to wait outside for you to finish up. I don't want my girls getting took ill.'

'He's an aborigine.' I scowled at her as I took the drinks. 'Not a dog. Just hurry up with them eels, can you?' Once she was gone, and I was sure we was out of earshot, I turned to Warrigal and held my beer pot aloft. 'Cheers for getting me out of a tight spot, Warrigal,' I said. Warrigal eyed me hard. He knew that I wanted him to lift his pot and chink it against mine in a gesture of friendship but he did not want to play. 'I know you only done it for your own ends,' I continued. 'You need me out of prison if you're ever going to find that jewel, I suppose. But I want you to know that I was pleased to see you when I did. Very pleased.'

Warrigal gave a small nod to acknowledge this.

'And I'm sorry you lost a decent boomerang over it,' I said with my beer still held out. 'I thought them things was supposed to come back to you?'

'Not when they hit,' he said.

'Oh, I see.'

'My father's boomerang,' he told me then. 'My dead father's.'

'Was it?' I shook my head at the shame of it. 'Which means I owe you double.'

His mean eyes did not leave my face and I began to wonder if he understood what it was I was encouraging him to do.

'In England,' I explained, 'when one cove wants to show friendship to another, say for instance if the first cove owes his freedom to the actions of the second cove, or if the first cove is sorry that he ran away from the second cove even if, as is sometimes the case, the second cove did try to kill the first cove when he weren't looking . . .' Warrigal gave a short quiet huff, 'then what they do to make up is to raise a glass like this –' I indicated my still raised beer pot – 'and chink them together to show that they is still great pals. That is a little custom we have here.'

Warrigal nodded again but still did nothing.

'Why don't we give it a go?' I continued. 'Come on, it'll do us good.' He did not move so I lowered my glass in defeat. 'Look, Warrigal,' I sighed, 'I know you don't care for me much. For some reason you've got it into your head that I can't be trusted.' He blew his nose on the stolen hankie I had given him. 'But if there is one thing I pride myself on, it's that I always takes care of my pals. If you was to behave like my pal, instead of like some paid murderer what might throttle me at any moment and who can never say a kind word, then I'd stick my neck out for you, believe me. Your problems would be my problems. In truth, your problems *are* mine. We both need this stone so let's stop acting like we hate one another and be tight for a change. You done me a good turn today and I appreciate it in spite of what you might think. And if the time comes when you need me to do you a good turn, then I won't hesitate.' Mrs Cunningham was heading back over to the table with her hands full of bowls and plates. 'But I'll only do it if we're pals,' I said, lowering my voice as she reached us. 'If we ain't, then you're on your own.'

The plates of pie and mash was put in front of us and a bowl of eel soup each was placed at the side. We said not a word to each other as Mrs Cunningham fussed around us, remarking on how starving we must be to have ordered so much. 'We'll need another chair,' I told her. 'A lady friend will be joining us later.'

After she had left I tucked a napkin into my shirt and picked up my knife and fork to tuck in. But then I heard Warrigal cough and looked up to see that he was looking at me with his pot of beer raised.

I smiled and lifted mine again.

'That's the spirit,' I said as we chinked them together. Then we turned back to our plates and feasted like bears.

Chapter 17

The Art of Shadow

Containing dark happenings and silent movements

It is no easy thing, the shadow. To follow a cove unseen through these tangled streets, what can seem dense and confusing even for us Londoners, requires a skill, speed and artfulness that few possess. Back in my youthful days, when it could be said that I knew the map of the city as well as any hackney coachman, I was often called upon by the Jew to shadow those who he took an interest in, to be the fly what hovers after you, ever unnoticed but always watchful.

But for a stranger to the city like Warrigal, who had been on these alien shores for less than three days, to shadow so vigilant a quarry as myself over such a distance was nothing short of miraculous. He was an expert tracker, this much I knew, but the outback of Australia was a vast space what never changed and where footsteps, fires and other human leavings showed up bright and could not be hid. London though was not the outback; it was loud, ever-shifting, crammed with people all heading in a multitude of different directions and at varying speeds. To track a man through that was something else and I was most curious to hear how he had done it. As we sat opposite each other, slurping up those vinegary eels and waiting for Ruby to join us, he explained what had passed since last I saw him.

'Too much noise,' he said, with the little finger on his knife pointing over at me as he cut an eel in half. 'Too noisy, too much moving.' This was in reference to my attempts at slipping away from him and out of the Greenwich window. I was ashamed at this as I had been under the impression my escape had been all stealth and soundlessness. It seemed that Warrigal had watched my every movement and I spied a rare smile play upon his lips as he mimicked the sound of me lifting up the creaking window and looking both ways before pushing my body through it. He then went on to explain, after sucking the longer eel half into his mouth, that rather than just grab my legs as I was halfway out of the room and pull me back in, he instead decided to see where I would lead him. He had hoped that I would take him straight to the Jakkapoor stone, suspecting that I really did know where it was, and he reasoned that he would gain more from me if I thought myself alone. So the very second I crawled out on to the veranda he dressed himself, was out of the chamber door, down two flights of steps and watching me from outside as I shimmied my way down the flagpole and into the wedding party beneath. Once I was out into the street he knew that this part of the track would be simple as he had shoes and I did not so he just kept to the shadows and begun trailing me.

'You stole shoes,' he said then much to my shame, 'from a beggar.' He then told of how he had seen me down by the docks, making out I was all pious as I walked among the crowds reading from the Bible. He had mingled among the homeless, always just out of view, lost among a host of dark faces, and watched as I made a hypocrite of myself for money. 'Then you got in a cab,' he told me as if daring me to refute any of these events. 'A cab to which nobody saw me clinging.'

I considered this to be impossible and said so. That cab ride took me all the way to Whitechapel and, even if it was the dead of night, someone would have noticed him. 'They did not,' he said before adding, 'London people all eyes front.' He went on to say how he had clung to the shaded part of the undercarriage and described to me the sights and sounds of the journey. 'Your roads,' he said, shaking his head in bewilderment, 'are mad things.'

He seemed to think that the whole city had been designed for the very purpose of throwing trackers such as him off of their scent. He then said that after I had alighted at Bethnal Green he had shadowed me to Ruby's house and watched as I had entered. Using the outside wooden stairs of the house opposite and then the guttering, he had scaled the building and perched himself on the roof, where he had a perfect view of the old Sikes place and he watched through the window as Ruby, whom he recognised from Smithfield Market, lit the fire and ran me a bath.

'I saw all,' he said after another chill had run through him and he had fought a sneeze. 'Bath, kiss, man, fuss.'

'I didn't kiss her,' I protested. 'I didn't have time.'

'Her man is big,' he told me and waved a finger. 'Bigger than you. Watch yourself.'

'So you just sat up there on that roof all night?' I asked, keen to change the subject. 'No wonder you're in such a state.'

He shook his head and told of how he waited up there, underneath a high awning to keep him from the elements, until he saw candlelight glow in the lower room and then he climbed down and approached the ground-floor window. Peering through, he saw Ruby showing me my bed for the night and waited until she had left. Then, knowing from his own need for sleep that I would be out for hours, he withdrew from Bethnal Green and found a carriage what would speed him back to Greenwich so he could see to our things, pay the tavern and visit Evershed's man.

'Timothy Pin?' I asked, alarmed.

He nodded. 'Pin, yes.'

'Why did you do that?' I cried in alarm. 'You didn't tell him where I was, did you?'

Warrigal nodded again and told me that he had peached to him that I had tried to escape, where I now slept and, worst of all, that I had no real clue as to where the Jakkapoor stone was. In that moment any tender feelings what I may have been developing for my timely rescuer was pushed to one side and told to toughen up.

'Well, that's just blooming marvellous, Warrigal,' I moaned. 'What'll he do now, eh? What'll he do to me? To you? To those at Honey Ant Hill? He'll have sent a telegram to Evershed already, I'm wagering.'

Warrigal reached into his inside coat pocket and pulled out a small envelope.

'Read,' he said as he handed it to me. It was unsealed, unstamped and bore my name written with a flourish across the front. There was no ordinary paper inside however but rather a small calling card, the like of which I had often found inside the wallets of flamboyant theatrical types what I had brushed against.

Dear Mr Dawkins,

Delighted to learn that you have arrived home safely from your productive time spent in the colonies and I very much look forward to making your acquaintance. Our mutual friend, Mr Peter Cole, informs me that you have taken an unpleasant turn and are recuperating in a retreat in the East End of London. How tiresome for you. He also tells me that your expectations prove not as great as any of us had been told. Dear, oh dear.

It is advisable, indeed essential, that you accompany Mr Cole to my address so we can discuss what is to be done about you. If instead you should decide that you would rather reject this offer of assistance then, rest assured, I will come to seek you out regardless.

These are hard times for you, Mr Dawkins. Best not to make them any harder.

Yours in friendship,

TP

'Decent of him,' I said as I handed the card back to Warrigal, 'to show such me concern.' Warrigal took the card and put it back in the envelope. 'So, you're in his line of work,' I went on. 'When do you think he'll want to kill me?'

'Doesn't,' Warrigal replied. 'Not yet leastways.' He returned the envelope to his coat.

I sighed and took a swig of beer to wash down the mash. Warrigal was looking more tired than ever. 'Ain't you been to bed yet?' I asked with real concern. Warrigal said that he had not even had time to shut his eyes back in Greenwich as Pin sent him straight back in a carriage to watch over me. He was concerned that I might have moved on while he had been away, but when he crept up to the window where he had left me he saw I was 'underneath a big woman, going nowhere'. A wider smile as he told me this.

He then went on to tell, his manner getting lighter as he spoke, that he had hidden all morning outside Ruby's house until she and I emerged to go finding. Then he made straight for the carriage what Pin had sent him back in, and what was still waiting in a nearby street, and told the driver to follow our omnibus. Once we alighted at Tottenham Court Road he left the carriage and followed me on foot but my wanderings, as I picked my many

Soho pockets, was too haphazard and unpredictable to shadow me unobserved. So he climbed up on to a tall building, using wooden stairs what zigzagged up the side, in order so that he could watch me move through that small vicinity from above. Whenever he needed to he jumped from one building to another or, if he had to he would climb down one and then spider up the next. Nobody seemed to spot him or, if they did, they did not know to warn me about him. Near Oxford Street he watched from a much lower rooftop as I tried to kiss Ruby and where he thought she had seen him. Then he managed to keep pace with me as I tore through the streets away from the peelers. He sprinted over the rooftops, making bold jumps between them where possible and on occasion almost failing to make the distance. One gap between these two very high houses was too wide for him and he fell short of it and tumbled downwards towards the street below. But he managed to grab on to an open window underneath and haul himself into a room where a screaming old man was squatting over a pisspot and tried to throw the contents over him in fright. But Warrigal was out of the door, down the stairs and out into the road in time to see me get grabbed by the cross-sweeper. He positioned himself around the corner so the peelers could not see him and then threw his boomerang. Then he headed off in the other direction so he could meet me on the other side of the fence.

'Bravo, Warrigal,' I said. 'I'm impressed.'

'Should be,' he said, and drained the last of his beer.

Just then, as I was set to remark with sympathy upon how terrible he was starting to look, I smelt a strong feminine scent come up from behind. It was one I had smelt somewhere earlier that day and I got out of my seat, as a gentleman should, and turned to greet Ruby and enquire as to what had kept her so long. But instead I found myself facing a different female, far larger than Ruby and in a blue dress what was all flashy and loose. She was sailing through the tables in Cunningham's towards us and smiling at the many girls what worked there as she did so. As she reached our table the smile disappeared from her face and was replaced with a threatening scrunch. 'You got my five shillings yet?' she asked. I hadn't recognised Greta with her clothes on.

'What you doing here?' I asked, all rude. 'Where's Ruby?'

'Ain't coming,' Greta sniffed. 'I ran into her three corners away, and when she heard that I was on my own way here she asked if I would come and see you instead. She wanted to get back home to read some book.'

I pulled a chair out so she could sit with us and I counted out ten of the coins I had pinched and I placed them in her hand. 'That's double,' I said and, in a decided effort to ingratiate myself with her, added, 'and you was worth every one of them.'

She smiled as she tucked them down a pouch hidden in the top of her dress and, with a little dip of the head, said, 'Thank you very much, kind sir.' She softened then, after being paid her due, and shouted to one of the girls she knew to fetch her a drain of whisky and water.

Once Greta had taken a few sips she told me that Ruby had a warning for me. Then she turned her head to Warrigal as if just noticing him. He was still wiping his nose and looking like Death was a close relative who could pay him a visit at any time. She moved closer to me. 'She says there is some dark fella following you about on the rooftops. This'll be him, I suppose.' So that was what Ruby had meant when she said we was being followed. 'Your old servant what tried to kill you, so she said.'

'This is him,' I confirmed. 'But he ain't my servant no more. He's a pal and he would not hurt a fly.'

Greta turned back to him, smiled to say hello and asked why, if he was my friend, was I letting him suffer like this. 'He's got the vapours on him,' she observed, and indeed by now Warrigal's black face was closer to ash than to coal. 'You should get him resting before he dies here in front of us. It's only human.'

On this we agreed and so I thanked Greta for the message and told her we would head back to Bethnal Green forthwith. She, in turn, thanked me for the shillings and said how she very much looked forward to doing business with me in the future. Warrigal stumbled a bit as we left Cunningham's. His eyes was heavy and he looked like he was ready to pass out at any moment. He must have hardly slept since we was at Saffron Hill, had been outside with a head cold on his first winter's day in England and, to top it all, had spent the afternoon running around the rooftops like a madman. He was starting to look somewhat overcome by it all. Once out on the street I managed to hail us a cab what would take us back to Bethnal Green and we climbed inside, and out of the bitter cold. I wanted to spend the journey back in discussion of how we could set about finding the Jakkapoor stone but it was no use. Warrigal was asleep before we had even left the Dials.

Chapter 18

The Rat Pit

I attend a sporting event and make further enquiries
as to the whereabouts of lost princes

'Cur!' roared Sikes, louder than any other. He was in the grip of
a violent frenzy, red-faced and mad-eyed, with spittle hanging
from his mouth. 'Get your teeth in, for gawd's sake! Come on,
you wretched creature, 'ave 'im like you 'ad the others!'

The outhouse in the backyard of the Three Cripples shook with
the weight of the bodies what was crammed within, all crowded
around a large pit made of apple-case boards and in which a vicious
dog scrambled around over a dozen dead rats in hot pursuit of
the one remaining. This rat, the final thirteenth, had been doing
a heroic job of dodging his destiny for several minutes and if he
could keep it up for one more then the dog would be yanked out
of the pit and the bets counted.

'Cur!' yelled Sikes again at the dog, as the last rat made to leap
over the wooden fence only to be thrust back down by the
surrounding gamesmen. 'You're four times 'is size! 'Ave 'im, cur!'

Despite this encouragement the dog, whose name for all I knew
really was Cur, was still not quick enough for the rat and the game
continued apace. Cur was all muscle and aggression and had seized
the other rats in his teeth clean and quick and they was dead before
he was on to the next. But he was panting with tiredness now

while the nimble rat darted to the left, the right and even through the unhappy mutt's short legs. Sikes continued cursing over the cheers of the crowd, what was all boisterous young men fired up with gin, and, save for those losing money over it, they was all whooping with delight at so spectacular a show. Stood close beside me was Georgie, now a foot taller than I was, and he put his arm around my shoulder in a show of affection and handed me his half-drunk bottle. 'Good to 'ave you back, Dodge!' he said, stupid with happiness as I drank from it. He had been telling me all evening how much he had missed me. 'You was . . .' he slurred, his finger on my chest, his legs unsteady, 'the best of 'em. Fagin always said you was the best of 'em.' The raucous noise inside that outhouse was building, the rat had turned desperate on its attacker and the dog seemed to be retreating from it. 'Top-sawyer, that's what 'e called you. Even after you was gone.' Stood just as close on the other side was Jem White, and I could feel him turn as Georgie said this. 'None of us,' Georgie carried on in spite of Jem's pricked ears, 'could touch you on any scent. Tha's what Fagin said.' He prodded my chest with every word. 'On. Any. Scent.' Jem snatched the bottle out of my hand and gave Georgie a dark look. Georgie seemed blind to this and glanced over to him, looking for approval. 'In't that right, Jem?' he said. 'What Fagin said.'

'Fagin said all sorts,' Jem said before swigging.

It was my first time back at the Cripples since my return to London and I was happy to be surrounded by the companions of my youth. As well as Jem and Georgie I had been reunited that night with Mouse Flynn, Mick Skittles, Herbie Sharp, Little H and the Chickenstalker, all of whom treated my reappearance in the old neighbourhood as if Christ himself had risen again and brought with him a case of his father's finest cigars. I had left

Warrigal at Ruby and Jem's house after I had returned from Cunningham's so he could sleep off his sickness, but Jem had been most rattled to see him. Was this not the same Warrigal, he asked in alarm, what just the night before I had told him had tried to strangle me and from whom I had fled? Yes, I admitted, it was. But that had been a misunderstanding. Warrigal and I had made it up now, we intended to speak no more upon the unpleasant business and we would thank Jem if he too could respect this decision. Jem grumbled a bit but in the end relented. This, I suspect, was because, in spite of his ill health, Warrigal had the look of the very devil about him and Jem, in spite of his bluster, was a coward. So Warrigal was put to rest and an evening's entertainment was arranged for those of us what, even now, was still calling ourselves Fagin's boys.

'Useless cur!' yelled Sikes on the other side of the pen as his dog failed to land his teeth in the rat once more. 'I'll kill ya, if the rat don't first.'

I was pleased with this rat for putting up such a good show. I, like most of the lads from Saffron Hill, had money on the previous dog, one that had belonged to the McAllister twins, to catch his thirteenth rat in quicker time, and if this rat could keep away from Cur just a bit longer then we would have won the bet. If, however, the rat should fall before that time then all the money would be taken by the hated Sikes gang crowded opposite.

We Fagin's boys was all orphans. We had been plucked from the streets by the kindly Hebrew because he had seen promise in us and we had been taught secret skills without having to discover them for ourselves. Other young thieves, those what had been born into established criminal families and whose reputations rested on the dark deeds of their older relatives, hated us for this. They felt that we was favoured by the old man, treated like grubby princes, in spite of having no connections of our own to draw on. We had no names, the other boys would say of us, we had no families. We only had an ageing Jew who did not really care for us.

I had a touch more respect afforded to me by such people on account of Kat Dawkins who, while a dangerous lunatic with a knife, was at least a distinguished whore and villain. But there was a feeling among the other gangs that a boy what rested under Fagin's roof could turn traitor at any moment because they was wastrels from other places, not true Londoners. We could, as far as anyone knew, be related to anyone and therefore lead disaster into the rookeries. Often we would find ourselves getting into scraps with gangs of boys from named families. And one such gang was here tonight, betting on a different dog in the outhouse of the Three Cripples. They was the Sikes gang, made up of the sons, brothers and nephews of the nastiest crooks about, and they was led by this here Ben, younger brother of the more famous Bill.

'A curse on you!' Ben swore at the indomitable rat as it again leapt away from canine teeth. Fagin's boys, my boys, laughed all the harder to see his frustration and every so often he, or one of his cronies, would look over and call us bastards. We put up a fine show of pretending not to be scared of him but there was no doubt that his mob was bigger than ours and that if things erupted we would be outmatched.

'Out of time!' yelled Mouse, still the most excitable of us, and he drummed his little hands on the edge of the pit and jumped up and down. 'He's got to be out of time by now, Bolter!'

Morris Bolter, a slimy-looking cove what I had never met before but who seemed to be most familiar to the others, was keeping track on a faded old timepiece and shook his head.

'T'ain't,' he replied in a stubborn country accent. 'Still loads to go.' Nobody in the outhouse believed this, including myself. Cur had been in the pen for much longer than the McAllister dog, we all felt this, and a number of the boys tried to snatch the watch from his hands, accusing him of favouring Cur. Bolter whined and held it aloft but this made the boys fight for it all the harder. Young Crackit, a menacing cove and son of a respected burglar, then fought to protect Bolter, which was as sure a sign as any that the shifty country boy was in league with the Sikes gang. A rumpus broke out, just some light pushing, shoving and name-calling, but it gave me the chance, as I puffed upon my clay pipe, to regard Fagin's boys in action with as much freedom as if they was fighting in the pen themselves. Could any of these, I wondered, have been given the Jakkapoor stone?

As I watched my boisterous friends punch and kick at harder men I could see what a corrupting influence an upbringing in the house of Fagin had been to these once innocent children. It had made malefactors of them all. There was not one among them, even Mouse who had once been so easy to scare and who could never go to bed unless one of the older boys had brushed it for spiders beforehand, that I did not now view as the basest sort of villain. They had become the men polite society was afraid of, rogues, ruffians and thieves all. They was a scourge upon the peace and tranquillity of the city. They was, in short, some of the grandest companions a person could wish for and I was glad to be amongst them once more.

'The winner!' boomed Sikes then and threw his hands in the air in triumph. We all turned from the fracas and looked back down into the pit where Cur had at last sunk his teeth into his prey. The rat screamed in the dog's mouth as Cur began worrying it and, it should be recorded, it still put up an almighty fight to the last. But it was no use – the game was over and the rat done for.

The rest of his gang began crowding around Ben Sikes in congratulation, patting him on the back and cheering. Sikes laughed and called over to where I stood. 'You know your trouble, Dodger?' he jeered. He had heard that I, to be flash in front of the rest of the boys, had placed more money on the McAllister dog than anyone. 'You ain't that fuckin' artful after all.' His gang all roared at that and a chorus broke out about how I should have stayed abroad. I was having none of it though and I strode straight over to this Bolter, who I had disliked from the very moment I had set eyes on him, and got out my own watch to match his. It was a gold one that Evershed had presented to me to help me pass as a gentleman and that Warrigal had now returned. I could see the gathered thieves was most impressed with it.

'By my reckoning,' I said, showing everyone around the fine craftsmanship of the piece, 'it's ninety seconds after what your man here says it is. Which means he's a cheat what dialled his long hand back to favour your dog. And I ain't tolerating no cheats!' I snapped the watch shut as Fagin's boys all cried support and the Sikes gang roared outrage. Another rumpus broke out as Morris Bolter had to defend himself against accusations of rat fixing and a fist landed on his face courtesy of Georgie Bluchers. In truth, he must have only dialled it forward thirty seconds as my own had been wound back a minute to favour our dog. But as he fell to the floor the Sikes gang all bundled over to help him and then the outhouse shook with real sport as we all laid into each other and a fine time was had by all.

'You know who I feel sorry for?' moaned Mouse hours later in the taproom of the Cripples. He was pressing a slab of steak on to the bruise on his cheek in an effort to soothe it and was leaning over the same table I had been playing cards on six years ago when I had last seen Kat Dawkins. Georgie had been trying to count out the cards for another game of cribbage but he had dropped them all over the floor and he was now slumped asleep on his hands and knees. None of us wanted to disturb him – he'd been very free with his fists all night, even after we had left the outhouse and stumbled in here for an after-fight drink. It was best, we all agreed, to just leave him in his hunched position until morning rather than risk him lashing out at us again.

At this early hour there was only myself, Mouse and Jem still awake as the Sikes gang had all headed off back to Jacob's Island and the remains of Fagin's boys was either passed out or had run off during the fisticuffs. Herbie Sharp had long since emptied his guts into a metal bucket and was now, for all we knew, dead in the gutter. From the main bar we could hear the few remaining revellers gather around the new piano as someone played out a singalong, and every so often Barney, the landlord, would stick his head into the taproom and ask us if we needed anything. I'd been paying for the gin all night, even before we had gone into the yard for rat-pitting, and Barney was sure to tell me how pleased he was I was back and how proud Fagin would be of me. I smiled at him and raised my pipe in drunken thanks before asking him if he would care to scuttle along and get us another bottle before bedtime as this one was nearly done. After he'd gone I leaned over to the glasses of Jem and Mouse and with an unsteady hand shared the dregs out between them.

'The rat,' said Mouse as I did so.

'What about him?'

'That's who I feel sorry for.'

'Why?' asked Jem, vexed by the sentiment. He had been cradling his face in his hands, ready to sleep, but was now awake again and reaching for his glass, an irked look on his face.

'Because if that sneak Bolter,' Mouse spat the name, 'had played fair and called time earlier,' he pointed his finger in stern judgment at Bolter, who was not present, 'the rat woulda been crowned champion.' I smiled at Mouse as he slurred this. He was still as soppy as ever, underneath the grime. 'The rat,' he went on, slapping the steak down on the table, 'should have won. I think he deserved to.'

'You're a fool then,' growled Jem, who had never found Mouse's whimsy to be as charming as I did. 'If he'd've won they just woulda stuck him back in his box and used him in the next game. Rats don't win, idiot,' he explained. 'They're doomed from the start.'

Mouse looked crestfallen at this remark and I thought it as good a time as any to raise a toast to something less maudlin. 'To Saffron Hill,' I said as I held my own glass aloft, 'and to good old Fagin.' Mouse and Jem lifted their own and chinked them against mine. 'And to Eddie Inderwick,' I went on, 'and to Charley Bates. Wherever those boys may be.'

This toast did not go down well and I had expected it not to. Jem sneered in disgust at both their names, Mouse went silent and even Georgie raised up his head and shook it. I knew from earlier that both these boys was less popular than before I went abroad and so I had raised their names now to discover more about why.

Eddie Inderwick was one of the older boys what had been nearing the end of his education at Fagin's school around the time that we was beginning ours. You might say he was our prefect, at least is how the more respectable schools around the land might have referred to an older boy what was so admired. Fagin was forever holding him up as a model thief to the rest of us. 'Be as steady as Eddie,' he would urge us before pushing us out of the door for our day's work, 'and as lucky.' When Eddie came of age he soon moved out of Fagin's lodgings and in with an attractive young woman named Sally Quick, who was as admired for her handsome looks and her thievery as much as he was. Still Eddie used to come back and visit the kitchen often, dressed up all flash. He would slip some money to his dear old teacher and give us boys all good advice about how to stay one step ahead of the traps. He was a hero, was Eddie Inderwick, and I wondered at how his name could now meet with such derision.

'Eddie get grabbed?'

'Some years back,' said Georgie. 'At Cremorne Gardens for pinching a wallet what had just dropped out of cove's pocket.'

'Only this cove was a peeler,' Jem continued for him. 'On his day off, if you can believe that, and he grabbed Eddie in seconds.'

'It was a trap, from the sound of things,' sighed Mouse. 'These peelers never play fair.'

'Is Eddie still in prison?'

'Nah,' said Jem. 'He was only put away for about six months. Nothing really. But prison done something to him and he was never the same Steady Eddie.'

'I saw him in a gin-house the week after his release,' Georgie told me. 'Grey skin, underfed. He had this massive bruise on his eye from a fight the night before.'

'Ben Sikes done that,' Mouse told him. 'He'd been getting comfortable in Sally Quick's bed while Eddie had been away, and there was this confrontation. Eddie started it; Ben finished it.'

'His hands was always trembling from then on,' said Jem, mimicking the shakes as he lifted his gin glass. 'Useless to us.'

'He got took up again for an attempt on a lady's purse, only this time it was no trap,' said Georgie. 'He had just lost the touch. He spent two years in Tothill Fields Prison and when he got out he no longer had the nerve for the more daring work. I hear he's a sorry thief now, stealing from old boats on the riverside, rolling over drunks, that sort of shamefulness. Most of his money goes to the Chinamen these days. You can find him at Wu's I should imagine, losing himself in the smoke.'

'And for this reason you all want nothing to do with him?' I asked in surprise. 'Just because he's an opium fiend?'

'He's still a pal.' Mouse shook his head. 'We just can't work with him no more.'

'It weren't him we was cursing,' Jem growled, and then sunk another glass. 'We was cursing the other one? *Your best pal!*'

'Charley?' I replied, taken aback.

'Yeah, Bates!' Jem said, and burped. 'The splitter!'

'Charley wouldn't split on anyone, Jem,' I said, and looked to the others for reassurance. 'He was staunch.'

'It's true, Dodge,' said Mouse in a softer manner. 'Charley told the peelers where Bill was hiding after Nancy's murder. Leaned out of a window and shouted his name to a whole mob what was hunting for him. That's why he ain't around no more. The Sikes gang'd settle accounts if he was to show his face.'

'Not just them,' Jem said, getting to his feet to address the room on unsteady legs. 'I won't have splitters in my gang neither. We'd settle him too if we got hold of him, eh, boys?'

The other two was half-hearted in their agreement but Jem did not seem to notice. He just stood there for some minutes and talked us through the many violent acts he would inflict upon Charley Bates should they ever meet again.

I was most intrigued by the news of Charley's flight, and not just out of disappointment at him being a white-livered splitter. I also suspected there might be another reason for his wanting to vanish from London just as things was getting nasty. A young robber doesn't head off on his own with nothing, I knew that. He takes the means to start a new life. And where would Charley Bates, prosperous thief though he was, get that sort of capital? Perhaps he had in his possession something very valuable. Something priceless.

'Fagin was wrong about that one,' declared Jem with bitterness. 'He used to be one of the old man's favourites. And he betrayed us.'

'Is that what you think, Jem?' I asked with too much interest. 'That Fagin thought of Charley as a favourite?' Jem misunderstood my question and turned nasty on me.

'Oh, don't you fret on it, Dodger,' he swayed over, curling his lip. 'You was always the *Top-Sawyer!*' He started mimicking the old Jew in a way I did not find humorous. But then impersonations never was Jem's gift. '"*Be more like the Artful, my dear,*"' he said in a voice that sounded nothing like the man. '"*The Artful this . . . the Artful that . . .*" Pah! It was like you was his own Jew son.'

At this moment Barney came back into the room with the gin bottle I'd asked for. He had heard Jem getting louder from the main tavern and was keen to stop any trouble brewing. 'What's all this then, eh?' he said in a friendly manner. 'Ain't we all good pals still?'

'Gerroutofit, you rotten Hebrew,' Jem barked at him. 'You're another one I can't abide.' The honest Barney flinched at these words as if he had been spat at. Both myself and Mouse was outraged by this verbal attack upon the good landlord and we said so.

'Don't go breathing your fire on him, Jem,' I told him straight. 'Barney's safe, safer than most. Just because Fagin never rated you as a thief don't mean you can speak to his friends however you care to.'

'Ignore 'im, Barn,' Mouse said. 'He lost some money on a dog, that's all.' Barney handed me the gin bottle and said that it was on him.

'But maybe drink it on the way home, eh, Dodge?' he suggested. 'And take your pal there with you. Bedtime for Barney.' The music from the bar had stopped by now and he begun snuffing out candles around the taproom. I took the bottle and stuffed it in my coat pocket what was hung on the rack. 'You can leave Georgie here,' said Barney, noticing that he had passed out underneath the table again. 'I'll get him a blanket and lay him out nice and comfortable.'

'Aah!' Jem groaned as he went to get up and shook his head in regret. 'You know I loves ya, Barn,' he said to the fine old man in a humbler tone. 'It's just the Dodger. 'E vexes me so with all his talk of being Fagin's favourite, reminding us all the time. Fagin never called *me* his favourite,' he said, his voice all self-pity. I tapped the last of the tobacco from my pipe out into a tin, coughed and told him that I could well believe that. Jem turned on me again, his voice raised and angry.

'I'm top-sawyer now, Dodger, not you. Maybe you was, once along ago, but not no more, y'hear. Not no more.' He punched his chest and stood like he was a savage warning off foreign settlers from his own land. 'Don't like it? Well, go back to the colonies and take the black boy with you. This ain't your city no more. You can cut away just like Bates did!'

'Oi oi oi.' A voice from the floor. It was Georgie, lifting up his face with a look of agony. 'What's this row about, Jem?' he asked, rubbing his head. 'Jack ain't like Charley. He'd never get scared and run off at the first sign of trouble.'

'You reckon, do you?' Jem said. He turned to me. 'Why d'you want to see Bates anyway?' he asked. 'So you and him can boast about how clever you both is? Chuckling together, like you always did, always about me.' He prodded my chest. 'Well, the Jew was wrong, weren't he? None of you was worth half of what I am – the blind old fool just couldn't see it.' He was getting right in my face now, daring me to fight him, using his gin breath as his first weapon. 'All the ones he loved turned bad, didn't they? All three. Your pal Bates . . .' He leaned in close and I backed away, which I knew was a mistake as soon as I did it. I couldn't have Mouse and Georgie see me cowering, not if I was to be their top-sawyer again. 'Always the giggling fool – in the end he was no more than a rat and a coward.' I stood still as he gave me all his front. I let him perform for a bit, knowing he would run out of steam. 'You . . .' he went on, in love with his own slurred voice, '. . . arrested for something as trifling as a silver snuffbox. Paffetic!' It would not take much to drop him, I knew. His feet was unsteady as he stepped forward; I was by far the more sober. 'No wonder Ruby went off ya! I've seen the way you looks at her. But a woman like that don't want those what are all mouth. She wants a man like me, what—'

Unfortunately Jem did not get to finish extolling his own virtues as Ruby's preferred lover. He was instead most rudely interrupted by my fist smashing up into his face. The surprise of it caused him to stagger backwards and crash straight down on to the table, scattering the gin glasses and the tobacco tin. He rolled over and on to the floorboards and the others all called out in surprise. Georgie rushed over to help him up and Barney ran about to see how many of his glasses had been smashed. 'My eyes, Jack,' said Mouse as I rubbed my knuckles, what had only just been starting to heal from their fight with Warrigal, 'you've gone and lain him out flat.'

I stepped over to see if this was so and as got close Jem sprang up again and came at me, landing a powerful blow to my chin. I fell backwards and landed hard but Mouse and Georgie was up and pulling Jem away from serving me more.

'Rah!' Jem struggled and he swore loud that he would kill me. But the boy was so stricken from the drink that his limbs would not let him stand his ground and Georgie had to put Jem's arm over his shoulder just to help him to a chair.

'We've been at the spirits,' he said. 'Time to call it a night.'

'You!' Jem pointed at me again, his throat rebelling against more than one word. 'Dawkins!' he managed. 'You is . . .' And then he puked all over his own lap.

We all of us cried out in disgust at this and Barney announced that the fun was over and that we was all to make our way home. Nobody wanted to argue. That small, airless room had long since lost its allure even before this had happened and we gathered our things to leave. Georgie and Mouse, after having helped wash the mess from off Jem's clothes, took an arm each and hoisted him out of the door, apologising to Barney as they left. Barney had fetched a bucket and mop out of a nearby cupboard and, when I collected my hat from off the peg, he called my name before I left.

'Jack,' he whispered, keen that the others would not hear, 'I meant what I said, y'know.'

'About what?'

'About Fagin being proud of you. For getting back here and looking as fine as you do. You really was one of his favourites.'

As he said this a memory returned to me of the previous night in Greenwich. It was of me sawing open that little Indian prince and finding it hid only a pebble inside, nothing more.

'So they tell me,' I said. And with that I bid Barney goodnight, tossed him a gold sovereign and left him alone to wipe up the sick.

Chapter 19

A Friendly Game of Thimble and Pea

Containing dealings with the Dollman

The Dollman lived just where I remembered from my childhood, in a slanting one-bedroom crib what overhung a tilting second-hand toyshop in deepest Clerkenwell. It was just after sunrise on a sleepy Sunday when I arrived there and the street was cold and deserted save for a watching cat and a vagrant asleep in the doorway of the shop. Not caring if I woke him I used my cane to rap down heavy upon the weathered door with its peeling pink paint. No answer. Undeterred, I walked through an alley until I was at the rear of the shop, climbed through a hole in a fence and was soon in a weed-covered backyard throwing pebbles up to the tiny window above. A man's head appeared at the glass, greyer and balder than I had expected, but it was a head what I recognised. He did not recognise me however and I heard his muffled shout, asking me what in fiery blazes I thought I was playing at.

'Dicky!' I called up, smiling and waving to show him that I had come in friendship. 'It's me, Jack Dawkins!' I could see the face turn quizzical and I told him to open the smeary window so we could talk proper. This he did and I repeated my name.

'Yeah?' he asked, adjusting his spectacles. 'And who's Jack Dawkins when he's at home?'

'The Artful Dodger,' I said. 'You must remember me. One of

Fagin's boys. I was in here all the time with the old man.' I saw recognition dawn at last upon Dick's face and it brightened as he asked me what I was messing up his garden for so early in the morning. This I found to be most droll as the untidy stone-yard had one or two bulbs growing in cracked clay pots but to describe it as a garden really was to put on airs. 'I want to talk to you, Dicky,' I said. 'About this doll.' I reached into my pocket and produced the two halves of the wooden prince. 'Let me in, it's important.' Dick nodded, told me to meet him around the front and he shut his window.

There was two reasons for why I wanted to rise from my bed in Bethnal Green so early and travel over to this small, curious address before the rest of the city had woken.

The first was on account of how this Dick, not only a manufacturer of cheap toys but also a man not averse to buying goods burgled from middle-class nurseries, had been a business associate of Fagin's and I was hoping he could shed light on a few things. The second reason, and this one accounted for the unsociable hour, was that I had no wish to be asleep in that house when Jem finally awoke.

He, Georgie, Mouse and myself had all made it back to his crib in Bethnal Green after our night out in the Cripples just hours ago and, although my head was stinging hard from too much gin, I did not want to lie there unprotected for long. The last time I had lain too long asleep in that house I had woken to discover a harlot plying her trade above me, but I fretted that on this occasion a more violent act would be my alarm. Because of how insensible the drink had made him, I had suffered no reprisals from Jem for punching him the night before. Instead, he just unlocked the front door and staggered, still smelling of puke, into the room he shared with Ruby and slammed the bedroom door shut after he pulled his shirt off and threw it on the floor. Mouse curled up to sleep on some cushions he found by the fireside, in a manner what suggested he was accustomed to sleeping there. Georgie meanwhile said that I could share with him the hard, one-pillowed bed that was in another room what only he had the key for, a room he used whenever he stayed over the night before a big burglary. So my night had been restless and unsatisfactory and this, coupled with my eagerness to distance myself from Jem, was why I felt that an early-morning social visit would be a very good idea.

The shop window of Dick's was still, regardless of the disrepair, as magical to me as it had ever been when I was a small kinchin. I remember gazing in then, all excitable, at the many brightly coloured wooden soldiers, dolls hanging from strings, the soft bears and alphabet blocks, and wondering which of these enchanting items I would be shoplifting later to sell in other districts. Old Dick never caught me though and he smiled at me now as he unlocked the many chains on the front of the shop. The vagrant in the doorway refused to respond to my friendly taps to shoo him away and so I just stepped over him once the door was open. Inside I was struck with the musty old smell of the place, a mixture of paint oils, sawn wood and the real animal hair what was used on the dappled rocking horses.

'Finer stock than Tackleton's,' I complimented him after we had shook hands. 'You'd never know this stuff was second-hand if it didn't say so outside.'

'Most of it ain't.' He winked, knowing I was safe. 'Much of it was lifted straight off the back of a Tackleton's cart last Wednesday. And you should see the prices they charge for 'em in the big shops. Compared to what I'm selling 'em for it's downright villainy.'

He then walked me through to a tiny back parlour what was also stuffed with stolen toys. This was where he made his own dolls and there must have been a hundred stringed wooden figures, Mr Punches, Joey the Clowns, devils, all dangling from hooks and clothes lines. As he began boiling up a kettle a voice squawked down the crooked stairs.

'Who is it, Dicky? What do they want?'

'An old friend, petal,' Dick shouted back up the stairs. 'Just saying hello.'

'Tell him it's a Sunday and come back to bed.'

Dick rolled his eyes as he poured my tea. 'Ignore Albert,' he said. 'He's new.'

'I won't keep you long, Dicky,' I said, after blowing on my tea. He pulled out some old wooden chairs covered in bits of cloth and tiny dolls' eyes. I brushed them off and sat down. 'I just wanted to know what you made of this,' I took out the two parts of my toy and showed him.

Before learning that Louisa Evershed had hidden the Jakkapoor stone inside a small wooden doll, I had always imagined that Fagin had got my toy from this here Dicky. It was very like the sort of thing what he made and because he and the Jew was so close it seemed likely that this was where it had come from. Dicky took out his steel-rimmed glasses and inspected the smiling prince, turning both parts around in his hands, sniffing at the paint and the inside wood.

'One of mine,' he said after a time, 'if I know me own handiwork. You ain't looked after it very well, I must say.' My heart sank as I realised I had been mistaken in ever thinking I had been given Louisa's doll in the first place. 'My wood, my paint, and look here –' he pointed to a tiny 'DD' scratched underneath the left foot. 'That's my little signature.'

'So Fagin did get it from you,' I sighed. 'Not from George Shatillion.'

Dick raised an eyebrow at the famous name. 'Oh, I made it all right –' he grinned then – 'but it weren't my design. I was manufacturing to order.'

'You mean Fagin asked you to make it special?'

'Heh. He did indeed. I recall I painted it for him most particular, this one and another. That was a peculiar afternoon. Most peculiar indeed.'

'How so?' I could not keep the interest from my voice, and Dick, always the frustrated performer, seemed pleased to have a keen audience.

'For one thing,' he said as he stood and crossed over to a dilapidated chest to search through the drawers, 'it was the only time he ever bought anything off me and not me off him.' Sticking out of the chest I could see the small wooden limbs of even more of his creations and Dick rifled through them in search of something. 'He was always the seller, was he not?' He turned to me and winked. 'And if he ever wanted anything, most times he'd send one of you boys in to lift it for him, eh, Dodge?' He waved his hand to say that I should spare him my denials and he went over to another pile of toys stacked upon a dresser. 'But the most peculiar thing about this occasion,' he paused for dramatic effect, 'was his companion.'

'Why?' I asked, aware that Dick was the sort who liked to have a tale teased out of him.

'Ah! Here we are.' He had shifted along to a big collection of assorted dolls hanging in a little nook and he hooked one off and brought it over to me. 'A good likeness, is it not?'

It was another wooden doll, the same size and weight as the Indian prince, only this one had a brown coat, thick black lines painted on his face giving him a fiendish expression, and a shock of red hair. It took me some seconds to make sense of it.

'It was for his execution,' Dick explained. 'I do a roaring trade on hanging days if I can make them fast enough.'

'This is meant to be Fagin?' I asked.

Dick looked hurt by my disbelief. 'Course,' he said. 'Don't it look just like him?'

The horrid creation he'd placed in my hands made me want to be sick. 'This is disgusting,' I told him.

'Thanks very much,' he grinned. 'I did put a lot of work in. I feel I captured the spirit of the man beautifully.'

'I mean, it's disgusting that you made a doll out of him for hanging day. He was a friend of yourn.'

'That's as maybe,' he said with indignation as he snatched it out of my hands, 'but old Fagin was never one to begrudge a neighbour the chance to spin a guinea. And besides,' Dick protested, 'me going poor was never going to save him from the gallows.' He went on to explain that whenever a villain is reported to be put to death there is always a market for such dolls. The ghoulish reasons for why people might wish to own wooden likenesses of the doomed he did not like to speculate on; he just knew that there was always a crowd gathered outside Newgate on such days what liked a souvenir. 'I made a dozen of Fagin,' he told me, 'for he was so very hated. And they all sold out, save for this one. I kept the last one back, y'know, for sentiment's sake but –' he shrugged as if he was about to rob himself – 'you can buy it off me if you fancy it, Dodge. But only because I know you and him was so close.'

'I don't want the rotten thing,' I said, not bothering to hide my outrage at the very idea.

'Then how about a Bill Sikes?' he said, and pointed to another brutish figure what was hanging high above the clock. 'Bill was the most popular murderer I ever carved, what with him being such a butch bastard and all.'

'I ain't come here to buy no dolls, Dick,' I snapped. 'At least no morbid ones like them. I want answers about this one here.' I waved the top half of my prince in his face again. 'I want you to tell me about that peculiar afternoon.'

'Please yourself,' he said, and sipped up his tea again. With his other hand he took the Fagin doll and began making a pantomime of him.

'So . . .' he turned the doll's head this way and that as if it was looking out for eavesdroppers, 'on one queer summer's afternoon in, oh I forget the year, in walks our dear Mr Fagin –' the doll jerked back and forth as if walking – 'into my humble shop to buy himself some dolls.'

'With a companion?'

'With a wooden companion,' he nodded, and he settled his tea next to a little red box on the table between us. 'A doll, with nothing special about it. One what had been made as part of the colonial craze we had at the start of the century. Indians was most popular then, redcoats too.'

'A doll like this one?' I said, holding up my divided plaything.

'That one,' said Dick, 'and the other one I made, was both fashioned to look just like the one he had brought in. He wanted two identicals.' I could not hide my surprise as he said this and Dick grinned and tapped his mug against the small red box. The lid sprung open and I cried out in fright as a dusty-looking Jack with a maniac face jumped out and began this drunken swaying. 'Heh,' said Dick, after I had composed myself. 'I done that deliberate.'

As I watched him try to stuff the Jack back into his box and wind up the spring I thought about the meaning of all this. Fagin had come in here, many years before, and asked Dick to make him two dolls to match this other one, what I had no doubt was the doll containing the Jakkapoor stone given to him by Shatillion.

And then he had handed me one of the false ones. What mad game was he playing at?

'Thimble and pea,' said Dick once he had finished fussing over his jack-in-the-box. 'That was all he told me about what he was up to. He said he was just playing a friendly game of thimble and pea.'

This referred to an old street game Fagin was fond of, one what he played with us boys often. It involved three thimbles, one of which would have a pea placed under it. Fagin would slide them about, in and out of one another, with such dexterousness that the player would lose sight of which was which. Nobody could ever beat him at thimble and pea; no matter how hard you tracked it the pea was never where you guessed it to be. I remembered that Evershed had told me that George Shatillion had met Fagin after he had tried to swindle the novelist on a street corner, and there was a high chance that it was with this game. It would explain why Shatillion named his next novel, the one what featured a character based on Fagin, after it. Was Fagin now playing Thimble and Pea with these dolls and the Jakkapoor stone? So that anyone looking for it would be given two false alternatives to chase after? He was a wily old fox and such behaviour would not be unlike him.

'I had to carve and paint these dolls so they could not be thought distinguishable from his own –' Dick took both halves of my doll from me – 'and place a pebble inside each one. I imagine –' he held up the top half of mine and peered into it – 'that the original contains more than just a pea, eh, Dodger?'

'Did he say anything about that?' I asked. 'About what was inside his own doll?'

He chuckled, placed it down again and took the Fagin doll over to his paint-splattered desk. There he stood it on the edge as if it was overlooking all the tiny pots of paint, oils and jars of water where the brushes stood. 'Chasing hidden treasure, are you?' He winked at me as he swirled a small brush around in a water jar. 'What exciting things you young men will pursue!' Dick dipped the brush into a black paint pot and begun touching up the lines of Fagin's face. 'He told me nothing more worth knowing. He just made his order and paid me handsomely. That is what I miss most about our dear departed. He knew how to reward services rendered.'

I took the hint, reached into my pocket and pulled out one gleaming gold coin. Dick was not impressed. 'One little sovereign,' he tutted, 'for a fortune's-worth of memories. My word, Dodger, must you insult me in my own home?' I flipped a second coin and he was more gracious about it. I then collected the two halves of my doll and bade him farewell.

'Are you certain I can't interest you in a doll of your old friend Fagin?' Dick said as I put my hat on. He had been dabbing at that doll as we had spoke, making it look as good as new. 'Or one of the others perhaps? As you can see I have a vast array of different characters!' I looked around the room, so cluttered with wooden men and women that I wondered if there was not one here for every soul in the city. And then a thought occurred.

'You got one of the Pimlico Pincher?' I asked.

'Not ringing any bells,' said Dick. 'Who is he?'

'She,' I told him. 'A jewel thief what was hung some time in the past five years. She must have sold well outside Newgate, I should think.'

'Never heard of her.' He shrugged. 'Which is rare, because women under the rope are good sellers oftentimes. What was her name?'

I did not want to tell Dick that I was asking after my own

mother and so I let the matter drop. As I turned to leave that high complaining voice from above called down again.

'Your rich friend going now is he, Dicky?' Albert said. 'Tell him to climb back in his carriage and leave us in peace.'

'He's off now, Albert,' Dick called back up. 'And he didn't come in no carriage that I saw.' He winked at me as he said this. 'He ain't found his fortune yet.'

'Then whose is that gothic horror waiting out the front then?' asked Albert. 'It's been there across the street all this time the rider's eyes haven't left our shop. Tell her to move on, she's giving me chills.'

I moved through to the front of the shop and peered out on to the street to see what he was on about. There, as Albert had said, stood a brougham carriage in as deep a shade of black as the horse what pulled it. The windows was curtained, the lamps at the side was still lit, showing me that it had travelled through the night, and it looked like it belonged to a funeral procession. Sat on the box-seat and holding the reins was a woman rider staring straight back at me, unblinking. She was tall, dark-complexioned and with a most severe expression. Nothing about that picture made me want to venture outside and join it.

'Well, you'd best be getting on then, young Jack,' said Dicky, as he got the door. It seemed he too could tell that the coach was trouble. 'I hope you find what you're looking for – I like to hear about happy endings. Off you pop now.' And with that he shoved me outside into the cold and away from his shop.

Across the road the coachwoman dismounted from her seat and stood on the pavement staring at me like a mesmerist. Trying to avoid her eyes I looked both ways along the still deserted street. Even the vagrant had gone now, scared him off by her in all likelihood. The cat remained on the wall behind the woman though, eyeing me just as hard.

'A fine-looking beast,' I said to her in reference to the horse not the cat. Somewhere in the distance church bells was chiming. 'Hope you and him have a very pleasant Sunday.' I doffed my hat to her, buttoned up my coat and began to stroll off.

'Late for the choir, Mr Dawkins?' A man's voice from inside the carriage, rich with scorn. I turned to face it and saw a white gloved hand pull back the curtain on the lowered glass window. 'I did not take you for a churchgoer.' I could make out a thin dark silhouette inside the coach, the long length of his hat and a metal object glinting in his left hand. I heard the click of a pistol. 'You won't find what you're looking for in a house of God, sir. I think you'll find a turn around the city with me will prove much more enlightening. We've been following you all morning and a refusal will not do.'

The small silver barker was pointed straight at me. It was no use trying to run, I'd be shot before my back was turned. And yet I was terrified of placing myself at this man's mercy. I knew full well who he worked for.

'This isn't a request, Mr Dawkins,' the voice said. The door was unlatched and swung open and the coachwoman walked over and held it. There was nothing else I could do but to cross over to the coach and climb inside as I was bid.

'Take us to the Mutineer, Calista,' the man said to the rider as she shut the door after me. 'I have a great many questions for Mr Dawkins of Dawkins Wool.'

Chapter 20

News of the World

In which you can hear a Pin drop

'Should it be necessary,' asked the man, as the horse began pulling us away, 'for me to introduce myself?' He lay the small silver flint-lock pistol on his lap and breathed out winter air.

'No, it ain't,' I answered careful. 'You're Timothy Pin. Evershed's man.'

Our knees was almost touching as we sat opposite one another in that small but plush carriage. And where the outside of the vehicle was death black, the inside looked like it was coloured to hide blood, with its cherry-red walls and crimson furnishings. There was large stains on the cushions already what could be from anything and the curtains on the windows was drawn so I could not tell where he was taking me. The man's face was as hairless as any I had ever seen. He had no eyebrows, no whiskers and, although his hat covered the crown, I doubted that there was a single strand upon his head. He was finely dressed and my thief's eye could not help but note that he had about his person a number of shiny items: a silver ring on the finger, a gold watch and chain in the vest-pocket, a stud in the necktie. Beside him was a thick satchel, like one a medical man would carry, only this was made of alligator skin and had locks of sterling silver. He reached over and unclasped it and began searching through all these papers.

'Tim Pin,' he said with a small nod. 'A humble servant.' Then he looked over to me and smiled wolfish. 'But not your humble servant, I'm afraid.'

I was most unsettled by now, what with the man, his pistol and his red furnishings. I wondered what my odds for survival would be if I was to just make for the door and hurl myself out when he was distracted. Not good, I considered, and so instead I chose a different move.

'Very happy to meet you, Mr Pin,' I said and I raised my hat in a manner most genial. 'I'm glad you've come to collect me as it goes, cos I was just now on my way to your address in Greenwich, as requested, to tell you all about my doings. You've saved me a lot of bother by seeking me out –' I gave him my cheeriest smile – 'and I'm obliged to you for it, sir. Obliged!'

He ignored me and carried on rifling through the satchel. At last he fished out a small round tin with a confectionary label on it and looked back at me. 'Why is the aborigine not with you?' he said at last.

'The British weather has laid poor Warrigal ill,' I replied. 'He's having a lie-in.'

'A shirker, eh? Disappointing. Well . . .' he inspected me, 'although you chose to ignore the kind message that I sent to you via Warrigal –' he waved his hand to silence my attempts at denial – 'I have received a number of messages about you from my employer.'

I stopped smiling and sat as far back from him as I could. I could glimpse through the crack in the curtains that the river was still on my right, meaning we had not crossed a bridge. So we was not heading towards his home in Greenwich but to another location. The horse galloped hard, making the carriage rock up and down, which only added to the discomfort of the situation.

'Bonbon?' said Pin as he popped the lid off the tin and, after folding back the paper, offered me one of the boiled sweets within. I refused and so he just took one himself and stared at me as he sucked.

'You have some explaining to do,' he said at last.

'I suppose I do,' I said, and tried to affect the air of a man what has everything under control. 'Right. Well, as Warrigal has already told you, the Jakkapoor stone was not where I thought it would be.'

'What an unfortunate assumption you made then,' he said, and I'm sure he would have raised an arch eyebrow if he had one. 'You've rather been wasting my employer's time, haven't you?'

'But it don't matter,' I rattled out in haste, 'cos I know who must have it. I know who has the jewel.'

'Who?'

'A lad called Bates,' I told him. 'My best friend when I lived in Saffron Hill. If I weren't Fagin's favourite, then Bates was most definite. So it's a good thing Evershed sent me back after all. So I could work that out and go fetch it off him.'

'You can assure us that this Bates was given the jewel, can you?' said Pin as he placed the cover over his sweet tin and put it away.

'Certainly.' I nodded. 'Either him or another lad called Eddie Inderwick.'

'Mr Dawkins,' he said, his hand resting on the barker again, 'would I be saving us all a good deal of time if I was to just blast your brains out here and now? It's a quiet part of town; it would be so easy to just drop you into the river afterwards.'

'Do whatever you care to, Mr Pin,' I challenged him. I had decided I was not going to let the man frighten me. If he wanted me dead he would already have killed me. 'But I told your employer I could find the Jakkapoor stone before Christmas, which is still three weeks away by my count.'

'And is there a chance you will have the jewel by then?' he asked as he drew back the curtains from the window.

'I'm confident, yes,' I said, noticing we was drawing close to St Katherine's Docks. 'You don't know what I've just learnt in that there toyshop.'

Pin lowered the glass of the window and spat what remained of the sucked sweet out into the street. 'I look forward to hearing it,' he said, and put the pistol away.

We soon came to a dirty row of houses so lopsided with disrepair that it looked as though the wind had blown them all into one another and only the large public house at the end was preventing full collapse. Outside this pub was where our carriage stopped and, if Pin had wanted the carriage curtains drawn so that I would not know to where I had been brought, he had wasted his time. We was at the Dancing Mutineer in Wapping. I knew of this pub and feared it.

The coachwoman, this Calista, could be heard dismounting the carriage and as she came round to open the door for us Pin wrapped a thick scarf around his neck. 'I own this establishment,' he said as he folded the cloth out so half his face was obscured, 'but I try not to be seen here.' The pub was shut at this hour but Calista unlocked the door and Pin gave her some orders while I was shoved through and into the front bar.

The Dancing Mutineer was notorious among criminals for its dark history, and Fagin had often said it was haunted by the ghost of Baron Beazle, better known as the Drowning Judge. As I followed Pin through the stone-floored bar and towards the stairs I could see through to the back window what overlooked the river. Beyond that on the shore of the Thames, dangling from a scaffold so simple in shape that a child could draw it, was the shortened noose with which he would have hanged those what had committed crimes at sea. At the top of the stairs was a private room, where Pin led me now, unlocking it with his own key, and through this window the wicked Beazle would stuff his fat face with pie and ale and watch the limbs of dying men he had condemned quiver and shake out their last. Now, in that small, musty room with its view of the river and the hanging post outside, was a desk covered in legal papers, ink pots and other used stationery.

'Sit,' said Pin, pointing to the chair what faced the river while he placed his satchel on the desk and sat opposite me. Then he opened the bag again and pulled out a copy of *News of the World*.

He pulled out a thin leaf of paper from within the pages and asked me if I would like to read his latest piece of communication. 'It was delivered to my home in Greenwich in the early hours of this morning by a young fellow who works in the telegraph office. Would you like to read it?' He turned the paper towards me and held it close. It was unreadable.

'These ain't letters,' I said. 'It's all dots, dashes and queer shapes.' Pin whipped the paper away and smirked.

'Of course you can't read it,' he explained. 'It wouldn't be much of a code if you could. Sensitive messages of this kind pass through many hands.' He placed it down upon the desk but my eyes was then distracted by a different text, what I did understand. I snatched it up and began reading with some urgency.

'One of yours, Dawkins?' asked Pin with amused surprise to find me so interested in today's story. My eyes was still distracted by the news as I asked him what he meant. 'That publication only concerns itself with the most nefarious crimes,' Pin continued. 'And I take it from the look of horror upon your face that one of your own is this morning's feature.'

'Nothing to do with me,' I said at last, and whistled in relief as I folded the paper over. 'Thank a ghost. But I think I know the poor victim's family, bless them.'

Pin waved it away in annoyance. 'Well, you can read it on the journey home,' he said, and turned back to his telegram. '*This* is much more pressing and it does concern you. It was sent from the Canary Islands.'

I had been to the Canary Islands myself when the *Son and Heir* had docked in Tenerife for a spell on my return journey from Australia. It was run by Spaniards, scorching hot and the only thing worth stealing from the markets was fruit. I could not imagine who would be corresponding with Pin from there.

'It confirms what I already knew,' he sighed. 'He'll arrive in two weeks or thereabouts.'

'Who will?'

'Lord Evershed.' Pin gazed out of the window then, towards Bermondsey on the opposite bank. He seemed as unsettled by this news as I was.

'What's he coming here for?' I asked. 'Warrigal is supposed to take the stone back to him in Australia.'

'He left some weeks after you. It seems he wants the jewel as soon as he can get it and will not wait another six months for the return journey.' He spoke then, in a quieter, more confidential tone than he had used before. 'Lord Evershed is a great man, Mr Dawkins, and our Empire owes him much. But there's something I feel that you must know about him which may help to explain a lot of the unusual business that you have found yourself caught up in.' I leaned in closer as he lowered his voice. 'His Lordship . . .' he whispered, 'is not of sound mind.'

He leaned back again and looked upriver towards the many clippers what was sailing in from foreign parts. There was a small silence which I broke.

'I'll be honest with you, Mr Pin,' I ventured with caution. 'That thought had crossed my mind already.'

'I blame George Shatillion,' Pin went on, ignoring me. 'If only that man had controlled himself and left Lady Evershed alone then all of this would have been avoided.' He waved his hand over the many pages of coded telegrams what could be seen bunched together in his satchel and his voice tailed off. 'Revenge,' he said instead, 'is a wild thing. It can never be sated.'

'Revenge on who?' I asked. 'George Shatillion is dead, ain't he? He fell off a cliff.'

Pin looked me square in the eye and said nothing. The truth fell upon me and I was surprised I had not thought it sooner.

'He was pushed then,' I said at last as I held his gaze in return. 'By you.'

Pin did not confirm this and he did not need to.

'I pride myself on being the perfect employee,' he said instead in a small whisper. 'I do as I am bid.'

I recalled then what Inspector Bracken had said to me that night in the stables. He had said that there was those in the police force what thought that the death of Evershed's wife was suspicious, and I found myself getting angry at the whole rotten business.

'What about Lady Evershed?' I asked. 'That you as well?'

Pin leaned his chair back and shrugged that one off. 'I was not in Lord Evershed's employ at that time,' he said. 'He has had many servants throughout the years. You and the aborigine are two of the most recent.'

He got up then and walked over to the window as if he expected Lord Evershed to come sailing up the Thames at any moment.

'We have a common interest, Mr Dawkins. The latest telegram makes it clear, as if it were not already, that failure will not be tolerated. We both need that jewel to be presented to him on the very day he arrives or there will be severe consequences. For myself as well as for you.'

'All this for one little jewel?' I asked. 'He's crossing the world just for this?'

'He wants to know where the Jakkapoor stone is, Dawkins, and by Christ we had better find it before he arrives. He thinks, do not forget, that you already have it.' Pin laughed and I could not tell at what. 'He thinks you were the child it was given to.'

'I'll have it by the time he docks, Mr Pin,' I promised him. 'I won't let you down.' But even as I said these words I doubted very much that they was true.

'You shall bring it here, to this public house,' he said, and wrote down the address for me so I would not forget. 'And we shall present it to him together.'

After that Pin made me talk him through what I had learnt in the toyshop. I explained that I had just discovered that there was two more dolls made just like the one what contained the Jakkapoor stone and it seemed that Fagin had done this to throw any jewel-hunters off the scent. Timothy Pin seemed most interested in this new information and after I had finished speaking he admitted that neither he nor Lord Evershed had known anything about this.

'What a puzzle this Hebrew was,' he mused after giving it some thought. 'So there is a chance that the jewel was given to a child, but that the child was not you.' He tapped his fingers on the desk. 'That would explain a few things.'

I told him I would not find it difficult to track down my old friends and before long I would be able to work out which of them was given the jewel and get it off them.

We was sat in that room for the best part of an hour going over the particulars and I made a good show of looking confident. But the more I thought about the chances of me ever finding this jewel the more impossible the task seemed and I had to work hard to not let the doubt show on my face.

After some time there was a knock at the door and the coach-woman Calista called through to say that she had fetched Warrigal and he was waiting for me downstairs in the bar.

'Very good,' said Pin, and he went to unlock the door. 'Calista has taken your trunk and bags from here to your residence in Bethnal Green. The aborigine is now here to ensure that you don't get lost on the way home. He is the man that you should fear if you fail to find the jewel, Mr Dawkins. Do not mistake him for a friend.' His eyes then dropped to my hands. 'Planning on taking that, are you?'

'You said I could,' I replied, holding up the newspaper. 'That is, if you or that coachwoman don't want it.'

'Calista can't read English,' he said as he unlocked the door. 'And I favour *Blackwood's*. Now, make sure you understand what I have told you in this room, Mr Dawkins. Get the jewel. Get it quick. Bring it here.' He opened the door and ushered me through. 'Nothing else matters,' he said, before shutting it after me. Then, after a second, it opened again just a little. 'And send Calista up,' he said through the crack. 'I want her now.'

Downstairs I found Warrigal propped at the bar drinking a jar of porter ale. He was perched on the stool in a manner much less tense than was usual for him and he seemed healthier than he had the day before. Calista was stood at the bottom of the stairs waiting to be told she could go up. I gave her the nod and up she went.

'Drink up,' I said to Warrigal as I approached. 'We've a priceless Indian jewel to find.'

'Finish this,' he said, and took another swig.

'You're looking better, Warrigal, I'll say that,' I pointed to the bar's large mirror with a whisky advert scratched on it so he could see for himself. 'Colour in your cheeks. Good night's sleep, was it?'

'Good sleep.' He nodded.

'What room was you in?'

'Room below theirs.'

'Greta's room?'

Warrigal nodded. 'Owe her five shillings,' he said as he drained the dregs of the pot.

Chapter 21

Desperate Characters

In which it is decided that some of us needs to take a trip

The News of the World

SUNDAY, 30TH NOVEMBER, 1845

M U R D E R

IN KENT VILLAGE.

SERVANT BLUDGEONED

AND BURIED IN THE NIGHT!

POLICE FOLLOW CLUES.

Never before have we seen an instance of burglary attended by so callous an act of Murder. The sleepy village of Riverhead, in rural Kent, is a quiet place ordinarily and yet an act of violence has occurred there that has shattered the peaceful idyll forever.

At the home of Mr David Parsons, a gentleman of large prop-erty, entry was forced on the night of Friday, 28th November, by two masked men brandishing pistols. Mr Parsons and his family were away on this particular night and the only person in residence was a servant girl, a Miss Fanny Cooper, who was bound by the hands with garden cord as the two ruffians proceeded to pillage The Cottage.

They were interrupted in their looting spree however by a Mr Colin Lees, a gardener who dwelt at the lower end of the property. Mr Lees, by all accounts a decent, God-fearing man, came to Miss Cooper's aid and fought with the intruders but, for all his bravery, he was fatally beaten upon the head. The murderers then clumsily attempted to bury his body in a vegetable patch.

It is strongly believed that the perpetrators of this wicked act came from London. Scotland Yard have therefore appointed their best Detective to track them down within the Metropolis. 'These are men of desperate character but they will be brought to Justice,' said Inspector Wilfred Bracken when questioned by reporters. 'The maidservant, Miss Cooper, is already helping us with our enquiries and I am confident that arrests will be made shortly.'

We wish the Inspector luck with his investigation and are hopeful that the two men will soon be apprehended and hung by the neck until Dead.

'Jem!' I shouted as I bounded up the stairs of his house, clutching the paper. 'Georgie! You around?'

Greta had let myself and Warrigal in and had said that the two of them was in the upstairs kitchen still recovering from the previous night's revels. Ruby, we was also told, was still in her bedroom reading a book and she was unhappy with Jem on account of the stink he had brought home with him from the Cripples. If she was out of sorts with him now, I thought, as I threw open the door of the kitchen and found the two wanted men sat eating bacon and eggs together, this new development was unlikely to improve her disposition.

'Back again?' said Jem as we entered, in a voice rough and dry. There was a bruise on his chin from where I had punched him the night before and he had a look on him that said that he was readying himself for the counter-blow. 'Ain't it time you and your valet pissed off and found your own crib?'

Georgie, whose mouth was full of breakfast, nodded me a more friendly hello but he seemed to be rattled by something. Then I remembered that he had not seen Warrigal before.

I strode up to their table and threw the paper down. Jem had his mug of coffee in his hand but stopped himself from drinking when he saw the headline. 'Someone needs to start packing their bags, Jemmy,' I said, 'but it ain't me.'

Jem grabbed the pages, holding the paper close to his face so he could read the tiny print below the headlines. His lips was moving along with the words and when he got to the part about Miss Cooper helping with enquiries he began shouting every swear word he could think of.

'Something up?' asked Georgie, still finishing his plate. What he imagined Jem was getting so angry about I could not say but he did not seem to think it concerned him too. His was not the keenest of criminal minds, I reflected, as I watched him lick the grease off his knife.

'That chit of yourn,' Jem shouted, and threw the paper at him. 'I knew we should have settled her too. Settled her like we did the gardener!' He got up and paced the room before stopping at the closed door what led into the bedroom.

'What's all this?' Ruby's voice piped up from within her room. The door opened and she stood there with her hair down and that book, *Teppingham*, in her hand. 'Who's done what to who now?' Heavy footsteps could be heard running up the staircase and then the other door of the parlour was thrown open with such force that it almost came off its hinges.

'Everything all right, Rube?' asked Greta, with a mean look in her eye. 'He at you again?'

'Fanny Cooper!' Jem said her name like it was curse. 'Georgie's girl from Crackity Lane.'

'Cheap Jane's sister?' asked Ruby.

'Yeah. She's splitting on us.'

There was astonishment from both ladies but Georgie, who was a weak reader but could make out the name of his sweetheart when he saw it in print, just shook his head. 'It don't say that, Jem,' he protested. 'It don't say that.'

'What else does it mean?' he roared. 'They've got her! They know it was a put-up job!'

'She won't talk,' Georgie insisted. 'Not my Fanny.'

'I'd wager that they've been to your crib already,' said Jem, still pacing about. 'The only reason they ain't here is that she don't know the place. Someone'll tell them though, mark me.'

'You'd best get out of London, boys,' I told them. 'This peeler, Bracken, is a terror. Warrigal and I met him the night we docked in England and he's a like a pit-bull terrier once he's got the scent. I should be very wary of him catching up if I was you.'

'He the one you beat up in the stables, Jack?' asked Ruby. I could feel, without looking at him, Warrigal's head turn to me. I fought hard not to catch his eye.

'That's the one,' I said. 'All the more reason to stay out of his way. He would not look very favourable upon finding the two of us here either.'

'We need to dash, Georgie,' Jem agreed, and he picked up a bag and started stuffing it with clothes. 'Jack's right – London ain't safe. They'll hang us like it says in the paper.'

'Hang you?' Greta scoffed. 'For burglary?' She went over to the table and picked up Ruby's red hat what was acting as a fruit bowl for all the apples she had collected from the market yesterday. 'Don't worry yourselves. Transportation most like. You'll end up in Jack's old bed, I expect,' she chuckled as she offered an apple to Warrigal. 'Nah. They don't hang burglars unless . . .' and she paused.

There was a silence in the room what Ruby, as low as a whisper, broke.

'Jem White,' she said. 'What have you done?'

She then walked over to where Georgie sat and snatched the paper out of his hand. The second she read the headline she gasped in fright. 'Murder?' she cried. 'Oh, Jem, you've killed a man!'

'It weren't me,' Jem wailed with impressive heroism. 'It was 'im!'

'Me?' asked Georgie.

'You! You and your rotten Fanny. What with your crashing about and her calling you Georgie, I had no other choice but to smash his head in.' The rest of the room went quiet. We all stared at Jem in silence. 'Don't give me that,' he said to us. 'What would you've done? There isn't one among you what woulda done it any different. I had no choice but to kill him.'

I reached over to the hat of apples what Greta was still holding and chose myself the ripest. Then I rubbed it on my shirt and took the seat he had just left. 'Well,' I said, 'as I believe I mentioned the other night, Jem. If I'd been there I'd've suggested offering the fellow a bribe to keep his trap shut. Also, I can't imagine thinking it would be a good idea to bury him in the garden of the same place in which you killed him. Still,' I said before raising the apple to my mouth, 'that's just me though. You're top-sawyer after all.' And I crunched into it all noisy, never losing hold of his eye.

Jem looked like he wanted to throttle me. His eyes was bulging with animal panic and his face reddened as he spat back, 'What you know about it? How many dead bodies have you had to get rid of?'

'None,' I replied. 'But Warrigal has. He does it for a living back in Australia and he ain't ever made the papers.' All eyes turned to my companion, who was leaning against the wall eating his own piece of fruit. Georgie and Jem was already afraid of him and I was enjoying making them even more unsettled. Ruby looked at Warrigal in horror for the first time. The news that there was now two killers in the room, one of them the man what shared her bed, was not sitting well with her. She had gone pale in the face and her fingers was raised to her mouth as if holding in a scream. Greta, however, did not seem rattled to hear about Warrigal's line of work.

'Is that right?' she said, sizing him up anew.

'I told him about your messy business on the way over here,' I told Jem. 'Asked him his professional opinion. He thinks you made a right old shambles of it.'

Warrigal nodded. 'Vegetable patch,' he tutted.

This was when Ruby stopped holding it in. 'Get out!' she screamed. 'Get out of here, all of you. You *murderers*!'

That word, when screamed by a hysterical woman, did nothing to lower the tensions of the room. Jem turned his anger from me to her.

'Don't you use that word on me, my girl,' he threatened, pointing at her. 'I've had me enough of loose-lipped women and, if I have to, I'll cut that tongue out of your pretty head.'

'You don't scare me, Jem,' Ruby shouted back. 'You sicken me. I regret ever having anything to do with you. I hope you burn in hell for what you've done! I hope you hang!'

She should not have said that. Jem reacted as though she had just set fire to the curtains. He strode towards her, fist raised, and Greta from the other side of the room shouted, 'No!' and made to stop him. But before he could reach Ruby I was out of my chair and landed an almighty punch into his chest. He doubled over and cursed me.

'That's the second time you've hit me since you've been back,' he moaned.

'You ain't touching her again,' I told him. 'That's all over.'

Jem lashed out, punching me under the jaw. All of the rage and fear he must have been feeling was in that punch and I crashed back against the wall. His hands was round my throat and his blood-rushed face was nose to nose with mine.

'You going to stop me, are ya?' he snarled, teeth bared. 'Well, who's gonna stop me from choking you?'

A blade had appeared at his throat. His hands released me and he looked to who was holding it. 'No,' said Warrigal. 'Need him.'

'Look, look, look,' said Georgie. He was holding up his arms as if to calm us all but his hands was shaking. 'This don't matter none. Fanny's safe. She loves me – I've promised her a baby and everything. She'd never blow on us, you'll see. In a couple of days' time we'll be sat in here laughing and wondering why we was all getting so worked up. You'll see.'

Outside a child's voice shouted something. We could not hear what it was, it came from the far end of the street, but we all turned to listen. Then another voice shouting the same word, closer this time, like a warning. A third voice now, a woman's, screeching it as loud as she could. And this time we heard it as clear as though she was the town crier. The sound of hoofs thundering down this crooked lane could be heard and the *clack-clack-clack* of many wooden rattles. A chorus of voices then, from every window of the rookery, all ringing out with that same dreaded word.

'*PEELERS!*'

We all dashed to the window and looked down upon the street and saw, to our great horror, two enormous police vans drawn by the strongest horses this lane had ever seen. The vehicles was crammed full of constables, three each on every box-seat and others clinging to the sides of the carriages, twirling their wooden rattles to alert us. The leading carriage had already reared its horses up just below us on the opposite side of the street and from out of the back leapt a dozen more of these tall formidable men in their long dark blue coats and top hats. They all pulled out their wooden truncheons from within the long-pockets of their tailcoats and began swarming around every door below, as if prepared to burst through all of them. At the reins of the second carriage, what had reared up close behind, was the tallest of the peelers. He was the first to look up to the window from which our six faces peered down. Inspector Bracken, looking more fearsome than ever in his brass-buttoned uniform, stood up taller than the rest and pointed towards us.

'That's the house, men,' he boomed to the others. 'Force entry if it is not granted freely!'

We jumped away from the window in wild fear. We could not have been any more terrified if we had seen hungry wolves prowling down below. It was Jem and Georgie that was in mortal danger, true, but there was not one of us that wanted the peelers asking us questions. Ruby and Greta was the least likely to be grabbed by the police – any stolen items found in the place could be blamed on the men – but it was not good for myself and Warrigal to be caught there. Bracken already hated me and if he could find any reason to poke his nose into my business then he would. The police was villains, we all knew that, and if the inspector could grab four men for a crime what only two committed I was sure the whole force would congratulate him.

'The cellar!' said Jem, and darted down the steps with Georgie close behind. I told Warrigal that we should go too. I knew from my dealings with Bill Sikes that this underground room was our only chance, and the four of us scrambled down the staircase towards it. As we reached the bottom of the stairs, and passed the front door, there was heavy thumping from behind it and Bracken's voice called through.

'Open up this door, Mr White!' he ordered. 'Or we shall be forced to break it down!'

We ran towards a small door under the staircase and Jem turned the rusty key what was there in the lock. 'We'll need candles,' he panted as the door opened up to reveal stone stairs leading down to nowhere but cobwebs and blackness. There was a table in the hall close by and he opened a drawer with many tallow candles and cleft sticks inside and handed them out to us. 'Lights,' he called out, most frantic. 'Gerrus a light, someone.'

'Fetch the battery!' shouted the voice from outside.

Ruby came scurrying down the stairs with a candle in a stick, her hand held over its flame so it would not blow out before she reached us. 'You're a rotten gang of villains,' she said as she lit each of ours, 'but I swear I won't split on you.'

'You better not,' warned Jem, and he vanished down into the cellar as soon as his was alight.

'They've got this great big battering ram!' shouted Greta, who was still watching the outside action from above. 'A huge iron thing,' she cried. 'Pulled it out of the van.' Her voice sounded as though she had never before seen such fun. Georgie's candle was soon lit and then Warrigal's and they both followed after Jem.

'I'll lock the door after you,' said Ruby as she lit mine last, 'and hide the key.'

'Thanks,' I said. And before I went I had to do one last thing. I kissed her again with some passion. She pulled away.

'Not *now*,' she said and shoved me through the tiny door. 'Go!'

I stepped down into that dark, damp cellar and saw the three others was lighting the candles what hung from clay walls. It was a foul-smelling place and I wondered if Jem had been keeping rotten meat down there. Just as she was shutting the door Ruby hesitated.

'Don't get caught,' I heard her say to me. Jem heard it too and looked up to her from where he was crouching by the wall.

'I don't mean to, you stupid mare,' he shouted up. 'Just shut the door.'

'*Chaarrrggge!*' we heard from above as Ruby shut us in and turned the key.

Then there was a smash so loud that it seemed to rock the very foundations of the place and I wondered if the whole house was going to collapse upon us. Dust and dirt fell from the ceiling of the cellar and Warrigal began coughing again. 'Here it is,' said Jem, who had been searching for something at the base of one wall. 'Give us a better glim, Georgie.' Georgie held his candle down to reveal a hole of two feet square what led into the neighbouring cellar.

Above us we could here the raised voices of the peelers. Their footsteps was hammering up and down the stairs to where Greta was, and Ruby could be heard crying out in protest at the invasion. Georgie went to stick his head through the hole but Jem pulled him back. 'Wait your turn,' he said, and crawled through, candle first.

'Open that cellar,' Bracken could be heard shouting. 'Where's the key?'

Georgie followed Jem, Warrigal went next and, as I began to crawl my own way through, I could hear the police trying to break in the door of the cellar behind me. By the time I was through and into the next cellar, what stunk even fouler than the one we had just escaped from, Jem was across at the other side, looking for another hole. Georgie and Warrigal was holding on to the walls with one hand and their candles with the other, edging their way towards him. It was as I had remembered from visiting this area in Bill's day. All of the houses in this part of Bethnal Green was connected to one another by hidden passages such as these.

'Stay away from the middle,' Georgie said to us as Jem crawled through the next one. 'There's a cesspool.' That explained the stench, although I could see nothing there. It was pitch black in this cellar, save for our four candles as we inched our way towards the hole. 'If anyone follows us,' Georgie said, before ducking his head through it, 'they'll step straight in that with any luck.'

I doubted this. I thought it unlikely, once the peelers had forced open the cellar door and realised where we had gone, that any of them would pursue further. Should they risk climbing head first through a hole what led from one dark room to the next, they would be placing themselves at the mercy of men whom they knew to be capable of murder, what might be standing over the other side, club in hand. More probable would be that they would charge around to front of the houses and try to be there waiting outside the right one once we emerged from our rat holes. We could not stay down here for long.

We moved through two more such cellars, what Georgie assured us was used by like-minded individuals what would be sympathetic to our plight. Then, at the fourth, the door above the stairs swung open just as Jem was about to pass through another hole. We started in fright and looked towards it. A rectangle of light shone into the dark room and a long shadow of a man was cast across it. The man spoke and I was surprised by how high his voice was.

'There's a window upstairs,' he squeaked, 'leads out on to the rooftops!' He stepped closer and we was all right relieved to see a child reveal himself, about nine years of age and lit from behind.

'Mother ain't in,' he went on. 'She's outside yours, gawping at the peelers.'

I was the first up the steps and I patted him on the head. 'You're a good boy,' I said as I passed into his house. I saw that even if the peelers had worked out what we was doing by now, they still had not made it to this door. 'What's your name?'

'Scratcher.'

'Well, Scratcher,' I said as my three associates tumbled out behind me into the narrow corridor, 'it's lads like you what've made this great country what it is today. Now where's this window of yourn?'

The window was in an attic bedroom. It backed out on to the houses behind and, once up there, I pushed the pane up and stuck my head out. It was true that we could reach up to the rooftops, but only by climbing on to a row of large spike nails what stuck out from this house and then by reaching up to another row of spikes what stuck out of the next house along. These nails had a small plank of wood rested on them what would act as a ledge and from there it would be easy to hoist yourself up to the roof beyond. There was a gap between the two houses though, down what it would be easy to fall.

'Looks a bit dangerous,' said Georgie. We was high up enough where, if we was to slip and plummet, the fall might not be fatal but bones would be broken and capture was assured. 'Maybe we should jump down.'

'And break our legs?' snarled Jem.

'Me uncle stuck them in good and strong,' said Scratcher. 'I get up there all the time.'

'You ain't as heavy as us,' said Jem.

Just then the sound of a woman's voice was heard entering the house below. She was telling someone not to shove and then some heavy footsteps could be heard charging in. Quicker than a blink,

Warrigal was out through the window and on to the spikes. We watched as he stepped from those to the row across and jumped upwards on to the ledge of the flat roof. I wasted no time in following him.

'Tell 'em we overpowered you,' I said to Scratcher as I ducked my head through his window and stepped on to the spikes. Warrigal had made it look simpler than it was though and Georgie had been right about the height. Below was a narrow alley and we was two floors up. The spikes themselves was lethal things and as I jumped from one row to the next I feared the plank what rested along them would snap. I did not linger there for long however and was up on the roof in time to see Warrigal springing from that one to the next away from me. I turned to see how the others was doing. Georgie was the next to dare it and he was stepping out on to the first row of spikes. I wondered why Scratcher's uncle could not have rested a wider plank of wood across both of them. It was obvious he had put them there for a situation such as this when the timing was most crucial.

'They're in the cellar!' said Jem from behind him. 'We ain't got long before they come up here. Move your fat arse.'

Georgie jumped from those spikes to the next but he did it so clumsy he nearly fell. I grabbed his arms and pulled him up from the untrustworthy plank but, as I was doing this, I heard the sounds of wooden rattles being clacked in the alley below. Three peelers was down there.

'Up there!' yelled one, pointing up at us. 'Alert the inspector.'

Georgie made it to the roof and took off after Warrigal. 'Jem!' I urged as he climbed out of the window. 'Hurry yourself.' Jem looked petrified and he just stood on the spikes not daring to look down as the peelers below shouted to him to give himself up. More peelers was pouring into the alley and it was only a matter of time before the ones in the house made it up to Scratcher's window. 'Now!' I shouted. He looked up at me with real fear in his eyes.

'I don't want to hang, Jack,' he said. 'Dear God, don't let me hang.'

'You ain't going to hang, Jem,' I promised him. 'But you need to jump quick. Here –' I held my hand out to him. 'I'll catch you. Just like I caught Georgie. Trust me.'

Jem nodded and reached his own hand out. But he stumbled and the jump was not made clean. He cried out in shock and slipped off the plank but not without grabbing a jutting spike with his hands. I grabbed his hand to help yank him up, but as I did this I could see many more peelers swarming into the alley below. I strained to pull him, as it looked like he still stood a chance, but he was heavier than me and it was not easy.

'Don't let me drop, Dodger,' Jem was pleading. 'Don't leave me.' I kept pulling but from down below I could hear Bracken barking orders.

'That's our man,' he told his constables. 'Ready yourselves to catch him.'

Bracken had not yet spotted that I was there and I did not want him to. Jem, with a bit more help, could still make it up as his left hand was clutching on to the rooftop, but the longer I stayed with him the more the chances was of getting caught myself. And then I remembered the bruise on Ruby's cheek.

'It ain't far down, Jem,' I said, and pulled away from him. 'They'll catch you.'

Jem screamed as I released him but he was still dangling with one hand on a spike. 'Bastard!' he thrashed about below me. 'I'll kill you for this.' There was a chance, I saw, that he could still climb up and come running after me.

I crouched down on the side of the roof, with my face pointing away to avoid detection, and I let my foot stamp down good and hard on to his fingers. He screamed then and dropped. I heard the peelers groan as his heavy weight landed upon them and then a big cheer went up, as they had got the man they was pursuing the most.

I got to my feet, peered over and saw that he was not hurt. And then I realised I was being watched from the window opposite. I started, fearing it was a peeler what could identify me, but saw instead just the innocent face of young Scratcher. He was staring back at me, his mouth open in wonder at my betrayal.

I raised my finger to my lips, made the shush sign to him and then turned and fled across the rooftops to safety.

Chapter 22

A Country Retreat

In light of recent events my companions and I decide to leave
behind the strife of city living and take to the road

I kept running across the rooftops for the whole length of the
street, balancing myself along the gutterings where I needed to,
jumping across the gaps, not looking down or behind me to see
if anyone was in pursuit. The further I scrambled the fainter the
shouts and rattles of the peelers became until I at last came to an
edge from where I could jump to a lower roof and then shinned
a water pipe down to a narrow by-lane. The people of this vicinity
was much kinder towards hunted men than the ones I had encountered the day before and if anybody saw me they did not alert the
police. As I ran down this lane and into a busy thoroughfare I
kept an eye out for either Georgie or Warrigal. I had lost sight of
them both after I had remained with Jem, but it was impossible,
I reasoned, for either of them to have taken a different path to
mine without falling. So I was certain that they too must have
headed into this street, what was a rush of people, carts and horses
chasing to and fro and would be so easy to disappear into. I crossed
the street to where a row of newspaper stalls stood, pinched a
copy of *The Times* to shield myself and walked up the road
pretending to read it. It was hard to watch where I was going and
before long I was tripped up by a beggar what was slumped on

the pavement in front of me. I stumbled and cursed him for not moving before realising that the trip was not accidental and that the man was no real beggar. Warrigal had made himself invisible in the most effective way that a man of his colour ever could, by sitting in broad daylight and asking people for money.

'Follow me,' he said, getting up and dusting himself down, 'to graveyard.' He headed towards the direction of Hackney and I followed behind as bid. For some reason, although the city was mine and he had been here less than a week, I felt as though he was more in command of it at this moment. 'No Jem,' he observed.

'Jem got took,' I answered as we crossed over towards St Peter's Church. 'And there was nothing I could have done to stop it.'

Warrigal gave me a quick glance and then pointed towards the churchyard. There a single mourner was crouched over the furthest gravestone pretending to cry. 'Other one,' he said.

We approached Georgie and I made the sign of the cross and knelt beside him. 'You need to get out of London,' I whispered. Georgie raised his head and asked where Jem was. 'Jem got took,' I said again, 'and there was nothing I could have done to stop it.' Georgie then wailed in what sounded like genuine sorrow and cursed the name of his once-beloved Fanny. As he did this two elderly ladies passed by the gravestone and remarked upon him. I shook my head at them in sadness and pointed at the carving on the stone. 'His mother,' I explained, and they expressed their sympathies and walked on.

'They'll hang him for sure,' he sniffed once they was out of earshot.

'I don't know about that.'

'They will, Jack. The bastards'll choke the life from him. Poor Jem.' He held his hands up to his face. 'He ain't a bad lad.'

I had to stop myself from remarking that, considering Jem had killed a man, was forever burgling houses and was happy to punch the woman I loved in the face, that we would struggle to call him a good lad. But, not wishing to intrude upon private grief, I patted him on the back instead and nodded along. 'There never was a truer friend,' I agreed with a great sigh.

We knelt there, he and I, while Warrigal looked on from under the shade of a tree, in silent tribute. But after less than a minute of that I clapped my hands together to move things along. 'Right,' I said, 'I'm starved. Let's get ourselves out of this district and to a friendly place. We need to work out what is to be done with you.'

Mouse Flynn lived in a nice house within a rotten vicinity, not far from Fagin's old place, with a woman named Agnes Dunn. Agnes was ten years older than him and was a gifted pickpocket herself and together they earned good money strutting around the Haymarket at night pretending to be quality and brushing against theatregoers. 'Sometimes,' Mouse laughed on introducing me to the love of his life, 'people mistake us for mother and son. But either way, it works.'

Georgie had told us on the way over that their cupboards was always well stocked with vittles and that Agnes was a hospitable sort, ever ready to harbour a fugitive whenever one should happen to drop by. Indeed, I found her to be a kind soul and I could tell, in spite of their age difference, that Mouse had done well to take up with her. He was still a child in many ways – on a small table in their parlour stood a pyramid of playing cards just like the ones he used to try and make when we was at Fagin's – so it was good that he had found himself the mothering sort to live with. She showed great sympathy to the three of us when we appeared on her doorstep and, after I had assured her that Warrigal was far gentler than he looked, she let us in and made us welcome.

'They're all splitters in Crackity Lane,' she scowled as she poured from a nice china teapot. We was all sat around her kitchen table and had been explaining the day's events to them both. 'Must be something to do with whatever spouts out of that water pipe they have there. You, Georgie,' she said, placing a biscuit on his saucer, 'is better off without the lying mop-squeezer. She don't deserve you.'

Georgie sighed all heartbroken and dipped the biscuit into the matching cup. 'I loved that girl, Agnes, and would have married her,' he sniffed, 'if I wasn't married already.'

Mouse was getting himself most distressed at all that we had told him, the dead gardener, Fanny's betrayal, the police raid, Jem's arrest, each part of the story seemed to make him more anxious than the last. Agnes sat herself by him and told him it would be all right, stroking his cheeks until he calmed himself. 'What'll we do without Jem?' he asked. 'He was our top-sawyer.'

'Don't you worry yourself about that,' I told him, sipping from my cup. 'I'm back now. And I say that first order of business is to find a place where Georgie can run to before the traps get him. And if I was you, Georgie –' I looked to him and shook my head in sympathy – 'and I thank the high heavens that I am not, I would try and book myself passage abroad somewhere.'

'What?' he cried. 'You mean another country?'

'That's what abroad means, yes. England's going to be too hot for you now, my son.' Georgie moaned at the unfairness of this but Agnes reached over and took his hand in hers.

'He's right, George,' she said. 'You want to get yourself on a boat over to that Europe. Change your name, start again.' Georgie wailed in protest.

'America then,' I suggested. 'They reckon New York is the perfect place for a bright boy such as you to go and make his fortune. I was thinking of heading off there myself at some point, and I ain't even killed anyone.'

'*I* ain't even killed anyone,' Georgie said, and got to his feet, knocking the wooden table as he did so and making all the nice china rattle. 'It was Jem what clubbed his head in. I just happened to be there, burgling the house. I'm an innocent man!' He faced the grandfather clock and placed his hands behind his head. We all went quiet as he pondered his situation and only the sound of the clock ticking could be heard, a reminder to me that I had my own business to attend to. Finally he turned back to us, tears in his eyes, and whined like a kinchin. 'I don't want to go abroad,' he pleaded.

I considered this and wondered whether he might not need to after all. Fanny Cooper had seen that it was Jem that was the killer and that Georgie was just an accomplice what had helped to hide the body and it was probable that she would have told the peelers this. I knew that didn't mean that they would not hang him but there was a chance, after Jem had swung, that they might consider justice to have been done and would stop searching for the other man. It was even possible, I dared to hope, that Fanny had not ever mentioned her lover's name at all and that Jem might not peach upon him either. If Jem was to betray anyone to the police it would be myself and Warrigal, even before I had kicked him into their arms. And we had only arrived back in England the day before the murder, which Bracken himself knew, so they would have difficulty making that stick. So if Georgie could just lay low somewhere safe for a year or two then perhaps he could come back to London in time. I told the others my thoughts and asked if anyone knew of a safe house on these shores.

'I have an Uncle Josiah,' said Agnes as Mouse got up and went into the bedroom. He could be seen through the open door searching through a large chest in the corner of the room. 'He owns a mill up in Coketown and employs all sorts. If I write you a letter of introduction, tell him you're a friend of the family and give you a false name, you could work under him for a spell.'

'Forget that,' said Mouse, walking back into the room with a piece of paper in his hands. 'This is better. A close pal in Northamptonshire what would put you up for free and never ask for no change.' He handed the paper to Georgie, who read the address all slow and with his lips moving. But I had guessed who it was and dared to hope I was right.

'Charley?' I asked.

'Yeah.' He smiled as he sat back down again and reached for his cup. 'That's the address he gave me the night before he scarpered. It's where his relatives live what own the farm where he now works.' Georgie and myself both cheered at this although not for the same reason.

'He made me promise not to tell anyone,' Mouse continued. 'He knew the Sikes gang would love to go up there and settle him for peaching on Bill. But he also said that if I ever found myself in a tight situation like the one that Georgie is now in, he would see to it that I could hide out at his place, give me work and shelter.' Mouse grinned at Georgie. 'I don't see why that offer wouldn't stand for you an' all.'

'Good old Charley,' said Georgie once this news had set in. 'He was always the best of us. Safe, honourable and without a treacherous bone in his whole body, I don't care what no one says.' His mood had become so jubilant now that I felt it would not be appropriate to remark upon how this appraisal of Charley's character was in sharp contrast to the words he had used to describe him the night before. Besides, however happy he was to be given

Charley's address in the north, it did not compare to what sweet news it was to my ears.

'Charley Bates,' I said aloud, and looked to Warrigal to see if he had understood how important this name was to us. He gave me a small nod. 'And you say you saw him the night he left London, Mouse?'

'Yeah.' Mouse nodded. 'That horrible night when Bill Sikes died and they came to take Fagin away. The night it all fell down.' He glanced over to his pyramid of cards. 'I was there in the den with a few of the younger boys and we was all crying about what would become of us, where would we go, who would have us now, all this. Charley runs in, face red with fear, all of a tremor, and starts packing his things into a bag. Myself and the other boys crowd around him, asking questions. What had he heard? Where was the Jew? Was Bill still on the loose? He was so shaken that we knew he must be not telling us something, but we did not yet know it was him what had blowed upon Bill. He just told us all to go back to bed and not worry about it and then, once he was packed, he dashed out into the night.'

Mouse was beginning to look quite upset at the retelling of this chapter in his life story, even more so than he had been on hearing about Jem's capture. Perhaps it was these memories what had made our morning's tale of doomed criminals so upsetting for him. 'As I said,' he went on lifting up the saucer and pouring some spillage into his cup, 'I'm in tears. I chase out into the night after him and I'm running barefoot down Saffron Hill calling out his name. Charley, who at first tries to ignore me and keeps on walking, finally turns and tells me to go back. But my sobbing is uncontrollable. It's all where are you going, take me with you, don't you leave too, this sort of thing. His hands are still shaking with the horror at what he'd seen and done that night, but he reaches over and gives me a cuddle, saying that he wishes I could come but he can't take me with him, what with it being so dangerous. Bill's gang, he tells me, will want to come after him on account of it being his fault that Bill has died. I tell him that I don't care, that I hated Bill too for killing Nancy, and Charley smiles and reaches into his pocket. Then he writes out that there address with a pencil and says that I can come and visit in time, once he's settled in, but I must promise to never tell no one about it.' Mouse paused in his telling and took a final sip. 'And I never have,' he said after he had drained the tea. 'Until now.'

'What sorts of things did you see him packing?' I asked.

'I dunno, Dodge. Clothes, watches, jewels, wallets . . .'

'Jewels?'

'You know, his findings and that. To live off, I imagine.'

'Any old toys?'

'Can't remember. He was packing everything what was his, perhaps to keep as souvenirs if he couldn't sell them. I was too busy sobbing to notice. I just cared that he was going.'

'Well then.' I leaned back on my chair and addressed myself to Georgie. 'This is a grand development. Even if he ain't there, his relatives will be able to point us in his direction. We'll be reunited with our old pal in no time.'

'Us?' Georgie asked. 'You coming too, Jack?'

'Course. I can't let you go wandering up north unaccompanied, can I?' I smiled at him. 'Who knows what trouble you'll get yourself into next without my good influence to show you the way. No, I must make sure you're safe before my mind will be at rest, and it's the perfect excuse to see my old pal Charley again.' I turned to Warrigal. 'And you're always going on about how much you'd like to see the rest of this beautiful country too, ain't you?' Everybody turned to Warrigal in surprise at this supposed interest in sightseeing. He just stared back at them and said nothing. 'That's the spirit,' I said as though he had nodded along with great enthusiasm. 'It's going to be quite companionable.' I got up and walked over to Georgie, who appeared to be getting most excited about the prospect of a country jaunt. 'And, what with the wonders of this industrial age,' I said as I leaned over his shoulder to see the paper, 'I'm sure we'll be up there in no time. Now, what's that address say?'

'Newley Farm, Eden Lane, Wildreed Wood,' I told the wagoner what we had halted in a field lane somewhere south of Kettering. It was half a week later and the rain was battering down upon our sodden hats as we looked up where he was perched. It was late afternoon, the short day was darkening and I was starting to doubt if we would ever find the wretched place.

'Never heard of it,' the wagoner shouted down to us. 'Ye sure it's in Northamptonshire?'

'Not any more,' I sighed. 'Look, can you take us to a tavern or some other shelter. Your ride's empty and we're drenched.'

'Sorry, young sirs,' he said as he lifted the whip to strike the horse. 'I mean, if it was just the two of ye, then p'raps, but . . .' And he threw a glance at Warrigal before the wagon trundled on.

'He's my valet, you ignorant brute!' I shouted after him as he headed off down the sloping lane without us. But it was to no avail; the three of us would have to walk to the next village on foot.

We had travelled up to Peterborough by train with no trouble and, in truth, until then the journey had been most pleasant. The Northern and Eastern Railway is a modern marvel and it was a civilised delight to share the journey from Islington with the other sophisticated first class passengers whose pockets had unwittingly financed our next few days. However, what with myself and Georgie being two smoky London lads what was unused to any England beyond its capital, we had not reckoned on Northamptonshire being quite so spread out. We had expected to only have to visit two or three farms before chancing upon our man, but we had spent the last three days riding carriages between countless farmhouses, villages and hamlets and meeting with no one what had ever heard of no Wildreed Wood.

'Why would a farm be in a wood?' asked our innkeeper that very morning in a manner not unreasonable. 'Where'd the cattle graze?' This point had not occurred to me and I was becoming most vexed with how stupid the country was making me feel. The innkeeper, however, seemed amused by our childish ignorance of pastoral ways and was quick to educate us. 'We keep our farms in fields oftentimes,' he chuckled before showing us to his door, 'and our clouds in the sky. Seems to me that address ye've got ain't no address at all.'

It was later, as we trudged along the rain-splashed lane in the wake of that wagoner, that I began to entertain the serious idea of just giving up and going home. It was clear now that the innkeeper was right, the address Mouse had been given was false and Charley had not wanted anyone to know where he had fled to. Our time in the north of England had been a miserable one; we had visited every farm from Oundle to Corby to Rushden to Wellingborough and had met with much silence, distrust and hostility from wary provincials. Warrigal, who had managed to blend in among the other servants and colonials of London with surprising ease, caused great consternation here in the country and that was before the locals had taken a good look at the dark, hunted expression Georgie had been wearing on his face ever since he had become a fugitive from justice. We had been refused as many lodgings at inns as we had rides on carriages and this had hindered our progress even more. Those few Christians what did agree to take our money in exchange for beds, food and answers still could not help us in our search. Farmers knew other farms – they were sure they knew all the farms on the way down to Banbury and those in all the surrounding counties – so if this one was real we would have heard of it by now.

A steeple rose up through the deep cutting of the lane, heralding another village what had not been visited yet, one what was tucked down between some hills, and I felt it was time to voice these concerns to my fellow travellers.

'We'll spend a night here,' I said, 'and if we get no joy Warrigal and myself'll head home tomorrow. Georgie, you can go west to Coketown without us.' Neither of them spoke back. They just kept their hands on their hats so as to not lose them to the hysterical wind and grunted in silent agreement.

This last village was smaller than any we had visited so far but, like most of the others, there was an ancient church, an old inn and it was surrounded by farmland. As we walked down the one road we could see a handful of villagers eyeing us with suspicion as we made for the crackling orange windows of the Roundhead Tavern. We neared the place, what had a sign flapping in the wind outside with the image of one such soldier on it, and we could see through the glass that there was a handful of dirty patrons, farmhands it was likely, all gathered around the fireplace and drinking from pewter pots while a young woman was tending to the bar. Other than that it was empty, which meant there was a strong chance of lodgings, so we shook the rain from our hats and coats under the shelter of the doorway and entered. The patrons, as they had done at every other inn we had stopped at in recent days, stopped their talking and turned to stare at us like we was three Cavaliers come back to start trouble.

'Good woman,' I said as I strode up to the barmaid, doing my best to sound genteel. 'My company and I are weary from walking in the wet. We require three beds and three hot meals. Pray don't refuse us, there's a good lass.'

The maid, who was a little older than us and did not look the sort to suffer much nonsense, considered each of us, her eyes settling at last on Warrigal. I leaned in close to her so that the men by the fire could not hear.

'Try not to draw too much attention to my friend there,' I whispered. 'He's a prince from one of the African colonies but don't feel like you have to curtsy, he don't want special treatment. Just act like he's one of us.' I winked at her and pulled back before looking around the tavern and nodding with approval. 'I think this place will do, your Majesty.' I turned to Warrigal who was sneezing into a handkerchief, 'I think it will just about do.'

'Look here,' said the maid, her hands on her hips, 'I don't care if he's an Arabian Knight. He pays the same prices as everyone else or ye and he keep walking.'

We ordered three jars of the local ale and some beef pies and went to sit in the snug of the bar while our rooms was prepared. The farmhands by the fire kept on glancing over at us and speaking amongst themselves in hushed tones and we all tried hard not to catch their eyes. I was concerned about Georgie who, as I had observed that night at the rat pit, still had his old fondness for fisticuffs and could be baited into a scrap with little provocation. But for now he appeared to be behaving himself and just drank back the beer while moaning about the weather.

'If I do get grabbed,' he said to us with a defeatist air, 'then I think I should like to be transported. It sounds nice and hot, Warrigal, where you come from.'

'Is,' said Warrigal with a small nod.

'I think I should prefer to be sent there then.' Georgie looked out of the window towards the drizzle.

'Same,' said Warrigal.

The beef pies was served by the maid, who went straight back to the bar as I unfolded the little piece of paper with the address on it. The pie was piping hot and so I got up while it cooled and walked over to speak to her again. I was now sure that the words scribbled there was just nonsense employed to appease a crying child, but there was no harm in asking one more person. However, as with everyone else, this girl had never heard of the place and declared it to be make-believe. This was the final word for me; I was too dejected to ask anyone else and so I scrunched the paper up into a ball and tossed it over the heads of the farmhands and into the flames of the fire. The men looked perturbed at this, as if I had done it to offend them, but I turned my back and went to sit down again.

'Get some more pints while you're up there, Dodger,' Georgie shouted over with a mouthful of cow. 'I've already done mine and so has Warrigal.'

Behind me, from the farmhands, there was this sudden sniggering. Perhaps it was Georgie's thick cockney accent that they was finding so droll, or perhaps it was the word Warrigal. Either way, I hoped that Georgie had not heard it; there was six of them and, although they had seemed intimidated by us when we first entered, the snigger showed that this was no longer the case. The barmaid, who was taking forever to pour the pints, seemed to be thinking along the same lines.

'Go sit yeself down, sir,' she said as she saw that the ale needed time to settle, 'I'll bring these over when they're done. No need to stay at the bar.'

I took my seat again and spoke to Warrigal. 'First thing

tomorrow,' I said, 'train back to London.' He nodded and we ate our pies in silence as Georgie started going on about what a shame it was that we would not get to see old Charley after all. As he was talking, the barmaid came over with the pots of ale and laid them down. As she did this the men by the fireplace began sniggering again and one of them started making this barking noise. 'What's that about?' said Georgie, snapping his head around to them.

'Just some foolishness,' she replied. 'Best ignored.'

A number of them began barking now and it was clear they was looking over to us in mockery. Georgie laid down his cutlery and stared back at them hard.

'They calling us dogs?' he asked.

'Calm yourself,' I said to him and then, in a lower voice so the maid would not hear, I hissed, 'You're in enough trouble.'

'They're not calling you dogs,' the barmaid said in a hurry. 'Look, I'll have a word and tell them to stop if it's bothering you. We don't want trouble.'

'You ain't gonna get none,' I assured her, my stare still fixed on Georgie.

'It's just . . .' The barmaid went to leave but then decided to stay and explain things to us. 'They think the name is funny because there is a dog around here called that. A sheepdog. So they're just having a chuckle over it. They don't mean no harm.'

'There's a sheepdog called Warrigal?' Georgie asked, grinding his teeth at the indignity of it. He was getting riled on Warrigal's behalf after just one pot of ale.

'No.' She waved the idea away with her hands as if this was nonsense. 'The other name. Dodger.'

'Dodger?' asked Georgie. He punched me in the arm and laughed. 'Dodger the sheepdog!' He shook his head. 'That's funny.'

'Well,' she went on in a lighter tone, 'he's a very funny man, Farmer Bates. Now, can I get you gentlemen anything further?'

'Yes,' I said after taking my first mouthful of pie. 'This here could use some vinegar if you have it and later on I should care for . . . Farmer Who?'

'Farmer Charley Bates –' the girl smiled – 'of Bates Beef.'

Chapter 23

Two Dodgers

Containing a visit to the Merriest Young Grazier
in All Northamptonshire

Charles Bates, the barmaid went on to inform us, was a local cattle farmer. He was the man what all the sniggering fellows in that inn worked for, whose beef was in the pie I was now eating and who had thought to name his dog Dodger. He was known for his cheerful manner and, in spite of his youth, had proven to be the most popular pastoralist around ever since he had inherited the Harrington farm following his wife's father's death three years before. It was not a large farm, about a hundred acres, and he was said to be in some debt. But they all loved Farmer Bates around here, I was told, even though he was distrusted at first for being from my wicked part of the world. He had proven himself to be a most generous employer of local men while always working as hard as any of them and so the village had grown to revere him above all others. This girl in particular seemed to think very high of my old friend and she only ever struck a sour note when mentioning the wealthy wife he had married, a Rose Harrington, who the barmaid declared was a snooty mare what put on airs. However, after she had gossiped for some time about Charley the barmaid became more guarded as I began to show too much interest in her favourite cow killer. She refused to give me directions to his farmhouse and asked if we three meant to bring trouble to the door of Farmer Bates. I assured her that we was just his old friends from London but still she replied with suspicion. 'If ye and he are such good friends –' her eyes narrowed – 'then how come he gave ye a different address?' This was hard to answer and so I thanked her for her time and let her go about her business.

For the rest of the evening she watched us most careful from behind the bar as if regretting how loose-tongued she had been. But, keen to show what a friendly and harmless band of coves myself and my companions was, I approached the six farmhands and introduced myself as Jack Dawkins of Dawkins Wool. I congratulated them on the sparkling wit they had displayed and offered to buy each one of the hard-working fellows a pot of ale. Before long, we was all the best of pals what kept no secrets from each other and they was happy to tell me all about Farmer Bates and where he could be found. His farmhouse was a fair walk away down a quiet lane, they informed us, what cut between two fields. You could not miss the old Harrington place though, it being the only dwelling down there.

It had stopped raining and, although now very dark, it was still early enough for us to go visiting. As we paid for our vittles and made to leave the maid looked uncomfortable, knowing that we must be setting off towards Farmer Bates's home. But there was no reason for us to be too secretive about our movements – we of course meant Charley no harm and our things was left in the tavern chamber so we was not behaving like wrongdoers. We put our hats and coats back on, bid the farmhands goodnight and headed out. A low stone-walled path led out of the village and curved down a dark lane and we had to trek a long way through thick wet mud before we saw the lights of the little farmhouse what lay between the two fields. Smoke was puffing out of the chimney and a smaller path led towards it and some stables. However, a thought occurred as we drew near that if we approached from that direction then Charley would be able to see us coming and, should he have something valuable to hide as I hoped he would, then he would be given plenty of warning to do it. Instead, I told the others, we would climb over the stone wall into the field and walk on the inside up to where the cow-barn was so that our arrival would catch him unawares. 'It'll be a nice surprise for Charley,' I whispered to Georgie, who also liked the idea.

The field was sludgy and so strewn with pats that our boots was squelching and caked in mud and worse by the time we drew near the cottage. I did not regret the furtive advance however as it afforded me a good opportunity to see into the lighted window of his home. The closer we got the more we could hear piano music. It was a simple tune being played, like one a child would like, and I began to spy the movements of a man walking about in the front room. We crept up close yet still hidden behind the wall and from this position I could see that a tall fellow was hanging decorations around the inside of the farmhouse. There was flickering lights what suggested more than just a lit fireplace and he appeared to be talking to someone what I could not see. I was still not close enough to tell if this was Charley.

'It's not a good idea for all three of us to just appear on his doorstep like this,' I whispered. 'Especially you, Warrigal. If he sees your face rearing out of the black night unannounced he's liable to think you're Spring-heeled Jack or some other fiend come to grab him. No, I'll go up alone and call you two over when I'm ready.'

I climbed over the stone wall and began pacing towards the house. I did not want to make straight for the knocker though; first I wanted to creep as close up to the window as I could and peer in without being seen. The thick mud on the soles of my boots muffled the sound of my footsteps until I could get close enough to see what I needed to. But before I was even able to see the face of the tall, gangly man of my own age what was hanging sprigs of holly and ivy from the wooden beams of the ceiling, I knew it was him. He was laughing at something another person was saying, a woman what was sat playing on the small piano, and they was conversing as she did so. I knew him from the laugh straight away; it was the very same loud, generous chuckle with which he had warmed up my childhood. It was Charley all right – good-humoured, light-hearted Charley Bates, my most favoured companion. I felt an ache to see how much he had altered during my time abroad and again cursed the magistrate what had rent me from those I held most dear and stolen my youth. I had not realised until this moment how much I had missed Charley, how he was as treasured a part of my upbringing as Fagin had been. The Jakkapoor stone meant nothing, I saw now, compared to the joy of this reunion.

The woman on the piano stool must have been his wife and I could see at a glance why the barmaid at the Roundhead had been so sniffy about her. She was a striking beauty. She was speaking to him as she played and was keeping him most amused as he went around the room preparing their home for Christmas. It was a magical scene, with a small tree like those what burglars used to describe seeing in rich houses during the festive season, standing proud in the corner of the room. This tree was alight with many tiny white candles what accounted for the flickering and also hanging from its branches was those twinkling glass baubles, all different colours, just like the ones that Fagin would hang from the door at this time of year. Once Charley had secured the mistletoe to the centre beam he gestured for his lady wife to join him for a kiss. She stopped playing, stood and crossed the room to him. It was then that I saw she was with child. I was beginning to grow uneasy with what I was seeing. I had a sudden memory of Fagin hanging his own coloured baubles up many years ago and myself and Charley asking him what the story was behind them. Fagin, who knew a great many things and was ready to make up whatever he did not know, had answered by telling us that the tradition had been begun by the forest people of eastern Europe. They had made the baubles to hang from the outside of their doors to ward off any evil spirits what should try to cross the threshold of the home. Folklore held that the sight of their own hideous reflections would be enough to scare the spirits away and they would not return for a whole year. I glanced towards the stone wall behind which Warrigal and Georgie was hiding and felt a sudden want to retreat. I stepped back from the light of the window, unsure of whether to knock or not. And then I saw something else that stopped me dead.

A dog barked and startled me. Both Charley and his wife turned to look outside and I heard her gasp in fright as I was spied. More barking, and Charley strode right up to the glass. 'Dodger!' he exclaimed, and then dashed out of the room. The barking dog ran up to the front door of the cottage and began scratching at it most violent so it could get to me. 'Dodger!' I heard Charley say again from inside. 'Wait!' I stepped around so I would be facing the porch as he opened. He was taking his time about it and so I was sure he must be putting that dog on a leash first. Dodger, I then remembered, was the name of the animal and so I called out so he would recognise my voice.

'Charley!' I said. 'Charley Bates! It's me.'

There was a small pause and then the door flung open and out bounded a Border collie, unleashed and teeth bared. It dashed straight towards me and scrambled to a stop just feet away. There it continued to communicate in loud aggressive barks its desire for me to clear off.

'Woah!' I cried in panic. 'Easy, boy!' I went to run and the dog made to chase me but I gathered enough wits to see that this was no natural attack animal. So I stood my ground, with my open hands on display, and tried to show him that I was a friend. 'Charley,' I pleaded, 'put him on a leash for pity's sake before he bites my leg.' I looked towards the man stood in the doorway, who was holding up a lantern with one hand and brandished something else in the other. It was a farmer's shotgun and he was pointing it square at me.

'Turn around and go back to London,' he warned me in his rough voice. 'Come near my family again and I'll blast a hole in your head.' From inside I could hear a baby crying.

'Charley?' I cried in panic. 'Don't be like that. We're pals.'

He raised his lantern so he could get a better look. 'This about Bill Sikes?' he squinted. 'Well, I don't care how you knew him. He was a murdering bastard and I'm proud of what I done.'

'So am I!' I said back. 'He deserved it for killing Nancy.' This was the honest truth, and I then added, 'And I'd a peached upon him myself if I'd been there,' which was not.

He paused and again lifted his lantern. The shotgun looked heavy — I supposed he used it for shooting sick cattle — and the two weights seemed to fight each other for balance as he took another step. I was still unsure if he had recognised me or had just been startled by a London voice and had assumed the worst. Finally he spoke.

'Dodger?'

The border collie cocked a confused head towards his master.

'You talking to him or me?'

He laughed then, the good old Charley laugh what I knew so well, and his shotgun arm dropped down. 'Jack!' he guffawed, and shook his head in merriment. 'Jack Dawkins! Old Artful! Lumme, Jack! What a surprise to see you here!'

I laughed too and made towards him, arms open for a manly embrace. But then the shotgun arm went up again.

'I didn't say come closer,' he said, blunt. 'I still don't want you inside my home.'

'But, Charley,' I begged. 'I'm your best friend in the world. And it's freezing out here. Have a heart.'

'What you doing in Northamptonshire?' he demanded. 'Why ain't you in Australia where they sent you?'

'I'm a farmer now,' I told him. 'Like you, only my line is wool. And I'm here to ask you some questions and for a favour. Honest though, Charley, I mean you no harm. Please stop pointing that thing at me.' I edged a bit closer towards him. 'I'm at your mercy.'

Charley eyed me hard but I could see he was starting to see sense. After thinking on it for some moments, he at last lowered his gun arm again and whistled in relief. 'I'm sorry, Jack,' he said in a softer tone. 'It's just that up here you get so tense about every little footstep and I can't take chances—'

Warrigal sneezed. Charley spun towards the stone wall and saw two hatted heads in silhouette watching us. 'Who's that?' he shouted, and before I could answer the lantern was dropped, the gun arm was up and a shot was fired. Georgie's hat went flying from off his head and they both vanished behind the wall again. His wife screamed from within the cottage, the dog dropped its head to the floor in fright and I grabbed at the gun. I at least now knew he was out of shot and so tried to wrestle it off him.

'You snake!' he shouted at me as he fought for it back. 'You've brought others here to do me in.' He had grown bigger than me, like Jem, but he could not take the gun back without a fight. Dodger the dog, however, had gotten over the shock of the blast and now jumped up to help his master. I tried kicking him away, but he was going to sink his teeth into me and so I pulled the gun away from Charley and tried to hit him with it. Then another blast rang out and I felt shot whizz straight past my ears.

'Get away from my husband!' a woman's voice cried out in a strong northern accent. I turned to see the pregnant figure of Mrs Rose Bates stood in the porch and reloading shot into her own rifle.

'It's just Georgie!' I shouted at Charley in desperation. 'Georgie Bluchers! He wants your help, Charley! Nobody's here to hurt you.'

'Who's the other one?' he shouted back, as deafened as I was it seemed. 'And why they hiding?'

'The other is a friend too,' I answered. 'His name's Warrigal, he's from Australia and he don't even care who Bill Sikes is. Tell your wife not to shoot me,' I said as I saw the woman was almost done reloading. He turned then and held his hand up to her.

'You explain yourself,' he growled to me, 'and make it good.'

I let go of the gun and stepped back, panting as I did so. Dodger had scarpered at the second shot, so I could take my time in speaking. 'Georgie is here because he's in trouble with the law. He wants you to hide him for a bit and let him work on your farm under a false name until the trouble blows over.'

'Oh, does he now?' said Charley, and let out an ironical laugh at the impertinence of it.

'Yeah, he does,' I said. I was bending over with my hands on my knees to get my breath back after the excitement. 'But that ain't why I'm here. I'm here to ask if you still have a little wooden doll what Fagin gave you when you was a kinchin. There is a chance that it has a little black jewel inside it and, if it does, I know a man in London what'll pay you handsomely for it.' I stood to my full height again and looked him in the eye. 'Give me that stone and I'll see that you get a decent reward. You can trust me on that, Charley. I'd want you and your wife to have it even though she has just tried to shoot me in the head.'

'What you on about, Jack?' Charley asked with a look of bewilderment. 'I ain't got no little wooden doll.'

'Yes, you do,' I said, and pointed into his home. 'It's the one I've just seen in there grinning out at me. You've got it hanging from the top of your Christmas tree.'

There was a long silence as he let that sink in. His wife just stood in the doorway looking at us with a scared expression and her heavy gun in her hands and the only sound heard was the crying baby from somewhere behind her. And then a voice spoke.

'That was a bloody good hat, that,' Georgie moaned to Warrigal from behind the stone wall. 'And now there's a hole in it.'

The sound of the gunshots had alerted the people of the village and in no time a group of men, including some of those farmhands we had met earlier, was running up the pathway towards the cottage, all wielding spades, sticks and other makeshift weapons. A man galloped past them on horseback with a shotgun of his own and reared up just outside the cottage. 'Farmer Bates!' he cried as he did so. 'Are ye all right, sir?'

By now myself, Georgie and Warrigal was all inside the hallway of the cottage and I was trying to explain things to his still terrified wife who also had their one-year-old son in her arms and was rocking him back to sleep while their oldest child, a girl of three, was stood behind her legs looking frightened also. Charley had decided to trust us, although like most English people he had baulked at the sight of Warrigal, and I was doing my best job of apologising to the couple and promising them that we had only ever come in friendship. Avenging a murderer like Bill Sikes would never be my business, I swore to them, and I would never divulge their address to those for whom it might be.

'We're all fine here, Eli,' said Charley, as he went outside to speak to the coming mob. 'A faulty shotgun, that's all, but nobody got hurt. Rose and the babes are safe.'

'Hetty at the Roundhead says ye've had visitors,' said the man. Our three pairs of muddy boots was stood outside the door in a row and I could see through the glass that he was straining to see in. 'An African prince or summat?'

'Just friends from London,' said Charley with a nervous chuckle. 'Nothing to worry on. Thanks for coming down though.' He headed out of our earshot towards the other men to say more of the same and so we was left stood in the hall with his Rose. She beheld the three of us with horror and looked as though she would be ready to pick up the shotgun and start beating the three of us. I smiled at her, gave a friendly wave towards the girl and then tried to break the awkward silence.

'You're a sweet one,' I said, motioning towards the elder child. 'What's your name?'

'She's called Nancy,' her mother said.

'Is she?' I said, taken aback by this. 'Well, she's a love. It's a very cosy little home this, Mrs Bates.' I looked around the hall. A lucky horseshoe hung from the wall and there was a picture of an old man in a field atop a large mare. 'That your father, is it?'

'How d'you know that?' she asked.

'Nice woman at the inn said you'd inherited the farm. So I thought tha—'

'Listen, Mr Whatever-you-said,' she interrupted, 'I don't care what that gossipy cow has told ye. I don't care for three strange men creeping up to our house at this hour unannounced. You say you knew my husband from his London days? Well, from what he's told me of his upbringing that can only count against you. So why don't we all just keep quiet until Charles gets back. That is unless you want to tell me about this reward you mentioned.'

'Reward?' Georgie asked me. 'What reward's that?'

'The reward for the jewel,' I said, and pointed at the shut door what led into the room with all the Christmas decorations, 'what I hope is hidden in plain sight through there. How about we all go through and I'll show you?'

Rose nodded and so I opened the door and walked over to the tree. There, dangling from a string tied to one of the top branches, was one of the three smiling Indian brothers. It was identical to mine and I unhooked it from the tree and listened for a rattle.

'There's something inside,' I said to Warrigal with such excitement it was as though St Nicholas had placed it in there himself. 'I need to open it,' I said to Rose. 'Has Charley got anything what can cut through wood?'

''Course he has,' she answered with no grace at all as she sat down in a rocking chair with the baby still in her arms. 'This is a farm.'

Just then the front door slammed and Charley was heard putting Dodger away before coming in to join us. 'They've gone,' he told us as he entered the room. 'Now where was we? Georgie! Jack!' He flung open his arms and gave us the big welcome I had been expecting before he'd taken out his gun and set his dog on us. 'I thought I'd never see you boys again!' After we had embraced most warm and remarked upon how much we had all changed Charley turned to his unsmiling wife. 'Have you all done introducing yourselves then?'

'I know that they're from that school for thieves you've spoken of.' Rose sniffed as she rocked the baby back to sleep and stroked the hair of the little girl stood next to her. 'That's enough to know.'

'No, but Rose,' Charley was quick to explain, 'these two ain't bad. They was the victims of that corrupting place, not the villains. Jack was my best friend back in those days. The Artful Dodger. I've told you about him often.' He turned to me and nudged my shoulder. 'I named the dog after you.'

'So I heard,' I replied with genuine gratitude.

'And Georgie . . .' He walked over to the where the big lump stood and threw his arm over his shoulder, 'Georgie here was the sweetest of the lot. He's as gentle as a kitten, old Georgie.' I nodded my head most fervent at this description of Georgie's character and decided that now was not the best time to mention Georgie was on the run for burglary and helping to bury a murder victim. Instead I changed the subject by turning to the aborigine in the room.

'And don't you let my pal upset you, little Nancy.' The child had been staring at Warrigal in horrid fascination ever since he had entered the house. 'He's as kind as Black Peter from the fairy tales. And besides –' I turned to Charley, keen to bring matters back around to business – 'he and I will be leaving for London first thing tomorrow. Once we've taken a peek inside this.' I rattled the doll again and asked if they would like to hear a story.

I was telling the truth about getting Charley a reward should the Jakkapoor stone be discovered inside his doll. Evershed was rich and would pay big money if he was to hear the jewel was in the possession of some honest farmer whose place was in debt. Charley deserved it, should he turn out to be Fagin's favourite and, as he would never have even known about the jewel without me, I considered that it was a fair deal for us to go halves. We all sat around the fire and, holding the doll in my hands, I proceeded to tell everyone there as much as they needed to know about why I was back in England and what I hoped to gain from the jewel if found. By the time I got to the part where the famous Jakkapoor stone could be hidden inside this very doll, Charley and his wife was desperate for me to just get it open and see the stone.

'Get a saw, Charley, quick!' his wife cried, but he was already on his feet and dashing outside to the stables. 'My word,' she said to herself while he was gone, linking her fingers as if in prayer. 'If this man will pay us what you think he will then it will solve all our money problems. We can pay off all of father's bad debts.' She looked at me in wonder. 'Oh, Mr Dawkins,' she said, 'if you're right then your visit here tonight will have been like that of an angel. I'm sorry for being so ill-mannered earlier.'

'That's all right,' I waved it off. 'Don't thank me yet.'

Charley burst back in with a long metal saw and told me to hold the doll over a wooden table. I did so, careful to ensure that whatever was rattling inside would not be damaged, and he began sawing in the middle while I held the head and Georgie grabbed the legs. He was most excitable as he began cutting it in half, even giggling as sawdust covered the table. Finally he had cut into it enough so I told him to stop and took it in both hands to let whatever was rattling just fall out on the table. Charley, Georgie and Warrigal leant in close as I snapped it in half while Rose stood behind with Nancy and the baby and tried to see over our shoulders.

'Well,' she asked in great anticipation, 'is it there?'

She must have seen her answer written in our collective shoulders as they all drooped in disappointment and we went quiet. Charley picked up the pebble, what was just like the one what had been in mine, and showed it to her.

'This don't look like no priceless Indian jewel,' he sighed, and handed it to me. I could feel the same wave of anger and despair coming over me that I had felt in that Greenwich hotel room when I had learnt that I was not Fagin's favourite after all. I was as hurt for Charley as I had been for myself. But that pain was outweighed by the frustration that I now had even less of a clue as to where the real stone was. I wanted to kick something and wished that Dodger was in the room.

Rose Bates, with her baby still in one arm, grabbed hold of Nancy's hand with the other and looked at me most fierce as she made for the door. 'I'm going to bed, Charley,' she huffed to her husband. 'I hope Mr Dawkins and his friends enjoy their stay in the Roundhead tonight. Tell 'em not to bother saying goodbye before they leave for London tomorrow.' And she slammed the door behind her. I turned to Charley, who was looking most downhearted and held the two halves of the doll he had kept as a souvenir for all these years in each hand.

'Sorry about getting your hopes up, Charley,' I said as he and Georgie took a chair each and sat down. I took the piano stool and Warrigal just leant against the wall by the window looking out at the night sky, his face away from us. 'It's still good to see you though.'

Charley gave me a sad smile and rocked in the chair that his wife had just got out of. 'You've been here for less than half an hour, Artful,' he said. 'And in that time I've been scared out of my wits, driven to violence, told I was going to be rich and then been made heartbroken that I'm not.' He laughed as he looked at the grinning head of the doll. 'You ain't changed all that much.'

Chapter 24

The Greens

In which some names come up, one of which
proves most important to this here history

'Eddie Inderwick,' said Georgie, slurping up the rest of his coffee and then looking at the three of us with great surety. 'He *musta* been Fagin's favourite.'

It was the following morning and the four of us was having a late breakfast in the Roundhead before Warrigal and I was set to return to London. We was sat around the same small table we had eaten at the night before and, with Warrigal as silent as ever, the conversation soon turned to the whereabouts of the Jakkapoor stone. We had not much time to spare before the wagoner what Charley had arranged to take us to Peterborough would be arriving at the inn so this was a farewell meal and my last chance to ask if either of my two childhood friends could help me in my quest for treasure. Georgie, it had been agreed, was to stay here under a false name and work with Charley as a farmhand for at least a year until the hot search for Jem's accomplice had cooled. Charley, as I had always known he would, was prepared to harbour him for friend-ship's sake although he made it clear to Georgie that he would not tolerate no thievery while he was under his care. Charley had become a proper flat in the past six years, that much was clear. This farmer business, moving up north to where his relatives lived, working for the Harringtons as a farmer's drudge, ingratiating himself with the family, marrying the eldest daughter, inheriting the farm – this was not just a dodge for him. As amazing as it seemed, he really was a proper farmer, not just pretending to be one for his own low purposes like what I had done. He had risen before the cocks had crowed that morning to tend to the cattle and had given orders to his farmhands to carry on without him before meeting us for this final meal. The barmaid at the Roundhead, Hetty, had been unwilling to serve us that morning when we came down from our chambers and had asked us to leave before we caused more trouble. Then, after Charley had strolled in and given her his reassurance that we was all right, she began busying herself around our table making herself most helpful and flashing her smiles at the handsome young farmer. The whole village afforded him a respect that I had never before seen a boy of such poor upbringing receive without having to live off crime for it.

Charley, with his good lady wife not around to snort disapproving fire at us for building up castles in the air, became most animated when talking about the whole business of the hidden jewel and George Shatillion. He told us that Rose had been reading him some of an old Shatillion ghost story called *The Lady of the Loch* earlier that year and he was laughing in disbelief at how Fagin had been intimate friends with the author of characters like Old Man McWorter and Wee Dougie Boyd. Now that the disappointment of the previous night had passed we had all begun to turn our minds back to who we thought had been given the third doll. The mysterious story had captured the imagination of both Charley and Georgie and they was full of ideas as to where the jewel may have ended up.

'Fagin was fond of Eddie, true.' I nodded. 'But if he's an opium fiend like you reckon then it's more than likely he's sold everything he owns to pay for it. He won't have it now. Who else might have been given the doll?'

'What about the Mullins twins?' asked Georgie as Hetty came to remove our plates.

'Don't bother with Alan Mullins,' said Charley after thanking her and telling her to put it all on his bill. 'Fagin hated him on account of his face. But Davey Mullins he liked. He preferred his look.'

'They was identical.'

'Not in the eyes they wasn't. You looked in Alan's eyes and you could tell what he was – a scheming thief. There was no hiding his villainy and Fagin despised him for it. But Davey had the eyes of an innocent choirboy and that Fagin could work with. That was the thing about the old Jew.' The four of us rose as through the window Charley saw the wagoner rolling towards the inn. 'He had two sorts of boys he liked. There was the likes of you, the clever thieves, the earners, the ones what never got caught because they was naturals at it. And then there was the innocents.'

'What innocents?'

'The ones it was up to him to corrupt. Those was his real favourites.'

We put on our hats and coats, waved farewell to Hetty, who herself only waved back to Charley, and went outside to meet our transport. The wagoner was the same one what had refused to take Warrigal the day before, but this time Charley told him to stop complaining and do as he was bid. He sniffed and said he wanted to unload some stale, musty-smelling hay into another wagon first and replace it with fresher stacks from a nearby barn. Warrigal and Georgie went with him to hurry things along while I stayed back to talk to Charley.

'Innocents?' I asked, annoyed by his last remarks. 'Who you talkin' about? None of us was innocent.'

Charley lowered his voice so nobody in the village, the village what now held him in such high esteem, could overhear him speaking of his tainted childhood. 'I was innocent,' he said, 'when I first got there. I'd never had a dishonest thought until I went to live in that place. That's what Fagin liked about me though. He liked corrupting boys and making us like you; that was his fun. I never minded at the time – I was getting fed and clothed and making new friends. But now I'm a father myself, well . . .' His voice tailed off. And even though his mouth was shut I could tell his teeth was grinding away within. 'I'll just say,' he said at last, 'that my kinchins won't be playing the snatching game at my house on Christmas day.'

'You ungrateful wretch,' I said in disgust. 'That man taught you skills for getting on in this life. He was father and mother to us all and his lessons was important. You can't expect to survive in this world without picking a pocket.'

'Tell that to Eddie Inderwick,' he replied, 'when you visit him in his squalor.'

'Eddie got caught,' I shot back. 'That was his luck. You married a farmer's daughter. That was yours. Look here, I don't want to row with you just before we say goodbye forever, but you're wrong. Fagin loved me the most because I was sharpest. He didn't have time for the greens.'

I had become most vexed by this suggestion that I was not the old man's best boy because it struck me as a wicked lie. Why would Fagin call me top-sawyer if he favoured another more? But Charley just laughed in response, not his usual warm laugh but one what was bitter.

'He loved the greens best!' he exclaimed. 'Remember how excited he would get whenever one of us would bring home a new one we'd found on the streets. "Your face is your fortune, my dear," he used to say to them and he'd treat them like they was made of china. He thought that they was best on account of where you could send them – into a church, to the theatre, into a rich man's home. An angelic boy could go anywhere, steal anything, that's what he used to say. That can't be said of you, Dodge.'

'Why can't it?' I asked, outraged by the suggestion. I was starting to think that the country air had affected his senses.

Charley just sighed and looked to the wagon what was set to take me away from him again. It was almost empty. 'Because you're like Alan Mullins,' he replied. 'You look like what you are.'

With this impertinence he had gone too far and I faced him in anger. 'Look like what I am?' I cried. 'And that's a thief, is it? Meanwhile you've got a face like the baby Jesus, I suppose?'

'Don't get upset, Dodge,' he said, trying to calm me, but it was too late for that.

'I'll have you know,' I declared loud enough for the whole village to hear, 'I have spent time in the company of proper society. Lords have confided their deepest secrets to me. Men of the cloth have invited me to dine with their families, even thrown their daughters at me for marriage if I cared to have them. Quality like that wouldn't let a common rustic like you set foot in the house!'

'Everything all right, Farmer Bates?'

Two hefty farmhands had appeared from around the corner of the lane what led down to his farmhouse and had chanced upon me in the throes of my anger. I corrected myself as they walked towards me, readying themselves like a pair of sheepdogs to chase me off should Farmer Bates give them a whistle. But Charley told them that everything was fine and assured them that I would be leaving soon.

After they had walked on he turned to me and spoke softer. 'All I meant was,' he said as the horses of the wagon trundled towards us and Warrigal threw our bags into the back, 'that Fagin liked those what was uncorrupted. He made it his sport to turn a good boy bad. The angels, they was his biggest weakness. And in the end it was an angel what was the death of him.' The wagoner pulled his horse up to where I stood and gave me an unfriendly look but Charley was still speaking. 'You should know, Artful,' Charley went on. 'You introduced them.'

This comment confused me. I had no clue as to what he was talking about. Georgie walked over to us. He was getting ready to bid me farewell.

'Introduced who?'

'Fagin and the boy what peached upon him,' explained Charley. 'You must remember. The one from the workhouse. You and I took him out to go finding one morning and he got himself caught. Oliver, I think his name was.'

As he spoke a dim light became brighter inside my memory. I did recall an Oliver, some pale little weakling what had got Fagin all agitated. He had got grabbed, if I recalled right, and taken to a wealthy home. Bill, Nancy and the Jew had gone to great trouble to snatch him back for reasons I had never understood. He had then been taken to aid Bill Sikes in the burglary of a home in Chertsey and he had gone and gotten himself caught there too. As far as I knew that was the last of the hopeless bugger. I had not thought on him since and had certainly never entertained the idea that he, not I, would be Fagin's favourite boy.

'You must not have heard,' Charley went on as I scratched my mind for more details on him, 'on account of you getting lagged before all the trouble began. I only blowed upon Bill and that was for murdering Nancy. But it was this Oliver what peached upon Fagin. He told the police all about our school and that was what finished us. He was the great destroyer.'

I saw him then. A small child shivering on some cold stone steps. I remember thinking about how he would starve if no kind soul thought to step in. I took pity.

'*Hullo, my covey,*' I had said. '*What's the row?*' And I had invited him home with me.

Georgie was saying goodbye to me now and Warrigal was in the wagon waiting for me to join him but my thoughts was still absent. I was thinking on that boy and nothing else, and I was not engaged with what was going on around me as we went to leave. Charley gave me a hug and said he hoped we would meet again although I could hear in his voice that this was not true. He made me promise to write though and let them know the moment it was safe for him to send Georgie back.

'I just wish,' he said as I climbed up on to the wagon, 'that I could remember the second name of that boy. You could look him up and see if he has the stone.' I told Charley that I planned to do just that and that I remembered the name now. It was all coming back to me in sickening clearness.

'*This is him, Fagin,*' I had said to my beloved master, all proud and unaware of the poison I was presenting, '*my friend Oliver Twist!*'

Part Three

Chapter 25

In a Puff of Smoke

Some different characters come and go
through the black London fog

Seven nights had passed since I last saw my lovely Ruby but I had not rested my head upon a pillow without thinking on that precious moment when she had finally told me she loved me. It was like something from a romantic novel and I was keen to take her in my arms again and repeat the experience, only this time without the cellar, the murderer and the army of police about to burst in on us. That she had not actually said the words 'I love you, Jack,' was a detail I was not letting trouble me. She could never have said that with Jem listening, I told myself, so instead said, 'Don't get caught.' And if ever there was a better coded phrase for 'I love you, Jack,' then these young ears had not heard them. There was a chance, I considered, that it was Jem that she had been speaking to or perhaps that she was addressing all four of us. But I decided to cast these thoughts aside as unromantic. With Jem gone, I said to Warrigal as our train pulled into Islington station late in the afternoon, Ruby was mine for the taking and I planned to head straight round to her house and unload my heart to her. Warrigal, a business-minded cove who had little time for the intrigues of young lovers, shook his head and told me no. We had wasted too much time up north, he said, we had still not found the jewel and we had less than a week before Evershed arrived in London. We would be better employed tracking down some of those names I had jotted down in my notebook, he told me, and asking them about the third doll. 'Eddie Inderwick,' he said and then, as if it was the most ridiculous name he had ever heard, 'Oliver Twist.'

This, I admitted, was a fair argument and I was very keen to track down young Twist for reasons that went far beyond the search for the jewel. But I reminded him that we also needed to retrieve our things what had been left at that address and so the hunt for the Jakkapoor stone would have to wait. We stepped on to the foggy streets and hailed a cab to Bethnal Green where I was sure that Ruby, my ever-constant sweetheart, had been longing for my return.

'Ruby's gone,' Greta told us upon answering the door. 'She don't want nothing to do with none of you lot.'

'Gone?' I exclaimed in disgust at the fickleness of woman. 'But Jem's only got took a week ago! Where has she gone?'

'She's gone back to work in the music halls, or so she told me before packing her bags. Said she wishes she'd never given all that up for a rotter like Jem.'

'Don't blame her,' I remarked. 'She was wasted on him. Now, what theatre has she gone to, so I can pay her a visit?'

'I dunno,' Greta shrugged. 'And I wouldn't tell you if I did. Now, are you going to come in and take what's left of your things inside or what?' She stepped away from the door and let us cross into the house, smiling at my companion with fondness as she did so. 'I see you're still with us, Warrigal.' She stroked the front of his shirt with her finger as he passed by her to go up the stairs. I could not help but notice she was not pestering him for his five shillings.

Every door of every room in that house was open and filled with chattering women what was not here last week. Many of them was in a state of undress and one was sat upon her pisspot in front of all the others and complaining to them about the price of cockles as water hit tin. Some of these women glanced our way and they did not conceal their hostility towards us. Others just acted like we was not there. They was a toughened set of females and I asked Greta, as she led us into the bedroom where our trunk was, if this was now a brothel.

'No, it ain't,' she said sounding scandalised. 'Well, apart from my room. And even that will have to change now these girls are here. This will now be a house where women come to get away from all that. And away from any bastards what mistreat them.'

Sat on a chair beside the bed where Nancy died, and in a manner most relaxed, was a tall woman with cropped hair what was dressed in gentleman's clothing. She was sat with her legs crossed, smoking a cigar, and was regarding herself in a hand-mirror. She looked over to us, a small smile playing upon her lips, as we went over to open our luggage, and something about her seemed familiar. It was not until Warrigal threw open the smashed lock of the trunk, revealing it to be almost empty, that I realised why this was.

'If I'm not much mistaken, madam,' I said to the woman as she held my gaze and drew on the cigar, 'those are my trousers you've got on.' She blew out a smoke ring and watched it float towards me.

'Is they?' she said.

'Yes, they is,' I replied, and pointed at her canary waistcoat. 'And that there is mine as well. The shirt and the cufflinks though belong to my companion. Be a friend and take them off for us, will you?' The woman looked to Greta and then turned back to me.

'You want me to get unrigged for you?' she said, all antagonistic. 'I just heard Greta tell you that this weren't that sort of place.'

'But it is the sort of place where you crack open the locks of others,' I said as if I had never before seen the like, 'and take whatever you care to without the decency to pretend like you haven't? I should be ashamed of such brazenness.'

'Jack,' said Greta, coming between us, 'the peelers broke your lock, not us. They rummaged through the whole place, and once they was done there was not a lot left in there. These girls came here at my invitation after Ruby left. And, yeah, we helped ourselves to what remained in your trunk, which weren't much. For all I knew you was never coming back.'

'Well, here we are. So, if you don't mind –' I turned back to the woman – 'I should like my togs.'

The tall woman stood and shook her head at Greta as though I was being most unreasonable. But, with the cigar still clenched in her teeth, she began pulling at her waistcoat buttons and asked Warrigal and myself to face the wall while she changed into something more feminine. This we did, all the while asking Greta about what had happened while we was away. As we spoke I found myself staring at that music-hall poster of Ruby's what was still hanging upon the wall.

Douglas Boyd, I recalled, was the name of the producer what had first introduced Ruby into the music halls and it made sense to me that she would try him if anyone. This place, Rafferty's in Wideapple Square, was therefore where I was likely to find her.

'I'm surprised she didn't take this poster,' I said as Greta was telling me all about the damage the peelers had done to the place.

'Ruby left all sorts, she was in such a hurry,' Greta sniffed. 'I expect she'll come back for it and the rest once she's settled. But you just leave her alone from now on, Jack,' Greta warned. 'She told me she's done with thieves like yourself.'

'She didn't say that, did she?'

RAFFERTY'S
GRAND MUSIC HALL
WIDEAPPLE SQUARE, LONDON TOWN

Mr. DOUGLAS BOYD PRESENTS
BENEFIT CONCERT!
WEDNESDAY, FEBRUARY 15th
FOR THE SOCIETY OF FALLEN WOMEN

RUBY IN RED
A SONG, A WINK AND SOME SAUCY BANTER!

SID FRIZELLE
IS
A MAN OF A MILLION CHARACTERS!

DEPINTO AND JONES
ARE
TWO HALVES OF THE SAME HORSE!

FANNY DORRIT
NO NONSENSE ABOUT HER!

THE CRUMMLES FAMILY
FEATURING THE INFANT PHENOMENON!
MRS HILDA HANNIGAN
TALKS TO THE DEAD!

GOD BLESS HER BRITTANIC MAJESTY

'As good as. Anyway, you can turn round now, your clothes is ready.'

Warrigal and myself turned back around and saw the clothes tossed on to the floor between us and the woman. She was sat back upon the chair looking at herself in the hand-mirror, in the precise pose that she had been in when we entered. Only now she was as naked as a babe and sniggering.

'Told you I'd change into something more feminine,' she said with a cackle.

We ignored her, picked up our clothes and threw them into the trunk. We still had plenty of money upon us to get lodgings else-where, but I hoped that Evershed had not made an inventory of what we had been given in Australia as he was not likely to get much back. Before leaving I asked Greta if she had heard about what fate had befallen Jem.

'He ain't been tried yet if that's what you're asking,' she said as she led us back down the steps towards the door. 'But he'll swing, I'm sure of that. I tell you, I never liked the boy – he used to hit Ruby and was a murdering bastard – but still I would not wish the rope on any poor creature.'

'Me neither,' I said before we stepped out into the chilly air. 'If only he had not got took. But there was nothing that could have been done.' I sighed and put on my hat before taking another look around this dark house where Bill had killed Nancy. It was now full of the sounds of women talking and I could hear some laughter from a room above. 'This place has a sad history,' I said to her before I left it forever. 'I hope that's all done with.'

'It will be –' Greta nodded all proud – 'now I'm in charge. There won't be no Bills or Jems worming their way back in here no more.' Then she stood in front of the door, blocking our path, and touched Warrigal's nose as if they was sweethearts. 'You can come by whenever you care to though, my handsome. Say you will or I ain't letting you out.'

And only after he promised not to be a stranger did she finally stand aside and let us go about our business.

'Fog!' I said as I rapped on a red door what was marked with three painted Chinese letters. It was late the next day and we was just off Limehouse Reach. The stone steps was thick with mud from the banks and gulls flew above from the nearby docks. The smells of rich spices all around was a treat for the nostrils and as night-time drew in these lanes was getting even busier with sailors and dockers out looking for fun.

'Fog what?' came the sharp reply from within.

'Fog everywhere!' I answered, having been told these watch-words by Georgie. Some chains could be heard rattling on the other side and the door was opened by a young Chinaman what I took to be one of the sons of Wu. 'Your name is Ling, if I recall,' I said to the pigtailed boy who was a few years younger than myself and dressed in a silk robe with a black skullcap. 'I'm Artful and I used to play cards with your father. He about?' The boy shook his head but I told him this did not matter as our business was with another man anyway. I flashed him some gold coins and asked if we could come inside. 'Looking for Eddie Inderwick,' I said to him. 'I'm told this is his home of sorts.' After pocketing them the boy admitted myself and Warrigal into the den and before the door was even shut after us we was breathing in the sweet fumes of opium. The boy pointed down a long corridor of door-less rooms what was overhung with many-coloured silk curtains and lit with Chinese lanterns. He told us to go behind the loose purple one hanging at the far end and, as we walked towards it, this heavy smoke puffed out from behind the other rooms. Behind most of them we could hear bubbling sounds and make out the figures of people lighting their oil lamps through the fine materials and lying back to smoke in the strong-smelling vapours.

I pulled back the purple drapes and stepped into the small room beyond, which contained three male bodies lain out on long wooden shelves but who was all difficult to identify on account of the heavy fug. I coughed loud to see if any of them would stir but none did and so I approached and leant in close to see which was Eddie. The first man was a grey-haired Lascar and the next was also far too old to be our man but the third, what was half-covered in a dirty blanket and muttering to himself in his sleep, was just about recognisable as the once-respected prefect of Saffron Hill. His thin pillow was damp from his sweat and he was wearing brown corduroy trousers with no belt and an open thick grey shirt what was missing buttons. I was much taken aback by how awful and aged he now appeared. This was the older boy what I used to admire so much and who I remembered as having the healthy glow of a sportsman. Now he was thin-skinned and sunken-eyed and his fitful sleep seemed most distressed as he gibbered something unintelligible. He held the opium pipe against his chest with one hand and the lamp it was attached to was all used up. I pitied him then as I crouched close beside and I wished there was some way to bring peace to his much-troubled mind.

'Eddie,' I said instead, and prodded him in the face. 'Wake yourself.' His eyes snapped awake and he glared at me in horror.

'Murder!' he cried, sitting straight up and trying to protect himself with the blanket. 'There's a murderer here!'

'Eddie, Eddie, Eddie,' I tried to shush him in a soothing way, 'I ain't a murderer. I'm Jack Dawkins, one of Fagin's boys what came after you. Remember?' Eddie's scared panting continued as he looked at me and then around the rest of the room as if reminding himself as to where he was. 'I don't mean you no harm,' I promised him. 'I'm a friend.'

'Jack Dawkins,' he whispered at last, saying the name slow as if testing it.

'That's it. The Artful Dodger, you knew me as.' I nodded again and smiled at him. He leaned his wet brow close to mine as if about to tell me an awful secret.

'Am I seeing things?' he asked.

'No. I'm back from Australia and grown tall.'

'Not you,' he shivered and pointed a bony finger towards Warrigal. '*That!*'

'Warrigal ain't a vision, Eddie,' I assured him as he shrunk from my companion. 'He's an interested party. We're here to give you some money in return for some questions answered. Are you fit to talk or should I slap you gentle first? It might help concentrate your mind.'

Eddie's face became as pained as an abandoned baby. 'Water,' he demanded. I saw a bottle by the sleeping Lascar, handed it to Eddie and watched as he poured it down his throat. Once it was empty he wiped his lips with his shirtsleeve and looked at the empty shelf opposite his in horrid fascination. 'There was a murderer,' he told me. 'Lying there. A man who was planning to murder.'

'Well, don't you worry, Eddie,' I told him. 'He ain't here to bother you now. And if he does come back then we'll chase him off together, eh, you and me. Now, I want to ask you if you've ever seen anything like this?' I reached into my pocket and pulled out the two halves of my doll. But Eddie's eyes was still on where this murderer had been lying.

'Told me everything, he did, as he sucked on his murderer's pipe.' His eyes was unblinking and he spoke slow. 'Who he was going to kill, why, how . . . the whole plot.'

'It's a doll what Fagin gave me,' I continued, ignoring this, 'and I'm hoping he may have given you one just like it.' I waved the Indian prince's face in his. He blinked and looked from the doll to me. 'Ring any bells? Fagin ever give you one like it?'

'Fagin!' said Eddie, his whole self brightening at the name. 'Good old Fagin.' His eyes shut and a broad smile spread across his face.

'Good old Fagin,' I agreed. 'You was always his favourite, was you not?'

'Heh,' he nodded. 'I was. He used to tell me that often.'

'Did he ever give you anything to prove it?' I went on, still holding the doll up. 'Like one of these?' Eddie looked to Warrigal again and then at the door.

'Is he here?' he asked. 'Has he come to take me back to his house?'

'No,' I sighed. 'Fagin ain't here.'

'Have you come to take me back there? Are we going home?'

'No. Eddie, Fagin's dead.'

Eddie looked stricken at this. He turned back to the empty shelf. 'Murdered?'

'In a way, yeah. They hung him.'

He groaned aloud and looked up to the ceiling. 'It was the nephew,' he cried. 'The nephew!'

'What nephew?'

Eddie pointed his shaky finger back to where this murderer had lain. 'That's where he's going now. To kill the nephew. Where's my pipe?'

'Your pipe is here,' I said, pointing to the thing what was coiled up on the bed like a sleeping snake, 'but your lamp is empty. Tell me about this doll and I'll give you some coins to pay for more. Did Fagin ever give a doll like this to you?' Eddie picked up the pipe and tried sucking from it. When he realised there was nothing coming through he slumped over and rested his hands in his face. 'You hear what I said, Eddie?' I continued, losing patience with his drugged state. 'About Fagin?'

'I don't know about Fagin,' he whimpered. 'Ask him yourself, why don't you?'

'I'm asking you!' I snapped, and then hit him hard across the face. 'Have you seen this or ain't you? Don't mess me about, Eddie. I ain't in the humour for it.' The Lascar and the older man both woke up at this and saw Eddie crying in a crumpled state against the clay wall. 'Go back to sleep,' I told them. 'This don't concern you.'

I had not meant to be so violent with him but I had been overcome with a sudden fury at what a wretch he had turned out to be. Charley had said that I would find the great pickpocket living in squalor and I was vexed that Eddie had proved him right. I grabbed his ragged shirt and started shaking him. 'You was our hero, Eddie,' I shouted at him. 'You was the one Fagin wanted us to grow up to be most like. You let us all down!'

He was snivelling now and his hands was up to shield himself from another strike what I was fixing myself to give him. Then a hand rested on my shoulder.

'Shh,' Warrigal told me. Then he nodded towards the curtain, where the Chinese boy was peering through to see what the fuss was. 'Too much noise from you.'

I breathed in and turned back to Eddie. 'Look,' I said with the doll still held out to him and in a softer but still firm voice, 'you've either seen one of these before or no.' Eddie looked at the toy and shook his head as if in horror. 'Very well,' I said, and got to my feet. I took some pennies from out of a coin-purse and chucked them on the floor near where he lay. He began scrambling around on all fours trying to pick them up. It was a disgusting sight. 'Have a pleasant evening, Inderwick,' I said with scorn and pushed the curtain aside as I stormed out. Warrigal followed as I strode through the heady fumes of the corridor and into the fog-filled night.

'Shameful!' I ranted as the hackney cab we had hailed in Limehouse neared Saffron Hill. 'Shameful and pathetic, that's what I call it.' Throughout the whole journey I had been venting my frustration and Warrigal had sat opposite listening in silence. 'To think of all the talent and education he was given! He was destined for greatness. I'm glad Fagin never lived to see the sorry sight he's become.'

That Eddie could not help me find the Jakkapoor stone was of course a terrible, if not unexpected, blow. But it was not just this what was getting me so emotional on that dark cab ride to the Three Cripples. I was raging about all of Fagin's boys, these lads what I had so missed while away in Australia and with whom I had longed to be reunited. I had spent years holding them up as the finest collection of companions a cove could have and yet ever since my return I had met with nothing but shabby failures and disappointments. Alan Mullins was in Newgate after getting himself locked inside a shop he was trying to burgle, Reggie the Dipper was living on the streets and Joe Scoggins had been killed in a knife fight what he himself had started. Jem and Georgie was clowns what had made such a mess of a simple burglary that they had brought the full force of the police thundering into the rook-eries, while Mouse Flynn was just a weakling hiding behind a woman's skirt. The only one of my childhood friends who had amounted to much was Charley and he had done this by fleeing London to work as an honest flat. They had all lost the steel they had shown in their youth and was now a broken collection of drifters, cowards and opium fiends and I wondered how I had ever considered any of them my equal.

Warrigal's face spoke of nothing as I ranted; he just sat opposite me and let me get it all out. And it occurred to me then that perhaps here was the only person what I could hope to call a friend. He had tried to kill me, this was an undeniable truth, and perhaps he still would if Evershed ordered it. But in the time I had spent with him he had shown himself to be capable and talented, smart and brave. It was a shocking realisation to discover that I thought more of him now than I did of any of Fagin's boys and I wondered what he made of me. If he did have to kill me, I wondered for the first time as the cab drew up outside the Cripples, would he be sorry or glad about it?

The smoke of Fagin's favourite night haunt was as thick with tobacco as Wu's had been with opium and, as I pushed open both doors at once in order to make as dramatic an entrance as was possible, the potent whiff of gin and beer hit me just as hard. I had wanted the patrons of the establishment to notice myself and my remarkable companion as we cut straight through to the bar, as I had been hoping that someone might have heard about my hunt for a doll and would have it there waiting for me. The Cripples was not busy on this particular night, there being just a few knots of rough characters about the place, all eyeing our fine tailorings with suspicion, and some prostitutes what took an immediate interest and began their approach. But I brushed them aside and addressed the landlord, what stood behind the bar pouring some whisky into a glass for me before I had even asked for it. 'So, Barney,' I said after I had took the glass from him and knocked it back, 'any news?'

I had visited the Cripples earlier that day with Warrigal and had asked Barney what he remembered about this Oliver Twist

character what had been the ruin of Fagin. He said that he remembered the boy well and was surprised that I did not. He did not
know what became of the lad after the trial, but there was a
crooked lawyer of his acquaintance what was familiar with the
case and he said he could ask him for more details. I paid him
good money to do this and now, less than eight hours later, I was
back and hoping for some joy at last.

'A peeler has been in here looking for you, Jack,' he said with
urgency. 'I told him nothing.'

I groaned aloud. This piece of news did nothing to improve
my mood as I handed the other glasses to him and Warrigal. 'He
asked for me by name, did he?'

'"Jack Dawkins, formerly of Saffron Hill."' Barney nodded as
he sipped. 'He was in here less than an hour ago. He knew a lot
about you, said you was sometimes called the Artful Dodger and
you went about with an Australian colonial –' his eyes turned to
Warrigal, who was sniffing at his glass as if unsure if he wanted
it – 'called Peter Cole.'

'Inspector Bracken,' I said, knowing that I had introduced
Warrigal by that name when we had met at the Booted Cat. 'Him
what took my mother as well as Jem White. That old ghost is
becoming a proper nuisance.' It was likely that Jem White had
told Bracken all about me and my movements, although I did not
utter this suspicion to Barney. I did not want to let any of my
people know that Jem might be holding a grudge against me for
any reason.

'This weren't an old man,' Barney corrected me. 'He was a
constable, not much older than you and very tall.'

'Marvellous,' I sighed. 'So by now he's told the whole
Metropolitan Police Service to keep an eye out for me. As if I
ain't got worries enough. Now tell me,' I said, changing the subject

around to why I came in here, 'what have you learnt about Twist.'

'Brownlow,' said Barney with a proud expression. 'That's the name of the cove what adopted this Oliver around the time of the trial, according to my source. So young Oliver will be going by the name of Oliver Brownlow now and not Twist.'

I jotted this down on to my notepad as Barney told me all that his lawyer friend could remember about this Brownlow. 'I'm told he insisted on taking Oliver to visit Fagin in Newgate on the night before the hanging,' he said. 'Which I feel was in poor taste.'

As Barney said this I could feel my blood heating once more. This cursed Oliver, the deadly viper at Fagin's bosom, had been one of the last people to have seen the tragic man alive while I, one of the few boys what truly cared for him, had already set sail to the other side of the world, oblivious to his fate. I was so angry in that moment that if Oliver had walked into the bar I would have done a Bill Sikes on him and damned the consequences. 'Where is he?' I demanded.

'Don't know,' replied Barney. 'He don't move in these circles no more, that's for certain.'

'Why has no one sniffed Oliver out before?' I asked after drinking my second glass and feeling the alcohol flame my spirit from within. 'Why ain't he been settled? They all talk about settling Charley for Bill's sake. Why has nobody been to see Oliver yet?'

Barney held out his hands as if asking what I wanted of him. 'Dodger,' he said, all soft. 'He's genteel now. A rich man's son no less. No one wants the trouble.'

'Well, I want it,' I said as I slammed the empty glass back down on the bar. 'And I'll get it.'

Just then a hand landed on my shoulder. 'It's your lucky day, Dodger.' I turned to see Herbie Sharp's gap-toothed mouth grinning at me in delight. 'The search is over.' And he reached into the large pocket of his check coat and produced a painted wooden doll what had a smile as wide as his. 'I believe I heard tell,' he said as he gave it to me for inspection, 'of some sort of reward.'

'Where d'you get this?' I asked.

'Fagin gave it me,' he said with no shame. 'Told me I was his favourite. I hate to give something so sentimental away in all truth, but these are hard times and I know your money's good, so . . .' He shrugged and waited for me to pay him.

I put the doll down on the bar and showed him my fingers. They had paint on them. 'Made this today, did you?' I asked. 'Or d'you get someone else to do it? Either way, it ain't what I'm looking for.' Herbie looked most downcast at this and asked me what the difference was anyway. I did not tell him that I was looking for a rattle what this doll did not have, but I said it needed to match the one what I had on me. He at last admitted that he had been trying all week to find one just like what I had been heard describing. 'Nice try though,' I granted him as we both looked at the doll's thin black smile, and I offered Herbie a drink.

Soon after that Warrigal and myself set off towards our new lodgings in Whitechapel. We thanked Barney for his help before leaving and buttoned our coats as we stepped out and walked towards Hatton Gardens where we hoped to hail a hackney cab. It was still early in the misty evening and this back lane was empty of any drunken revellers. However, behind us on the other side of the street some loud footsteps could be heard keeping pace with ours. The moment I heard them I could tell that whoever they belonged to had been waiting for us to leave and, what was more, that he wanted us to hear him. The steps sounded too strong and deliberate and the night was too cold for them to belong to some idle wanderer. I turned my head to look, careful not to seem suspicious, and saw a tall hatted figure walking in the same direction on a dark patch of pavement between two lamp posts. I did not need to ask if Warrigal had spotted this too; I knew he would be even more alert to such followers than I was and after we had crossed over into a number of different streets to see if he would take another route, Warrigal motioned for us both to stop. We had paused at a sign of three hanging balls and we pretended to look into the pawnbroker's large window to see what was on display. There, in the reflection of the glass, we saw the man what followed us walk under the light of a gas lamp opposite and there was no doubting the uniform now.

'A constable,' I whispered to Warrigal. 'Not Bracken.' The peeler had stopped and could be seen looking over to us, not bothering to disguise his interest. 'We should run,' I said. And then, 'Should we run?' Warrigal said nothing and the peeler began crossing over to us.

'Evening, all,' he said then in a voice what was slow but commanding. 'Don't you dash off now, Dodger.' I recognised this voice but I could not tell from where. We still had our backs to him and I made to bolt but Warrigal stopped me. He was right, I knew. We was doing nothing wrong and we still had that pardon from the Governor of New South Wales. It would be better just to act like we had nothing to hide and see what he wanted. There was another gas lamp on this side of the street between us and he paused before stepping into its spotlight. I turned around to face him, in the hope that I could place that deep voice, but I could not see who was under that dark-blue stovepipe. He was not too far away from us but, in the black fog of the night, all I could make out was two lines of glinting gold buttons running down his uniform and the silver buckle on his big black belt. He was tall, that was for sure, and about my age.

'Can I help you, officer?' I asked him.

'John Dawkins,' he said, all disappointed. 'You don't know me?'

This rattled me to my bones. I did not like that he was calling me by my given name and not Jack. But the voice was becoming more familiar. It was a man's voice but I had known it as a child. I squinted some more so I could see him through the killer fog.

'I have something here,' he went on, reaching into his long-pocket, 'which I'm told you and your friend want back.' I could see him starting to pull out a wooden item from it what did not look to be a truncheon but I still could not make out what it was through the mist. He stepped closer into the light and his face became clearer. I recognised it then, although it had grown much more handsome with age and had the same beardless, thick-whiskered style of all peelers. And I was more amazed by this than anything else I had encountered.

'No,' I said, and took a step back from him in astonishment. I had wanted to see him again, that was true, but not like this. Not with him wearing that.

'I told you not to dash,' he said, seeming to sense how close I was to flight. Then he laughed, a small and bitter laugh. 'You always dash. Remember that time you took me pickpocketing.' He shook his head as if hurt by the memory. '*To show me how it was done*, you said. Trying to corrupt an innocent boy into becoming a low crook like yourself.' He was in the full glare of the light now; there was no mistaking him. '*But dash don't mean dash*, you said. *It means walking off in-con-spic-u-ous*. And that you did, Dodge. You just left me there.'

I said his name in disbelief. The peeler grinned when he heard it and gave a slight dip of the head in acknowledgment.

'That's *Constable* Belltower to you,' he said with smugness. 'And you was right about me, little brother. I never was made to be a thief.'

Chapter 26

The Biggest Gang in London

In which half is still half, even if it ain't the best half

'Horrie!' I said, coming to my senses at last. 'What are you doing dressed in that uniform? You look proper ridiculous.'

He stopped smiling and put whatever the wooden object was back into his truncheon pocket. 'I look like what I am,' he said, thumbing his chest all proud. 'A soldier of the city.' Although I confess I was most stunned to see him stood there wearing enemy colours, this did not mean I was going to be showing him much more respect than I ever had when we was young. This was my own half-brother after all, what I had once seen lose a battle of wits with a cart-horse about which of them should pull the other one home.

'So it's true what they say,' I whistled in disbelief. 'The peelers really are taking anyone these days. Things must be desperate.' I smiled to show him I was only jesting and opened my arms to see if he would come and give me a brotherly embrace. I had hoped that this would give me a chance to feel for what it was that might be in his pocket. Was it the third doll? I wondered. Fagin had not even met Horrie, let alone known him well enough to ever declare him a favourite, but after seeing him dressed like this anything seemed possible. I could find out what the object was if he would just let me get close enough. Instead though he just stood there with a meanness in his eye. This approach of his, it was clear, was not for the purposes of affectionate brotherly reunion.

'Never wanted me in your gang much, did you, John?' he said with what sounded like real hurt. 'Now look at me. I'm in the biggest gang in London.'

'But how?' I asked. 'Don't take this the wrong way, Horrie, but the only peeler I could ever imagine you ever becoming was for potatoes. The last time I saw you, you was getting arrested for chucking stones at acrobats. How did you go from that . . .' I waved my hand over his whole appearance, 'to *this*?'

Warrigal and myself had now stepped away from the pawn-broker's and was occupying the centre of the wide pavement, giving Horrie the chance to walk around us slow as he talked, enjoying showing me where the power was. 'They don't take on thieves in the Metropolitan Police, if that's what surprises. But, as I say, I ain't no thief.'

This was true, he was not a thief, at least never a very good one. But Horrie was a thug, and a tall one at that. And what was any one of those other constables what had leapt out of the police vans at Bethnal Green and swarmed after us if not just tall thugs dressed up smart? The more I thought on it, the more I could see him fitting in well among them.

'That day when I got took for throwing stones,' he said as he circled us, 'was the best day of my life. Those boys took me back to the police office and gave me a proper hiding.'

'Nice of them.'

'It was. They punched some sense into me.' He was behind us now and I felt a threat of violence breathing down my neck as he spoke. 'For me, a poor fatherless boy what never had no discipline, it was good medicine. I thanked them for it in time, once my cuts had healed.' He came round the front now and stopped again, facing me. 'That was my punishment, see, for throwing the stones. And I took it like a man. But by the time they had finished pounding on me I had won their respect as much as they had won mine.' He smiled again and held his chin up high. 'I've always wanted to be a bobby ever since they first came to be. That's why I loved the punch shows so much. I used to enjoy seeing crooked Mr Punch take his beating from the policeman – it felt right and just.' He had walked up close now, close enough to show me how much taller he was. 'Anyway,' he said at last in a friendlier tone, 'ain't you going to introduce your friend to me? I am family, after all.'

'Warrigal –' I turned to my companion and made the introduction as if we was at a society ball – 'allow me to introduce to you my brother Horace Belltower, a person of some importance, it would now appear.' Warrigal raised an eyebrow at the confirmation of his being my relation. 'I know,' I said in embarrassment, 'there ain't much resemblance.' Then I turned to Horrie. 'And my valet's name is Warrigal,' I said, 'and not Peter Cole as you may have been told.'

'How d'you do, Mr Warrigal,' said Horrie, raising a finger to his temple in mock salute. 'You're from Australia, I'm told.'

'And who woulda told you that?' I asked, as if I did not know.

'My superior officer.'

'Inspector Bracken.'

'That's the man.' Horrie grinned. 'You've met him. Well, now he wants to meet you again, John. Tonight. He asked me to come out and fetch you both, on account of us being blood and that. He's waiting at the station right now.'

'Are you arresting us, Horrie? On what charge?'

'No charge, John.' Horrie shook his head. 'You're not arrested yet. But I've promised the inspector I would bring you to him and you wouldn't make a liar of me, would you?' He nodded for us to stroll with him in the direction of Skinner Street. 'Let's walk.'

I felt that Warrigal and myself had no choice but the situation was most uncomfortable. I did not like to be in the company of no peelers at the best of times but in particular not when one was my older brother Horrie who I knew had no love for me. As we strolled down to Newgate and towards the nearby police station with our unlikely but insistent escort I could hear the sound of the prison death bells ringing out. These signified that another unfortunate soul was to be executed early next morning and I wondered if Horrie knew how much this path would unsettle me. He seemed to enjoy the route himself and was full of how he had at last fulfilled his life's ambition to become a police constable.

'As you can see,' he went on as we saw the dismal prison loom up in front of us, 'I've altered much since last we met.'

'Can't argue with that,' I said, fighting the urge to tell him that he still stank of bad cheese. 'You're a changed man.'

'But you, John . . .' He shook his head like a disappointed parent. 'You ain't altered a bit.'

'I'm a prosperous sheep farmer,' I protested, 'with a full pardon from the Governor of New South Wales.'

'So I'm told,' he said. 'And chummy here is supposed to be your valet. But I know that you and him was out picking pockets in Oxford Street just over a week ago. And you ain't got a pardon for that.'

Jem, I thought, must have told the peelers that fact in revenge for my kicking him into their arms. I did not let it trouble me however; there was no proof against us.

'A woman reported having her pocket picked whilst riding the omnibus on the Friday before last. She was lucky enough to see

the perpetrator again in the company of two of my brother officers what took chase of him. He got away, but their description
of the felon didn't half sound a lot like you.'

'Do me another turn, Horrie,' I scoffed. 'There are a thousand
thieves in London what look like me. That's why I'm always getting
the blame for things I never done. Is that the best you got?'

'No,' he said and he stopped walking just as we reached the
high-walled corner of Newgate Prison. We was stood under a
bright lamp what shone clear enough for us to be seen by two
guards what stood outside. Horrie reached into his long-pocket
again and smiled. 'We got this.' Then he pulled out a long wooden
item, so well painted and carved that it was unmistakable as the
one we was familiar with. It had a bend in it.

'New truncheon, is it?' I said as he held it out for us both to
see.

'This was thrown at one of the officers by an accomplice of the
pickpocket as he made his escape. No one in the force had any
idea what it might be at first, but it was sent from station to station
to see if anyone could place the funny thing. You know us bobbies.'
He grinned. 'We love a good mystery.'

I was most careful not to glance at Warrigal as Horrie spoke
but I was sure that he would not react to the sight of his dead
father's boomerang. Instead I kept my eyes fixed on Horrie, who
was very much enjoying dragging this all out.

'It was Inspector Bracken himself what at last solved it for us.
He was so interested in the thing that he even took it to the British
Museum to have a word with the people there. It's a native throwing
stick, they told him —' he looked to Warrigal and smiled as if all
this was a lovely coincidence — 'from your part of the world.'

Warrigal said nothing, as ever. Horrie just held his gaze until
at last Warrigal looked away as if uninterested.

'They always come back,' Horrie sniggered, and put the boomerang away again. He began walking us towards an area with many peelers strutting about and police vans coming to and fro. It was not a place I would walk past on any night if I did not have to. 'The inspector has taken an interest in you, John. Know why?'

'Yeah,' I said as we passed the outer gates of Newgate. 'I was unlucky enough to meet him on the night I arrived back in England and he took an unfair dislike to me. He's the man what arrested our mother, Horrie, as you no doubt know. She hung for it, so he said. She would have spent her last night alive in there, I would have thought.'

I pointed over to one of the small grated windows of the prison and felt myself getting angry for what he had become. He was her favourite – she had always shown that to both him and me – and now he had become a policeman and allied himself with the very same man what had destroyed her. I tried to keep my anger masked but it was not easy. Horrie had betrayed our people and I would never forgive him for it.

'The inspector is a great man,' he went on, as if going out of his way to aggravate me. 'And he's shown me many kindnesses. After arresting our mother he made enquiries about me, her son what had gotten into trouble with the police but was now struggling to become one himself, and he took me under his care. He showed me how to conduct myself as an officer, taught me right from wrong at long last, and without his approval the force would never have accepted me. 'The new police needs boys like you, Belltower,' he always says, 'just as much as it needs men like me.'"

Horrie went on to tell me about Bracken's many accomplishments and it was only when he told me that he sometimes took tea with the man and his wife that I decided that I could no tolerate this no longer. I stopped in my tracks and turned on him.

'He killed our mother, Horrie,' I said, my voice raised and blood up. 'By arresting her, he killed her as good as if he'd just wrung her neck there and then. And there you are, drinking from his teacups.' Horrie just looked back at me, doubtless surprised by how passionate I was being about a woman what had never been worth much as a parent. 'You ain't got no loyalty,' I went on. 'You ain't got no respect for the dead and you ain't got nothing to be proud of. You're a fucking disgrace!'

Horrie looked like he was ready to bash me for this but he stopped himself in time. Then he sighed and shook his head as if nothing could be done with me. 'He's a father to me now, John,' he said. 'And to a lot of the young constables. Just like that old Jew was a father to you and the others. Can't you understand that?'

'What I understand,' I said, still bold with anger, 'is that this man you're speaking of is the same one what brutalised me on the only night he met me. Told me to stay out of the city of my birth even though I had a full pardon for my crimes. He'll be the death of me as he was for our mother if he can be. He's an evil sod, Horrie, don't be fooled.'

'Oh yeah?' Horrie said, and then pointed towards the door we had stopped under. There was a police sign hanging over it. 'Well, you can tell him all this yourself if you're up to it. He's inside waiting for you.'

Inspector Bracken seemed to have grown taller than when I had last met him and it was some seconds before I realised that this impression was likely to be on account of the hat. He was dressed in full peeler uniform but it was clear he was of a higher rank than anyone else in the station. He was stood up as Warrigal and myself was led into a small and stuffy police office and he looked the two of us up and down as Horrie shut the door behind him. We was the only four people in the room.

'I recall telling you,' said Bracken, his manner as stiff as ever, 'to stay out of my city.' There was two chairs what faced the desk he was stood behind, but neither me nor Warrigal chose to sit on them. We just stood there opposite him, all defiance.

'If you want to see my pardon again then you're welcome to,' I said with even less civility than he had spoken. 'I don't mind if you make a fool of yourself once more.'

There was a short silence as Bracken regarded me like something he wanted to snap, but I refused to be intimidated by him.

'And that queer stick what the constable has just shown us,' I went on, 'ain't nothing to do with neither me nor Warrigal. We ain't seen it before and I don't care what the British Museum has told you.'

His eyes left me and he looked over to Horrie, who had crossed over and was standing now against the adjacent wall, ready to act if need be.

'I have read that pardon of yours once,' said Bracken at last as he flicked his eyes back to me. 'And it told me more than it meant to. It told me that you have fallen into bad company, Mr Dawkins.'

'No surprise there,' snorted Horrie from the wall. I shot him a mean look as Bracken ignored him and went on.

'As I told you on the last time we met,' said the inspector, 'your character witness is known among the police force. He's even more notorious than Bill Sikes once was.'

'Lord Evershed?' I replied in scorn. 'He's an aristocrat. A hero of the Empire. He's friends with the Governor of New South Wales among other people. And if his word is good enough for the Governor, then it should be good enough for you.'

'It is roundly believed by a great many officers . . .' he paused before continuing and his eyes darted over to the door as if afraid that someone might overhear this next part, 'that he was responsible for the death of his first wife.'

'You said as much before,' I replied. 'And, whether he is or not, it don't have much to do with me.'

'Why doesn't it?'

'Because it was years ago,' I replied fast. 'I was only a kinchin then.'

There was a small movement to the side of Bracken's mouth. I cursed myself for speaking too quick.

'You know a lot about it, Mr Dawkins,' he said, and I wished I was just keeping quiet like Warrigal was doing. 'Why?'

'I dunno.' I shrugged. 'I just heard the story, same as everyone else. She took her own life.'

'Or had it taken from her,' Bracken said. I did not reply but returned his glare. I could not start talking to the police, not with the mouthful I had just given Horrie outside about working for them, but nor did I care if they suspected Evershed of murder. He was not my friend and I saw no reason to defend him.

'His wife had betrayed him, did you know that?' Bracken asked after a long pause. 'With a famous man – George Shatillion.' Another silence as he searched my face for a reaction. 'This is called a motive.'

I was finding staying silent to be most difficult as it was not a natural state for me. I don't know how Warrigal could stand it.

'He left for Australia soon afterwards so any investigation was difficult, particularly considering his peerage. George Shatillion became a recluse for the next seventeen years and rarely left the house apart from for the occasional walk. Perhaps he suspected his life too was in danger. Earlier this year, on one of these walks, he fell to his death from a high cliff in circumstances that strike me as improbable. I believe that people walk along that path often and rarely stumble.'

'What,' I said when I could contain myself no longer, 'are you telling me for?'

'Because, Mr Dawkins,' said Bracken in a more urgent voice now, 'you are involved in something and I must know what it is. After seeing his name on your pardon I telegraphed a friend of mine in Australia who is aware of Lord Evershed to ask if anything suspicious was occurring. He wrote back to say that Evershed had set sail to England for the first time since leaving all those years ago and that he will be docking here any day.' Bracken looked to be getting the most excited I had ever seen him. 'He's back, Dawkins, and I think you know why. Tell me.'

I am ashamed to record that I almost considered it. I would have been so relieved to see Lord Evershed get taken by the peelers and to therefore be free myself from his tyranny that it almost seemed worth the moral transgression of telling the police all I knew about the man. But of course there was nothing I could tell Bracken about these murders that would mean much anyway. Timothy Pin would just deny it and Evershed would have me killed soon after. The only thing I could really tell him about was the business of the Jakkapoor stone and the threat against my life if I should fail to produce it. But none of that would have interested the peelers. It was not illegal to believe in mad curses and the police would not be inclined to offer protection to me of all people. So I just remained silent for a while longer and Bracken spoke again, this time in a softer tone.

'You should not consider the police force to be your enemy,' he said. 'It may interest you to know that a man we arrested recently, a burglar named Jem White, tried to blame his crime, a murder that took place at a cottage in Kent, upon the two of you.

I happen to doubt that this is true because the crime took place on the very night after I encountered you both at the Booted Cat and it seems unlikely that even you would have been out burgling that soon. But I could have ignored that instinct and arrested you regardless. I chose not to because I do not like to charge people with crimes they did not commit.'

If he said this in the hope that I would burst into tears of gratitude then he was left disappointed. This move of acting hard towards a person only to then do them a small favour was a trick often employed in criminal gangs in order to gain power over vulnerable minds. My mind was not that vulnerable however and I asked him instead if we could go now.

'I've promised my valet that I would take him to the music hall,' I said, and reached for my pocket watch to see what the time was, 'before the last curtain falls. So is there anything else?'

Bracken's face hardened again and he stepped around the desk and came towards me. He reached into his coat pocket as he did so and pulled out a card.

'Know this then: if you refuse to cooperate with us then you shall be considered an accomplice of Lord Evershed's.' The card had the address of this very police station on it and he placed it into my hand. 'Should you change your mind however, and come to us with any information we can use against him, then the Metropolitan Police Service will look more kindly upon you.' He stepped back and gave Horrie the nod to open the office door. 'Do not be fools.'

Outside the station Warrigal and myself had to button our coats up as the night had become colder still while we had been inside. We walked away from the police vicinity and looked for a cab to hail. The interview with Bracken had depressed me further and I needed cheering up.

'Boomerang,' Warrigal complained once we was sure no peelers was about.

'Well, you're the one that chucked it,' I said back. 'You've nobody to blame but yourself.'

I looked up and down the road to see if there was any hackney carriages approaching and I wondered if we was being followed by any other policeman, uniformed or otherwise. I was still lit up from the whisky at the Cripples and this was making me even more suspicious than usual. My thoughts fell upon whatever Ruby might be doing.

'I'll tell you what, Warrigal,' I said as I checked my timepiece again to see if it was still early enough to see the final acts. 'I said we was going to the music hall and I meant it. You ain't seen much culture during your short time in London. How d'you fancy taking in a show?'

Chapter 27

The Man of a Million Characters

Where things start getting most theatrical

Lord Albert Tipsy, with his monocled eye, red leathery nose and hair what looked as though he had been caught in an explosion, tottered his unsteady way towards the drinks cabinet. He was dressed in elegant yet trouserless evening wear and mumbled something about a letter he had been sent what had got him most upset. 'It is from my beloved,' he announced in slurred aristocratic tones as he reached the cabinet and found it propped up against a silver cocktail shaker. 'It reads, "To my darling Tipsy." That's me,' he explained between hiccups. '"To my darling Tipsy, I am leaving you."' He looked at us then, his face a very picture of unhappiness. '"I shall only return under the condition that you desist in poisoning yourself with alcohol."' He let the letter drop to his feet and appeared to be most heartbroken and then he turned his back to us as his shoulders seemed to shake with sobs. But when he turned back again he was just shaking himself another cocktail and grinning like an idiot. His only applause for this bit of deft comic business was that, from up in the gods, someone threw an orange at his head.

'Bring on Ruby in Red!' shouted a chorus of hard male voices from above. The orange was followed by a volley of different missiles: half-eaten apples, coins, even a boot. Poor Tipsy tried to struggle on through his act, and burst into a rendition of the music-hall favourite 'Blowing Away the Cobwebs', but this late-night crowd of mostly men only wanted to heckle and boo. There was soon a rain of coins falling down upon him, all of them meant to hurt rather than reward Tipsy for his tomfoolery, and one struck him just below the line of his wig and cut him.

'Fuckers!' he shouted in his true cockney accent as he clutched his bleeding forehead. His face filled with rage as his monocle pinged off into the centre of the pit, earning him his biggest laugh of the night. 'A pox on all your filthy whore-pipes!' And then he fled the stage followed by thunderous cheers and clapping.

Rafferty's had always been one of the rougher music halls and they had these large spikes sticking out from the edge of the stage what was there to protect the performers. This did not stop some of the more intrepid spectators around us in the pit from trying to climb over them to collect the thrown coins as the drinks cabinet and other props was removed. Warrigal and I was sat in a dark corner overhung by the gods so we could not be viewed by those what sat above and we was far back enough to be able to spot any possible police tails what might have entered after us before they could mark us. Warrigal attracted his own share of attention from the rest of the crowd but this was more on account of the manner in which he carried himself rather than by his colour. The place seemed to be full of the servant class, mop-squeezers and fart-catchers, what was taking the night off from waiting on their masters and mistresses and among these was several dark-skinned coves gathered together in their own groups. But Warrigal had long since abandoned any appearance of servility towards me and the sight of him and myself, both dressed as flash as each other and whispering back and forth as if in plot, marked him out as more than just another colonial prize for some grand house.

'Ruby's on next,' I told Warrigal over the din of stamping feet from the Gods above. 'It says so on the poster outside.'

When the cabman had drawn up outside the theatre just ten minutes earlier I had been most pleased to see Ruby's stage name emblazoned across the angled bill posters in as large and as colourful letters as it had been on that poster I had seen in her crib. I guessed that she must have come back to this Douglas, the producer what had given her a job as a singer in the first place, and he had forgiven her for leaving and put her straight back to work. This worried me as perhaps old Douglas expected to receive more than just a good show in return for this generosity.

Once the coins and fruit splatter was swept away from the stage another man bounded on from the wings and addressed the audience in a booming voice. 'The Inimitable Lord Tipsy, ladies and gents,' he declared all proud, and he held a hand out to the other side of the stage from where the stricken comedian had made his retreat. 'A pity he had to leave us so soon – he was just coming to the funny bit. And *now* –' he clapped his hands together and spoke fast before another attack commenced – 'back for her second performance of the evening . . .' The boys in the seats above went wild now and his words could only just be heard above their raucous hooting. 'Behave yourselves, my fine fellows,' said the smiling man, wagging a finger as a small band behind him began to play. 'She's a lady, don't forget. For I give you – the sensational – *Ruby in Red*!'

As soon as she danced on to the stage I could see what the fuss was about. I could not imagine London possessing a maid with a face and figure more pleasing than the fair warbler now upon the stage. Her voice was stunning and she was wearing a very fetching scarlet dress what was cut in a way what revealed her wonderful bare legs high-kicking away, which sent the audience into a frenzy.

They had been right to make her top of the bill, I thought. I could not help but notice one crucial thing about her though. This was not my Ruby Solomon.

'This is not my Ruby,' I pointed out to Warrigal, who I imagine had already noticed. 'There must be more than one Ruby in Red,' I supposed. 'It's the only explanation.' I was vexed at discovering a stranger on the stage in the place of the girl I had come to see and I wondered if this really was the right music hall what Ruby had told Greta she was returning to. Perhaps she was dancing in another show.

'This is the last of the vittles,' said a voice from behind me. It belonged to one of the many young girls what was walking around carrying trays of bruised oranges and limp ham sandwiches and she spoke without apology. 'But we're still charging you a ha'penny for 'em.'

I turned around to tell her that I would prefer some whisky instead and there I saw her.

'Jack,' she said, recognising me in the same instant and almost dropping her wares in surprise. 'What you doing 'ere? I thought you'd left London for good.'

'Missed you too much.' I smiled back just as I had in the meat market when she had said the same thing. I got to my feet and went to embrace her, which was not easy considering the tray of stale sandwiches which blocked my way. A drunken fellow walked towards her with a penny in his hand, but Ruby, who was busy telling me how pleased she was to see me, gave him the whole tray of food and said he was welcome to the lot before she turned back to me.

'I thought the peelers had took you like they took Jem,' she said. She did look relieved that I was back although she seemed less pleased to notice I still had my ever-present shadow with me.

Her attitude to Warrigal seemed to have changed since I had mentioned that he was a killer back in Australia. 'Well, I'm glad you're all right, Jack,' she said, ignoring him.

'You and me both,' I told her. 'And I thought what better way to enjoy my liberty than to come and see you perform your act.' Ruby's smile dropped as I thumbed towards the woman in her place. 'Only it seems this thieving mare has stolen your stage name.'

'She ain't stolen a thing,' Ruby said in a quieter voice and shrugged. 'She's Ruby in Red, always has been. I just pinched the poster and made out it was me. I've only ever worked here as a sandwich girl.'

'Oh,' I said, and after a small silence added, 'That's a funny thing, you both being called Ruby.'

'Her name ain't Ruby, it's Esmeralda. Douglas Boyd gave my name to her because it sounded better. I asked him if I could have a chance to perform my songs upon the stage but he said I had a voice as fresh as the guttering.'

'Cheeky bugger,' I said. 'Show me where he is. I'll have some strong words with him.'

'You'll be lucky to find him. He vanished about a year ago owing this music hall a fortune in ticket sales. Ain't been heard of since. Shame really – after Fagin and my old Uncle Ikey he was the only man to ever show me a kindness. I was lucky that Rafferty gave me my job back, considering I only ended up here because Dougie saw to it. Speaking of which –' she reached over to where some drunken theatregoers had cleared her tray of the last sandwiches and took it back – 'my work hours are done. I need to fetch my bunce for the night.' She went to leave. 'Enjoy the rest of the show, Jack. See you about.' I grabbed her by the arm before she left.

'I ain't come here for no show, Ruby,' I told her. 'I've come here to talk to you. I've something I need to tell you.'

'I don't know, Jack,' she said, and pulled away from my touch. 'I'm busy now and I've got a new life. I'm living back in Saffron Hill with this family. They're good people and I'm glad to be free of Jem and all that for now.'

'Yeah, but I ain't Jem,' I told her.

'I didn't say you was, but—'

Some of the crowd began to shush us now for talking during the performance and even Ruby in Red could be seen scowling at us between kicks for talking so loud. My Ruby said sorry, bowed her head and made her way out of the theatre and I followed her close behind. Warrigal, of course, followed me and we all went round to the back of Rafferty's, Ruby telling me all the while that I was not to follow. I refused and so she said we could come backstage while she waited to get paid and she disappeared up some iron steps what led into the rooms above. This backstage area stank of sweat and spirits and the unpainted walls was as good as covered with old bill posters what boasted of former glories. It was late in the programme but there was still a number of tired performers there slumped on chairs and staring at their own unsmiling faces in these large mirrors as they wiped off their stage make-up. Bright discarded costumes of all sorts was strewn around the floor for others to collect for the wash as Ruby led us through the different rooms, saying hello to all she passed. In one room a man dressed only in his undergarments was leaning backwards on a wooden chair in front of a large mirror as a woman dabbed his forehead with some damp cotton. The grey wig of Lord Tipsy was on the dresser in front of him, his face was smeared with old man make-up and when he saw Ruby enter he asked her where in hell Rafferty had got to with his money.

'For half an act?' she scoffed 'You've a cheek.'

'I was under attack!' cried the comedian in outrage. 'I can't be expected to keep performing under those conditions. You tell Rafferty I'm not leaving until I've had my bustle.'

'Contracts is contracts, Sid.' Ruby shrugged as she pointed towards a dilapidated piece of furniture what Warrigal and myself could wait on. 'You sit there while I look for Rafferty,' she said to us, ignoring the outraged wailing of the man at the dresser. 'I won't be long.' She and the other woman then left us in that dressing room sat behind this Sid who was now holding the cotton to his own head and flashing us an evil glare through the mirror in front of him.

'These weeknight audiences are fucking barbarians,' he complained once the door was shut after them. 'And Rafferty's is the biggest pisshole there is. I don't know why I play here.'

'Well, some people are no judge of talent,' I said back, all encouragement. 'But I for one thought you was very droll. I should have liked to have seen more, Mister . . .'

'Sid Frizelle,' said the man, brightening in an instant. He spun on his chair, away from the mirror, and faced me eye to eye. 'The man of a million characters.' He waved his free hand with a flourish. 'Most of them drunkards. But I can do blind men too if the money is there.' He looked to Warrigal and then back to me. 'What talent agency are you from?'

'I ain't,' I replied, causing his smile to vanish with a blink. 'I'm just waiting for Ruby.' Frizelle scowled at me and turned back to his mirror.

'Then you should have brought flowers,' he said in spite. 'The dirty puzzle will go with anyone for flowers.' I was about to tell him to watch his mouth before I realised that he was likely to be referring to the Ruby now onstage rather than the one what served sandwiches so I just let him stew there.

Just then the door opened again and my Ruby told him that the other Ruby was taking her bows and would soon be up. 'She'll need this room to change in,' she said to him. 'You've had long enough.'

'Don't you talk like that to me, young lady,' he squawked back at her. 'I want my bunce. Wee Dougie Boyd ain't around to stick up for you no more! You're lucky Rafferty took you back.' Ruby rolled her eyes and left us again but, as she had promised, we was soon joined by the radiant figure of her namesake, her face alight with the exhausted satisfaction what comes from a successful performance.

'Fuck off, Lord Tipsy,' she said to Sid, and began taking off her dress. 'I need that mirror.' Sid had now produced a small bottle of whisky and drank from it saying nothing. 'And who are you two?' Ruby in Red asked, looking at us.

'We're here to see to it that this Rafferty pays Ruby her money,' I told her. 'There'll be trouble if he doesn't.'

'Give us a hand with these clasps then, lover,' she said, and turned her back to me. I moved close to her, as I was bid, and helped her to take off that dress. The clothing fell away from her, revealing the sort of sensational lingerie I had only before seen stolen from shops. 'I'm sweating like a pig in this,' she moaned, kicking the dress away. 'And there's really no need to get in any fisticuffs on my behalf – I've been paid already.'

She went behind a portable changing screen to get unrigged as my Ruby came back in, counting some coins and saying she was ready to leave.

'So Rafferty is handing out the coffers,' exclaimed Sid. 'Has he got mine?'

Ruby just put her money in her reticule and turned to me. 'What was it you wanted to say, Jack?' she yawned. 'I'm working two jobs now. I'm selling meat at the market first thing tomorrow and then I'm straight back here. I need to get home and sleep.'

'You shouldn't walk home alone,' I told her. 'Warrigal and myself will be happy to escort you. There might be thieves about.'

'I don't want you to escort me,' Ruby said with a sudden firmness. 'I'm happier by myself. Now say what you came here to say and we'll bid each other goodnight.'

I had not wanted it to be like this. I had been practising this declaration in my head for over a week and I had not imagined making it in a room where we was overheard by Warrigal, a sour-faced comedian and another woman what was draping her stockings and underthings over the top of a changing screen while I spoke. But I could see that this was the only chance she was going to give me and so I just blurted it out quick.

'Ruby, I love you and I want you for mine.'

She looked back at me and said nothing. At his place by the dresser Sid Frizelle swivelled around once more to face us and behind the changing screen the other Ruby stopped rustling and all was stillness.

'Well, you can't have me,' said the one behind the screen at last. 'Not without bringing me flowers.'

'He's talking to the sandwich girl, you stupid cow,' said Sid, and then he turned back to see how my Ruby would respond. She just stood there and looked most awkward until I reached out to take her hand. She pulled it away.

'I'm sorry, Jack,' she said, 'but no.'

'What do you mean, no?' I responded. 'You mean yes. You feel the same way, Ruby, you must do. You've been sweet on me ever since we was kinchins. You mean yes.'

'I mean no.'

I looked at her then to see if she was at jest. It seemed she was not.

'So you ain't sweet on me then?' I asked, unwilling to believe it. 'But I . . .' I looked over to Warrigal, then to Sid and then to the other Ruby what had stepped out from behind the screen in her silk robe to watch us. 'But I'm top-sawyer,' I said at last. The two performers exchanged a glance, unsure as to what that meant.

'I loved Fagin,' said Ruby after a time. 'He was the only father I ever had. And you was his favourite so of course I loved you too. But not like a sweetheart. More like a brother.'

She said these last words as though they was meant to be some sort of consolation to me but that was not how they landed. I did not want to be loved like a brother. I already had a half-brother and he did not love me one bit. I could not think of anything she could have said what would be more insulting.

'I've been reading this book,' said Ruby as I struggled to understand her. '*Teppingham* it's called – you was there when I was given it. And it's helped me to see things straight. A woman should not surround herself with villainous men; that's the lesson of the story. She should hold herself higher and give herself to he who values her.'

'I value you,' I replied. 'And I always will.'

'I won't have no more criminals in my life, Jack. I'm sorry. I do love you sometimes, I loves you to bits. But I just can't have it.' She looked to be getting herself most upset by saying all this and I was certain that this was all just some foolishness and she would come to her senses in a moment. 'I want honest people about me from now on, Jack. Please don't look so upset.'

'Honest people?' I asked in bewilderment. 'We don't know any honest people.'

'I do,' she answered with a little more toughness than before. 'John Froggat for one.'

'John who?' I did not at first recognise the name.

'He who lives with his family in Fagin's old house. John knows who you are. You went there once, he told me.'

'Him what sells metalware?' I asked in disgust. 'How do you know a flat like him?'

'I've known him and his family for some years. After Fagin died I used to visit the old place and he saw me standing outside once. He invited me in and we had tea together. I met his mother and his uncle. They're all very nice people.'

'He ain't that nice,' I remarked. 'He threw me out of my childhood home.'

'I live there now,' she told me. 'After you and the others fled from our crib in Bethnal Green I packed my bags and went to him. He's often asked me to leave Jem and move in with him in the past. And now I have.'

'Oh, I see,' I said in indignation. 'And this has been going on for some time, has it? Even while you was with Jem?'

'Nothing has gone on between us,' sighed Ruby. 'At least . . .'

'At least what?'

'Well, he's sweet on me, if you must know. And he's asked if I'll let him court me.'

'And now you're living with him!' I cried out in disbelief. 'Well, he's a fast worker, I'll give him that.'

'He's a decent Christian man, Jack. I live in a spare room and that's how it'll stay for now.'

'Will you court him?' I asked.

'I don't know,' she sighed. 'Perhaps. In time.' Her eyes moved from me then and it was as though she was talking to the far wall. She confessed something in a smaller voice. 'He's asked me to marry him.'

Just then a large red-haired man appeared at the door and looked at all of us before he turned to the comedian and pulled out a wallet.

'How much is it then, Sid?' he asked in a thick Irish brogue.

'Shut your big gob, Rafferty,' Sid replied, holding up a finger for silence. 'This is *terrific!*'

'Marry him?' I asked her. 'You can't marry a man like that. He's poor.'

'I didn't say I was going to,' she protested. 'I don't know how I feel about him. But he can make me happy.'

'*I* can make you happy, Ruby,' I said as she went over and collected her cloak what hung from a peg.

'Perhaps you can,' she said as she put it on, 'but you can also make me sad. I don't want that.'

She made for the door 'But I can give you things,' I called out to her before she went, making her stop. 'Diamonds, pearls, gold necklaces. Whatever you ask for.'

Ruby looked with pity to see me making such a fuss but I did not care. She shook her head as though I was just not listening to her. 'I don't want your stolen trinkets, Dodger,' she said just before she passed by where Rafferty was standing. 'I want a good man.'

'But I can be that too,' I promised her. 'It don't look hard. I'll be honest if you want.'

Ruby looked at me then and her face hardened. 'No, you can't, Jack Dawkins,' she said before she left the room. 'You're a villain and you always will be.'

She left and I just stood there in the middle of the room unable to speak. Sid Frizelle cleared his throat and turned to Rafferty. 'Three crowns,' he said in a hushed voice, 'or I ain't leaving.'

I had been rocked by what Ruby had just said, not only by the rejection of me but by her decision to live with a man so very different. I had been happier when she was with Jem, because he was nothing but a lesser copy of myself. John Froggat was something else, however. I could not hope to compete with goodness.

The false Ruby, the one whose real name was Esmeralda, snatched the whisky bottle from Sid, poured some into two glasses and crossed over to where I stood.

'Never mind, lover,' she said, and went to hand me one. 'She don't know what's good for her. Personally I like a villain if he can promise me diamonds. What was your name again?'

I shoved her aside and dashed out into the corridor after my Ruby. I chased after her out of the theatre and she had reached the side alley by the time I caught up with her. She turned to face me as I clattered down the iron steps.

'Don't make this harder than it need be, Jack,' she said. 'I still care about you. I'd hate for us to fall out.' I stepped towards her and tried to make her see sense.

'You're being a fool, Ruby,' I told her. 'And you'll realise it in a few days after you've had a chance to calm yourself.'

'I am calm, Jack. You're the one what's getting in a state.'

'I'm not in a state,' I assured her. 'Just . . . just let me come visit you at Saffron Hill some time tomorrow and we'll talk this over. I'll come see you and we—'

'You can't visit me. John won't allow it.'

'I don't care what Froggat will allow!' I shouted back at her. 'It ain't his house. It's Fagin's!'

Ruby shook her head and told me I was wrong. 'There's nothing there for you no more,' she said. 'It's a different place now.'

I collected myself and tried again. 'There are some things for me still there, Ruby,' I said. 'Some remembrances of my child-hood what are hidden in the attic. I need to go back and get them. So you've got to let me visit.'

'Don't lie, Jack,' she said. 'You've already been there and taken anything you wanted. John told me how you visited him one night and asked to stay in the attic, and I saw you the very next day in Smithfield Market. Warrigal had one of Fagin's old dolls sticking out of his pocket so I know you've already collected anything you wanted.'

'That ain't what I'm on about,' I shot back at her. 'That was for something else. I need to fetch my old tin box with all my . . .' And then I stopped talking.

'What?' she said, and looked at me with impatience as I froze. 'Is that all you have to say? Can I call myself a carriage now?' I stood there for a few more moments saying nothing. I had worked myself up into such a state that my mind was moving slower than normal.

'How did you know it was Fagin's?' I asked at last.

'How did I know what was Fagin's?'

'The doll,' I answered. 'What was sticking out of Warrigal's pocket. That could have been from anywhere.'

'Let's not drag this out, please,' she said, and turned to walk out on to Wideapple Square. 'There's nothing more to say.'

The theatre was emptying now. There was a large crowd spilling out into the cold night and looking for their own transport, but she barged her way through them and whistled for a hackney. I came up behind her and grabbed her shoulder. She spun back to me and shouted. There was tears in her eyes.

'Leave me alone, Jack,' she cried. 'I want nothing more to do with you. Won't you listen?'

'How did you know it was Fagin's, Ruby?' I insisted. 'Tell me how you recognised the doll.'

'What does it matter?' she groaned. 'I'm going home.'

'All right, go to John Froggat then. I don't care if you marry him and spawn a million Froggats. But just answer my question before you go. How did you recognise the doll?'

'Because Fagin gave me one just like it,' she replied in exasperation. 'It's a treasured possession if you must know.' I released her shoulder as a cab drew up along us. Ruby was talking to me with real disdain. 'And I've looked after mine better than you have. Mine's still in one piece. I saw yours again when you stayed at our crib and it was broken in half. That's the trouble with you, Dodger,' she said after she had told the driver she wanted taking to Saffron Hill. 'You don't respect nothing.'

Chapter 28

A Black Heart

What was lost is at last found

Ruby climbed into the carriage and I did nothing to stop her from leaving. She did not look back at me through the uncurtained window once she was inside and I just remained on the pavement and watched the horse pull her away from me. I could have told her about the doll if I had wanted to, about how there was a priceless treasure within her possession; there would have been enough time. But she had hurt me and I did not want to.

I was surrounded by theatregoers all shoving and shouting over one another to hail the next cab what drew near and their bustle broke me out of my spell. I spun around to go and look for Warrigal, only to discover that he was standing right behind me in the crowd.

'Warrigal,' I spluttered fast, 'Ruby has the Jakkapoor stone!'

'Heard,' Warrigal said nodding, which surprised me as I had not seen him about until now. 'Follow,' he said, and pointed to another carriage.

I was unsure I wanted to do this. I did not want to go chasing after Ruby when she had just rejected my advance and, further-more, I was unsure how Warrigal would behave if she refused to hand it over.

'We know where she lives,' I told him. 'Let's go home, rest and head straight over there tomorrow. She ain't going nowhere.' I whistled loud enough for every passing horse to hear and, before he could protest, I had got inside a hackney and he had no choice but to join me.

The cruel words what Ruby had used to rebuff me had caused such pain that on the journey back to our new lodgings I could not even rejoice at the unexpected luck of tonight's discovery. I was in agony just thinking about how she might be making John Froggat her preference and not me and before long this agony had turned into anger.

'She don't deserve no Jakkapoor stone,' I swore to Warrigal as the carriage trundled along. 'Shatillion wrote that Fagin left it to a child because they was his favourite. There's a joke! Now she won't have nothing to do with no thieves and she was given a thief's treasure and don't even know it. Well, I ain't letting her keep it so she can sell it on, oh no. I'd rather steal it off her. See how she likes that.'

I crossed my arms and put my feet up on the upholstery opposite. Warrigal looked at me with an expression I had never seen on him before and it was hard to tell what it signified. If I did not know him better, I thought, I would suspect him of feeling sorry for me.

We had secured new lodgings in Whitechapel and as we came to the end of our journey Warrigal hit the roof of the carriage with his cane for it to stop and then we made our way to Flower-and-Dean Street through many dark alleys and crooked byways. Once we was satisfied that we was not being followed we crept up the outside wooden stairs and turned our key as quiet as we could. We was renting these upstairs rooms from an elderly Irish couple what lived below and around whom we did not wish to raise any suspicion. Neither of them had seemed the questioning

sort, and if they had we would have looked for lodgings else-
where, but we still did not wish to alert them to our comings and
goings. As the door inched open we entered our small corridor
as gentle as we could so as to not cause any floorboard creaks. We
was paying for two bedrooms and a large parlour and, although
some moonlight shone in through the cracks in the curtains, the
place was otherwise lightless.

'I'll strike a candle,' I whispered as I fumbled about on the
parlour dresser for a matchbox. I looked behind me to see if Warrigal
was going to follow me into this room or just go straight to his
bedroom but I could not hear any movement. 'So we can talk
more of this,' I explained.

'Allow me,' said a voice then from the corner of a room as the
sound of a match struck. Startled, I jumped away and saw the thin
silhouette of a man sat in the studded leather chair with his legs
folded. 'I would be very interested to hear all about your recent
adventures myself.'

In the corridor I then heard the sound of a small struggle and
saw the glint of silver. They was cast in shadow but I could make
out a figure of a woman standing behind Warrigal with a small
pistol pressed against his head. In her Spanish accent she told him
not to move.

The seated man lifted his glowing match up to light the three-
candled lamp what stood next to the chair. In doing so he revealed
his smooth hairless face to me. 'I must say,' Timothy Pin sighed
once he had illuminated himself some more, 'I am growing heartily
sick of chasing you two fellows around.'

Warrigal was pushed into the room by Calista the coachwoman
and we was both told to take a seat on two wooden chairs what
they had already positioned in the middle of the room facing Pin.

'Lord Evershed's boat docks at St Katherine's some time

tomorrow,' Pin said as Calista busied herself lighting the other candles in the room. 'Are you two even aware, as you flit about London in so carefree a manner, of the terrible consequences that face you both if the Jakkapoor stone is not to hand when he asks for it?' Pin had a tall silver cane propped up beside the chair and pointed it towards Warrigal. 'He'll be particularly disappointed in you, good sir. Remaining in contact was very much part of your role. There will be some very unhappy scenes in Honey Ant Hill as a result of your failure, I can assure you.' He did not wait for a reply, which was just as well as I doubted Warrigal was going to give him one. 'I sometimes think,' he sighed, 'it would be easier doing business with a pair of monkeys.'

'I know where the stone is,' I told him, much faster than I should have. I should have kept silent for longer, like Warrigal was doing, but I was frightened of this man who had broken into our new address what we had tried so hard to keep secret. This man, with his clean diction and rich words what he used like they was for cutting, could kill us any time he wanted to. 'Well,' I corrected myself, 'I know who has it.'

'You have told me this before. About Mr Bates and Mr Inderwick.'

'Charley did have the other empty doll,' I told him. 'We went to see him up north – that's what we've been doing. So now I know that the one remaining must have your jewel in it and tonight I discovered where that is.'

'Where?'

'Fagin gave it to one of his orphans as George Shatillion wrote that he did. And she still has it now.'

'She?' said Pin, and tilted his head in disbelief. 'Impossible. The autobiographical fragment that Shatillion's biographer gave to me, and that I then sent to Lord Evershed in Australia, did not mention that the child Fagin gave the doll to was a girl. It told us many other interesting things but not that.'

I regretted saying 'she'. I had meant to get the stone off of Ruby without having to tell Pin or Evershed anything about her, but now I had mentioned it I could not see the harm. Perhaps Pin would go round to her place tomorrow and offer her money for it, more money than I could. Then he'd have the stone, she'd be better off, and I'd be free to go.

'Fagin didn't keep girls,' I explained. 'He kept *a* girl.'

Pin glared at me hard. I saw a violence growing in his eye as he was no doubt wondering if I was lying to him.

'Her name is Ruby Solomon,' I went on regardless. 'Ruby like the jewel. And Fagin always treated her like one. I used to think she was his daughter, he used to guard her so close.'

'Ruby Solomon,' Pin repeated the name slow. 'She sounds Jewish.'

'She is,' I replied. 'Or at least her mother was. Now she even lives in Fagin's old house in Saffron Hill with no idea she has the jewel. It's still in the wooden doll as it ever was. Warrigal and myself are going round first thing tomorrow to try to get it off her.'

'Will she give it to you?' asked Pin.

'Oh yeah,' I nodded. 'We're in love.'

Sat beside me I could feel Warrigal's head turn to look as I said this.

'She has relatives, you say,' said Pin. 'But the child that Shatillion wrote of was an orphan.'

'Her mother is dead and there was an uncle what she never sees no more. I don't know about the father. That orphan enough for you?'

'An uncle?' asked Pin. He leaned back in his chair and crossed his hands as he seemed to think. 'Would that be an Uncle Ikey by any chance?'

'Uncle Ikey, that's it!' I cried aloud. 'That proves it – she's always on about him.'

Pin grinned then and clapped his hands. 'It sounds like we have her all right. She sounds like the one.' He stood up then and began to pace the room. 'Ruby Solomon,' he said the name again, warming to it. 'We weren't expecting a girl, but Shatillion's document refers simply to a child so she might be the one. If she has the jewel, as you think she might –' Pin stopped pacing and appeared to address no one in particular – 'then my employer's torment will at last be at an end.'

'Hurrah for that,' I said, glad that things was at last going so smooth. 'Then it's happy endings all round. When Evershed gets here, myself and Warrigal will have fetched the jewel off her and we'll say no more about the whole messy business. There's a bottle of wine in the parlour – we should all have a drink to celebrate.'

Pin turned on his heels to face us and pointed his cane at me. 'You and I shall be inseparable until the jewel is recovered, Mr Dawkins. We shall visit this address in Saffron Hill together so I can see the jewel with my own eyes. Then we'll take it to Lord Evershed. I had planned to meet his boat at the docks in the afternoon but I can leave that to Mr Bungurra.'

'And who might Mr Bungurra be?' I asked, not liking the sound of him.

'Mr Bungurra,' Pin sighed as if struggling with his patience, 'is the gentleman sat to your left.' I turned to look at Warrigal and he gave me a tiny nod to confirm that this was he. I had been travelling with him for over six months and it had never occurred to me that he might have a surname of his own. 'He will no longer be required to keep you on a leash, that happy task now being mine. And should it transpire, sir,' he said with his hands now resting upon his cane, 'that this girl does not have our jewel after all –' he glanced over at Calista, who was still holding the pistol – 'then your employment will be terminated very swiftly.'

Should any of the poor people of the Warren, the part of the rookeries where Fagin once lived, have peeked out of their windows before sunrise on the very next morning then they would have seen something moving through the fog what would have appeared to them like a phantom. The black private coach of Timothy Pin, what was so opulent and unnatural for this part of the city, crept its way through the broken-down district, pulled by a horse what was just as menacing and as black. I looked out through the red lace curtains as I sat beside Timothy Pin and I told him how it was possible that Ruby would hear of our coming before we got there, as slum-dwellers was known to shout about any irregular carriages what approached by way of warning. This, I said, could be good for us as it would alert Ruby to the affluence of the man about to make her an offer on her old doll and she would be inclined to take him more serious. Pin said nothing but just looked out of his window at some dirty kinchins what was gambolling in the street and seemed alone in his thoughts. Then, when we was just two streets away from her address, his cane hit the roof, the carriage stopped and he leaned out to tell his driver Calista that she should let us alight here so we could continue by foot.

'I do not wish for her to hear us coming,' he told me as he climbed out and instructed Calista to return to St Katherine's Docks and join Warrigal, who was waiting for Evershed's boat to dock. 'I would rather us appear inconspicuous.'

'Then you should roll around in the dirt a bit,' I said, looking at his finely cut grey suit, 'and leave your silver cane in the coach.'

Pin did not agree to roughing up his coat but he did remove any shiny trappings of wealth from view.

'I still have this about my person, however,' he said, and unbuttoned his coat to show me. There, tucked into the inside long-pocket of his coat, was the small silver pistol he had pointed at me when we first met. It was small enough to be hidden in the hand and I imagine had been fashioned for secret underhand killings. 'Remember that before you think to run from the scene.'

There was a thin slimy alley just across from Fagin's old house down which I knew lay our best path of approach. Pin and myself crept up to the end of this and we peered around the corner towards my childhood home. The house across from us, what was just to the left of Fagin's, was boarded up and looked to be empty and there was a run-down old vegetable cart positioned between us and the street what also seemed abandoned. This meant we could stay there for a while watching the house and trying to make sense of who was home.

'It sounds as though,' whispered Pin after some time, 'somebody inside that house is skinning a cat alive.' This was in reference to the terrible sound what had been coming out of one of the rooms and what had got louder and more strangulated after Mother Froggat was seen leaving with a big basket of laundry in her arms.

'That'll be Uncle Huffam,' I said. 'An old blind man what plays the fiddle.'

'He's deaf too from the sounds of things,' winced Pin. And then he shoved me backwards as the front door opened again and two more people stepped out together. 'Is this her, Dawkins?' he demanded. 'Is this the girl?'

Ruby stepped out of the front door wearing a light blue dress, much less flashy and expensive than usual, and I was vexed to see she was in the company of the man Froggat. She held open the door for him as he passed through with his hands full with that tray of metal objects he sold. The two of them stood on the doorstep for some moments and exchanged words in low voices as though they was in plot. They seemed an unlikely pairing, I thought, as I crept over to where the vegetable cart was to see if I could make out what they was saying. He was some ten years older than her and he was not what you would call handsome. I poked my head over the top of the cart to get a better look and I saw her hand raise up to his shoulder in a small tender way what she had never done with me. And then he looked up and down the street, in a manner most furtive, and leaned his tall self down towards her as if about to impart a secret.

He kissed her then, in full view of the whole street, upon her pretty lips. She did not resist him. There was no stiffening of her body, no attempt to turn her face away, like she had done with me. She had responded to his advance in a manner most warm and her hand now touched his cheek all gentle. I stepped away from the scene and returned to Pin at the edge of the alley.

'Remind me, Mr Dawkins,' said Pin as my own hand raised up to my face, 'did you say you were in love with this lady or that she was in love with you?'

The night before, when she had looked me in the eyes and had told me that she was not interested in no more villains, I had not been willing to believe. I had just imagined this was because the pain of Jem was still fresh and that she would come around in time. I had not believed that a man like Froggat would be able to win her hand and had assumed she was just thinking about his proposal for form's sake. But on seeing them together like this as their kiss came to its end, and then hearing that giggle of hers echo up the quiet lane, the light of my love was snuffed and done with.

'She ain't nothing to me,' I told him in a dry voice. 'So are you going to get that stone from off her or what?'

Ruby and her man then stepped away from the house and they crossed the street with her arm linked into his. They was walking towards where we was hidden, and Pin pushed me deeper into the alley so I could not be seen.

'Not with this fellow around,' he whispered, and leaned against the corner of the alley as they strolled towards him, shielding me from their view. I turned myself out of their path and, as I heard their two pairs of feet coming towards us in perfect step, a sharp painful sensation ran through me and I moved back and hid further along.

'Morning!' I heard Ruby say to Pin in a bright and happy voice what contrasted with the tone she had struck with me on the night before. I saw then that the sad face she had worn when rejecting me outside Rafferty's music hall was only a mask what she had most likely removed before her carriage had even returned her to Froggat's. I was the one upset, I now realised, while she could not care.

''Appy morning to ya, guvnor and milady, gawd help me so it is, I do say.'

This, I realised after a confused second, was the horrible sound of Timothy Pin pretending to be a local. John Froggat, the man what had stolen my love, grunted a reply and the betrothed couple passed by without stopping.

'An attractive girl,' said Pin, once they was out of earshot. I stepped back on to the street and watched the pair walk away from us. 'The face of a heartbreaker.'

Ruby giggled again at something Froggat was murmuring and I felt the fury rise up within me. I would have done anything for her, I thought in shame. I would have given up thievery, had she so willed it. I had even broken a criminal code and kicked another thief into the arms of the law just so that she and I could be together, and she had repaid me by linking arms with another. I had been made a fool of and I hated her for it.

'If you want, Mr Pin,' I said, 'I'm happy to break in there now —' I pointed over to Fagin's old home — 'and just take the rotten jewel.'

Ten minutes later I had gained entry to the empty house what stood next to the one I wished to burgle. Timothy Pin continued to wait outside and keep watch for the return of Ruby, John or the mother, but he had given me his small set of skeleton keys. These, he reckoned, could open any Bramah, Chubb or other lock and he said he had used such a key to gain entry into my lodgings. As he had boasted, one of them had opened the door of this unoccupied house and I moved through darkness and cobwebs to get to the top. The windows of the place was all boarded up and I could hear rats scurrying around as I felt my way up the stairs to the top floor and looked for a way into the attic. This house was almost identical to the one what I had grown up in and so I was able to find my way about even with so little light. Once in the attic I looked for the small window what led on to the roof, forced it open and poked my head through. I looked around to assure myself that there was no way I could be spotted and then pulled myself out and on to the roof.

I knew from experience that I could move along the guttering to get to the roof of Fagin's house, as I had been taught how to do this in the other direction by the old man himself should there ever be a police raid. I also knew that his roof had a hidden entrance underneath some loose tiling for the very same purpose, and it was not long before I had uncovered it and lowered myself through.

I dropped into the attic, where I had slept just weeks ago on my first night back in London, and crept all soundless towards the trapdoor what led below. This hatch was tough to prise up with my fingers and I was concerned that Uncle Huffam, whose painful fiddling I could now hear coming up from below, would hear me. But he continued to play as I released the door and then lowered myself into the natural light of the landing. As my feet touched the worn-out rug underneath I heard a loud screech what made me jump within my skin. That black cat what now lived here jumped out from a corner, ran past me and raced down the stairs towards where Huffam was playing.

'What is it, Boney?' I heard Huffam say as his fiddling stopped and the cat ran into the door of the kitchen. 'Big rats again, old boy?' I stood frozen upon the landing while I waited to hear if Huffam would come to investigate but after a short silence he resumed his music and I could carry on moving towards one of the doors on this top floor, knowing from memory which of the floorboards beneath me would squeak, and avoiding them. I tried the handle of the door, it opened with little noise and I stepped through.

The air seemed thick with honest labour as I entered this room; there was a wooden workbench with saw-marks all over it and many metal items in these boxes all around. I knew Ruby's doll would not be in here and I picked up one of the saws and stepped out again. I recalled from my last visit that the door opposite led to John Froggat's bedroom and I had the depressing thought that perhaps Ruby was already keeping some things in there. Perhaps his room was already hers, regardless of his Christianity. This room was also unlocked and one glance around his stark bedroom told me, to my undoubted relief, that there was no feminine presence in here either. I looked about me, at the religious tracts what rested on the bedside table and to the pencil sketchings of boxing fights what he had pinned to his walls, and I wished I could set fire to the place. I hated this man and was glad to leave and shut the door on his chamber unsearched.

Ruby must be staying in the vacant room below this, I reasoned, the one what Froggat had told me his late brother had lived in and that years earlier I had shared with Charley, Jem and Mouse after we had all grown too big for the attic. This room was behind the kitchen where Huffam was still playing his fiddle and, as I reached the bottom of the stairs without being heard, I could see him through a crack in the door. He was sat in his rocking chair facing away from the door and lost in his art. I tiptoed past the door, with the saw in hand and watched only by the cat. I reached the room, turned the handle and found it locked. So I pulled out the bunch of skeleton keys what Pin had given me and tried each one. The last key unlocked the door and I pushed it open as quiet as I could.

The room was Ruby's – there was no doubt of this from the very first second I entered it. It smelt of the expensive perfume that she had worn when she had embraced me that morning in Smithfield Market. I felt a tremendous sadness come over me as I recalled how happy she had been to see me then and I soon found myself sitting on her bed. Since that time I had often imagined walking into her bedroom and now here I was at last, but as a common thief and not her lover. My eyes cast about the room, which was the lightest in the place on account of her fine white curtains, and I recognised some of the clothes, jewellery and linen what she had had in Bethnal Green. From the kitchen Huffam continued scraping on his fiddle but it seemed as though he could sense the sad mood of the house and he had moved on to a very mournful ballad. If I had not been there on a criminal errand I would have banged on the wall and told him to knock it off.

Through the crack in the door I noticed I was being watched. Boney the cat padded in and cocked his head at me and I felt, in my self pity, that he was perhaps feeling some sorrow for me also. I patted the bed for him to come over but instead he jumped up on to a small chair, then on to the dressing table and moved along it before climbing up to a taller chest of drawers. He passed a number of her things as he did so, brushes, hand-mirrors, boxes of jewellery. It was only after he had passed by a smiling wooden doll, what was almost identical to the ones what Charley and myself had been given, that I snapped out of my gloom and recalled what I was doing there.

Up in a blink, I crossed over to the toy, picked it up and held it close to my ear. With one deliberate rattle I heard that there was something inside what sounded heavier than the pebbles contained in the other two. In that glorious second all my melancholy lifted like the fog and I was desperate to crack it open and see if the hunt for the Jakkapoor stone was now over. I had made the mistake before of leaving this house without knowing for certain if the jewel was recovered and I was not going to do that this time. And so, with the sound of Huffam's fiddle covering the strokes I held it down with one hand over the edge of Ruby's table and began sawing with the other. I should take it up to John Froggat's workbench, what was already so covered in saw marks that one more would not be detected and cut it open there, I thought. But I was far too eager to know.

And what, I asked myself as I worked upon it, would I do if I should open this doll up to find no jewel inside? Where would I hide if I found another pebble? I would not be returning to Timothy Pin, he would be sure to kill me. Instead I would have to escape over the rooftops and leave London forever. Perhaps even leave the country.

Then, as the teeth of the saw travelled through the prince's chest, I asked myself an even more important question. What would I do if I did find the jewel inside? Should I hand such a priceless treasure over to a man like Lord Evershed and then go about my business? Neither Warrigal nor Pin was with me now – there was nothing to stop me from fleeing the country anyway, but with this prize to sell. The girl I loved thought nothing of me and I had few friends what was not either dead or living in Northamptonshire. There was no reason I could think of for me to go back to Pin anyway.

And then, just as I was coming to the point where I could snap the doll with my bare hands, I remembered that there was a reason. I heard the word in Warrigal's voice. *Consequences*, he had said. If Evershed does not get the jewel then his people on Honey Ant Hill could suffer. Timothy Pin had even reminded him of that yesterday. If I was to flee now, then this threat against Warrigal's loved ones would always rest heavy upon me. And I had promised him we was friends.

During a pause in the music I swept up the sawdust and placed it into my pocket. If possible I did not want Ruby to know straight away that she had been robbed. I hoped that it was only when she went to look for her doll that she would notice the loss.

And then the music continued and there was no more putting it off. I held the doll with both hands, cracked it open with one swift motion and tipped the contents into my hand. A black jewel, heavy and shining, fell out of the wooden prince and lay in my palm. The black heart of Jakkapoor. It was beautiful.

I closed it into my fist, raised it to my lips and kissed it. In my long trade as a pickpocket I had held many jewels and other treasures but none had moved me as much as this one. I could see now why Evershed had wanted it so much when he saw it there in the temple of Seringapatam some forty-odd years before and why his pursuit had been so hot ever since losing it. What he had said about the stone was true. It called to you.

I wasted no more time. I put the jewel in my coat pocket and made to leave the room and lock it after me. This was made harder by Boney's refusal to exit with me and I spent three silent minutes trying to convince the belligerent cat that it should follow me out into the hall. At last he ran through my feet and went up the stairs before me and I turned the key all soft and made my way towards the staircase.

I came to the kitchen door and just as I stepped past it there was a sharp screech along the fiddle and Huffam stopped playing. I froze and looked towards the old blind man, who lifted his head up from his instrument and addressed the wall in front of him.

'So you're back, are you?' he said in a mean, thin voice. 'Back to visit your old home. I knew you would be.'

I did not move an inch and just stood there not wanting to even be heard breathing.

'You're a wicked one. I heard you shuffling about in that girl's chamber. Leave her in peace, why can't you?'

He shook his head in disgust and began waving his bow stick at where he seemed to think I was standing. I made to step away and he spoke again.

'She speaks fondly of you, would you believe? She's the only one who does.'

This made me stop dead. I was amazed that Ruby had mentioned me to Uncle Huffam. I wanted to hear more.

'My nephew John tries to set her straight, he tells her how wicked you are, but she will not listen to him. She says you're not all bad. She loves you, she tells us!'

I felt my heart becoming light again and I wanted to ask him why then, if she loved me so much, had she shunned me.

'You treated her kindly, she says. Her and a great many others. She's sorry you were choked.'

My hands went up to my neck as he said that, to the marks where Warrigal had tried to garrotte me.

'But you're a damned soul, aren't you, old man? Damned to haunt this place forever.'

My heart sank as I fell upon what the old fool was saying. He thought I was Fagin's ghost.

'You'll be back here,' he called after me as I turned from him and ran up the stairs. 'You're cursed to walk this space forever whether you care to or not!' I reached the top landing but could still hear him as I hauled myself back into the attic.

'*You'll be forever coming back!*'

Timothy Pin was still loitering by the vegetable cart and I approached him from behind. I had not exited the way I had come in as I had been so startled by the old man's ravings that I had just fled the building and climbed over four different rooftops before shimmying down a gutter. I tapped Pin on the back and he jumped around with his hand inside his coat pocket resting on that unseen pistol.

'I was about to come looking for you,' he spat in agitation. 'I thought you had been fool enough to take flight.'

'I wouldn't do that, Mr Pin,' I told him as we both disappeared from the view of the house and headed back up the alley. 'I know there would be consequences if I did.'

'Do you have the stone, Mr Dawkins?' Pin pressed me as soon as we was clear out of anyone's sight. He stopped walking and grabbed my coat collar with his free hand. 'We have nothing further to discuss if you do not.'

'I don't know,' I shrugged as I reached into my own pocket and pulled out the black heart of Jakkapoor. 'It look anything like this?'

I held the stone up to his face and saw his expression change from panic to wonder. He took it with his own hands and viewed it from all angles.

'It must be,' he said holding it with reverential care. There was real awe in his voice. 'Surely this can be nothing else. Was it where you said it would be?'

'In the doll, yeah,' I nodded.

'We had best hurry away before she notices the loss. When do you think the girl will be back?'

'She works at Smithfield Market by day,' I told him. 'That's where she was headed just now I'd wager. Then she goes from there to sell sandwiches in the music hall in the evening. So she won't come back here until gone midnight.' Pin placed the jewel into his left pocket and I moved away as he did so. 'Well, there you have it and my job here is done,' I said, doffing my hat to him. 'Thank Lord Evershed for the pardon when you see him, but I might as well be on my way.' I made to leave but Pin grabbed me once more.

'His Lordship will want to confirm this is indeed the jewel before you're set free, Dawkins,' he said. 'This could be a likeness and you're trying to pass it off as the real stone. For all I know, you never even went into that house.' He forced me further up the alley and I thought about that deadly pistol he still had in his other pocket. 'Your aborigine friend has been instructed to meet Lord Evershed at the docks and wait with him until Calista arrives with the carriage. Then they are to travel to the Dancing Mutineer,' said Pin referring to the public house in Wapping where he had taken me on our first meeting. 'Lord Evershed could be on his way there now expecting to be presented with this jewel and we can both be thankful that we secured it in time. There would have been a mighty reckoning if we had failed.'

The alley led out on to a busier street and he held his arm up to hail a hackney cab but none came. This was a low part of town and it was all donkey carriages and carts pulled by men or dogs. 'His Lordship will be very pleased with what you have delivered, Mr Dawkins,' Pin said at last when a small horse-drawn carriage for two drew near. 'You'll have made an old man very happy.'

Chapter 29

The Dancing Mutineer

Containing the lesson of the story. The lesson of every story

It was Fagin what had first told me of the dreadful history of the Dancing Mutineer, the pub what I had learnt years later was owned by Timothy Pin. When I was a small kinchin what had just come to live in Saffron Hill he told all of us boys the story of it before bed and why it was a place where thieves was too scared to go.

It was on one of those nights when we was all too excitable to sleep on account of the great thieving adventures we had got up to during the day and we would have been stamping, scrapping, shouting and making all manner of mischief above the room where he slept. He poked his head up into that attic room and told us that it was far too late for fun and games if we was to be up and out first thing tomorrow.

'Early birds, my dears,' he would say, pointing towards the jackdaw what I had carved into the wooden beam from where the lantern hung. 'Early birds.' We boys, what loved it whenever he would come up to say goodnight to us, pleaded with him then to tell us one of his frightening stories and promised we would sleep all the softer for it afterwards. Fagin, who never needed much persuasion to spin another cautionary tale, then climbed the rest of his bony self into our attic and made us get in our beds before he continued.

'Should I tell you, my dears, more of the terrible Baron Beazle?' Fagin cackled once we had settled ourselves and he had positioned himself under the one lamp for full effect. 'Or, as he is better known, the drowning judge!' After making us promise that we had steel enough to listen to the story of this hanger of seafaring thieves he continued to tell us about the heroic Magnus Craft what had fallen into the clutches of the navy and been brought home to England to face justice. 'Captain Craft,' Fagin told us, 'was a fine pirate and he and his crew had plundered their way across the South China Seas like champions. They had buried so much treasure under the earth of tropical islands that the greedy British Empire decided they wanted it for themselves and would not rest until they had found it. Craft was clever though and spent years dodging his pursuers with his crew of hearty young pirates, many of them boys as young and as fine as yourselves. But, and here is where the story turns sour, he was led into a trap by a man he once trusted, his own midshipman, what had been paid by the navy to betray the good captain. He had been peached upon, my boys, by one of his own. Now what do we all think to that?'

A chorus of disapproving voices rang out as we all clamoured over the others to describe what bloody vengeance we would each carry out on anyone foolish enough to play such games among our little crew. Fagin grinned with pride and continued.

'Very good, my dears, that's the spirit. Now Captain Craft was taken back to London and found himself up in front of the Admiralty Court, presided over by the cruellest man in the land, the black-hearted Baron Beazle.' Some of the younger boys pulled up their blankets at the mention of this man we had already heard so many bad things about. 'Beazle wanted to know where the captain had buried all his treasure but Craft, being a brave pirate what only cared about the fortunes of his crew what was all still free upon the ocean waves, refused to answer him. So Beazle decided that a common hanging was too good for Craft. Instead he had him taken . . .' there was a long pause before Fagin made a leap towards us in his scariest voice, '. . . *to the drowning chamber!*'

We boys all cried out in mock terror and Fagin chuckled at us before going on to explain how this chamber worked. 'The chamber is the cellar of a pub, my dears, but this is no friendly establishment like the Three Cripples, oh dear me, no. This pub is the Dancing Mutineer, a place feared by everyone in our profession and with good reason too. It still stands to this day on the bank of the Thames near Execution Point, but the way in which the condemned men meet their doom when sent to the Mutineer is not always by way of the noose. It is much slower and more painful. When the tide is low they are taken down into the dark steps of the cellar and chained to the walls, where they are left, but not before their executioners have opened the tiny sluice gates that face the river. As the tide comes in, the water rises, filling the chamber. Poor Craft was left there to scream out his lungs as the water poured in and rose and rose up to his chin. Chained to other walls was the skeletons of other pirates who, like him, had fallen foul of the Baron.' Fagin stood then as tall as he could and snuffed out the lantern light. Light still beamed up from the trap he had climbed up through and he crawled back towards it. 'Did he survive or did he perish, my dears?' he said as his bottom half descended down it. 'How would you like to hear that the story ends?'

'He was rescued,' I said. 'By a woman what loved him.'

'By his crew,' said Georgie Bluchers. 'They blew open the river wall with dynamite and stole him away.'

'He told them where the treasure was,' said Charley Bates. 'And the Baron let him go.'

'He drowned,' said Jem White. 'Like a rat.'

The only part of Fagin still seen in the attic now was his head, and the light from below illuminated his red hair making him look like something from a bible picture book. His left arm reached over to the trap door ready to shut it after himself. 'All fine ideas, boys. Anyone of you could be the next George Shatillion with fine ideas like that.'

'So what happened?' asked Mouse. 'Did he live or did he die?'

'The thing is,' said Fagin as if telling us a terrible secret, 'it don't matter how it ends. How it ends ain't the lesson of the story. The lesson of the story, the lesson of every story, is these three little words.' He raised a finger and tapped the air with each one. '*Don't. Get. Caught.*'

And then he pulled the trap door over himself and left us with darkness and dreams.

The place in Wapping where the Dancing Mutineer stood was a deserted vicinity made up of ship-building factories. And, while it was true that some among the criminal community avoided the place for superstitious reasons, many law-abiding persons would also steer clear just because it was horrible. Dockers and factory workers would frequent it after a day's labour, but it was less than a week before Christmas and the street was deserted.

'Lord Evershed is here already,' said Pin in a nervous voice as our small cab reached the pub and we saw Calista waiting outside with her carriage. 'Dear God, I hope he's in a good humour.'

'You look more scared of him than I am,' I said as we squeezed out of the box on wheels what we had been travelling in and Pin paid the driver. He did not reply but breathed out as we entered the pub and walked through the bar, where Warrigal sat alone drinking a whisky, and then led me up the staircase. He walked towards that office room where we had spoken less than two weeks before and where he had admitted to me that he thought Lord Evershed was not of sound mind. Pin placed his hand on the handle, glanced at me for one second and then opened the door to meet his employer.

'Lord Evershed,' he said in a strong voice as he strode into the room with me, 'I do so apologise for keeping you waiting. I trust your voyage was not too hellish.'

Evershed was stood in the middle of the room with his back to us. He was dressed in black trousers and waistcoat but there was a long military sword sheathed in a gold-plated scabbard around his waist. On the table was a long-barrelled flintlock pistol, black with a golden butt, what looked old enough for him to have used as a soldier in India. He was looking out of an open window to the river beyond and a small fire in the grate was struggling to stay alight against the draught. When at last he turned to face us he seemed even older than I remembered him being in Australia although his face was still brown from the sun. If he recognised me at all then he made no sign of it.

'This city,' he said to neither of us in particular, 'is even more squalid than I remember.'

There was a silence then as Pin seemed unsure of how to respond. 'I know,' he said at last. 'It's ghastly. But once our business is done you shall see no more of the dreadful place and return to Longwinter in the country.'

'It's all still whores and vagrants, as far as I can see,' Evershed went on as if he had not heard him. 'Whores and vagrants.' He moved over to the desk then and stood behind it, looking at the two of us. He had not shut the window after himself and the cold December air filled the room. 'I waited in that dockyard for one hour *all on my own* until your blasted driver arrived. It's a good job she knew me from my portraits.'

'Oh dear,' said Pin. 'Was Warrigal not there to keep you company, Your Lordship? I sent him along ahead of us for that purpose.'

'Warrigal was late,' barked Evershed. 'He arrived after she did. Said he got lost, the wretch.'

'He's only been in London a month, Your Lordship,' Pin bowed his head. 'It was my fault for sending him. But I could not greet you myself as I had an urgent task to attend to with Mr Dawkins here.'

Evershed's head turned towards me for the first time. 'Was it him after all then?' he said to Pin in disgust. 'The one who was given the doll? This fellow?'

'No, Your Lordship,' Pin explained. 'Mr Dawkins and another boy were both given a similar doll to throw us off the scent. But the jewel was given to a different child entirely.'

Just then there was a sudden bang and I spun around. Warrigal had walked in and the door behind had been slammed by either him or the wind. He stood there, with his hands together, as if awaiting instruction.

'Then why is he still here?' asked Evershed, his eyes still fixed upon me. 'And not the correct child?'

'Because Mr Dawkins here,' said Pin, unbuttoning his coat, 'was extremely helpful to us in the end, Your Lordship. Without him we never would have discovered the identity of the true recipient.'

Evershed turned away from me then and looked with eagerness to Pin. 'You have it then?' he asked. 'It's true?'

In reply Pin reached into his pocket and pulled out the jewel I had given him. 'It is my great pleasure, Lord Evershed,' he declared with his chin held high, 'to present you with what was always yours by moral right. I give you, sir, the Jakkapoor stone.'

Evershed said nothing but moved around the desk and close to Pin. He took the jewel from him and inspected it.

'It is the real jewel then, Your Lordship?' asked Pin after Evershed had stared and sniffed at it for some time.

'Oh yes,' murmured Evershed. 'It's the very one I liberated from Seringapatam as a much younger man. It's unmistakable.'

'I am pleased, Your Lordship.'

'You've done well, Timothy,' Evershed said, and then turned away from him. 'I thank you for this.'

And then, with one swift and strong stroke, he threw it out of the open window and straight into the Thames.

'Fucking thing!' he said, and turned back to us.

I cried out in horror. 'What did you do that for, you mad bastard?' I had forgotten all about the danger of the moment, so outraged was I by the travesty of this action. I almost wanted to barge past him, jump out of the window and dive in after it. 'I've spent the best part of a month looking everywhere for that!'

I looked to Timothy Pin to see if he was as shocked as I was.

He gave me a small shrug. 'Revenge is a wild justice,' he said as if he had expected that.

'I've never wanted it,' grunted Evershed. 'I don't believe in silly curses, Dawkins, I'm not a child. So,' he turned to Pin. 'Tell me his name then. And where the bastard can be found.'

'*Her* name, Your Lordship. The child was a girl.'

'Wrong, Timothy!' Evershed shouted in sudden anger. 'George Shatillion wrote that the jewel was given to his bastard. Bastard means boy!'

'I assumed so too. But the girl Dawkins led me to walked past us in the street just hours ago. Her name is Ruby Solomon. I got a good look at her face and I'm certain that she is the one.'

'How can you be?'

'Because her likeness to your late wife is startling,' replied Pin.

I stood listening to all this dumbstruck. I was still confounded by the tossing away of a priceless jewel and could not begin to make sense of this talk of bastards and Ruby.

'The hair is the colour of Shatillion's, Your Lordship, but the rest –' Pin stopped and then looked to me – 'belongs only to your late wife. I even remarked to Mr Dawkins that she had the face of a heartbreaker.'

'Hold up a second,' I said after I had at last roused myself out of confusion. 'What we on about?'

'We are discussing the illegitimate child of George Shatillion and Lady Evershed, Dawkins,' sighed Pin as though I was a child at a big table what needed adult talk explained to him. 'A love child that your Mr Fagin was paid to hide from Lord Evershed in fear that the truth would make His Lordship even more murderous.' Pin turned back to Evershed and apologised for the interruption.

'You think Ruby is George Shatillion's daughter?' I asked in bewilderment. 'Because she ain't.' Evershed seemed as unsure of this claim as I was and turned to me for the first time since I had entered the room.

'Why can't she be?' he asked.

'Because she had her own family,' I told him. 'A mother and an uncle.'

'Last night Mr Dawkins told me about the girl's uncle,' Pin said to Evershed as if he was the prosecution and I was the defence. 'His name was Uncle Ikey.'

Evershed kept his eyes on me and asked if this was true. I said nothing and tried to work out the importance of it.

'Just as Shatillion mentioned in his autobiographical fragment, Your Lordship,' Pin went on. 'Recall that he wrote that although he wanted the world to think that he had been living as a recluse in his latter years he had in fact been visiting the child under a series of aliases. One such alias was a character modelled on Ikey Slizzard, his character from *Thimble and Pea*.'

Evershed nodded slow and tapped the walnut desk with his fingers in a slow thoughtful way.

'Ikey Slizzard?' I gave a small laugh at the mention of this villain from Shatillion's first book. 'That ain't even a real person!'

Pin turned and explained things with relish. He was talking to me but I felt that his words was more for his master's ears. It sounded like he wanted to remind him of how clever he had been in uncovering all this.

'In his fragment George Shatillion wrote of a child he sired with Louisa Evershed. Until then nobody had even known of this child's existence as Louisa had given birth to it during the period after she had run away from her husband. Shatillion had abandoned her at this point but it seems that he feared Lord Evershed's sworn vengeance. He had heard of His Lordship's temper and guessed that an attempt would be made on Louisa's life. So he took the child away and hid it.'

'Didn't save her,' sniffed Evershed, who was now sat behind the desk and playing with a piece of jewellery. It was, I noticed, the same gold locket what he had shown me that day in Australia as we walked together along the River Hawkesbury. The one what contained the picture of his murdered wife. 'And it didn't save him either,' he said, and snapped it shut.

'Indeed it did not,' Pin went on. 'And although Shatillion had been successful in shielding his offspring from our view, he evidently believed that there would come a time when her identity could safely be made known. To this end he detailed the whole saga in a document which he at some point planned to send to his trusted friend and biographer, Hartley Mellish. Mr Mellish received this document after Shatillion had unexpectedly fallen to his death and contacted me about what he had read there. It was not a cheap bit of business buying it off him, I can tell you.'

Pin seemed disappointed in Shatillion's old friend, as though this mercenary behaviour was somehow worse than his murder. He seemed to be enjoying the sound of his own voice though and, as he stood there showing off, I found myself wanting to punch him in the gob.

'The document explained how he had taken his baby from Louisa quite against her wishes as well as the jewel which was hidden inside that doll.' Pin indicated the top half of Ruby's gift what poked out of my pocket still. 'Shatillion then handed the child over to a man who kept so many orphans that one more would never be noticed. He had met your Mr Fagin many years before and knew that the old villain had one redeeming virtue. He knew how to look after children.

'Shatillion continued to pay Fagin with many jewels and trinkets throughout the child's life as long as the Jew kept watch over his charge and ensured that the doll remained with the child. It was to act as a signifier, he explained, to prove who the child was should the day ever come when he would want to.'

Pin then turned his attention to Evershed, who just stared at the shut locket not appearing to even listen.

'When Dawkins told me she had an Uncle Ikey then I knew it must be her, Your Lordship, and that the uncle was in fact her father, George Shatillion. From this and her face I knew she was the girl even before the jewel was revealed.'

'Bravo, sir,' said Evershed in a voice without joy. 'You have me convinced. It's a girl then.' He put the locket away in the top drawer and stood up. 'A pity. It'll be harder with a girl.'

'What will?' I asked, stepping backwards. But I was already feeling sick with the realisation. Evershed never wanted me to deliver a jewel. He wanted me to deliver a name. And I had done it.

Evershed crossed over to a hatstand and removed his greatcoat what hung there. 'You have her address, Timothy?' he said as he began to put it on, cloaking his uniform. 'I want to attend to this at once.'

'Oh yes,' replied his servant. 'But she won't be there now.'

Perhaps they wanted to see her for harmless reasons, I considered. So that they could tell her whose daughter she was and make amends for the slaying of her true parents. But I very much doubted this.

'She works at Smithfield Market,' Pin continued talking to Evershed. 'We have Mr Dawkins to thanks for that information too.' He turned to me and smiled.

'You're going to kill her?' I cried in disbelief. 'That's where you want to go now?'

'Where better?' he replied as he looked over to the door where Warrigal was standing. 'It's crowded, lots of noisy, screaming animals and there's blood everywhere already. Such markets are a gift for the professional assassin.'

'But why?' I shouted at them. 'What's she ever done to hurt you?'

Evershed had his coat on now but it was still unbuttoned and the tail was hanging over the mighty sword he carried on his hip. His old face dropped with shame.

'She has done nothing to harm me, Mr Dawkins. Nothing at all. But she is the product of a union that cut me more deeply than any battle wound. Shatillion thought he could hide her from me and in doing so he would win. He left her on Earth as mockery of me.' His expression hardened then and he began to button his coat. 'But I am the Empire. And the Empire will not be mocked.'

'You're a mad old bastard!' I pointed at him. 'A lunatic what wants locking away. You ain't nothing else!'

'I never expected you to understand, Mr Dawkins,' he sighed, 'which is why neither of you were ever told my real motives. I felt the lost-jewel story would make more sense to rougher souls.'

I turned to the man by the door. 'You didn't know either, Warrigal?' I asked him. 'We can't let them do this – it's murder. You've met Ruby, you stayed in her home! She was kind to you and helped to nurse you back to health when you was ill. We can't let them kill her.' Warrigal said nothing. He just stood in front of that door and in his hands was that long shining blade that he had carried at the bottom of our trunk.

'Don't let him out of this room, Bungurra,' Pin ordered him. 'Kill him if he tries to get past you.'

I spun back to where he and Evershed stood and warned them not do this. 'I won't let you kill her. It's wrong.'

'Weak,' Evershed scoffed and turned to Pin. 'Finish this, Timothy.'

Timothy Pin put his hand into his left-side coat pocket. 'His Lordship and I thank you for your services, Mr Dawkins,' he smirked. 'But you are now relieved of your duties.'

Then his smile vanished.

His hand came out of his left pocket and went into his right. Then he opened his coat to see if what he was looking for was in there. But he no longer had it. It had not been in his possession since he had shared a ride with me in that small cab.

'Did your mother never teach you, Timothy,' I said as I pulled that small pistol of his out of my own pocket and pointed it at his bald head, 'not to sit so close to a pickpocket?'

Both of them was most alarmed at this reversal of fortune and Pin cried out in fright.

'You bloody fool, Timothy,' Evershed cursed. 'You damned amateur.'

'I'm sorry, sir, I didn't feel it.' Pin looked most astonished. 'How did you do that, Dawkins?' How was it possible?'

'Well, they didn't call me Artful for nothing,' I replied, and pointed the gun from him to Evershed. His weapon, the larger flintlock, was on still on the desk and I could shoot him easy before he reached it. 'Warrigal,' I called over. 'Open that door and step away from it, there's a good boy –' I kept my eyes fixed on Evershed so there was no doubt who was taking the shot – 'or the Empire falls.'

Evershed stared back at me bull-like. 'You haven't the stomach for the kill,' he challenged. 'You're not a soldier, just a thief. Put down the weapon. You look ridiculous with it.'

Warrigal had not moved but I sidestepped towards the other gun so no one could fire it after me. 'I'm leaving here now,' I said to them all. 'Try and stop me, and it's curtains for the man with the money.'

Evershed snorted. 'We'll see about that, shall we?'

And then he swung back his coat, grabbed the handle of the sword and charged.

I had not expected this and, as he came at me roaring, I stepped away and fired the pistol. But Evershed was right – I was unused to firearms and my aim was unreliable. The ball shot from the barrel of the tiny gun and struck him in the shoulder. It was a small wound and he had no doubt suffered worse in battle. But it was enough to send him staggering backwards and crashing to the floor as Timothy Pin seized the moment to tackle me. He came at me but I swung the butt of the pistol into his head. He cried out in pain but still shoved me over to the fireplace and tried to restrain me.

'Bungurra!' he yelled. 'Help me, God damn you.'

I shoved Pin back and then punched him with as much force as I could muster, straight in the side of his face. He fell back and I turned to Warrigal to see if he was next. Evershed was clutching his shoulder and crawling towards his pistol shouting, 'Kill the boy!' but Warrigal hesitated at his post with that knife.

I did not wait to find out what Warrigal would do. I turned to the open window, the only other exit, ran towards it, jumped on the desk in between and launched myself out. We was two floors up but I cleared the few riverboats moored below and fell down with terrific splash straight into the drink. The sensation was like death.

The Thames, I discovered at that moment, is London's greatest monster. The freezing, rushing, pulling shock of it overcame every other concern as I sank like a stone into its powerful filth. My whole body rebelled against the thick water and I kicked and thrashed my way back up to the surface in desperation, fighting against the strong currents what was wanting to pull me deep. At last I swam to the top and took a great gulp of air as I tried to find my bearings. The Dancing Mutineer had somehow moved to the right but I looked up to the window I had jumped from and saw the bald head of Timothy Pin staring out from it. I could not hear well, on account of my ears being full of river water, but I did make out the sound of Evershed barking orders. A shot rang out and as some water splashed next to me I saw that Pin had the black gun in his hand. It would be some moments before he could reload the shot and I did not waste time.

There was some old wooden dinghies tied up along the side of the bank further downstream and I began thrashing towards them to help me stay afloat. Once I reached these I dragged myself along until I came to some small stone steps what led to an old shipyard where I pulled myself up and out of the disgusting river. I was gasping heavy as I climbed the steps but there was no time to linger and I took off my coat what was now made cumbersome with river water and threw it back in the Thames. Then I climbed over the fence and into the shipyard and ran through, with water dripping from me, in sheer terror for my life.

The place was deserted save for a number of derelict workmen and ageing sea dogs loitering about and I knew I could not rely on these sorts to come to my aid. I ran between two half-built hulls, keeping my head down as I did this so as not to be seen by any onlookers what might point pursuers in my direction. I jumped over coils of rope and loose timber and made for the yard gate what led out into the road but it was shut. But as I approached it began to open and someone entered the yard. I hurled myself down behind an upturned boat as Warrigal, knife in hand, came looking for me.

I crawled on all fours to the stern of the boat and peered around it to see if he had spotted me but he had headed in a different direction and was walking past a tall tower of scrapped vessels what he seemed to think I was hiding behind. The only way out of this yard was through the gate he had entered through but he would see me if I made a dash for it and could cut me down with ease. So I decided that a game of hide and seek was the better plan and crawled backwards, away from the boat, and looked for a place to conceal myself. It occurred to me that I could crawl under one of the many upturned boats and hide within, but this would be placing myself at a disadvantage should he find me. I was still dripping water and it was a matter of time before Warrigal, an expert tracker, would see these drips and close in. I would have to fight him before long and I searched around for a weapon. There was a small hut near the corner of the yard, at the very opposite end to where Warrigal was searching for me, and I ducked down and made towards it. The wooden door was falling off its hinges and inside was all these oars and sculls stood up, just waiting to be used in my defence. I was quick to choose which was the best suited to my purpose; it was short and thick and good for swinging, and I dashed around to behind a large locked shed where the metal items was kept. There I hid and clutched the oar and waited for his approach. A swift surprise attack was the only way I was going to best a man with a knife.

Warrigal stalked to this end of the yard now and I readied myself to jump out and swing the oar in his face. But as he drew near to where I was hidden and was about to spring from, he stopped dead and spoke. He did not shout the words, as he would if he had thought I could be lurking anywhere in the yard. He talked low and steady as if knowing I was close by.

'You drowned, Jack Dawkins,' he said in his croaking accent. 'I drowned you.'

I remained still. I was unsure what he meant by this as his English was never good and there was a chance he was telling me he would still drown me yet.

'Stay dead,' he said, and I heard him moving backwards towards where he had come from. 'Stay dead and go away.'

And with that I heard his footsteps return towards the gate. I peered around the corner of the shed and saw him leave the yard. Then I dropped to my knees, let go of the oar and breathed out hard as I realised, to my great relief, that he had spared me.

Chapter 30

Wild Justice

Featuring scenes of bloody butchery

Although it took me a good minute to recover from my near-fight with Warrigal, a fight I was sure I would have lost, I could not bring myself to stay in that place for too long. I was gripped by uncontrollable shivers from the swim and – what was more important – Ruby was in peril and it was I what had put her there.

Lord Evershed was no longer on speaking terms with sanity, this much was clear. I had thought him mad back in Australia when he told me he thought that the Jakkapoor stone held supernatural properties, but this false lunacy had been eclipsed by the true one. Someone who would want to kill a person because of an eighteen-year-old grudge against their parents was not a cove what could be reasoned with and I knew that for Ruby the situation was grave. I did not doubt that as soon as Warrigal reported that he had silenced me for good then Evershed and Pin would head straight to Smithfield Market in their carriage and try to sniff her out. Her only hope was for me to get to her first and steal her away to safety.

Once I was sure all was secure I crept out from behind the shed and made for the gate, thinking about how I would never forgive myself should she be harmed on account of my recklessness. I was already ashamed of my behaviour earlier that day, for breaking into her home and stealing her treasured gift from Fagin, and now I had as good as peached upon her to some murderous villains. I had betrayed the only person left alive what I still cared for and I had never before felt such guilt. It no longer mattered to me that she had swept me aside and given her heart to another. It only mattered that I loved her.

I trod through the gate of the shipyard all cautious, still suspecting that Warrigal might be lurking behind it as a trap. But as I poked my head around the corner so I could see into the street I heard the thundering noise of hoofs coming towards me and I darted back behind the fence as the carriage passed by. I had enough time to see it was Pin's black coach with Calista at the reins and two figures sat inside. So they was still going to Smithfield to do away with her, I thought as my hopes faded. There was no sign of Warrigal however and so I knew I had to still be watchful.

As soon as they had rocketed off I dashed out into the lane and tried to work out what to do. I was not far from St Katherine's Wharf where Evershed had docked, and I began running towards it knowing that there would be far more people there what might be able to aid me. I would have told anyone my troubles at that moment if it would have helped Ruby, even, God forgive me, a policeman. But I also knew it would be impossible to explain the madness of the situation to anyone and expect them to act with the speed required.

I ran into a lane what was as deserted as the one I had just come from, save for some dogs on chains barking at me to stay away from their property. It was hard to run as my wet clothes was heavy and my legs burned with chafing. I was just considering removing my trousers and other clothes so I could move with more ease when I saw someone on a horse what came galloping in the other direction. I cried out for him to stop, in the hope that he would hear my story and give me a ride to Smithfield in time to rescue Ruby. I was waving my arms in a manner most frantic as he approached, and I tried to position myself in his way, but he spurred his horse to run faster and I had to jump to the side before I got trampled. I shouted some choice curse words after him as he disappeared up the street but my spirit was knocked and I dropped to my knees on the dusty ground in despair. The situation was hopeless, I told myself, I would never make it to Smithfield in time to save Ruby.

Just then I heard the sound of a horse's whinny and noticed that along this quiet dockside street was a small stable what appeared unguarded. I ran up to it to see if there was anybody about what I could appeal to but none was seen and inside was this large brown horse with a saddle already on it. I could see through the narrow windows in the stable door that it was just the sort of animal I had been taught how to ride back in Australia when the Empire still thought it could make a proper farmer of me. If only I could get to it, I knew, then I could ride it well enough to get me to Smithfield. There was even a chance I would get there before Evershed, knowing the lanes as well as I did. But the walls of the stable was brick and it was attached to a building what seemed to be empty of human souls. The stable door was thick wood and the windows was too narrow to squeeze through. The doors was secured with a large Chubb lock and, as I took it in my hands, I felt there was no way I could expect to smash it off.

And then I remembered that I might not need to. My hands went for my left trouser pocket, hoping hard that they had not fallen out of my pocket during my swim in the Thames, and there, to my great joy, was what I needed above all else. I pulled the chain of skeleton keys out of my pocket, the set what Timothy Pin had given to me to break into Ruby's house with, and what

I had never returned to him, and I tried the lock. It turned on the first try and the horse was mine.

It was true that I had been taught how to ride in Australia but, I soon realised as I struggled to get the nag to head the right way up the quiet lane, I had not learnt my lessons well. The mare was a belligerent beast at first and getting her to take me away from the vicinity of her home was a trial I did not have time for. I swore and cursed at her for not doing as I asked, which may have made matters worse. However, once we was out into the rush of Upper Thames Street I calmed myself and she became more responsive and we was soon racing at great speed and weaving through the other traffic. I imagined that Calista would have taken the busier route along Cheapside and that their carriage was too big to dodge through other vehicles and could not move as nimbly as I was doing. I dared to hope that I could reach Smithfield before them and I made the horse take some narrower lanes what I knew. These cut through the poorer districts and caused many unfortunate coves to have to leap out of our way as we galloped past and an apple merchant what was crossing the lane in front of us overturned his cart as she leapt over it. By the time the horse had made it to over to Newgate Street she and myself was thinking as one and her final dash to Smithfield Market was a magnificent display of equestrian majesty. I pulled her up as we reached the edge of the market and she grew unsettled again as the awful sounds of animal suffering came out from the drover's rings.

'This is a bloody good horse,' I told a young butcher's boy what had watched us rear up as I went to dismount. 'She's for riding, not eating.' I handed him the reins and made off into the market crowds.

Smithfield was even noisier and more populated than on the last time I had come here and it was hard to push through as my eyes searched each stall of the open space for where Ruby might be working. There was many girls of her age selling meat and I saw several what I thought was her through the crowds, only to be see realise how mistaken I was when I got closer. As my eyes searched around I slammed into a man twice my size, looked up to face him and was startled to see he had covered me in blood.

'Watch where you're going, son,' warned the butcher with the bloody apron and I understood what Pin had meant about this being the perfect place for a kill. Anyone could stride through this place of screams with murder stains all over them and nobody would question it.

Not only was I searching for Ruby but I also kept watch for Pin and Evershed. Although myself and the horse had moved fast through the city I could not be sure if we had beaten them to this place or if Warrigal had gone ahead of them. They may have already found her, I feared, which was why I saw her behind none of the stalls. The more I searched the more frantic I became until I began to feel most sick. I passed by a man with a live pig in his arms what was fighting for its freedom and the sound the animal was making was diabolical.

There was a crate of dead poultry resting on the ground beside one stall and I stepped on this to see over the many heads while ignoring the owners' complaints. I surveyed the sweep of the market, the many pens and stalls what was spread out around me, but could not see Ruby anywhere. And then, just as I was about to step down from off the crate, I saw at the sausage and bacon corner Lord Evershed entering the market ring. He was grimacing in pain and walking with his hand holding some dark towels pressed against his shoulder. He was a tough old bastard and it seemed my gunshot had not disabled him. Beside him was Timothy Pin, and Evershed looked to be issuing him with orders to search the market in a different direction to himself. I saw, from watching his hand movements as he rested himself against a brick wall, that Evershed was tired and wanted to rest. I lowered my head so there was no chance of either of them seeing me and then heard a voice calling my name.

'Jack Dawkins,' it said. 'My goodness!'

I turned and saw her then and she looked just the same as she had that day in this very market three weeks ago. She was wearing the same outfit, although her expression was much more annoyed than it had been then. However, I was so glad to see her alive that I just jumped down from the box and ran over to her without caring.

'Ruby, I've got something to tell you that's important. But we need to get out of here first.'

'Oh no, Jack,' she said with dismay. 'Not this again. I do still like you, but I can't—'

'It ain't that,' I said, speaking fast and grabbing her wrist. 'Some people are coming to hurt you and we need to *move*!'

Ruby resisted and her face became more aggressive. There was people pushing past all around us and it would not have been easy to get her to shift even had she wanted to.

'Did you break into my room this morning?' she challenged me and pulled away.

'Huffam tell you that?' I asked.

'No, he did not! I saw it myself when I went back to change into this dress. My doll ain't there, the one you was on about last night, and there's sawdust everywhere.'

'Yeah, that was me,' I admitted. 'And you have no clue as to how sorry I am for it. Come with me and I'll tell you the whole story.'

'I'm not going nowhere with you, Dodger,' she said. 'You're trouble.'

'How very right you are, young lady,' said a voice coming out of the crowd behind her. 'He's a damnable nuisance.'

I saw the glint of the blade moving towards her before I saw Timothy Pin; it was low and ready to strike. But my fist was on his wrist before it could reach her red dress and I punched him good and hard right in his posh face.

Ruby screamed as she saw me assault a finely dressed gentleman in a public place for what must have seemed like no reason. The gathered throng of marketeers all turned and cried out in disapproval but there was no time to explain as Pin was quick recover himself and still had the knife in his hand. He swung at my face with it but I darted out of the way and returned with another punch right under his chin. The strike caused him to drop the blade and stagger backwards, crashing against the fence of a pigpen.

'I boxed at Cambridge, Dawkins,' he sneered as he jumped up again, wiping some blood off his face. 'Did you?' And then he adopted the pose of a well-trained pugilist and raised his fists up to me.

But if he thought that Broughton's rules would defend him against a boy what had learnt how to fight in the slums then he was much mistaken. I charged right into him and showed him how it was done in the rookeries. He seemed most taken aback by the ferocity of my attack as my left fist struck into his face and the right landed straight in his gut. He tried his counter-attack and landed some strikes of his own but my blood was so hot that I did not even notice them. I felt as though I was taking on the whole ruling class with every hit and at last, once his smooth hairless face had been battered enough, I threw my final punch and knocked him backwards through the wooden fence and into the pen with the rest of the swine.

A cheer went up from some of the rougher onlookers and,

although the owner of the pigs swore at me as he struggled to stop his livestock from escaping, I was given many compliments from coves what had been impressed to see such quality street fighting. I turned my back on the defeated Pin, who would not be getting up in a hurry, seeing how he was busy being trampled by trotters, and looked for Ruby. The crowd was even thicker now with butchers patting me on the back, but I just glimpsed her red hat some distance away and vanishing off in the other direction. I cursed aloud to see that she was headed out of the market and towards where I had last seen Lord Evershed.

I barged my way through the throng and took after her. It was not easy as my way was obstructed by all sorts of dithering coves what slowed me down, but I shoved them aside and kept following. Ruby was far ahead now and I saw her pass the spot where Evershed had been and continue in the direction of her home. There was no sign of either him or Warrigal and I kept running as she went left into Cow Cross Lane. But, just as Ruby turned the corner and vanished from view I saw the terrible vision of that large black coach cut across from the opposite street. Through the open window I could see Evershed leaning out and giving Calista instructions to pursue. I shouted out Ruby's name in panic and ran towards where they had gone but before I could get to the corner I was pounced upon by three tall men in uniforms.

'Where is he, Dawkins?' barked Inspector Bracken into my face as two of his constables held me up against a brick wall. 'Where's Evershed?'

'Let go of me, you stupid bastard!' I shouted, and tried to punch and kick myself free of them. 'They're going to kill her!'

'You mean Miss Solomon?' asked Bracken as several other peelers came running towards us from the market with their truncheons out. 'You've seen her? She's still alive?'

'She went that way!' I pointed towards where I had just seen the black carriage go. 'Hurry! They're going to kill her.'

'Was it Evershed?' Bracken demanded as he looked in that direction.

'Yes,' I told him. 'And he's as mad as a clown. He's in a black carriage with some woman driving it. That way!' I was struggling to break free and take chase myself when I saw Warrigal appear from behind the policemen. He too was running to where Ruby had gone and I shouted to the peelers to grab him. 'That's one of them!' I cried. 'Stop him!'

'We know,' said Bracken as the peelers released me and then footed it towards Cow Cross Lane. 'He's with us.' And then I noticed that the peelers was not running after Warrigal at all. They was running with him.

I ran to the corner myself, praying to every ghost I had ever known that there was still enough time to save her. But, as I turned into the long lane, I saw that she was at the far end of it and already at Evershed's mercy.

The carriage had stopped moving, the door was open and Evershed had stepped out of it and into the street. He was talking to Ruby and, although I could not hear what they was saying, he was holding up that gold locket from its chain, the one with the picture of Ruby's mother inside. Ruby took the locket to see, unaware of the danger, as Evershed stood there clutching his wounded shoulder.

'*Franklin Evershed!*' boomed Inspector Bracken as he, myself, half a dozen peelers and Warrigal all looked down the lane towards them. '*You are under arrest, sir!*'

Evershed spun around to see us all heading towards him. Then he turned back to Ruby and shoved her hard against a brick wall. She screamed and dropped the locket as he flung open his coat and pulled out that old musket I had seen in the Dancing Mutineer. He pointed at her head and fired.

The blast rang out and there was a splash of blood as she fell to her knees in front of him. I cried out in horror as we all continued charging towards him and he threw the gun down and made to get back in the carriage. But Calista did not wait for him and before he could climb in, the horse was whipped onwards and the carriage left him in the street abandoned.

'*Bitch!*' he cried out after her and turned again to see us closing in. Then he reached for his sword and pulled it out of its scabbard before heading off in the other direction. Bracken and his peelers all ran past where Ruby was lying and continued in pursuit of Evershed as he made it to a narrow alley and disappeared down it. I was the first one what stopped to aid the fallen woman.

'Ruby!' I cried as I saw her slumped against the wall with the gold locket lying at her feet and her hat over her eyes. There was a hole in the hat and blood dripped down the lower part of her face. I could not contain my upset as I crouched down and touched her cheek.

Behind me, as I sobbed and told her I was sorry for everything I had ever done, I heard another set of footsteps make it to where she lay. My eyes was watery but I could sense that Warrigal was there and I was so full of anger that I was about to turn on him and charge him with not getting there sooner. From up the alley I could hear an almighty battle taking place and the sounds of policemen shouting for the man to place down his weapon.

Warrigal peered down to Ruby as a police van trundled down the lane behind him and I saw more peelers jump out, these ones with firearms, and head to where the cries was coming from to aid their brother officers. Warrigal just pointed at Ruby and spoke in a soft voice.

'Red,' he said. And then I remembered when I had heard him say that last. I pulled her hat off to reveal a thick rare cut of steak what was sat atop her head and dripping its juices all down her face. I took it off and saw there was a musket ball embedded within.

Ruby's eyes blinked open and she spoke to me in shock. 'Jack,' she said as I whooped with delight and kissed her unharmed head. 'Who was that maniac? What did he mean by saying I looked like someone he once knew?' She struggled to stand up and looked towards the alley what Evershed had run off down. 'What was all that about?'

As she asked this we heard the tremendous roar of Lord Evershed ring out from somewhere and all our heads turned to where it came from. Then some shots was fired and the roar was silenced.

I turned back to Ruby and helped her wipe the blood away. 'Whatever it was,' I said, not knowing what to tell her, 'it's all over now.'

Ruby took the steak from me and bit her lip. 'Please don't tell John that I'm back on the lift,' she pleaded as she put it back in her hat. 'He wouldn't approve.' I laughed and promised her that I would do no such thing. I was just so relieved to see her alive again and I told her how happy I was.

'Not as happy as I am, you thieving little shit,' said a rough voice from behind me. I was yanked up by two strong arms and then thrown hard against the wall beside Ruby. I fought against this manhandling but my arms was forced behind my back and I felt some rusty prison manacles being locked onto my wrists. 'You're coming down the station, baby brother,' Horrie said as he turned me round to face him. 'We got some questions need answering.'

Chapter 31

God Rest Ye, Merry Gentlemen

In which I am at last freed from Satan's power

'Fucking Hellfire!' said the Prime Minister of Britain. 'This is going to take some fucking explaining.'

Although I could not in truth see Sir Robert Peel for myself as I sat in a police cell some hours later, I could hear his broad Lancastrian tones echo from the room next door as he tried to make sense of what he was being told. He had been speaking to Inspector Bracken for some time and it sounded as though he had been dragged away from some important public function to come down here and attend to this mess.

'I shudder to think what Her Majesty is going to say about it all,' he moaned as I heard his footsteps stomping about. 'Evershed was a friend of her father's and she doesn't care for me much as it is.'

I was in this cell with Warrigal, who lay on a small truckle bed and stared up at the ceiling. I myself was sat on a chair and looking out of the barred window to the white sky what hung over the city. It would be snowing soon, I thought to myself. It always does in time for Christmas.

'He was a friend of Wellington's as well,' Peel continued ranting at the Metropolitan Police, a force he himself had created as Home Secretary. 'And now he's been shot dead in a dirty alley by my own damned officers like he was a rabid dog. I'll never hear the fucking end of it.'

Inspector Bracken was heard clearing his throat. 'Yes, Prime Minister,' he said. 'It is unfortunate that Lord Evershed drove us to take such action. But as you have been informed, he wounded three of my constables, one almost fatally. And we had just witnessed him trying to shoot an innocent woman in the head.'

Warrigal and myself had spent the last few hours being questioned as to what we both knew about His Lordship and we had managed not to incriminate ourselves. Warrigal had not told me what he had been up to earlier that morning when Pin and myself had gone to Saffron Hill to fetch the Jakkapoor stone and he was late collecting Lord Evershed at the docks, but it was starting to sound like he had been very busy.

'And the reason you had armed officers in Smithfield Market looking for Lord Evershed,' Peel's voice was heard asking, 'was because an Australian aboriginal told you he would be there?'

'Indeed, Prime Minister,' Bracken confirmed. 'A Mr Warrigal Bungurra.'

'A reply, Inspector,' said Peel with a hard sigh, 'that raises more questions than it answers.'

Bracken explained to Sir Robert Peel who Warrigal was, how he had met the two of us some weeks before in the Booted Cat, and how we had since been approached to cooperate in an unofficial investigation into the murder of Louisa Evershed and George Shatillion. He then told how, in the early hours of this morning, Warrigal had strolled into a police station when he should have been waiting for Lord Evershed and asked to speak to Inspector Bracken. Bracken was not there and Warrigal could not stay long, but he left a message to say that Lord Evershed would be arriving in England on that very day and would be going to the Dancing

Mutineer pub in Wapping. He also said that Evershed had threatened to arrange a massacre at an aborigine settlement in Australia. I looked over to where Warrigal was lying to see if he was listening to this all but he just kept staring at the ceiling. 'You're a dark horse,' I said.

'Mr Bungurra would not wait for me to arrive at the station, Prime Minister, as he did not want to be missed. But he told the sergeant on duty that he would try to keep Lord Evershed and his companions at the Dancing Mutineer until we arrived. However, due to some incident involving Jack Dawkins jumping out of a window, he was unable to do this. Evershed and Pin had left Wapping before we got there and only Bungurra remained. Bungurra then travelled with us to Smithfield Market and said that he had since learnt that Evershed intended to kill a woman called Ruby Solomon. I asked him if he would testify against Lord Evershed in a court of law and he said that he would. But only as long as both he and Dawkins were cleared of all wrongdoing.' There was a pause as this seemed to grate upon Bracken. 'With some reluctance,' he continued, 'I have agreed to honour this condition.'

I looked over to Warrigal again as I heard this. 'Thanks,' I said. He just looked over and nodded.

'We have not been able to apprehend Timothy Pin, sir,' said Bracken after Peel asked if anyone had been arrested. 'He's the man we suspect of having killed George Shatillion by pushing him from a cliff. He was last seen getting beaten up in a pigpen in Smithfield and has since vanished. The lady driver of his black coach is still at large also.'

'This incident is bad, Wilfred,' said the Prime Minister before leaving. 'It's bad for the force. See to it that you can prove that there is absolutely no doubt about the rightness of your actions in shooting Evershed. And try to keep things as quiet as possible.'

And so it came to be that Warrigal and myself would not be arrested provided we both agreed to go along with everything the police wanted us to say about Lord Evershed, which, as luck would have it, was also the honest truth. Our tales of his tyranny and evil was more than just believed by the Metropolitan Police, they was welcomed. We was kept in that station for some days after the incident going over our accounts of Evershed's villainy, and Ruby was brought down to tell them the little she knew as well. It was Bracken, not myself, who told her what we had heard about her being the illegitimate child of George Shatillion and Louisa Evershed, and I cannot imagine how she took the news.

The key turned in the iron door and Horrie stuck his head in. He had been looking in on us most regular ever since he had dragged us to this cell, providing us with toiletries and regular vittles, but if he was feeling bad about trying to arrest his own flesh and blood he was good at hiding it. He had given me some dry clothes however, to replace the ones what I had jumped into the Thames with. 'That lawyer is here again,' he told us now. 'The one what stinks of gin.'

Jacob Slaithwaite was the lawyer what Barney in the Three Cripples had mentioned knowing and he had sent him down on hearing of our unfair detention. Slaithwaite was the man what had defended Fagin after his arrest six years ago so I was not expecting great things from him. He shuffled into the cell behind Horrie, coughing his hellos and apologising for his head cold. He was an elderly man what should not still be practising law at his time of life, but the worn-out shoes, threadbare coat and battered briefcase he walked in with told me he had no other choice. There was a small writing desk in this cell with chairs on either side of it and he sat on one as I took the other.

Jacob breathed out in exhaustion as he watched Horrie leave us and shut the cell door after him and then reached into his coat pocket. 'Thank goodness he's left us in peace,' he wheezed pulling out a silver snuffbox. 'I do hate the peelers.' I waited as he took a pinch of snuff and let the sensation of it hit him.

'So, Jacob,' I said after he had replaced the top back on and left it on the table, 'what news have you got for us?'

'All good,' he said, and grinned at me so I could get a good look at every gap in his teeth. He reached into his briefcase and pulled out the pardon what the Governor of New South Wales had written out for me. 'This,' he said, and held it out, 'is still watertight. Just because the man named as your character witness lost hold of his senses and ran amok with a great sword does not mean this official pardon can be overruled. Otherwise they'd have to start overruling all sorts of decrees and that would never do. So you are allowed to stay in England for the rest of your days if you wish it.' He then again turned to Warrigal and cleared his throat. 'That is, if you commit no further crimes.'

'Don't you worry on that score, Jacob,' I told him. 'I'm a changed man.'

'Very good,' said the lawyer, not seeming to care either way. 'Mr Bungurra will be expected to remain here for some time as he is helping the police with this Evershed business. But you, Mr Dawkins –' he winked and got to his feet – 'cannot be detained here for one moment more. You can walk out of this building with me now if you care to.' He banged on the door for Horrie to let him out again.

As Horrie took his time in letting myself and Slaithwaite out of the cell I stood up and held out my hand for Warrigal. 'You needn't to go back to Australia, you know,' I said to him as we shook. 'My pardon stands for you an' all. You should stay here and be a Londoner if you like. You already know your way around and we was a good gang you and me. A gang of two.'

Warrigal nodded and repeated those words as though he liked them. 'Gang of two.' He smiled.

But, despite this, he told me that as soon he was allowed to go back to Honey Ant Hill then he would do so. 'Australia is home,' he said with firmness. 'And there is an end to it.'

So we said goodbye once more and then, not being able to stop myself, I reached my arms around him and gave him a strong embrace.

'Thanks for not killing me, Warrigal,' I said. 'That was a good turn you done me.'

And then I was led out of the cell and the iron door fell shut between us.

I held the big plum pie, the fruitiest one they had in the shop, out in my arms as I heard the front door being unlocked. I was dressed in the smartest, most colourful suit, what had been laundered just for this day, and beside me on the pavement was a bundle of other gifts, some wrapped, one not, what I had spent the last hour struggling to transport to this very door.

'God bless us!' I cheered as it swung open to reveal the man of the house. 'Every one!'

John Froggat took one look at me and slammed the door shut again.

I had expected this and so was not going to let it spoil my festive mood. I lowered the pie under one arm and rapped again upon the door with the other. After a short pause it opened once more.

'I say, God bless us, ev—'

'Why are you here, Mr Dawkins?' Froggat demanded. 'You are not welcome.'

'Well, Mr Froggat,' I said, glad to have engaged him in conversation at least. 'I have come here to pay my respects to you, your family and your fair lodger and to present you with these gifts as a gesture of goodwill to all men.' I pointed to the one unwrapped gift what I had stood up against the others and was so shiny and new. 'That one is for Uncle Huffam.'

Froggat eyed the gift with suspicion. 'Looks expensive,' he said.

'It was.' I nodded. 'And I have a shop bill to prove that it was honestly paid for.'

'And was the money you used to paid for it honestly acquired?'

'Let's make life easy for us all and imagine yes. Mind if I come in?'

Just then my name was called and I saw Ruby coming down the stairs behind him. 'Jack.' She smiled as she walked up and touched Froggat's shoulder. 'How lovely to see you.'

'You an' all,' I said, and meant it. This was the first time I had seen her since Evershed had tried to shoot her and missed. She was every bit as beautiful as ever and I tried hard not show how bitter it was to see her acting all familiar with John Froggat. But, unlike in stories, I had to accept that just because you save someone's life it does not follow that they are therefore obliged to give it to you. I had come here expecting friendship and nothing more.

'I've brought you a Christmas present,' I told her. 'One I hope you'll like.'

'I hope it ain't the fiddle,' said Ruby, nodding towards the unwrapped instrument, 'because I can't play a note.'

I laughed and picked up the bow and stick after handing her the pie. 'This is for old Huffam,' I said, and looked to John Froggat, who was still blocking my entrance into his abode. 'Let's go inside and give it to him, eh?'

Froggat was reluctant to let me in but at last stood to one side after Ruby told him she had forgiven me for breaking into her room on account of how the police had told her I had stopped a man from knifing her in broad daylight. So he helped me carry in the gifts while still regarding me like I was a stray animal what might disgrace myself on the rug.

'What a beautiful pie!' gasped Mother Froggat when she saw what Ruby had carried into the kitchen. Then she saw me following in behind and shrieked. 'Him again! Get him out before I call the police!'

'Now, now, Mother,' said John, walking in behind me. 'Mr Dawkins is here delivering gifts of the season. As Christians it is our duty to give him another chance, and I'm sure that pie will be most welcome once we have eaten the goose. Also, he has brought something very special for dear old Huffam.' I went over to the old blind man, who was sat in his rocking chair, and let him feel the brand-new fiddle for himself rather than telling him what it was. Huffam was delighted to feel the soft polish of this instrument, so superior was it to the one he already had, and he began trying to play it with the stick.

'Lord help us,' groaned Mother Froggat as the painful sounds began filling up the house. 'Now he'll never shut up.' She looked to John, who had a very small smile on his lips as he saw how happy his elderly relative was made. 'I suppose we'll have to have this young villain for Christmas dinner now –' she thumbed towards me – 'if your lady friend should wish it.'

'Thanks very much,' I said before John could answer no. 'That would be most charitable. But first I have something I would like to give Ruby.' I looked to her across the wooden table where she was eyeing me with some suspicion. 'A gift what is of a most personal nature,' I said before asking if I could see her alone for a minute.

Ruby and myself left the others to prepare the Christmas meal and she took me into the little parlour so I could present her with what I had. She sat on an old upholstered chair and stroked the cat as I reached into my pocket, but she jumped when she saw what I dangled from the chain in front of her. The last time she had seen it was just before Evershed had tried to kill her.

'It's your mother, Ruby,' I said as she took the golden locket what had I had collected from the scene. 'And there is a strong likeness.' She gazed upon the face of the woman what had given birth to her and she became most emotional at the sight.

'I still can't believe it, Jack,' she said after she had looked at her for long enough. 'That George Shatillion was my father. That he took me away from my mother and left me to grow up in the rookeries. Do you think he even loved me at all or was it just some big game?'

'He left you the Jakkapoor stone,' I said. 'And he kept watch over you as your Uncle Ikey so he must have felt something. And that's not all.' I told her then about what I had realised when going over the whole saga during my time in that police cell. About how Timothy Pin had said that George Shatillion had been disguising himself as a number of characters to watch over Ruby.

'When I was up in Northamptonshire Charley said something that I only recalled yesterday. He had read a Shatillion novel, he told me, one what featured a character called Wee Dougie Boyd. And I was wondering if—'

'Wee Dougie Boyd!' she said, rising to her feet and causing the cat to scarper out of the room. 'That's the same name as my old producer at the music halls!'

'The one what gave you a job, yeah.' I nodded. 'And who went missing around the time that George Shatillion died.' Ruby was flabbergasted to hear this and began pacing around the room going over the possibility that it might be true. How many other people had she met in her life that was George Shatillion in disguise? she asked.

Soon John Froggat came in to tell us that dinner was almost ready and Ruby showed him the locket and told him our suspicions about Douglas Boyd. He seemed most amazed to hear of this and, as she carried on chattering away to him and telling him all that she felt, I saw what a peaceful life she might have with a man like him. I decided that I should leave the two of them alone and I went out of the door and headed for the kitchen.

I was not feeling too festive as I moved away from Ruby and her other man and crossed the hallway towards the sound of Huffam's fiddle. I was still very much infatuated with the girl but I could tell that she was indeed better off without me. Uncle Huffam was playing what sounded like a strained rendition of 'Comfort and Joy' and the sound was making me even more melancholy. I paused for a second in that hallway before going to join him and Mother Froggat around the Christmas table and tried to recall the lyrics.

And then as I passed the bottom of the stairs on my way to the kitchen I took a sudden start. I spun my head around and looked up to the top of the staircase but nobody was there. It was just a damp stain on the back wall what had tricked me in the light. I could have sworn, however, that I had just seen an old man stood there, fixing me with a most curious look. It was a look that seemed to be asking me how my day had been, and what nice shiny things I had found for him this time.

End of Book One

Acknowledgements

The first five chapters of this novel were written as part of a creative writing masters course taken at Kellogg College, Oxford. I would sincerely like to thank the course director Dr. Clare Morgan, the tutors and, most importantly, my fellow students for helping to create such a wonderful writers' community in which to experiment.

Thanks to everyone who read and commented on the book while it was being written, including Anna Jones and Kent DePinto. A special thank you to my great friend Christian Regnaudot who has been my most faithful reader ever since I first began writing and whose many suggestions have proven invaluable.

Many thanks to my agent Jon Elek for believing in the book at such an early stage. And to my editor Jon Watt for his huge support during the later stages.

The love and encouragement I have received from my family during the development of this novel has been beyond measure. My deepest thanks are for them.

Final thanks must of course go to the immortal Charles Dickens for creating such an irrepressible character. His Jack Dawkins is a superb creation and it has been a great and rare pleasure to spend time with him.